6

DANDELION FIRE

Also by N. D. Wilson

Leepike Ridge
100 Cupboards

N. D. WILSON

DANDELION FIRE

➢ Book 2 of the **100** CUPBOARDS ⬱

RANDOM HOUSE 🏠 NEW YORK

Text copyright © 2009 by N. D. Wilson
Jacket illustration copyright © 2009 by Jeff Nentrup
Diagram illustration copyright © 2007 by Jeff Nentrup

Published in the United States by Random House Children's Books,
a division of Random House, Inc., New York.

Random House and colophon are registered trademarks of Random House, Inc.

Visit us on the Web! www.randomhouse.com/kids

Educators and librarians, for a variety of teaching tools, visit us at www.randomhouse.com/teachers

Visit www.100Cupboards.com

Library of Congress Cataloging-in-Publication Data
Wilson, Nathan D.
Dandelion fire / by N. D. Wilson. — 1st ed.
p.   cm. — (100 cupboards ; 2)
Summary: Presents the continuing adventures of Henry York, who has been living in Kansas with his cousins, where he discovers doorways leading to other worlds and becomes involved in a multi-world struggle between good and evil.
ISBN 978-0-375-83883-5 (trade) — ISBN 978-0-375-93883-2 (lib. bdg.) —
ISBN 978-0-375-83884-2 (tr. pbk.)
[1. Magic—Fiction.   2. Space and time—Fiction.   3. Doors—Fiction.
4. Family life—Kansas—Fiction.   5. Cousins—Fiction.   6. Kansas—Fiction.]   I. Title.
PZ7.W69744Dan 2008
[Fic]—dc22
2008003037

Printed in the United States of America

10 9 8 7 6 5 4 3 2 1

First Edition

For Heather Linn
amo te mea nais

1. Library/Adria/Lost
2. Cylinder/Aksum/Alt Pres
3. Wall/Mistra/CCM back
4. CV/Telmar/Alt Pas
5. Square/Ur/Damage
6. Barrow/Lindis/Pres
7. C. Lane/Yarntom/Vary delay?
8. /Endor/
9. Vestibule/Buda/Pre-war
10. Balcony/Fontevrault/apprx. C loss
11. Larder/Milan/Alt?
12. Lunar A./Carnassus/Alt Pas?
13. Spiral/Lahore/Ruin
14. Kastra/Damascus/iii
15. Litter/Napata/Alt Pres
16. Stern/Tortuga/Static
17. Rail/Arizona/Now
18. Treb/Actium/Constant
19. Hutch/FitzFaeren/Alt Pas?
20. Closet/Reba/Pres
21. Friez/Karatep/Broken
22. Deep Shaft/Masada/Varies
23. Viper/Edom/Alt
24. /Cleave/
25. Falls/Rauros/Alt
26. Drop/Ein Gedi/Alt 2M back?
27. Sealed/Daqin-Fulin/?
28. Bom J./Goa/Pres
29. Dome/Sintra/Alt pas
30. Hall/Cush/Damage
31. Partition/Globe, H-let/True pas? Alt?
32. Garden/H. Sophia/Pre-minaret alt
33. Wet/Henneth Annun/Alt
34. Encyc./Uqbar/Partial Pres
35. Lower Castile/Transito/Sealed pres?
36. Rotten/Heriot/?
37. Water Tunnel/Germa/Varies
38. Tempore/ /Alt pres?
39. Lake/Acacus/Now
40. Bowl/Skara Brae/Now
41. Lab/Knoss/Alt Pas. back 4M?
42. inner p./Arcturus/Surging
43. Mound/Lerna/Now
44. Sewer/Topkapi/ back 5C, true
45. Mouth/Marmara/Alt?
46. ?/Angkor/Varies
47. Hall/Midge/Other
48. Fern/Bootes/Damage
49. /Cleave/

50. Peat/Grus/Trailing
51. Hole/Nara/Alt now
52. Konya/Huyuk/Shifting alt
53. Granary/Mohenjo/Lost
54. Pool/Basra/Slowing alt
55. Grave/Lagash/Damage
56. Commonwealth/Badon Hill/Same
57. Hostel?/Bovill/Now
58. Hollow/Iguazu/Shifting Now
59. Narbonne/Carcassone/back 3C
60. Daxiong/Ningbo/Now
61. Barn/Lower Sol/Alt pres
62. Gate/Procyon/Flux
63. Lighthouse/Alex/Alt Pres
64. Sheer/Henge/Never
65. Moss/Morte/Surging pres
66. ? /Kappa Crucis/Lost
67. Nave/Dochia/Alt Fut
68. Column/Thucyd/Alt
69. Corrund. shaft/Myanmar?/ ?
70. Pump/Rayfe/Fast
71. Vat/Kimber/Alt now
72. Southern Cit./Boghazk/Alt pas. back 3M
73. Bank/Amster/yesterday
74. Wells/ Premier Cullinan/Lost
75. Yellow Pine/Tindrill/ ?
76. Temp/Mysore/Alt pas. back 4C
77. Post/Byzanthamum/When?
78. Shifting/ San I.O./Shift spring
79. Gunnery/Brush/Static
80. Crush/Corvus/Dead
81. W.house/Cam?/Bubon
82. Mill/Gilroy/Alt trailing L
83. Reka/Skocjan/Back? Alt?
84. Bell/Delphi/Other
85. Base/Massis/Alt back 3C
86. Canal/Tenochtitlan/Alt pres
87. Bog/Malden/Damage
88. Blue/Cataldo/Alt fut
89. Loft/Strickne/Now
90. Sub Pill. 56/Persepolis/Alt pas. back M
91. Frame/Tana Kirkos/Partial Lost
92. ?/Ellora/Damage
93. Mine Spurr/Tordrillo/Now
94. Mid/Izamel/Flux Alt
95. Veranda/Millbank, Rhod./Alt pas
96. Model/Saqqara/Lost
97. Cliff/Achil/Now
98. Offs./Epidauros/Constat Aristo

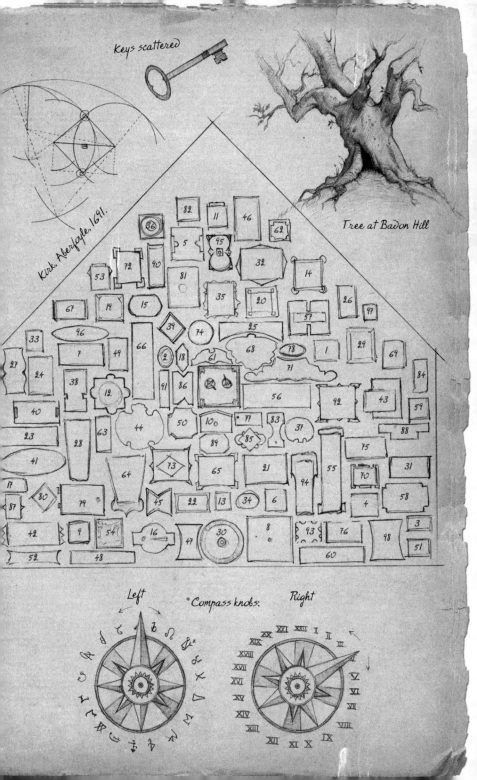

Keys scattered

Tree at Badon Hill

Kirk Aberfoyle. 1691.

*Compass knobs:

Left   Right

DANDELION FIRE

CHAPTER ONE

Kansas is not easily impressed. It has seen houses fly and cattle soar. When funnel clouds walk through the wheat, big hail falls behind. As the biggest stones melt, turtles and mice and fish and even men can be seen frozen inside. And Kansas is not surprised.

Henry York had seen things in Kansas, things he didn't think belonged in this world. Things that didn't. Kansas hadn't flinched.

The soles of Henry's shoes were twenty feet off the ground. He had managed to slide open the heavy door in the barn loft, and after brushing the rust and flakes of red paint off his hands, he'd seated himself on the dust-covered planks and looked out over the ripening fields. Henry's feet dangled, but Kansas sprawled.

Henry had changed in the short weeks since he'd stepped off the bus from Boston, been smothered by Aunt Dotty and taken to the old farmhouse, to the attic—to a new existence. He looked different, too, and it wasn't just the cut across the backs of his fingers. That was scarring worse than it needed to only because he couldn't stop himself from picking at it. The burns on his jaw were a lot more noticeable and had begun scarring as well. He didn't like touching them. But he had to. Especially the one below his ear. It was turning into a divot as wide as his fingertip.

What had changed most about Henry York was inside his head. Things he had always known no longer seemed true. A world that had always felt like a slow and stable and even boring machine had suddenly come to life. And it was far from tame. He'd uncovered a wall of doors in his attic room, and now he didn't know who he was. He didn't know who his real parents were or whether he was even in the right world. He didn't really know anything. Strangely, that was more comfortable than thinking that he did.

One month before, fresh off the bus from Boston, he would have been nervous sitting where he was, slowly bouncing his heels on the wall of the barn. One month before, he wouldn't have believed that he could hit a baseball. Something wheezed beside him, and Henry turned. One month before, the world was still normal, and creatures like this one didn't exist.

The raggant sniffed loudly and settled onto his haunches. His wings were tucked back against his rough charcoal skin and his blunt horn was, as always, lifted in the air.

Henry smiled. He always did when he looked at the animal. It was so proud and so very unaware of how it looked. At least Henry thought it had to be. Shaped like a small basset hound but wearing wings and a rhino's face and skin, it was far from beautiful, but that didn't stop it from being as proud and stubborn as a peacock. Like an otherworldly bloodhound, it had found Henry, cracking the plaster in the attic wall from inside a cupboard. The raggant had started everything. Whoever it was that had sent the raggant had started everything. Henry couldn't even imagine who that might be.

"Do you know how strange you look?" Henry asked, and he reached over and grabbed the loose skin on the creature's neck. It felt like sand-based dough, and as he squeezed, the raggant closed its black eyes and a low moan sputtered in its chest.

"I want to see you fly," Henry said. "You know I will." He glanced down at the ground and then back at the raggant. He could push it. Then it would have to fly. But it just might be proud enough not to, proud enough to tuck its wings tight and bounce in the tall grass. "Sometime," Henry said.

The afternoon sun was falling, and Henry knew it wouldn't be long before the barn's shadow stretched across acres. Worse, it wouldn't be long before the fields and the barn and all of Kansas became part of his past. His parents had been back from their ill-fated bicycle trip for a while, and he still hadn't heard from them. That wasn't too unusual. When they were just getting back from their photographed adventures, he rarely ever heard from them. The fact that they'd actually managed to get kidnapped this time would make their return crazier, would keep him safely off their minds for that much longer. But it couldn't last. If they'd had any say in the matter, he never would have been sent to stay with his cousins at all. Now that they'd returned, they wouldn't leave him in Kansas for school or even through the summer. He'd be back in Boston, on some new vitamin diet and meeting a new nanny, and then back to boarding school. Maybe a new one. His third.

Parents. He still thought of them that way. Would they ever have told him that Grandfather had found him in the attic? Not likely. Henry didn't care that he'd been adopted. But it was hard not to care that his parents had never really been parents—not like Uncle Frank and Aunt Dotty were to his cousins. Henry had always known exactly where he was on his parents' list of priorities.

Yesterday, he'd seen his parents on television. He'd been stirring his cereal and listening to his youngest cousin, Anastasia, complain about Richard when Uncle Frank called him. He'd hurried, and when he stepped into the room, Frank pointed. There, on a stiff couch in a television studio somewhere, sat Phillip and Ursula, smiling and nodding. They each had hands crossed on their knees. Ursula kept glancing at the camera. She looked like Henry's aunt Dotty, but with all her edges hardened. The two of them talked about their amazing endurance, the difficulty of bicycling through the Andes, how they had never given up hope of finishing their trek even after being abducted in Colombia, the size of their book deal, and their discussions with film agents.

In a general way, Henry remembered all they had said. But there were two things that sat in the front of his mind, every syllable in concrete.

"Are you closer now?" the woman had asked them. "After going through all of this together?"

Ursula had leaned forward. Phillip had leaned back. "You know," Ursula had said. "We've both changed a great deal during this whole process. We really need to get to know each other again. But first we need to get to know ourselves."

Phillip had nodded.

Henry was pretty sure he knew what that meant.

And then the woman had asked about him.

"Now you all have a son? Is that right?"

"That's right," Phillip had said.

Ursula had smiled. "Our little Henry."

"That must have been quite the reunion. What went through your minds when you saw him again?"

"Oh, it was wonderful," Ursula had said. "Elation. Pure maternal elation."

"Thrilling," Phillip had said.

It had been strange, watching his parents lie. Uncle Frank had slapped his shoulder afterward and Aunt Dotty had squeezed him. Anastasia had opened her mouth, but Penelope, the oldest, always the most concerned, had pinched her before she could say anything. Henrietta had tucked back her curls and stared at him.

The two of them had opened the doors together, had knelt in the attic and stared into strange worlds, and still she always tested him, curious if he'd be weak. Henry knew she was waiting to see if he'd be sad. He hadn't been. Not then. Richard, always out of place, had stepped quickly out of the room.

"What am I going to do?" Henry asked the raggant. "I won't get to stay here, and you can't come with me even if you try. You'd get sold to a zoo. Or a circus."

A hot breeze crawled through the fields, rolling the surface like thick liquid. The raggant didn't open its eyes, but its nostrils flared.

"Richard is worse," Henry said. The scrawny boy who'd followed him back through the cupboards into Kansas weighed on his mind a lot. "Unless he lives here forever, he'll have to go back through the cupboards. Maybe not home, but somewhere else. Unless Anastasia kills him first."

Below Henry, from the other side of the barn, came the sound of an old door rattling open.

"Henry of York!" Uncle Frank yelled.

Henry turned. "Yeah?" Footsteps crossed the plank floor below him. They stopped. Old ladder rungs sighed.

Five feet from where Henry and the raggant sat, Uncle Frank's head emerged. Henry smiled at him, but Uncle Frank didn't smile back. He was looking past his nephew, out the open doorway and into the fields. When he'd pulled his thin body up, he scratched the raggant's chin and then sat down beside Henry. His eyes wandered across the sky and then down through the wheat sea.

"Careful, Henry," he said. "Place like this can get in your bones. Even if you don't care for it, leaving can hurt more than it needs to."

Henry looked into his uncle's face, lean and leathery, with his eyes hooded toward the horizon like a sailor looking for land he knows he'll never find. His face didn't really explain his words. It never did. His uncle had tumbled into Kansas as a teenager, another victim of the cupboards. Henry wondered how long it would be before he looked like Frank, until he looked like something borrowed and never returned, out of place but settled in and dusty. At least Uncle Frank had memories. He knew what he'd lost, though he didn't talk about it. Henry didn't even have that.

Frank popped his knuckles and leaned back. "You can smell when the fields go green. And gold. Sound different, too. Green field rustles. Gold rattles."

"When's the harvest?" Henry asked.

"Soon," Frank said. "When the gold aims for white. You'll see the combines roll even if you don't see 'em finish."

Henry watched the wind work. "I have to leave, don't I?"

"Yep."

"I wish I didn't."

"Well," Frank said. "If wishes were horses."

Henry looked at him. "Then what?" he asked.

"Then I'd have a horse."

Henry almost smiled. He'd expected something like that. Beside him, the raggant snored. Still sitting up, its jaw hung open; its head sagged, nose no longer in the air. Henry eased it onto its side. "I wish I knew how long I have," Henry said. "I don't even like being in the house. Every time the phone rings, I think someone's on their way to pick me up."

"July third," Frank said. "Two weeks. Got a letter today."

"What?" Henry asked. "Why the third? Who sent the letter?"

Frank straightened his leg and dug his hand into the pocket of his jeans. He dropped an envelope, warm and wrinkled, onto Henry's lap. "Came up here to tell you. It's from a lawyer. Phil and Urs are parting ways. They've got some sort of custody arranging to handle next week. They'll figure out which one gets you, and then you'll leave."

Henry opened the letter and stared at it. It was addressed to his aunt and uncle, and there wasn't anything more to it than Uncle Frank had already told him.

"Two weeks," Henry said. "I'll miss the fireworks."

"Could be shorter," Frank said. "Moon goes halfway round the world in two weeks."

The two of them sat, and the raggant snored. After a while, Frank stood and stretched.

"Anastasia will call for you when supper's set," he said, and stepped toward the ladder.

Henry nodded. He didn't watch his uncle leave.

When Anastasia's voice reached him, Henry's legs still hung out the doorway, but he was on his back. He sat up and looked at the letter in his hand. He folded it up and slid it into the envelope.

"Henry!" Anastasia yelled again.

"Coming!" he said, and then flicked the envelope out onto the wind. He watched it spin as it dropped to the swaying tall grass beside the barn. "Go where you want," he said, and he stood up.

He left the raggant sleeping and climbed down the ladder. Anastasia had already gone back inside.

The table was crowded, but only Anastasia seemed to want to talk. Henry and Richard sat on one side, facing Henry's three cousins. Richard was wearing a tight yellow sweatshirt with a cantering pony on the front, forcibly borrowed from Anastasia. He was picking at the blue cast on his wrist. Uncle Frank sat with eyes unfocused and fork frozen in his hand while Aunt Dotty spread a smile, scooped buttered noodles, and passed plates. Henry looked at Penelope. She pushed her long black hair out of her face and smiled at him with lips clamped tight. Beside her sat Henrietta, curls loose and chin on her hand. She was staring at Henry again, but when their eyes met, she looked down to where her plate would be as soon as her mother gave it back. Beside her, Anastasia, shortest in her chair, chattered cheerfully.

"When Henry leaves, we'll have to keep the raggant, won't we? You should have named him a long time ago, Henry. I'll write you a letter and tell you what we name him. Do you want me to do that?"

Henry looked at her and shrugged. She looked at Richard.

"What are we going to do with Richard?" Anastasia asked. "He can't live here forever, wearing my clothes."

"Don't be rude," Penelope said.

Anastasia looked shocked. "I'm not being. Mom?"

Dotty nodded. "Be polite." Passing the last plate, she sat back in her chair and puffed stray, frizzing hairs off her forehead.

"I'm not being rude," Anastasia said. "I'm just being honest. We should send him back through the cupboards."

"Anastasia!" Dotty said.

Richard looked up, his thin, blotchy face even blotchier above the yellow shirt. "If I am going to be discussed," he said with eyebrows raised, "I would rather not be present."

"No," Dotty said quickly.

"I want my clothes back," Anastasia muttered.

"Frank?" Dotty asked. "Could you be here, please? In this world, with us. Just for now."

Frank took a deep breath, coming awake. "We couldn't send him back if we wanted. Not without the big cupboard in Grandfather's room, and that bedroom door is magicked right back to unbudgeable, isn't it? I'm not trying the chain saw again, and the attic cupboards are too small even if we folded him in thirds."

"I can't believe we're talking about this," Dotty said. "Frank Willis, you promised to plaster over those cupboards, and no one was to even think about traveling through them. Do you *want* something to happen?"

For a moment, Frank sat perfectly still, his jaw no longer chewing, his hand in the air above his plate. Then he spoke. "Doesn't matter. Don't have Grandfather's key." And he spun himself another forkful of noodles.

Henry was thinking the same thing. He had a wall of doors in his attic bedroom, none of them leading to Boston, one of them leading back to his birth-world and the world the raggant had come from. But it didn't matter. The cupboards up in his attic were like little windows, linking other places to this one, but they were no good to him unless they channeled through the cupboard in Grandfather's room, the one big enough for him to crawl through. He had Grandfather's journal with the combinations to connect each of his little doors to the bigger cupboard, but without Grandfather's key, there was no point.

"Henrietta's got the key," Anastasia said. "I've told you a hundred times, but you won't listen."

Henrietta banged her fork down onto the table and rolled her eyes. "I don't have anything."

"It's not in any of her normal hiding places," Anastasia continued. "But I'll find it."

Henry stood up. "Do you mind if I go up to my room?" he asked his aunt. "I'm not real hungry."

Dotty looked in his face, her eyebrows lifted. "What are you going to do?"

Henry halfway smiled. "Nothing," he said. "I don't have Grandfather's key."

When he reached the big second-story landing, Henry stopped. Anastasia's voice was mixing with Henrietta's, but he pushed the noise out of his head. He was looking at Grandfather's knobless door. Chopped and chewed and even cursed, it was still shut tight, impossible to re-open without the key. Any hope of finding where he'd come from was behind that door.

Henry walked around the railing and stood directly in front of the mutilated wood panels. With his toe, he prodded the tangled mess of carpet where Frank had dipped the chain saw. He'd lain right there with the hands of Nimiane of Endor around his neck. Her blood had burned his face like acid. His throat constricted at the memory, and his stomach queezed. Shivering, he hurried back around the landing to the steep attic stairs.

There were worse things than going back to Boston.

In the long, coved attic, Richard's sleeping bag and a small stack of borrowed clothes were piled against the wall beside Henry's closet room. Richard had wanted to sleep on the floor at the end of Henry's bed, but this arrangement was as close to room-sharing as Henry was willing to go.

Once inside his room, Henry went through what had become his entrance ritual. He turned on his light and stood back to examine the wall of cupboard doors. Ninety-nine doors of all shapes and sizes looked back at him. His eyes were first drawn to the center, where the door with the two compass knobs ruled the wall. It wasn't the most ornate of the doors, but, with the right combination, it could channel any of the others through the larger cupboard downstairs in Grandfather's room. And it had been the raggant's entrance into Kansas.

After letting his eyes run over the deep grains and bright inlay, flaking varnish and rusted hinges, the different colors, textures, and shapes, Henry next stepped to his bed. He pulled it away from the wall, where it hid half of the bottom two rows. He held his breath, forced himself to crouch at the foot, and looked directly at the black door on the bottom row with the gold knob in the center. Door number 8. The door to Endor.

Henry finger-checked the four screws Uncle Frank had used to seal it, stood up quickly, and pushed his bed leg back against it. Then he breathed. He knew that Nimiane wasn't behind that door anymore. She was behind whichever door his cousins had randomly selected while he and the witch had been unconscious. He'd heard the story, the description of the bat hitting her head, her cold skin. Anastasia still insisted that they should have stabbed her in the neck. But they hadn't. Afraid she would wake up, they'd fished her through the big cupboard and into some unlucky world. She wasn't in Endor anymore, but Henry still found the screws reassuring.

When Henry was breathing again, he found door number 56, the door to the place called Badon Hill, and opened it. He sat on his bed and waited for the air from that other place to drift in. It always did, and when the smell of moss and rain and a wind that had toppled breakers and poured through trees surrounded him, then Henry considered himself to actually *be* in his room.

Henry lay back on his bed and sighed. The doors frightened him, but they drew him as well. Behind one was the world where he'd been born, where he had siblings. At least six older brothers, if he believed what the old wizard had said in the cold throne room when he'd first gone through the cupboards. He looked up the wall at door number 12. Richard had crawled into that world behind him, and the wizard had known who Henry was. He would be able to tell Henry where he was really from. But he'd been horrible. Henry shifted his thoughts away from the memory and back to the doors in front of him. There was no reason to think that he'd come from a nice place, that the bent old man eating grubs on his dark throne had told the truth, or that his family was alive, and if they were, that they even wanted him. Wanted babies weren't usually shoved into cupboards.

But there was still the raggant. Raggants were for finding things. Someone had wanted to find him.

Henry took a deep breath and puffed out his cheeks.

Why had Uncle Frank stopped trying to get back? Was he afraid, too? But Frank had Dotty and his daughters. No one was going to put him on a bus back to Boston in two weeks.

"Two weeks," Henry said out loud. He looked over to the corner of his room, where one week ago, Frank had left a small roll of chicken wire and a five-gallon bucket of plaster. The wire was to cover the cupboards and strengthen the plaster. Frank hadn't touched it since he'd put it there. He'd mixed the plaster, but then left it. Now the bucket was as solid as a boulder.

"I could come back when I'm eighteen," Henry said. But he didn't think Frank could put Dotty off that long. A couple years, maybe, but not more than five.

Someone was coming up the attic stairs. Henry sat up on his bed and quietly shut the open cupboard.

His bedroom doors swung open, and Henrietta stepped into his room. She had the raggant tucked under one arm. It dropped quickly to the floor and jumped onto Henry's bed.

Henrietta sniffed the air, and her eyes drifted to the cupboard to Badon Hill. They hadn't talked in a while, and for a moment, they were both silent.

"Henrietta," Henry said. "I need Grandfather's key."

She met Henry's eyes and stared right through.

"There's no point in lying to me," Henry continued. "Things got really crazy at the end, but I know I didn't keep it, and you were the only other one who could have."

Henrietta crossed her arms and looked at the wall of

doors. Henry rambled on. "I'd be happy to stay here, but I can't. Two weeks, Henrietta, and then I go back to Boston and then back to school, and over the summers they'll store me somewhere, and I won't be able to come back until I'm old enough to move out or go to college." Henry took a breath. "I can't be here when they come for me. I have to go through the cupboards. And you have the key, Henrietta. You have to give it to me."

Henrietta sat down on the bed beside him.

"I know," she said. "I buried it behind the barn."

CHAPTER TWO

Henry was supposed to be watching for Anastasia and Richard, but he didn't think there was too much risk of being found. He had followed Henrietta silently out of the house while the others were watching television. If they did start looking for him, they wouldn't start behind the barn.

So, while Henrietta dug, he sat on a rusted seat loosely attached to the fragmented bones of an old plow. It was piled against the barn along with chunks of moss-covered concrete and a tangle of unrecognizable metal.

Henrietta was on her fourth hole. After the second one, she had straightened up on her knees and demanded that Henry either go inside or stop watching her. Now Henry was leaning back against the barn and watching the weather. It was hard not to.

He had never been outside in a storm. Not really. In about five minutes, he thought, he would be.

The early evening sky was divided in two. The east was as bright as it had been at noon, but the west was overflowing with charcoal clouds, flat-bottomed and towering. The wind that had rolled through the fields most of the day now rushed, bending and shaking wheat all the way to the horizon. The barn creaked behind Henry, and tall grass swirled around Henrietta, clinging to her hair while she dug.

Henry had carried the raggant down with them, but it had nosed off toward the old irrigation ditch that marked the edge of the fields. In the grass, it was invisible.

"I left a bottle on it," Henrietta said. "I swear I did." She grimaced and tried to push her hair out of her face. "It's not here now." She turned in place, examining the ground.

The sun was edging below the western clouds, and its light chased the wind across the fields. Every green and gold intensified while the clouds grew darker, saddled on the glow. A long, low rumble vibrated in the air, and Henry felt it in his chest.

"Is this going to be a tornado?" he asked. "Should we go inside or something?"

Henrietta looked up. "No," she said. "Just a thunderstorm. Not a big one."

Henry stared at the clouds, at the fields, and at Henrietta's blowing hair, all of it edged with solar gold. The moment dragged its feet in passing, and Henry savored each second, wanting to keep more than any memory would be able to give him. He almost felt like he could, like time would freeze for him, like the sun would hang just above the horizon and the storm clouds, laden with hail and rain and night, would rest in place, content to float on sunlight.

White and gray caught Henry's eye, and he turned slowly. Blake the cat had joined them, and he lay on his side in the bending grass, batting at a dandelion as golden as the sun. More golden. It had a yellow fire all its own, and the sun was adding to it, frosting it, wrapping its light around the weed's petaled head. Blake batted again, and Henry slid off his seat and knelt in the grass. The moment would die young, but not yet.

The dandelion was glowing. It couldn't just be the sun. Henry blinked, and the glow was gone. He was staring at a bright little lawn pest and nothing else. He let his eyes unfocus, something in his mind relaxed, and time rushed through, leaving him untouched. He wasn't staring at the dandelion, he was staring through it, at something else, behind it, in front of it, filling the same space.

Henry's head throbbed, and he almost blinked again. The rest of the world drifted away. The wind was gone, and his bones ignored the thunder's drums. There was a word singeing the tip of his tongue, a thought nearly captured by his mind.

And then he saw it.

At first it looked like fire, like the flower was burning. But nothing wilted away, nothing blackened and turned to ash. It lived in the fire. Or, the fire was its life. But as Henry stared, ignoring tears that streamed out of his unblinking eyes and a pain carving its initials inside his skull, he saw it differently. He was looking at a thing, a shape, a symbol, a writhing, changing word, a scattered, bursting story. And then, for a moment, it all came together, and he was hearing it. He was seeing a dandelion. Hearing a dandelion. Hearing the orange and the yellow, seeing the sour milk crawling in its veins, tasting its breath.

Henry put out his hand.

Somewhere, in another world, hail was falling, stinging his neck and ears. White smeared in the corner of Henry's eye, and Blake was gone.

"Got it!" Henrietta said. "Henry?"

Henry's hand was over the dandelion, and he could feel no heat. It wasn't real. Inside him, he had known that already. He touched it.

The world ripped. Light and sound surrounded him, lifted him up, and threw him on his back.

He was unconscious when he landed.

It was embarrassing for Henrietta, rooting around on her hands and knees, trying to find something that she had hidden. Embarrassing, first, because Henry had known she was lying, and lying is always embarrassing. It would have been worse if he'd known everything she'd been planning. She'd intended to steal Grandfather's journals from him before he left, and then, with the key and the cupboards and the compass combinations from the journal all to herself, she could have gone anywhere. Of course, not being able to find the key brought its own embarrassment. With Henry just sitting there, mouth-breathing and picking at the burn scars on his face, the whole experience was much worse.

So she'd snapped at him. He'd stopped staring at her, and the wind had calmed her down. She could hear the thunder already, but she knew it wouldn't be a big storm, not if the sun could get below the clouds.

Henry got down in the grass, but he hadn't gotten down to help. He was playing with Blake. Henrietta swatted at the grass in front of her, and, as it moved, she saw the place she had been searching for, where the glass Dr Pepper bottle lay on its side, still nestled halfway into the earth.

As she ripped it out of the ground, hail began to fall. The skeleton key, sealed in a plastic bag, was only a few inches down. Her fingers burrowed quickly.

"Got it!" she said, and loose earth fell on her lap when she pulled it free. She turned. Henry was kneeling on the ground with one hand out in front of him. He was crying. "Henry?" she asked.

The raggant burst through the tall grass, snorting. Lightning flicked in the clouds, and the bolt struck. Too fast for Henrietta to tell if it rose from the ground or fell from the sky, it was simply there in front of her, cracking its jagged whip between heaven and earth. She didn't hear the thunder, she felt it, like a blow, and she was on her back, deaf and blinking, hail stinging her face.

Gripping the key, she rolled over and crawled to Henry. His feet were bent beneath him and his arms were splayed out in the grass. The raggant crouched by his head, hooding itself with its dark wings. Henrietta looked at her cousin's face and panicked. He hadn't been struck. She knew he hadn't been struck. The bolt had been right there, but it hadn't hit him. She would have seen it hit him. Henry's face was white and lifeless. His mouth and eyes were open, his pupils were barely pinpricks.

"Henry!" she yelled, and slapped his cheek. The hail surged, small stones falling in a cloud. They left tiny spots of red on Henry's skin and fell into his mouth, striking teeth and lips.

"Henry!" Henrietta yelled again. Hailstones, melting, rested in his open eyes. She grabbed at the raggant's wing, pulled it over Henry's face, and pressed one hand against his chest. Relief surged through her when she felt the slow pound of life inside, but he needed to breathe. She grabbed his shoulder and pulled him onto his side, letting his legs straighten. The hail was already fading.

"Breathe, Henry! Cough! Do something!" She banged on his back. The lightning couldn't have touched him. If it had, his shoes would be all melted and his hair would be frazzled. His fingertips would probably all be split wide and charred. She felt his ribs expand, and she sat back. Probably just shock. He scared easy. Then she saw his hand. His right palm was peeled open. It wasn't bleeding. The skin was curled back around a two-inch slice, and all the edges were black. Small blisters dotted his palm, and larger ones crowded the freshly exposed skin inside the wound.

Henry's body shook. His legs jerked, and he levered himself up and turned toward Henrietta, blinking.

She frowned at him.

"What happened?" he asked.

"Lightning," she said. "You went into shock or something."

"Did it hit me?"

"No," she said, and glanced at his hand. "I don't think so."

Henry tried to stand but couldn't. Henrietta gripped his shoulders, and he staggered to his feet. Together, they tripped around the side of the barn, and, while the last of the hail turned to rain, the two of them moved slowly toward the back of the house.

Henry's joints were throbbing. His head felt chained to the ground. His vision clouded, and his stomach boiled. He grabbed at Henrietta, and she kept him from falling. She couldn't keep him from throwing up.

He knew he was inside when the rain stopped and Henrietta's voice erupted beside him.

"Mom! Dad!" she yelled. "Henry's sick!"

Henry leaned against the kitchen wall. Voices and people swirled around him, and his eyes burned. So he shut them, trusting in the hands that pushed and pulled, lifted and moved. He ignored it all and was alone in his head.

Alone with a dandelion.

*   *   *

Opening his eyes was not possible. His mind had no desire to try, and even if it had, his eyes didn't feel like they'd comply. But he could hear.

"Frank, I think we should take him to the hospital." Dotty's voice wavered. "Henrietta didn't think the lightning hit him, but what else would lay him out like this?"

Henry felt a rough hand on his face. Frank's hand. "Doesn't have to hit you. It's a current. It can hit something else and still find a way into you."

"We should take him in."

Henry felt his bed creak when Frank stood up. "We'll wait till the morning. Sleep is better than bouncin' in a truck for forty-five minutes just to have a doctor tell us he needs his rest."

"I can't believe you just let him sleep beside all these awful doors," Dotty muttered. "They give me the shivers. I never liked being up here, even when they were behind plaster. And speaking of plaster, Frank . . ."

Frank sighed. "Ease up now. He's leaving in two weeks. I'll get it done."

Henry vaguely listened to his aunt and uncle descend the attic stairs, and his mind rolled back in his head, searching for dreamlessness, where there could be no pain.

Instead, his doors opened and new voices entered.

"Henry." Richard's voice was just as pompous when you couldn't see him. "If you can hear me, I'm very sorry for your pain."

"Get out of the way, Richard," Anastasia said. "I want to see his hand."

Henry's hand was lifted, a bandage slid away, and Anastasia caught her breath. "That looks like it hurts. Did you see the lightning come out, Henrietta? He must have looked like a wizard."

"He wasn't struck by lightning." Henrietta's voice was flat. "I saw it. The lightning was just as close to both of us, and I'm fine."

"Henrietta." Penelope's voice was soothing. "I think he has to have been struck. Maybe just by a little side current, but something did that to his hand."

Henrietta sniffed. "I would have seen it. If a bolt of lightning had shot out of his hand, I think I would have noticed."

"I think you're jealous," Anastasia said. "You've always wanted to get struck by lightning, or sucked up by a tornado or something."

"I think we should leave him," Penelope said.

"I think you should leave him, too," Henrietta snorted.

"I'd like to stay with him," Richard said. "I could sleep on the floor in here tonight."

"Get out, Richard. Right now. You too, Anastasia. Bye-bye, Penny."

The doors clicked shut, and Henry felt Henrietta sit down on the bed beside him.

She sighed. "Are you faking, Henry?"

Henry swallowed and tried to lick his lips. His

tongue felt like it belonged to someone else, someone much larger than he was.

Before he could say anything, two thumbs pressed down on his eyelids and pried them back. Light and air, both made of pain, funneled into his eyes.

"Ow!" He tried to sit up, but only made it partway. Henrietta still held his eyes open. He swung at her with his left arm, and she let go and slid away.

"You were faking," she said quietly. "I'm glad. I was getting worried."

"I wasn't faking anything," Henry managed. His tongue was tripping over his teeth. He kept his burning eyes open, and Henrietta slowly slid into focus.

"You were pretending to be asleep."

"No," Henry said. "My eyes hurt."

Henrietta leaned back toward him and whispered, "Listen. It's okay. Everyone thinks you've been struck by lightning. Mom won't even be kind of suspicious. We can explore the cupboards tonight."

Henry collapsed back onto his bed and shook his head.

"It's okay," Henrietta said. "I'll let you rest, and I'll come wake you in a couple hours when everyone else is asleep. I've got Grandfather's key, you have all the combinations in the journal; we should get started. Two weeks will go fast."

Henry shook his head again and dropped his arm across his eyes.

"If they think you're really sick for too long, they'll probably send you back to Boston sooner."

"I'm not faking," Henry said. "Go. Please."

Henrietta stood slowly and tucked her hair behind her ears. Henry looked at her from beneath his arm.

"You're really hurt?" she asked.

Henry nodded.

"Then I'm sorry," she said, and turned to leave the room.

Henry shut his eyes, but they still burned. He tried to breathe slowly and drift away, but his little room oppressed him. Everyone had gone, but the heat of their breath and chatter remained.

With a sudden burst of resolution, Henry rocked and levered himself up. His joints burned like they were full of salt, and his vision dimmed as the blood left his head. For a moment, he sat on the edge of his bed, waiting for his dizziness to settle. When it did, he braced his hands on his knees and groaned as he straightened. After finding his balance, he slid carefully to the foot of his bed.

Henrietta was amazing. Even if he hadn't been struck by lightning, or whatever it was that had happened, he wouldn't have wanted to explore the cupboards willy-nilly. There was only one cupboard he wanted to go through, and that was where he intended to be in two weeks, no matter what was on the other side. He blinked his watering eyes and gripped the latch on the door to Badon Hill. It slid under his weight, and the door swung open. Then, breathing hard, he braced himself against the wall of cupboards and waited for the cleansing air to come.

It didn't. Henry could smell nothing but the sour closeness of his attic room. He placed his hand in the mouth of the cupboard, but the air was still and warm. He reached through and his knuckles scraped against a rough board at the back. There was no moss, no soft earth or confused worms. Not the slightest breeze. The cupboard had been cleaned and sealed from the other side. Henry put his hand on the back and pushed. The board didn't move, but his fingertips brushed against a thick piece of paper tacked onto the wood. He tore it free, leaned his back against the cupboard wall, and stared at it. His eyes went in and out of focus, and he blinked quickly to keep them from clouding over.

There was a crest at the top, the same green man that had sealed both the warning letters that had come through this cupboard before. But this time there was a slight difference. The bearded man's head was still set in the middle of the circle, and vines wrapped around his head and climbed out of his nose, ears, and mouth, but in the middle of all the leaves draped over his chin, there was something else. Henry widened his eyes and blinked more tears down his cheeks. The man was sticking out his tongue.

Like the others, the message was typed, but it was

much shorter, and it looked like a form letter with blanks filled in. And it was signed thoroughly, with an extra little handwritten note at the bottom.

A LERT

Under suspicion of tampering and transportation, this TREE has been:

CLOSED FOR MAINTENANCE (and monitoring)

Violators will be persecuted.

Fines will be administered up to and including:

CONFISCATION OF BREATH, MIND, LIFE, or EQUIVALENT

Authorized by the Committee of Faeren for the Preservation of Ancient Monuments:

Ralph T. R. Radulf, Esq., IX, Chair

Ralph Radulf
(Chair)

Don't think we won't.

Henry read the note once. He tried to read it through again, but no amount of blinking could clear his eyes.

He left the Badon Hill cupboard open and crawled slowly back onto his bed, wincing and beginning to feel extremely sorry for himself.

He turned off his lamp and settled his face into his pillow.

He did not see the beam of yellow light shining out of the small post-office box below Badon Hill. And if he had, he wouldn't have cared.

CHAPTER THREE

Henry smelled fire.

His lamp was not on, but his attic room flicked with orange light. He sat up on his bed. Everything was wrong. His space was narrower, and his doorway was wider. His nightstand was missing entirely. So was the end of his room.

He slid up onto his pillow and put his back against the wall. The cupboards beside him, doors he didn't recognize, stretched across the room and stopped where they always had. But instead of another wall, there was another place.

A low fire burned under a stone mantel, providing the only light. A high-backed chair crouched on either side of the fire, and in one of them, there sat an enormous man. His face was hidden.

Henry inhaled slowly. He was dreaming. He had to be.

The man leaned forward, pressing his fingertips together, half of his long, sideburned face still shrouded in shadow. "No," he said, and his voice gave Henry chills.

"The dream is mine. I come to give you gratulations. Your morphosis begins."

Henry said nothing. He didn't understand.

"This change," the man continued. "What power set flame to your flesh?"

Henry looked around his imitation room and then squinted at the man beside the fire. Dream or not, he didn't want to be here.

The big man slid forward in his seat. His voice quickened. "What did your eyes ken?" he asked, and he sounded greedy. "You have seen natura's mage, and your body revolts. It shall die or be changed. What did you see?"

"I was struck by lightning," Henry said. He stood up and stepped toward his bedroom doorway.

"Henry?" He could hear his cousin's voice on the other side.

"You will stay, yet." The man's voice deepened. He rose from his chair, filling the little room. The fire dimmed behind him. "The walls are of my imagine. They will not breach."

Henry's hand was on a knob. The doorway was trying to disappear. Instead it flickered and narrowed back to its usual self.

Henry stepped into nothingness, and he closed the door behind him.

Henrietta knew her parents wouldn't want her to wake Henry, so she hadn't asked. She'd left Richard and Anastasia bickering over their breakfast and hurried up to the attic. She tapped lightly on Henry's door, and when she didn't hear any response, she went in.

"Henry?" she asked.

Henry was facedown on his bed. His arms were tight against his sides. Henrietta dropped onto the bed beside him and poked his shoulder. "Henry? Wake up." She stood, slid her hands beneath him, and rolled him onto his side. "Are you feeling better?" she asked. "Up now! We've got places to see."

Henry's eyes were swollen shut and sealed with crusted grime.

Henrietta backed into the doorway, but she couldn't leave, and she couldn't look away from Henry's face. Blue webs of veins stood out behind his lifeless skin, and his dry lips were swollen and splitting.

"Henry?" she asked again. His eyes were the worst part. The eyelashes that were still visible beneath the in-flated lids were glued to his cheekbones, tangled in gunk that his tear ducts had pumped down the sides of his nose, around the corners of his mouth, and even across his temples and into his hair. Patches of the flesh-toned eye glue had hardened on his pillow.

Henry's body stiffened. One leg rose an inch off the bed, and a moist groan rattled in his throat.

"Are you awake?" Henrietta asked.

"No," Henry slurred. "I'm dead."

Henrietta moved back to the bed. "Um, Henry, can you open your eyes?"

The skin of his bulging eyelids quaked briefly.

They looked like they'd been stretched around plums. "No," he said. "I can't." He licked his lips and winced, then put his hands up to his eyes and felt gently around the sockets.

"They're huge," he said. He started scratching carefully at the crust, and Henrietta grimaced and turned around.

"I'm gonna get you a rag or something," she said. "I'll be right back."

Downstairs, Henrietta ran hot water over a washcloth and looked at her own eyes in the mirror above the sink. She felt worse now, for thinking that Henry had been faking. But she had seen the lightning strike, and if any had hit him, it had to have been some invisible strand. And she'd never heard of lightning giving anyone puffed-up, goopy eyes. Usually they just died or went deaf or had troughs plowed in their skin that made it look like the bark on some old lightning tree out in the fields. It had been the troughs and the charred, split skin that had made her realize she didn't really want to get struck by lightning. She'd checked a book out from the library, and the first picture was all it had taken. Under the right circumstances, she was still willing to consider being sucked up by a tornado.

Maybe Henry had allergies. She smiled. Maybe he was allergic to pollen, he had hay fever, or something. Allergic to pollen and lightning.

She was spending more time in the bathroom than she needed to, but she wasn't exactly in a hurry to look at Henry's face again.

Upstairs, Henry heard her climbing back to the attic. He had managed to sit up on his bed, and he'd scraped his eyelids mostly clear. Pinching the soft flesh, he lifted, leaving eyelashes stuck to his cheeks. Then he lifted higher. He blinked, lifted his lids up again, and rolled his eyes. He saw nothing. Not darkness. Nothing. Exactly the same thing that he saw with his elbow or the back of his knee. He felt his throat constricting in panic. He tried to swallow his fear back down, but it was rising too fast, moving into terror.

"Henry, that's disgusting," Henrietta said. "Put your eyelids down. Your eyeballs will dry out."

Henry pulled them up higher. He could feel his eyes moving, ricocheting around. "I can't see," he said simply. "I can't see. Henrietta, I can't see." His knee started bouncing wildly. He tugged hard on his eyelids, tugged against the stretching pain.

"Stop it!" Henrietta yelled. "You'll make it worse!" Henry felt her hands on his, the pain in his eyelids stopped, and he knew his eyes were shut. Warm wetness swallowed his face. "They looked fine," Henrietta said. "They weren't even bloodshot. I thought they'd be pretty nasty, but it's just your eyelids. Give 'em a minute."

"I'm blind," Henry said. "God, no. I want to see. I want to see. Open my eyes. Henrietta, open them."

"Shhh," Henrietta said. "Hold on. Does this feel good? I'm just wiping some of this stuff off your face, then we'll try again."

"Now!" Henry yelled. "Now! Get your hands off my face!" Henry swiped at Henrietta's arms and pushed her as hard as he could. He heard her stagger and hit the floor. Grabbing at his eyes, he tried to stand up. "I want to see," he whispered. "I want to see, I want to see. Right now. I'm going to see."

Henrietta was crying somewhere, and he could hear people running up the stairs. He lifted his lids, but he knew that he couldn't have. There was nothing there. Then, suddenly, he realized that he must have more eyelids. Another pair. His old eyelids must be underneath. They were still shut. He dug into his eyes with his fingers, pinching, feeling for more skin.

"There they are," he muttered. "There they are, there they are. They'll open." He tripped and staggered forward. His elbow hit something hard, and his head followed.

Strong hands gripped his wrists and pulled them away from his face.

"Henry," Uncle Frank said. "Enough. Breathe. Now. Breathe."

He was lowered to his back on the hard floor, and his arms were pinned to his chest. Frank's rough hand ran over his forehead. His thumb scraped over Henry's eyebrows and then the surface of his eyelids and cheek-bones. Henry felt one eyelid open.

"Henry?" Frank said softly. "What do you see?"

"Nothing," Henry said, and his breath spasmed in his chest. "There's another eyelid inside. You have to open it. Please. Can you?"

His eye shut, and he was lifted to his feet. Frank wrapped him up from behind, pinning his arms to his sides.

"Girls," Frank's voice said. "You're on your own. We'll call from the hospital. Dots, find a number for Phil and Ursula."

"I'll come," Richard said. "I won't be any trouble."

"Fine," Frank said. "Hurry. But you'll be in the back."

Henrietta hated crying. Nothing was stupider than crying. The old brown truck had left an hour ago. Her mother had been in the driver's seat while her father held Henry tight, the washcloth over his eyes. Richard had been on his back, rattling around in the rusted-out bed.

Penelope and Anastasia had followed her up to the attic. She'd cried because she was mad, because Henry had hurt her, because she'd been terrified, because she had to. Anastasia, pale, had watched silently and hadn't been rude once. Penny had hugged Henrietta, held her, and Henrietta hadn't pushed her away. Not at first.

They were both gone now. She'd asked them to leave, politely, and they had. She was by herself, sitting on the end of Henry's bed, and she was still a little shaky.

Everything inside her wanted to say that Henry would be fine, that if he'd just sucked it up and stopped freaking out, his eyes would have been normal. But she knew that probably wasn't true. Maybe. Either way, she hated it when people lost control. It made everything worse. So did crying.

Henrietta flopped back onto Henry's bed, but jerked up at the touch of the wet pillowcase. She picked the pillow up to flip it over, and froze. There was a piece of paper on the bed, stamped with the same green man seal that had been on the faeren letters. She read the "A Lert" quickly, and then slowly, and then she stared at the signature and the note.

She sighed and flipped the paper away from her. Henry had been trying to go through the cupboards by himself. What else could they mean by "tampering and transportation"? Of course he'd been trying. He got mad at her when she did anything on her own, but he would never include her in anything if he didn't have to. The only reason she even knew about the cupboards at all was because she'd caught him chipping the plaster off his wall in the middle of the night.

But she had the key. Henry may have tried to get through the small doors, but it wasn't possible. He needed her. And now he was either blind or going nuts or both or faking everything but his swollen eyelids. She could have helped him. They could have gone through dozens of cupboards by now.

She wondered where he kept Grandfather's journal. Probably tucked under his socks, where he kept everything.

Henrietta slid down the bed toward his nightstand-dresser and reached for the top drawer. Before her hand touched the handle, three sharp cracks burst from the cupboard wall behind her. She jumped and turned, scanning over the cupboards' formation. None of the doors were open.

Three more cracks rattled in the wall, and on the second, her eyes caught something behind the glass in the little post-office box. She moved back to the foot of the bed, crouched, and stared at the cloudy panel. The end of a stick, a cane, slid up against it from behind and rapped sharply. Then it withdrew. After a moment of silence, a folded piece of paper replaced it.

"Henrietta?" Anastasia's voice came up the stairs. "Do you want to come down? What are you doing?"

Henrietta twisted and spoke over her shoulder. "No thanks," she said. "I'm just thinking."

"What about?" Anastasia asked.

Henrietta stood up and moved to Henry's dresser. His sock drawer was empty. Socks only. "Just Henry!" she yelled. One drawer down, beneath Henry's T-shirts, she found what she was looking for: the two volumes of Grandfather's journal rubber-banded together and a small key.

"Zeke called for Henry," Anastasia said. "Penny's talking to him."

"Good," Henrietta said. She moved quickly back to the post-office box and inserted the key. With nervous hands, she pulled out the heavy paper and reshut the door quietly.

"Have you seen the raggant?" Anastasia asked. "I don't know where he is."

"Dad says he leaves sometimes. He always comes back." Henrietta looked down at the folded paper in her hands. "I just want to think right now, Anastasia. Why don't you look for him? Check the barn. He likes the loft."

Henrietta waited. Anastasia would come all the way up, or she would go away. She couldn't just keep yelling up the stairs.

"I don't know," Anastasia said. "Maybe I will. I hate it when Penny talks to Zeke. It's so boring to listen to, and I don't want to just sit around thinking about Henry being blind. It makes me feel sick."

Henrietta bit her lip and didn't say anything.

"Fine," Anastasia said. "I'll go bug Penny."

Henrietta turned the paper over in her hands. It was rough, almost fuzzy around the edges, and its surface was textured like a window screen. It had been folded and was sealed with a sprawling tree in black wax. She slid her finger beneath it.

The page was asymmetrical, and a stamp of the same tree was set near the top. The note was sloppily hand-written and spots of ink were flecked throughout.

H–

Ablution grant me. I am pressed. Our brief converse and your able departing have suaded me of your worth. If, deedly, you first sighted mage in the fork tungs of the storm, then you have need of my ansbettment. Not, and you will perish in the morph. In my own second seeing, I gibbered mad and blindful to the gaping tomb. I can hold you back. Those who keep you cannot ken such pain, nor what you now become. Bide. I prepare a way.

–D

Henrietta didn't know what *ablution* was or *ansbettment* or *the morph*, but she didn't need to. Henry had been talking to someone, and she knew who it was. She'd seen one of his letters before, and it had sounded just as halfway nuts as this one, wicked even. *Fork tungs* were probably lightning, and that meant that Henry had been talking to him last night, last night after he'd sent Henrietta away. And whoever this weirdo was, he was going to try to help Henry leave.

Henrietta was confused. It would have been easy to think that Henry was doing his own exploring and trying to make his own way out of Kansas without her help. The two letters looked that way. But his eye panic had been real. He had no reason to fake blindness. Unless he was working on some kind of plan.

Chewing her lip, she looked around the room. She needed to stop thinking. She needed to make a decision and do something. If Henry was being a weasel, she had every right to explore on her own. If he really was sick and couldn't explore himself, he would need her to do it for him. If he was dumb enough to trust the letter guy, then she should intervene.

Henrietta picked up Grandfather's journal and turned to the diagram of the cupboards. Then she stepped back and looked up at Henry's wall and down at the ink on the page. Grandfather's key was in her pocket. She could do it right now if Anastasia didn't catch her. She would.

She picked a door on the wall, a small, almost diamond-shaped door near the compasses in the center. It was labeled 18 in the journal. She looked at its name. Treb/Actium/Constant. She would just go through far enough to get a feel for the place. She wouldn't do a full explore. That would mean loading a backpack and getting ready and everything, and she didn't want to wait and end up changing her mind. She had to do it right now.

Henrietta flipped pages until she found the combinations. Then she knelt on the end of Henry's bed, inhaled slowly, held her breath, and twisted the left knob through all the symbols until its large arrow was in place over the horseshoe-looking thing with little circle-ends. And then she turned the right knob, clicking slowing through the Roman numerals until it was on IX. She double-checked the combination and slid back off the bed. She picked up the two pieces of paper and, along with the journals, tucked them under Henry's pillow. Then she turned and hurried down the attic stairs.

On the landing, she waited, listening. She could hear Penny talking downstairs, but no Anastasia. She checked the bedroom that she shared with her sisters, and when she was sure Anastasia was either downstairs or outside, she went to Grandfather's door.

Though her father had thoroughly mulched its surface trying to get in, it was as solid as it had ever been. Henrietta ignored her shaking hand and slid the key into the small hole in the wood. It turned, and the door swung open silently. She stepped inside, put the key in her pocket, and shut the door behind her.

Henrietta swallowed hard. The last time she had been in the room, both of her parents had been unconscious on the floor. A stain as dark as oil marked where her father had bled. The room was silent and dusty, books lay on the floor where they had fallen the last time she'd gone through the cupboards alone, and the end of a short rope stuck out from beneath the bed. Against the wall, beside the bookshelves, was a plain cupboard door, halfway open and large enough to crawl through.

Before she could change her mind, Henrietta got on her hands and knees and crawled into the door. The inside of the cupboard was dark and silent, and her breath tasted like dust. She inched forward, waiting.

*   *   *

The rank smell hit her in the face, the smell of sewage and hot salt water, of burning wood and tar and flesh. Voices followed, screams and yells, commands and curses. Splitting timbers.

She felt the floor moving beneath her, and her hand found the back of a small door. She pushed, and the door swung open. Golden heat struck her in the face as she squinted out over hundreds of men scrambling across the deck of a heaving ship. Some were armed with swords or bows, and others were stripped down to loincloths, wearing blood and sweat while they crawled around huge-timbered catapults. While she watched, frozen in shock, a storm of arrows ripped through the crowd of men. A crash like subterranean thunder shook the ship, and the deck roiled and lurched. A huge galley, spined with oar blades and twice the height of the deck in front of her, ground its way through the prow, first rolling the smaller ship almost on its side, and then plowing its bow beneath the water. The ship dove, levered forward beneath the weight of the galley, and Henrietta bounced and slid head and shoulders out of the little door. Splaying her legs, she wedged her arms against the cupboard walls. She could feel the deck writhing beneath her and the crackling of enormous beams, twisted to explosion. She had to squirm backward, back up the increasing incline. Back to Kansas. Back to now.

A man, glistening in his bloody skin, landed on his stomach in front of her, a broken arrow sprouting from his neck. He clawed at the deck as he began to slide, and his fingers grazed her face. Then, with the last strength of the dying, they closed around her hair.

Henrietta grabbed at his wrist, but the man's weight had already done its work. Her feet slipped free, and together, the two slid down across the slimy deck, down to the hungry water.

CHAPTER FOUR

Henrietta collided with something solid, and she gasped for air. She was hanging on to the beamed base of a catapult fastened to the tilting deck. Her legs were underwater. Her hair was free, and the man who'd dragged her into this world had disappeared. Drums were beating, men were groaning, and the wood beneath her still crackled in its contortion. The huge galley's five rows of oars were backing water, leaving the smaller ship to find the bottom.

Looking up the inclined deck, Henrietta could see where she'd come from. A small door hung open in the housing of another catapult on the other side of the shattered mast. That's where she needed to be, before she was shot, stabbed, or the entire ship sank beneath her.

The deck was mostly clear. The unwounded living had taken to the sea, and Henrietta could hear them praying and cursing behind her in the waves. She refused to look in the water around her, or to think about what was bumping against her back.

The big galley pulled its ram free, and Henrietta felt

herself, felt the entire ship, sink farther into the water. The wreck was becoming more vertical by the second.

She couldn't grip the deck with her hands, and her feet slid all over the planks. Henrietta turned, unwillingly, and looked at the bodies in the water around her. Most wore very little, but one man, floating facedown, had a knife handle sticking out of a belt in the small of his back.

Henrietta hooked the corpse with her toe. She tugged the little bronze-colored knife free and gripped it tight.

The water was at her ribs.

She drove the knife between two planks, as high above her head as she could reach. Then, scrambling her wet shoes over the deck surface, she managed to get most of the way out of the water. She found a splinter with her left foot and pushed higher, ignoring the pain as the deck shard dug through the sole of her shoe and into the ball of her foot. Working the knife loose, she reinserted it above her and pulled up again, kneeling on the steep deck before finding another painful foothold. She was climbing. She could do this. Her arms were shaking, and she might puncture her foot any second, but she could do this. She was closer to home.

The open door she had fallen through looked surprisingly small. Too small. But she refused to think about it. She had come in, so she could go back.

Halfway there, with another fifteen feet to climb, she stopped, relaxed her body against the still-crackling deck, wrapped her arms around the base of the mast, and panted. Looking out over the sea behind her, she realized that the ship wasn't in the open ocean. Islands dotted the horizon, and hundreds of ships were moving around them, crawling like centipedes on their oars.

The water had climbed with her, lapping at the deck beneath her feet. And it hadn't taken any rest. Again it reached her shoes. She gathered herself for another push, and as she did, the ship sighed beneath her. Something had changed. The ship was surrendering, sinking faster, diving below the waves.

Henrietta dropped the knife. As the water swallowed her shins, she pushed herself up and lunged for another hold. She caught it, splayed her feet, and lunged again. Each time, the water caught up to her as the ship dropped, and each time, she clawed her way above the surface, until finally, clenching her teeth and with the sea up to her thighs, her fingers caught the inside of the small doorway.

It was much too small for her.

Henrietta closed her eyes and forced her rubber arms to pull once more, forced her legs to drive her forward while her feet slipped on the wet planks. Her grandfather's room was just above her. She could get there. She kicked up, and her head was inside. The water was frothing around her waist. Her hands found the edge of the cupboard on the other side, and her fingertips felt carpet. One last surge, a groaning, vein-throbbing pull, and she spilled through onto Grandfather's floor.

Exhausted but panicked, she picked herself up and

ran out of the room and up the attic stairs, leaving Grandfather's door open behind her. Staggering into Henry's room, she fell against the cupboard wall and, with one hand, spun the compass knobs, not caring where they stopped. Then, with quivering legs, she hurried back down to the landing and, leaning on the rail, returned to Grandfather's room.

Inside, the carpet was a swamp, and water still dripped from the cupboard. She hoped it wouldn't drain through the ceiling in the living room, but who really cared if it did? She wasn't drowning in it. She wasn't floating through the middle of some bizarre sea battle with no hope of ever coming home. She shut the door and turned to the bathroom.

"Henrietta?" Penelope yelled. "Are you okay?"

"Yeah," Henrietta managed, and her throat clamped shut. "I'm," she said, and swallowed, "just gonna take a shower."

"Zeke came over!" Anastasia yelled. "Come down and tell him about Henry."

"In a minute," Henrietta said. She walked into the bathroom, locked the door behind her, and leaned against the sink. Her clothes were ripped and coated with grime from the deck—oil and blood and salt water. On her face, finger tracks, painted in blood, striped down her forehead and cheek where the man had touched her before he fell. She felt a sob in her chest, but she swallowed it down. Instead, she turned on the shower, and, shivering, she stepped in.

She stood in the shower and watched the filth run off her clothes and off her shoes and swirl around the drain. Then, hesitating, she put her hand to her face and rubbed away the blood. Cold fear and relief surged through her. Her legs shook, finally refusing to hold her up. Kicking off her shoes, she huddled in the tub.

Grandfather's key was in her pocket. Digging into her leg.

Henry lay perfectly still. He didn't know if he was awake or asleep, but he knew that he was listening. And he wanted to keep listening. So he didn't move.

A woman was talking. "The sedation we gave him will have worn off by the time he wakes up. I'd rather not redose him, but we can if you need us to."

"We'll be fine," Frank said.

"We don't know that." Dotty sounded nervous. "We don't know how he'll be tonight."

"I'll give you something just in case," the woman said. "You don't have to use it, but you may want to. Panic, in this case, is not a symptom, it's the cause."

"You really think it's all in his head?" Dotty asked. "His eyes looked so awful, and that burn on his hand?"

Henry heard the woman shifting. She was tapping something, and her feet squeaked. "We ran every scan that we can. His brain is clear of abnormalities, and he has no discernible nerve damage. The glucose levels in his urine were a little high, but his blood tested fine. His eyes weren't actually that bad, either. The swelling went right down, and they react perfectly normally to light. If his eyesight had been damaged by a lightning strike, swollen eyelids would be an unrelated symptom. Quite honestly, my bet is that he had a mild allergic incident that triggered massive anxiety. A panic attack. He believed himself to have been struck by lightning, and, after the swelling, he believed himself into blindness. If he doesn't regain his sight soon, I think you should start by taking him to a therapist."

"The burn," Frank said.

"Excuse me?"

"What about the burn?"

"Well," the woman said, "I can't explain the burn, but I can tell you that it is not like any lightning injury that I've ever seen, and it's certainly not serious. It looks ugly, but it's rather shallow. It's not infected, and it's already healing over. It may play a role in his panic, but it is unrelated to his other symptoms."

"Madam?" came Richard's voice, nasal but bold. "Ahmm, yes, excuse me."

The woman was laughing. "What can I do for you?"

"I'm afraid you are mistaken. I cannot believe that Henry York would falsify his blindness."

Henry could have climbed out of bed and hugged him.

"Oh, his blindness is real. It's just that his anxiety is causing it."

"Henry is not inclined to fear."

Henry swallowed. This, unfortunately, he knew to be false, but Richard continued. "I have stood beside him in extreme peril. Only I was standing more behind him than not. He did not panic and imagine himself to be blind. He did what had to be done."

"Richard, honey," Dotty began, but Frank was chuckling.

Richard sniffed. "If I lay blind upon the bed, and you told me that the weakness of my mind had been the cause, I would believe you. Not Henry." Richard kept talking, but his voice grew quieter, more distant. And then it stopped. They'd left the room.

Henry was embarrassed. Embarrassed because he knew Richard was wrong. He was entirely capable of a panic attack. But this wasn't one. He wasn't panicked. He opened one eye and squinted up at . . . nothing, where there should have been ceiling tiles and fluorescent lights. He was blind, and that was that.

Worse than being blind was being blind and being told that he wasn't really. Worse than that was being blind and being taken home from the hospital, where his cousins would be told that he wasn't really, that his mind was only playing make-believe.

Penelope would pity him. She'd probably offer to read to him. Anastasia would ask him why he didn't just stop it and start seeing again. Henrietta would think he was weak. She already did. Henrietta would know she was right.

And Richard—loyal Richard would stand with his scrawny arms crossed and his thick lips pursed, and he would defend the honor of Henry York, knight of the realm. That would be the final touch. Richard's defense would make everyone want to believe Henry was nuts.

A pit grew in Henry's stomach as he finally realized the worst. His cousins would tell Zeke Johnson. Zeke, who had taught him to play baseball and never laughed at him, who had belted a witch and saved Henry's life. Zeke would finally look down on him. And all the guys at the ragged baseball diamond would wonder why Henry didn't play anymore.

Henry thinks he's blind.

All in a moment, Henry wished he was back in Boston. He wouldn't be sent to school if he was blind, and when he was lying on the couch in his mother's new apartment, there would only ever be one person there to think he was weak. The nanny would look at him and shake her head, but he wouldn't see and he wouldn't care. He wouldn't know her.

Or maybe it would be a man. Someone strong enough to control him when he had his regular panic attack.

When they came back, Henry was sitting up on the side of the bed, wondering what he looked like in his little gown.

No one asked if he could see.

Everyone left while he redressed himself, or he thought they did, and then Aunt Dotty took his arm and led him through the halls. He sat in a chair beside Uncle Frank while Dotty talked to someone about his parents' insurance.

"Couldn't get ahold of 'em," Frank said.

"Who?" Henry asked.

"Phil and Urs. We got all old numbers. Dots couldn't find that lawyer letter, or we would have called them."

"You gave it to me," Henry said. "And I threw it in the field before the storm."

"Right," Frank said. "Well, that's probably the best place for it. Could be useful out there."

Henry sat up in his chair. "Uncle Frank," he said. "Do you think there's nothing wrong with me?"

"Of course there's something wrong with you, Henry." Henry listened to the sound of his uncle scratching a stubbled jaw. "Right now, I'd say your eyes are wrong. If lightning didn't do it, then something did. But I'm glad they're not busted. There's a difference between busted and just not working."

"Do you think they'll start working?"

"I do," Richard said. Henry had forgotten he was there.

"Don't know," Frank said. "Have to wait and see, I guess."

Henry sagged back down in his chair. "Or wait and not," he muttered.

"All set!" Dotty said. Her hands picked up Henry's, and he stood, waiting to be guided. A smooth arm slid beneath his, and he was turned.

Smelling his aunt, Henry listened to the world go by. The television faded behind him, and the automatic doors slid open. People passing, talking, and then the air crawling over his face and around his ears, his shoes on asphalt, cars starting, stopping, turning, and eventually, the squeal of the truck door opening, the sighing springs in the old seat, the smell of dust older than he was in the upholstery, the doors slamming, and the muffled thumping of Richard in the truck bed. Finally, the click of the key and the slow throbbing complaint of the engine before it exploded into life.

The explosions would pull them home.

Henrietta walked downstairs. She'd pulled her wet hair back into a tight ponytail, and she was wearing an old sweatshirt she'd stolen from her father months ago.

Zeke and her sisters were sitting around the table. They'd given him a glass of lemonade, but it was all ice now. He was leaning his lean frame back in his chair, passing an old baseball hat from hand to hand. A line in his short hair showed where he usually wore it.

"Hey, Henrietta," he said.

She smiled and stood beside Penny's chair. Zeke knew everything about the old house and the attic cupboards. At least he knew as much as Anastasia and Penelope. He'd ruined his wooden bat on the witch's head. The blood spatters had burned Henry's jaw.

They were all looking at her. Her face had to be different. She'd just watched people die. She'd almost died with them. Her sisters never would have known what happened to her. But they would have known that she'd done something horribly stupid. How much water would have come through that door? Henry, Kansas, could have become a saltwater lake.

Penelope stood up and pointed to Zeke's glass. "Like some more lemonade?"

"Sure," he said. "Thanks." And he handed it to her.

"Henrietta," Anastasia said. "Tell him about Henry's eyes. Do you think he'll be—" Anastasia stopped.

Henrietta put her arms around Penny and squeezed her tight. She didn't know why it was embarrassing, hugging her sister, but it was. She didn't care. She could feel tears building up in her eyes, and she quickly blinked them away. She wasn't going to do that again. Letting go of her sister, she stepped back, puffed out her cheeks, and looked at the three faces watching her.

Penny was smiling. Zeke didn't look surprised at all. Anastasia's mouth was open, and she stared blankly.

"Sorry," Henrietta said. "I think I'm going to lie down. Henry's eyelids were swollen this morning, and he couldn't see. That's all I know. Did Mom and Dad call?"

"Just when they got there," Penny said. "They didn't know anything yet."

Anastasia leaned forward onto the table. "Do you think he was faking?"

"No," Henrietta said. "He wasn't."

Zeke set his hat on the back of his head. "But he wasn't struck by lightning?"

Henrietta shrugged. "Something messed him up pretty good." She turned back toward the stairs. "I'm going to lie down," she said again.

She stopped on the second-story landing and looked over at her bedroom door. Then she climbed the attic stairs.

In Henry's room, she dropped onto his bed and slid her hand under his pillow. She was not going through any more cupboards by herself. Ever. At least not until she had read through Grandfather's journal. And, depending on what was in it, maybe not then.

She'd read the first pages before, the apologies to Frank and Dotty, the admissions of deception and hypocrisy, and the stuff about her great-grandfather's notes. But she ran her eyes over it anyway, and slowed down when she hit something new. It didn't all make sense, but it didn't matter. She was going to read for the parts that did.

> . . . You will rediscover the cupboards, and you will find it necessary to explore them. This is written so that you may avoid harm, such as is possible in such undertakings, but particularly the mistakes made by my father and myself.
>
> This house and these cupboards were my father's lifework, as well as his life destruction. If you care to see his notes, they are all tied up with string and tucked away under a loose

floorboard beneath my bed. All of them are there, from his first swirling epiphanies and elegant theoretical modifications of Euclid, Pythagoras, Ptolemy, and Sharaf al-Tusi to the last of his incomprehensibly mad droolings. The house and the doors became my work, but my father's madness quenched my desire in the end. He was never able to make all the doors work. For good or ill, I completed his design.

I cannot hope that you, Dorothy, or you, Frank, could ever understand the whole of it, so I will simply say this: my father applied the motion of real lines through space to a form of spherical geometry. He became able to shortcut points in space. As for time, what is time but space in motion? Your eyes are glazing, I know. But humor a dead man. My father could not create such connections. He could only find, rearrange, and exploit them. The magic (it was all mechanics to him—but it took the potent relics of FitzFaeren for me to make it all work) is in the wood or the iron or the stone. Such things are not as isolated in time as we are. A tree is alive in all of its rings. An old oak may watch an ancient ritual, see blood shed, and feel it rubbed on its bark. Fell it centuries later, shape it with skill, and it may take you there, where it still lives, in the darkest of its memories.

Such connections are frequently violent; they

are scars, the results of evil and wrongness. Some connect to a moment. Some connect to a place. And so the warnings begin: Do not travel the cupboards unless you are braced to witness murder, wander tombs, and crawl through bone-filled ruins. The doors are not evil. But they remember it.

Do not think that what you are seeing is illusion. Where you are is always now. You may be beheaded in Topkapi, or drown beneath a trebuchet in Actium along with the slaves chained to the oars. Both of those doors always connect to the same moments of danger.

Henrietta sat up on the bed. She had been drifting off, but now her eyes were wide. She could have read this sooner, but what kind of a warning was it? You can drown in Actium? Moment of danger? Why not, "You'll crawl through onto a ship as it is crushed and sinks. Hang on or you'll be lost forever"? That would have been helpful. At least now she knew that her grandfather didn't exactly overstate things. And she knew she never wanted to find out what Topkapi was.

Still sitting up, she read on.

Do not think that you are simply in your own past—I cannot think that is possible. There are many presents and many pasts, but only one world. It is like a tree. No, it is like a bramble in a ditch, or tumbleweeds tangled beyond sorting. It may be three, it may be twelve, but for any purpose, it is only one now. There are "worlds" that have the same pasts as our own but have forked into their own branch. In truth, I believe that all of these places, these "worlds," at least those that you may access, share a single past, a clean stalk that has now lost all order. Violence beyond reckoning has been done to it. Maybe I overestimate the chaos. There are really only a few "worlds" available through the cupboards. Many of the doors lead to locations in the same time and on the same plane.

Do not think that you can damage your present. I do not believe that we can travel into our own pasts. Any damage done is done to the future of others. Lord knows, I've done enough.

I meant this to be well thought out and ably executed, but now I find that I have less desire to continue warning you, and a deeper urge to simply unburden myself of guilt. I have no priest, and so you must hear my confessions, even though I will already number among the damned when you do.

FitzFaeren, beautiful FitzFaeren. Those people and those halls were all destroyed because of me and what I took. Crawl through that way, and you will see the most vivid of *hauntings, the memory of the wood and of the place. You will even see me, or some image of me, fleeing my own work, scrambling back to the safety of my bedroom. Eli has forgiven me, or so he says, but I cannot.*

Henrietta had seen those halls. She had seen the dancing and heard the music. She had chased Eli, the short old man, out of Grandfather's bedroom and back to that place. Eli had called her grandfather a fool.

She wanted to set the knobs to FitzFaeren and go slither into the cupboard downstairs to watch the dancers. She wanted to look for her grandfather. Why had she let Eli leave? He could have explained all of this.

Downstairs, she heard loud voices. Her sisters'.

Henry was home.

"No," she heard him say. "You're not helping me. I can do it by myself. I'm fine."

Her father said something she couldn't make out, and the house was silent of everything but slow footsteps on the stairs.

Henrietta waited. Even if Henry was in a bad mood, she wanted to talk to him. His feet found the attic stairs, and she listened to them complain as he climbed.

After a minute, his doors swung open and Henry stepped in. He looked much better. His eyelids were only a little heavy. She smiled at him and immediately felt guilty for it. His eyes were wide open, but they rolled around the room, groping for images they couldn't find. She swallowed, wondering what to say. Maybe she should cough.

Henry felt his way to the end of his bed, and then the cupboard wall. Running his hands over the cupboards, he crouched slowly, until he'd found the door to Endor. His fingertips sought out each screw and felt all around the edges of the door. He seemed satisfied and straightened up, breathing heavily, and groped for the door to Badon Hill. He levered it open and stuck his hand inside. Suddenly, gritting his teeth, he punched, hard, and Henrietta heard the crack.

Henry pulled his fist out and sucked on his knuckles.

"Hey, Henry," Henrietta said.

Henry jolted and nearly tripped.

"What are you doing in here?" he asked quietly.

"I was—I was reading Grandfather's journal. I went through a cupboard today. While you were gone. It was really stupid, I know. I almost died. I thought we should read the journal before we did anything else."

She waited for him to ask for the story, or repeat her own insult, or at least get angry that she'd looked through his drawers. He didn't. Instead, he sniffed.

"You're definitely not from number 18," she said, and tried to laugh. "It's a sea battle. Listen," Henrietta continued, "with your whole blind thing . . ."

"I don't want to talk about it."

"Well, we'll have to figure something out."

"You going to get me a guide dog? I already have Richard. Just leave. I want to lie down."

Henrietta stood up quickly and backed out of his way. "Sure," she said. She tucked the journal under his pillow, and then she dug in her pocket.

Henry crawled onto his bed and sprawled out, face-down.

"I'm really sorry," Henrietta said.

Henry snorted. "You didn't do it."

"No," Henrietta said. "I'm not sorry you're blind. I mean, I am. But I meant that I'm sorry for lying. About the key."

Henry didn't say anything. Henrietta waited, but she didn't think he wanted to hear anything else. She would talk to him again later. Tonight, maybe. But probably tomorrow. She stepped out of his room.

"Your stuff's under your pillow," she said, and she shut the doors.

Henry thought he'd done well. She might think he was weak, but he hadn't acted weak. He had acted tired. He hadn't acted. He was tired. And he had no idea what time it was. He hoped the dinner hour was past so he wouldn't have to refuse to go sit at the table.

He slid his hand under his pillow. There were Grandfather's rubber-banded journals, but something else was on top of it, something cold.

His fingers closed around the key.

CHAPTER FIVE

Henry rolled onto his back, clenching the key. He couldn't believe Henrietta had actually given it to him. Of course, she wouldn't be too worried about him using it. He was blind. She could afford to give it to him now.

Without thinking, he lifted the key up to look at it. Frustrated, and more insulted by his blindness because he'd forgotten about it, he dropped his arm back to the bed. But as it fell, he saw something move. His eyes had captured motion. He waved his arm and caught the faintest blur where he knew his hand had to be. Dropping the key, he held his hand still in front of his face. It was his burned hand. He couldn't see his arm. He couldn't see his wrist or hand or the room. In the nothingness in front of him floated his burn. Only it wasn't just a burn. It was a symbol, and it was moving.

Henry couldn't have taken his eyes off of it if he'd wanted to. There was nothing else to see, nowhere else to focus. The symbol held colors, every color, and they slipped out as it moved, not quickly, from shape to shape, crawling and morphing like a glowing snake spelling out some strange alphabet. But somehow, while changing, the symbol was never really changed. It was always itself, traveling through moods, and ages and times—speaking a life cycle, a patterned history of greens and golds and grays.

Henry knew what it was. His head throbbed as he looked at it, and he remembered the pain. This was a picture, a word, a name, the life of a dandelion, and he was looking at it, seeing it in a way that he had never seen anything. Knowing it.

Suddenly, in a burst of fear, Henry put his hand down and tucked it beneath his leg. His whole body ached from the pain of looking at it, and his hand throbbed. But more frightening than the pain was the sheer incomprehensibility of what had happened to him.

He remembered everything. He remembered Henrietta digging for the key and the storm and the wind and the sun-gilded fields. He remembered seeing a flicker in a dandelion. He had stared and throbbed and seen, and then he had touched. And Henrietta had shaken him awake. And he'd gone blind.

Henry had seen magic before. He slept beside little doors that couldn't be very well explained by anything else. He'd seen his uncle Frank's ax beaten back by magic. The blood of a witch had burned its way into his jaw. He'd watched a mailman's pant legs through his attic wall, and he'd smelled Badon Hill. But still, in Henry's mind, magic was something wrong, something bent, dangerous, something that could be kept someplace else if you remembered to screw the door shut.

Dandelions were not magic. They couldn't be. They were here. They were normal. You couldn't shut them up someplace or even keep them out of your lawn. If they were magic, well, then everything was.

Henry shivered, choked, and then crawled onto the floor. He was going to throw up. He'd done that in this room before, terrified by a world unlike anything he'd ever been told. He was going crazy, or the world was. There were no other options. And he didn't like either.

Crazy or not, he didn't want to puke. He sat up on his knees and tried to breathe like a sane person—long, slow, even breaths. It helped. Maybe he should see a therapist. He probably was mental. What kind of blind person could only see one burn? A dandelion burn.

His door creaked open, and he looked up.

"Henrietta?" he asked. "Richard?"

Something snorted, and he relaxed. "C'mere," he said, and put out his good hand, waiting for the raggant's sagging side. Instead, something hard and blunt and a little frayed butted into his palm. He pulled on the creature's horn, slid his hand up its head, and scratched behind its twitching ears.

Fur brushed against his other hand, and he knew that Blake the cat had come upstairs as well. Blind, crazy, and with knots in his stomach, Henry still smiled. He scooped up the two animals, held them tight like charms against panic, and lay back on his bed to think.

With one hand, Henry kneaded the raggant's back.

Blake licked the other. The world was the crazy one. He hadn't given a miniature rhino wings, or cats sandpaper tongues.

I'm normal, Henry thought. *Normal. Normal as a dandelion.*

There were three options, as far as Henry could tell. He could explore the cupboards blind and probably die or at least get permanently lost. Which didn't sound too terrible right now. Or he could wait for his parents, or one of his parents, or one of their lawyers, to come get him. He could leave the raggant behind and never mention his dandelion insanity again. If his eyesight returned, he could come back to Kansas when he was eighteen. If it didn't, then his parents would have him spending a lot of time with therapists. Or he could ask Henrietta to help him find where he was from. But he wasn't sure how any of this would help him. He wanted to see. In Kansas or Boston or Badon Hill, he just wanted his eyes to work. And there was no one he could talk to about that.

Henry sighed. He wished he had read through his grandfather's journal. He'd skimmed through most of it, looking for his name, but he hadn't been in any hurry to read the whole thing. He didn't like the cupboards, and from what he'd read, he didn't much care for his grandfather, either. He would have read it before doing any exploring. But he hadn't even wanted to explore. He'd wanted to go to Badon Hill.

He couldn't read the journal now. He could ask Anastasia to read it to him, but that would be pure tor-ture. Penelope would insist that they tell her parents everything. Henry didn't think Uncle Frank would mind that he'd kept the journal, but Aunt Dotty would. And she could put a stop to anyone reading it. Henrietta was too much to deal with right now.

The journal wouldn't help him, anyway. He needed someone who would know what was happening, some-one who could tell him why he could see his burn float-ing through the air like a living word and nothing else. Or, if they didn't know why, at least someone who could tell him what to do next, someone who could mix him something nasty and vomitous to drink and dance around and shake some bones in a monkey's skull.

He needed someone magic. Not some goofy voo-dooist, like the people in his parents' travel videos who dressed up in yellow feathers and papier-mâché for the tourists' cameras. Real magic, magic like, he didn't know what. Like the wind. Like the storm and the colors and the dandelion. Magic that could change you, that could turn caterpillars into butterflies and tadpoles into frogs and wood into coal into diamonds. He needed someone who could . . . make wood stronger than a chain saw.

Henry sat up, and the raggant tumbled off his lap and onto the floor like a sack of mud. It groaned and sputtered, snorted twice, and began snoring.

Eli. The little old man's magic had kept Grand-father's door shut for two years. And he had known

Grandfather. He might even know how Henry had come into Kansas or which cupboard he'd come through. If Henrietta hadn't chased him away through FitzFaeren, Henry might already know all the answers. He wouldn't be blind in an attic with less than two weeks before he lost his chance to find out who he really was and where he was from.

He shouldn't explore the cupboards. He should look for Eli in FitzFaeren. And he should read Grandfather's journal before he did. Someone should read it to him.

Henry stood up and felt for his doors. When he'd found them, he stepped out into the attic.

"Richard!" he yelled, and while he waited for an answer, he lifted his hand up and watched. Dandelion soul floated through space.

Henrietta slouched on the floor beside the muted television as it worked its way through commercials. Her mother stood behind the couch, wearing yellow rubber gloves still wet from the sink. Her father was sitting in the middle of the couch, separating Richard and Anastasia, and Penny was also on the floor. She was reading. She was always reading.

"I think I should take some food up," Dotty said. "He needs to eat. Someone should be sitting with him. He shouldn't be alone."

"I'll sit with him," Richard said.

Frank slapped a hand on Richard's knee. He was wearing tight pink sweatpants, castoffs from Anastasia.

"Stay here for now," Frank said. He tipped his head back and looked at his wife behind him. "Dots, we spent the whole day touchin' him and breathin' on him while people he couldn't see stuck him for blood, ran him through tubes, had him pee in a cup, and prodded around his eyeballs. If he wants his space right now, I can't blame him. We can offer him some grub in a bit."

"Do you think he's okay?" Dotty asked.

Frank looked back down. "No," he said. "I don't. He'll need to see other doctors, and keep seeing other doctors until one finally says that he's not nuts and that it's just that there's a little beetle that's hatched in his head, and it's put its foot in just the wrong spot. Henry's got a lot more prodding ahead of him. But it doesn't have to start till tomorrow."

"Can that happen?" Anastasia asked. "A beetle inside your head?"

"No," Dotty said. "It can't."

Frank nodded. "It happens."

"You'd have to inhale an egg or something," Penelope said. "When it hatched, it'd just crawl the wrong way in your sinus cavity and get into your brain." She put down her book. "Dad, I could go read to Henry. I wouldn't be crowding him."

Frank shook his head.

"Frank, I'm really worried about him." Dotty lifted a yellow hand to her forehead. "But there's not a beetle in his brain."

"Something's in it," Frank said. He reached back and found his wife's hand. "I'll check on him in a bit."

"Richard!" Henry's voice found its way into the room.

Richard jumped up off the couch and looked at Frank. Frank smiled and nodded, and the skinny, pink-legged boy hopped over Henrietta and ran for the stairs. After a minute, when the television's sound was back on and her mother had left the room, Henrietta rolled onto her knees, crawled to the door, stood up, and walked quietly after him.

Henrietta didn't have to climb the attic stairs. She could hear perfectly well from the bottom.

"No," Henry said. "We're not going for good. I just want to look around. Well, I want you to look around for me."

"What if we see him tonight?" Richard asked. "Will we chase him like Henrietta did?"

"No. We won't chase him like Henrietta did. I just want to talk to him. And I don't think we'll see him, anyway."

"Then why are we looking?"

"Listen, Richard. I want to find Eli. But I don't just want to rush off into a strange world. We need to check it out first, get a feel for the place, is it night, day, all that stuff. We are not going to hunt around in the dark. Not there."

"We should talk to Henrietta," Richard said. "Seeing as she's been there."

"So have I. I had to save her when she got stuck. You know the story."

"And I saved you when you got stuck."

"Right," Henry said. "Sort of."

"So why don't you ask her to help?"

"Because," Henry said, "I need someone who will do what I say. I'm blind, Richard. She'd leave me standing in the dark and rush off to look at anything that made her curious. Which would be everything. That's why."

"Right," Richard said. "And you want me to snitch a flashlamp."

"A flashlight, yes. And batteries. Can you do that without anyone noticing?"

"At home, I kept a pet hare in my shirt for four days without anyone noticing."

"A hair? Like, from your head?"

"No. A hare, as in hoppity-hop. They did find the hare, though. And they made Cook put it in my stew."

"Oh," Henry said. "Sorry. I have something for you to read to me. Now, hurry and get the flashlight and come back."

Henrietta heard Richard come out of the attic room. She scooted across the landing and into her own bedroom before Richard was on the stairs. She could grab him and threaten him into silence so she could come along. Henry was blind. He might never know. But it might be more fun to catch them in the act and watch

Henry try to be all righteous about leaving her out. Or she could just tell her dad and let him catch them. But then she wouldn't get to see FitzFaeren again. That's where they were going. That's where she'd been stuck. That's where Eli had escaped. They wouldn't find him. He'd be long gone by now. But even if he was standing right in the ruined hall, waiting to bump into them, they didn't have a chance of catching him. Not if Eli had gotten away from her.

Richard walked by, and Henrietta let him go. She would follow them in.

Richard's voice was extremely annoying. He was incapable of reading aloud without sending his pitch up to the ceiling and buzzing his vowels in his nose. Henry tried to be interested in how the cupboards worked, but he just wasn't. And his grandfather's writing, at least when Richard read it, never seemed to breathe.

He'd fallen asleep twice, before he finally rolled over toward Richard's voice and put out his hand.

"Thanks," he said. "You can go to bed now. I'll wake you up later."

Richard gave him the journal and whispered his excitement about the upcoming exploration.

"Yeah," Henry said. "Shut the door tight, please."

The doors clicked shut, and Henry slid the journal into a backpack empty of everything but one flashlight. The key was still tucked under his pillow. He wouldn't take that into FitzFaeren. If something bad happened, which it wouldn't, Uncle Frank would need to be able to get into Grandfather's room.

Lying on his back, he crossed his arms over the backpack and lay still. He'd already had Richard set the combination on the compass locks and put his shoes beside the bed. Everything was ready. He felt as good as he had since Uncle Frank had handed him the lawyer's letter. He was actually going to do something. It might not help. It might not accomplish anything at all, but it was something.

Uncle Frank had come upstairs, and Henry had been practically cheerful. He'd told his uncle that he'd seen something blurry—true enough—and Frank had sounded happy when he'd slapped Henry's shoulder and said good night.

Realizing that his light was probably on, Henry rolled onto his side and felt for his lamp, tracing the heat in the air with his fingertips until he found the switch. Nothing changed when it clicked off.

In the darkness, he lifted up his hand. The brand was still there, bright and curling, closing in on itself and expanding.

Henry watched the colors until his pulse was drumming inside his skull. Then he put his arm down and shut his eyes.

The dream started in Henry's toes. They were bare, and they were wet. Henry curled them, felt them dig through something cool and spongy, felt water seep up between them.

Wind stroked his face, strong but not violent. Constant. He pulled in a deep breath, a lungful, a headful of his imagining. It was sweet, with salt around its rim.

The soft applause of a thousand rustling trees surrounded him, and he ached to see them, to shake off his blindness and watch the silver-bellied leaves flick and twist on the wind's wake.

Why couldn't he? He was dreaming. He knew he was. So his eyes could work.

He blinked, but something was in the way. Not on the outside of his eyes, something back behind them, between his eyes and his soul, a curtain of darkness.

He ripped at it with his mind. He put his hands on his head and imagined himself digging with his fingers, prodding the inside of his skull with a stick, hoping to weaken, burst, whatever seal was in place.

His right hand was hot on his temple. He pulled it away and looked at it. His burn flamed up bright, and by its moving light, he could just see the outline of his hand.

Henry lifted his hand and plunged the fiery word into his eye. The pain seared and he opened his mouth to yell, but there was no air in his throat. He gargled agony, but the itch behind his eye was scratched, and the relief overwhelmed the pain. He pulled his hand away, breathed, and moved it to his other eye.

Henry's legs gave out, and he dropped to his knees, but he wouldn't move his hand, he couldn't. Not until his block, the itching membrane, the brain scab that closed off his eyes had been burned away. He ground the palm of his hand against his eye, twisted the heat it held into his head, and fell gasping onto his back. His hands dropped to his sides.

Lying there, with moisture crawling through his clothes and soaking his scalp, he opened his eyes on Badon Hill.

The thick-bellied trees towered above him, groping into the sky with their distant leaves. On one side of him, they climbed even higher where the ground rose steeply. Above him, the canopy was not as dense, and as he turned his head to the other side, he saw only blue, scattered with fast-roving clouds. He was at the base of the hill, on the edge of the island, where the trees met the sea.

"Boldly done," a man said. "Though madness outside, a dreaming."

Henry sat up quickly and climbed to his feet. He had been lying on a dense bed of moss. The hill, almost a mountain, rose up quickly on one side; on the other, the moss led to a cliff's edge. Below it, in the water, Henry could see a dock with a small boat tied to it. In front of him, with legs spread and arms tucked behind his back, stood an enormous man.

He wore black boots up to his knees and a long black coat. Blue trousers stretched to bursting around his thighs. His nose was large and hooked, but it still seemed small above his protruding jaw and between his thick, curling sideburns. He was tall already, half a head taller than Frank, but he was made even more so by his hat, with a flat, round brim around a tapering chimney. A silver buckle was set on the front. The man was smiling.

"Are you a Pilgrim?" Henry asked.

"Pilgrim," the man said, feeling the word with his tongue. "I seek, yes. Even the hard ways. Entering your dream was uneasy. I am called Darius."

Henry took a step back. "Why are you here?"

"I come," Darius said slowly. "As you are a seventh, a pauper son, a lastborn. I would help you."

"Other people have said that." Henry shifted his bare feet nervously. "What does it even mean? A seventh?"

"To many ones, nothing. It means they were the seventh-begotten son, that when their father is put to grave-sleep, they shall receive the last heritage, the pauper's portion, a rag's nothing. To others, to you, to me, it is potens. It is the twain sight, the second seeing." Darius brought his right hand around from behind his back and held it out toward Henry. "It is this." On his broad palm, there was a scar, almost a brand. As Henry stared, he could see that it was moving, writhing like a slug in pain, brown and slow. A dark whisper stood out in the air above it.

Henry didn't want to be any closer to the big man, but he couldn't help himself. He stepped forward, staring at the dark flicker, trying to read it. The thick fingers closed over the scar, and Darius lifted his hand to his face. Pulling gently at the curling hair on his cheeks, he smiled. At least his mouth did. His eyes had hardened.

"You would know what word-flame courses in my blood. You would know the force of my own morphosis."

"Um," Henry said. "I was just looking. You were showing it to me."

"I," Darius said slowly. The smile was gone, and he leaned forward while Henry backed away. "Be the greatest of the magi, of all the lastborn in this age of tempore's swamping, in the world in which my lungs draw wind. Not since the Endorian sons walked madless has a man wielded so thickly of natura's mage without shatter. Their potens was greatened because they staved off death, they wove it into their very sarx, their bones, and their bloods. Even now, they live on, deathless in the boneyards of Endor, madful only, addled and entombed, but soul and flesh still stitched as one. Breathing."

Henry wanted to run. To jump off the cliff and wake up in the water. He knew he could walk right out of the dream, he'd done it before. But he waited. Darius had a burn like his. He was evil, or nuts, probably both, but he knew more than Henry did.

"So you're strong," Henry said. "I'm sorry, I don't understand a lot of what you say. I did get that."

Darius straightened up and smiled. "I meant no braggadocc." He spread his arms, but kept his right fist closed. "I will speak more simpily. You have flung a legend wide for me—one I have long sought. You have freed the last Endorian daughter. Together, twain, we will find her and learn the secret of the deathless—the secret of morture—and death harnessed within will gift us life unbroken."

Even in the dream, Henry couldn't stop himself from shivering. He glanced at the cliff, and back at the grinning sickness in front of him.

"The witch tried to kill me," Henry said.

"Yet you live," said Darius.

"Her blood burned my jaw." Henry swallowed hard. He didn't think he'd get sick in a dream, but he felt like it. "She's evil."

Darius dropped his arms and stepped toward Henry, looking at his face. Henry slid away, toward the cliff.

"Speech is leapt to journey's end," Darius said. "But much road waits. First, you must live on. You are yet blind in waking life, and the mage in your blood will shake and rattle soul from body. It has not ended. A warpspasm comes before the second seeing, and it would seal your eyes forever."

"I don't understand," Henry said.

Darius stepped closer, frustrated. "You have seen it already, natura's life-magic, you have touched it. You will die. Or you will breathe on and wake, able to see the world and the mage beneath, able to grip, to taste, to speak what you see, to pierce illusionaries."

Darius stopped in front of Henry and lifted his

right hand. Henry felt its weight as it dropped onto his shoulder. He tried to turn. It was time to wake up. Time to leave.

"Come to me," Darius said quietly. "My seventh son. I will gird you."

CHAPTER SIX

Henry was frozen. He couldn't twist, he couldn't turn, he couldn't even roll his eyes. They were locked in the big man's stare, gripped by his all-pupil blackness. He could feel heat, the tingle of the man's slug brand, working its way down through his shoulder into his bones.

His dream bones.

Henry, terrified and motionless, grew angry. This nightmare was his nightmare. He could change it.

"I'm dreaming you," he said to the black eyes. He could see nothing else.

"I, you," the eyes said.

"I can turn," Henry said. "I can leave."

He couldn't. The eyes smiled.

Suddenly, in the panicked fury of an animal trapped, Henry's body quivered. He'd managed to move. He'd leaned forward, still staring up into the eyes, and they no longer smiled.

Henry's teeth ground. "Leave," he said, and his mind snapped free, painting a new dream.

Darius's arm slipped off his shoulder as the big man stepped back. The arm jerked up and removed his hat. He spoke. At least a voice like his did. His enormous jaw was clamped shut.

"I'm a Pilgrim," he said, "off to Plymouth. April showers bring May flowers." He turned and stepped toward the cliff. "And . . ." He was fighting it, trying to shake the pressure of Henry's imagining. "*Mayflowers* bring . . ." He was off the cliff. "Me."

But he didn't fall. The dream quaked, and sky and sea and crawling clouds all disappeared around him. He stood in blackness, turned, and stared into Henry's eyes.

"Your dreaming is sealed. A way has been prepared. You come."

"I can wake up!" Henry yelled. "I can."

"You will," Darius said. "But where?"

He was gone, and all of Badon Hill with him.

For a moment, Henry held the moss. Blackness surrounded him, but the cool, wet green beneath his feet, the beginning of his dream, remained.

A crack echoed through space, followed by Richard's whispering voice. "Henry? Henry? Are you ready? Are you okay?"

The voice faded. The echo died. The moss was gone. And still, Henry slept.

Richard had never fallen asleep. He had tagged along after Henry before, but this was the first time he had been included by invitation.

He lay in his sleeping bag on top of a small pile of

blankets that served as a mattress, and he listened for Henry to call him.

Henry was a loud sleeper. He moaned and hummed and occasionally kicked. The kicking made the floor shake. Richard got up twice to check on him. Both times, he'd cracked the doors just a bit and peeked in. He couldn't see anything, but he could hear better. Henry wasn't awake.

The third time, Henry sounded angry. Angry and in pain. And there was a crack. He'd kicked something maybe. Hurt his foot.

"Henry?" Richard whispered. "Henry? Are you ready? Are you okay?"

Nothing.

Richard slid quietly into the room and shut the doors behind him. The room was stuffy, but perfectly silent. Henry had stopped his mumbling. He'd stopped moving.

Richard switched on the lamp and looked down at his friend. Henry was clutching the backpack to his chest, and his eyes were clamped shut. They were oozing a bit again, but they weren't swollen. Richard bent over and touched them carefully and was glad that they seemed normal.

The air was moving. Blowing past him toward the cupboards, harder, faster, almost whistling. The post-office box was open.

With a sudden throbbing surge, the room blurred.

Richard felt like he'd left his stomach somewhere far behind as he flew toward the cupboard wall, too fast to even throw up his arms, though he tried.

He needn't have. He was unconscious before he hit it. Only he didn't really hit it. He went beyond it, into another room, and hit another wall, someplace else.

In a swirl of dust, his body piled limply onto Henry's, and the two of them lay, unaware, in a yellow room.

Henrietta worked very hard to help her sisters fall asleep. She didn't respond to any of Anastasia's comments or questions or whispers. She'd even ignored an old rag doll that her younger sister had lobbed across the room from her bottom bunk.

When Anastasia had given up, Henrietta tried to work on Penelope. She used her tiredest voice.

"Pen, how long are you going to keep your reading light on?"

"It's not that bright," Penelope said. "Roll over or something."

Henrietta sighed and rolled over, thumping heavily. "But how long?" she asked. "You're not going to stay up till four again, are you? I remember when you did that reading that old *Black Rose* book. You were a total crab for days."

"That's because the book was awful."

"You were awful," Anastasia laughed. "Wasn't she, Henrietta?"

Henrietta ignored her. "How long, Pen?" she asked again.

Penelope slapped her book shut. "Good night," she said, and clicked off the light.

"Henrietta," Anastasia said. "Henrietta?"

Henrietta didn't say anything.

When her sisters were both breathing heavily, Henrietta slipped out of her bed and cracked open their bedroom door. Then she pulled on a pair of jeans and set her shoes beside her bed. Finally, she positioned herself so she could see Henry and Richard when they walked around the landing. She could already hear them talking upstairs. And thumping. They weren't exactly sneaking.

She waited. She tried to be patient and waited some more. She got up, opened the door a little wider, and slid back onto her bed. The attic had grown silent, and she struggled not to drift off. When she'd jerked awake too many times, she sat up, wrapped her arms around her knees, leaned her head against the wall, and, staring at the door, fell asleep.

When Henrietta woke, she had a headache. She was lying flat on her back with her head on the footboard and one leg up against the wall.

Anastasia was snoring, and Penelope was buried in her blankets. Predawn gray filtered through the bedroom window and out onto the landing.

Henrietta levered herself up painfully. As quietly as she was able, she got her feet over the edge of the bed and rocked herself to standing. Rubbing her neck, she tiptoed to the door and looked out over the landing. It was empty, and Grandfather's door was shut. Henrietta slipped out of her room, latching the door behind her, and hurried to Grandfather's room. She put her hand on the door and pushed, but it wouldn't budge. She stepped closer and leaned her ear against it, but there was nothing to hear beyond the crackle of the house's joints beneath her feet.

Frustrated with herself for sleeping, and growing irritated with Henry to compensate, she moved to the attic stairs, held her breath, and began toeing her way up the edges as quietly as possible. When her head rose above the attic floor, she stopped and studied Richard's sleeping bag in the dim light. After a minute, she took another step and studied again. The bag was lumped up enough that he could have been in it, but she could hear no sound of breathing and not a hint of movement. She took the last few steps quickly and stood beside Henry's doors. The rumpled bag beside her was empty.

At first push, Henry's doors bowed but wouldn't open. She bounced against them and was sprung back.

Putting her mouth to the crack between them, she whispered.

"Henry? Henry?" When no one answered, she stepped back and put more force behind her shoulder. With a pop, the doors sprang open, and she stepped into the room.

The lamp was on, but it had fallen over. Henry's

blankets were piled against the wall. The bed was empty. The floor was bare.

Henrietta sat on the bed and picked up the pillow. The journal was gone, but the letters were there, and on top of them sat the key.

Well, at least they'd left that. She wanted to catch up to them, and as quickly as she could. It wouldn't be long before everyone else was awake, too, and wondering where they were.

She smiled as she tiptoed down the stairs. She would be completely nonchalant. *Hey, guys, you might want to get back. It's almost breakfast.*

At the bottom, she moved to her own bedroom door, turned the knob carefully, and slipped inside. Her shoes were still on the floor. Not bothering with socks, she finger-levered her feet into them and crept back out, past her parents' room, past the bathroom, and fumbled with the old skeleton key in front of Grandfather's door.

When she stepped into the room, she couldn't help glancing around herself, peeking behind the door and on the other side of the bed. The room was always otherworldly, but shadowed like it was with predawn light, it sent her skin crawling. And this time it smelled horribly dank, moist, and mildewy.

The boys had left the cupboard door open, which only made sense. You wouldn't really want to shut it after yourself.

Henrietta tucked the key into her pocket and closed Grandfather's door behind her. Then she stepped toward the cupboard door, and the carpet squelched beneath her. Water was oozing up around her shoe, but her own crazy escape already felt like ancient history.

Rising up to her toes, she moved through the carpet swamp, squatted in front of the door, and slid herself in.

The music began just as it had the last time she'd crawled into FitzFaeren. Surrounded by the blackness of the cupboard, she listened to the strings and the rhythms of the dance they moved and guided.

When her face found the back of the door, she pushed it open without hesitation. And there, in front of her, was the scene that she had been itching to see again. The enormous beamed hall sparkled with the light from hundreds of candles around the frescoed walls and columns and hanging on the enormous chandeliers. The towering windows were black with night, but they reflected the swirl of dancers moving across the floor.

Henrietta knew that she couldn't simply wait and watch. If she was going to burst Henry's bubble, she should find him soon. Waiting too long would mean she would be in as much trouble as Richard and Henry. More. Her father would be harder on her.

So she watched the small women spin in dresses brighter and smoother than any flower, and she watched the men with their boxy, short-sleeved coats. She hunted the room for the face that she knew had belonged to Eli, and then, before she found it, she forced herself to grab the edge of the cupboard and pull herself through.

The music died. The candles were gone. And the people and the windows and the night and most of the roof and chunks of the floor. It was like standing inside the bones of a huge whale. The ribbed beams still spanned the hall in many places, four or five stories above her. Most of the columns still stood, but the majestic windows had become nothing but oversize holes. Light filtered through clouds and into the desolate place, and all of the wood it found, once bright with stain and inlay, once rich, stood out dull, rotten, bleached, and weathered gray.

High above her, Henrietta could hear the traffic of pigeons. The sound was common in a Kansas barn, and she liked it there. It made her feel like the barn was still alive, still used. Here, it was an insult, a final desecration.

Grandfather had written that he'd destroyed this place. Henrietta wondered what he had meant. She hoped he'd been wrong.

Henry and Richard were nowhere in sight. But she really didn't think they could have gone far, even if they'd come through hours ago. Henry was blind, after all, and he knew that the floor was as solid as a spiderweb. He wouldn't want Richard to go quickly.

At first Henrietta stood and listened, hoping that she would hear some pop or crash just to give her an initial direction. A breeze stirred the pigeons, but otherwise, the rotting hall was perfectly still.

Carefully probing the floor in front of her, she made her way farther out into the room. Some of the wood planks crumbled, some sighed or popped, but when the wall was well behind her, she stopped and listened again, turning carefully in place.

There were three large doorways yawning into the hall. A dozen smaller ones were spaced between them. As Henrietta turned, she began to give up. The place was big enough that she could head off in one direction while Henry and Richard returned from another. They wouldn't know that she'd followed them, and nothing would keep them from resetting the compass locks.

Even though the hutch that she'd crawled through wasn't more than forty feet away, she felt a twinge of fear. For a moment, she thought she should go back, kick off her shoes, and crawl into her bed. Henry and Richard could fend for themselves. But then, through one of the large doorways, there came a crash, followed by laughter and voices.

They were coming back.

Henrietta bobbed and shifted her way to the hutch and then turned, leaned her back against it, crossed her arms, and waited.

No one came.

She heard the laughter again, but it hadn't come any closer. They were taking way too long. She wouldn't be surprised if the whole family was panicking right now because Anastasia had discovered them gone.

Staying close to the wall, Henrietta began moving around the room, toward the gaping doorway. She passed entrances to alcoves and hallways and collapsing stairs always leading up. She ran her fingers over carvings soft with rot beneath her touch. At each door, she was tempted to slow, to stop, to look, but she only glanced and moved on, toward the tall entrance at the end of the hall and the echo of voices.

Walking around the edge of the room took her longer, but she did get there, and without risking the gapped planks out in the middle.

She stood for a moment with her back to a column and collected her thoughts, rehearsing what she would say. But then she heard footsteps, careful, methodical footsteps coming toward her through the doorway.

It was either find or be found. She had to do it now. With a deep breath and a smile, she stepped into the doorway and crossed her arms.

Two men, not much taller than she was, looked up from their feet. Both had short black beards, and they carried pry-bars and hammers. They stood, frozen in surprise.

"Um," Henrietta said. Her smile faded away, but she forced it back. "I'm just looking around."

The men looked at each other and nodded. Gripping hammers, they stepped toward her.

CHAPTER SEVEN

Henry woke to the sound of voices. One he knew immediately, the other was new. And easier to understand.

"Prepare it," Darius said. "Pestling potions is for your likes."

"Sir," said the other voice. "You know nothing of him. If naming rites have already been performed, then a blood-bonding is impossible. It will be his killing. Splay his throat and spare the ingredients."

"Endorian blood crawls beneath his skin, and he lives on. Touch the burnings on his face and ken where death dripped. The twain sight came upon him through storming bolts, and he is not yet ash, nor even mad. Your strength is naught beyond vaporing steam beside his flame. He will be second among Lastborn. He will be a seventh son to me."

"You have no other sons," the man said quietly. "And to become second among us would require a nomination and at least a two-thirds voting at the society's midsummer banquet in order to express dissatisfaction with my service."

"Ass," Darius said. "Ass! You are no true witch-dog,

no better than a pharmator for mixing love draughts. You have my blood, prepare the rite!"

A door boomed shut, and Henry flinched with the echo.

"Darius the mighty witch-dog," the man's voice muttered. "Darius the seventh bastard son of a village priest. No better than a pharmator? You're no more a witch-dog than you are gran to the Fisher King."

Henry's shoulders ached. He was shirtless. His arms were sticking straight out from his sides and he had to move them. He tried to shift himself, to lower his arms just an inch or slide his body up. But he was bound. He flexed, and straps around his elbows and wrists and forehead held him in place. His legs were fixed as well, at the ankles and knees, and something thick pinned his hips to the surface beneath him.

He tensed his body slowly, trying to feel the strength of his bonds. The straps creaked like leather.

"The daimon wakes," the man said. "The straps won't give. They are charmed, and even if they were not, they would be strong enough for most."

"Am I in the post office?" Henry asked. "Why am I tied up?"

"The post office?" The man laughed. "No. Darius said you were not mad. But then his mind, so diseased itself, is no measure for others."

Henry opened his eyes. They were swelling again, and they itched horribly. He squinted them tight, squeezing out moisture.

"I need to rub my eyes," he said. "Why am I tied up?"

Henry heard the clink of glass and the shuffle of feet. Then a rough cloth pressed into his eyes and wiped his cheeks. "Your eyes' sorrow will increase. You are tied up so that your joints will not unhinge, so that you will not pluck out your eyes and the brains behind or bite the fingers from your hands or rip your flesh and pry at the bones within. The time of your warpspasm approaches. Your mind may addle, but in the straps, the worst will be the snapping of a bone. An arm, a thigh."

"I don't think I want to do this," Henry said. He wasn't sure if he should believe the man. "A warpspasm?"

The cloth went away and returned warm and wet. "Darius said he spoke to you of it. It is the coming of your heritage—it will try to escape you, it is not comfortable in man's flesh. Survive it, and you may keep it, though it will not settle easily. It is always like gripping a storm."

Henry swallowed, and his throat burned. "Can I have a drink?"

"It will only fuel the vomiting, but you may."

A bottle was uncorked, and liquid glugged in its neck.

"Here," the man said. "Suck this sponge. I will sop it again if you need."

Henry opened his mouth, willing to drink anything, but expecting a little bath sponge, something from a kitchen sink. Instead, a lump the size of his fist kissed his lips. He squeezed it with his teeth and jerked in surprise.

Sour and tart and biting, the fluid tightened up his tongue and pooled in the back of his throat. He gagged and swallowed and gagged again, and the liquid hit his burning throat. It felt better there, once past his tongue, so he sucked on the sponge and swallowed again. Then he spat it out. The sponge rolled down his cheek and rested against his neck. The man picked it up.

Flexing his shriveled tongue, he scraped it against his teeth but couldn't remove the taste. "Water would have been fine," he said.

"Ha!" the man laughed. "Better to face what you face than to swallow a draught of water. Water is for scrubbing, for sailing, and for cattle. Wine and vinegar for men, unless you desire sickness."

Turning his head to the side as far as he could, Henry spat. And then spat again. He could remember his dream clearly, and everything that Darius had said. It was starting to seem like the big Pilgrim had been telling the truth. He hoped no one would try to follow him. Of course, nobody could. Richard had already set the compass locks to FitzFaeren when he'd gone to sleep. They wouldn't know where he was. He didn't know how Darius had gotten him here, but he knew it hadn't been with Grandfather's mechanics. Darius, as weird and as evil as he may be, really had power. He wouldn't have needed to click any knobs.

The man touched Henry's bare stomach, and Henry jolted.

"What are you doing?" Henry asked.

"It is necessary," the man replied. "Clench your teeth. I had hoped to do this while you dreamt."

At first Henry felt only cold, but the cold spread down to his hips and up to his ribs. It began to bite, and when it bit, it bit like fire.

"Wha—" Henry tried to ask, but his jaw clamped tight. He arched his back the little that he could, trying to shake the sensation off of his skin. But it wasn't only on his skin. It was inside, digging down into his belly.

"Be still," the man said. "Darius would have a naming rite before your morph's complete. He's a fool, but I must prepare it. You feel the first potion, the first flesh-blending."

"Why?" Henry managed.

"He would bind you to himself. If you die in the warpspasm, he can absorb your spirit's portion of the sight. If you live, you will be his. His blood will be in your veins, his symbol in your flesh."

Henry was trying to control his breath, but it jerked unevenly. His diaphragm convulsed. Gulping hiccups came when he tried to speak. "Not," he gasped, and his ribs shook, "really?"

The man said nothing, but Henry's question was answered. The cloth that had been used to wipe Henry's eyes was shoved into his mouth. Something else bit into Henry's belly. A blade. Slowly parting his skin, curving and looping back on itself.

Henry yelled into the cloth. He clamped his teeth, roiled his body, and then stopped in shock. He knew, somehow, that the brown burn, the writhing slug on Darius's hand, the symbol he would not let Henry see, would be forever with him, as long as he was alive, whether for days or years. But he would not belong to Darius. Damn Darius. Damn all potions and lies. Damn the pain.

He felt his blood surge inside him, drumming through the rivers of his body. His flesh quivered and then sagged beneath the man's sharp tracing. Something else was coming, something he didn't know and couldn't begin to control.

His eyes rolled back in his head. Every joint in his body cracked and revolted, eager to swing free, to fold backward. His teeth ground through the rag in his mouth, and his tongue writhed, squirming back into his own throat.

Henry vomited, choked, and vomited again.

The seizures rocked him, contracted and strained and twisted every sinew, tore through his senses, and he knew nothing.

Henry was pain. He was lying on Badon Hill. Below Badon Hill. A chalky cliff rose above him, and beyond that, trees. He was on a beach of stones, and he couldn't move. He heard a man laugh and a dog bark. Beyond his feet, he saw them, the man and the dog, the man smiling and carrying a small, squirming bundle with one tiny, bare foot kicking freely, the big black dog running above and behind as they climbed a narrow trail up the cliff.

He knew that dog. He'd dreamt it before, and he'd seen its bones by the big gray stone at the top of the island mountain. Sadness overwhelmed him. Dogs shouldn't have to die. People should die. People had to. He already had.

Henry opened his eyes on a cloud of confusion. Light and sound and smell all swirled around him. He blinked dry eyes, and widened them.

He could see.

A ceiling above him was struggling into focus. Black beams. The walls were stone. Despite the acid burning in every muscle, he tried to sit up and found that he was still in straps.

"You live," a voice said.

"Unstrap me," Henry said. His mouth tasted like vomit and rags, but it had been swabbed out. His face had been wiped clean. "No more cutting or potions. Just unstrap me." Windows were set high up in the wall, and Henry stared at the white light that streamed through them. He would have smiled, he would have laughed and grinned, if his jaw hadn't felt broken and if his belly hadn't been stinging. If he hadn't been strapped to a table in a madman's world.

The man stepped into view. He was small, middle-aged, and normal-looking for any world. He wore glasses that would have made him look like a math teacher if there hadn't been blood on his shirt. His face was without expression.

"Forgive me," he said. "The warpspasm, less power-ful than Darius had hoped, came too early. It has passed, and the naming rite, half-prepared, is impotent. It is bet-ter for me if you had died. Darius will kill us both."

"Well, I'm glad I didn't," Henry said. "And I have a name already. Can you unstrap me, please?"

The man leaned forward, holding a vial over Henry's mouth. "Drink this," he said.

"Why?" Henry turned his head. "What is it?"

The man didn't answer. Instead, he pressed the glass to Henry's lips. Henry clamped them shut and shook his head, staring blearily into the man's eyes. The man sighed and stood up.

"You're trying to kill me," Henry said.

"It is the only way. I do not desire Darius's wrath, but then I do not desire him to supplant me with you. I'd hoped you would die. I still hope."

Henry was fighting back panic. If the man wanted to kill him, he could. "Listen," Henry said. "If you kill me, Darius will know. Just let me go. Make it look like an es-cape."

The man laughed. "No one shakes those straps."

"Darius could," Henry said quickly. "And he thinks I'm powerful. He thinks this whole thing started when I was struck by some magic lightning or something. But it didn't, it was just a dandelion. But let him keep thinking. He wants to already."

"A dandelion?"

"Yes. A little weed. Not lightning."

"And you will never return?"

"Not if I can help it."

The little man crouched out of Henry's sight, and then the sound of heavy pins rattling on the floor echoed through the room. Henry felt the leather loosen and pulled one arm free.

The man stood back up and jerked the straps loose one by one. Then he took Henry by the hands and helped him sit up. Henry winced at the pain and looked down at his belly, at the shallow symbol carved into his stomach. It looked almost like a tree, not at all like what he'd glimpsed on the big man's hand.

"It's not bleeding."

"No," the man said. "The first mixture stops it. Darius would have rubbed another one into the wounds during a later rite."

"I need bandages and a shirt," Henry said.

"Sorry, there is no time. I have released you, and that is all I can do. You are three floors above the streetway. You were brought into this world through the Sulie Post Management Station, two milongs from here. Keep south, and luck be with you."

The man turned quickly away from Henry and walked back to a small table buried beneath jars and bottles and bowls. A lumpy orange sponge sat on one corner. Henry watched the man choose a jar and dip one finger carefully inside. Then he turned around.

"Begone," he said, and dabbed his finger beneath his tongue. For a moment, he stood, staring Henry in the eye before his legs began to quake. He staggered back, grabbed at his table, spilling bottles and bowls to the stone floor. Glass splintered, and shards spun toward Henry's bare feet. The little man collapsed into the wreck, kicking. After a moment, the man was still—his slow breathing the only sound in the room.

Henry's eyes were burning, tears streaming down his cheeks, but he didn't mind. He could see again. And he had other things to worry about. He shifted his weight on tender feet.

He had to find stairs. He had to get down three flights of them without being caught and get out into the street. Then he needed to figure out which way south was and find a post office two milongs away. More problems would present themselves then. He didn't need to think about them now.

He couldn't remember what he'd been wearing when he went to bed, but now rough canvas trousers hung just past his knees. The waist, big enough for two of him, was cinched tight with a string. He wore nothing else but the bruises where straps had held him through his seizing and the cuts on his belly.

Henry tried to walk, but his joints felt compressed, slow and full of fluid. His head was ringing, his heart was pounding, and the cold stone floor looked to him like the softest, sweetest bed in the world. He had survived the warpspasm, but he felt dead enough. The whole second-sight thing was nonsense. If anything, his vision was worse. He looked down at his burnt palm.

The life stood out from his scar, golden and bright, moving in its story with all the personality of fire. He watched green bursting growth, watched it flame and burn to feathered ash. From the ash came green again, again and again, flaming and dying and being born. This story, this life, was embroidered in his skin.

He straightened up as best he could, head ringing more than ever. The room was out of focus, gray, swimming beneath his feet, walls rippling and falling in place, and he knew that life like the life in his palm was everywhere, that it was moving all around him, words and stories writhing and telling and being told. He could step into it and be carried away. If he did, he would be ripped in two. He would be stepping into a waterfall, a raging river, trying to catch Niagara in his skull.

Henry shut his eyes, balancing carefully, and breathed, listening to the ringing in his ears and his heart pounding in his temples. He was pain all over, and watching his burn had made it worse. But he had never felt or seen anything like it, anything so heart-stoppingly beautiful and so dangerous, a towering cliff calling him to jump, a sleek serpent calling him to touch, an ocean swell calling him to sink. A story to carry him away and erase him.

He had to move his bruised body. He limped away from the table. He needed to get back to Kansas first, and then he could pick dandelions. Or go to Badon Hill. Anywhere but here. He stopped.

Had he come through with his backpack? Grand-father's journals, all of the combinations, would be here forever if he left it. Struggling to keep his eyes focused on the right plane, he looked around the room. For the first time, he noticed charts, painted with diagrams and hung like tapestries all along one wall. They were layered thick on top of each other, and they reached the floor. Chains were draped over them, perhaps to keep them flat in a breeze when the high windows were open. A huge iron box squatted in a corner.

The man was breathing loudly, but a puddle of blood had formed beneath his head and was already skimming over, thickening in the air. There were no closets, unless he counted the iron box, no shelves beyond the cluttered table and the table where he'd been strapped. But be-neath the potion table, beyond the man's legs, there was a box with slatted sides.

Henry picked his way through the broken glass and tipped the box so he could see inside. A pair of gray sweatpants were wadded on top, along with his under-wear. Beneath them, he found a white T-shirt and his backpack. No shoes.

He pulled the T-shirt on quickly, wincing as it rubbed against his cuts. Not because they hurt, the pain was only slight, but because the sensation of the cloth flapping them open and shut seemed like it should hurt. A lot. He unzipped his backpack and glanced inside. Grandfather's journals were rubber-banded together, and a flashlight was cozied up next to them. Henry slung a strap over his shoulder and began to tiptoe back to the door.

His hand was on the latch when he heard voices. One voice.

"My son will be called Xerxes. I give no thinking to another. And every fratre must be in presentia regale."

Henry looked frantically around the room. He could slip behind the charts. The iron box was probably locked. The latch moved in his hand. He jumped into the corner, and the door was flung open into his face.

A servant, short and robed in gray, stepped into the room and placed his back against the wall next to Henry, holding the door open. Henry was breathing onto his shoulder. He couldn't slide any farther behind the door, so he bit his lip and waited to be found.

Darius, hatted and caped, strode into the room.

From behind the door, Henry could just see half of the big man's head and his left shoulder. He wanted to shrink, to disappear into the wall or the servant's robe. If the wizard turned, if he looked back at his servant . . . Henry didn't finish the thought.

"What is it?" a voice asked from the hall.

Darius said nothing. He took another step, further into view, and froze. He turned sideways, and Henry watched the man's hawked profile, his curling sideburns and enormous chin. He took off his Pilgrim hat and ran a gloved hand through his thick hair.

Henry blinked. There was a glimmer around Darius,

around his face, his legs, his entire shape. Henry blinked again, felt his eyes singe, and he saw.

Darius shrugged off his cape and threw it against the wall in fury. But he was not enormous. He was tall, and his skin was stretched tight over his bones. His hair was thin, straggling away from his bald crown, and his ears stuck out from his head. His nose hooked long and low, but below it, there was no chin. His mouth simply drifted back into his neck, and where a chin should have been, there was a large piece of bone, or ivory, carved in the shape of a protruding jaw and held on with a strap around the back of his head.

"Up! Rouse him!" Darius yelled, and a fat man, the voice from the hall, hurried into the room and over to the body.

Henry watched Darius's legs as he paced. They were not the full, muscled things that Darius projected. They rattled in his boots, and at his rear, the seat of his trousers flapped empty.

"He will not wake," the fat man said. "Still, the boy cannot have flown far."

"He is no boy!" Darius roared. "He is my son. My blood runs in his veins!"

"Not just yet," the fat man said quietly.

Darius ignored him. "His former blood, his yester-people did this. He cannot have so freed himself. I did not think of a rescuing." Darius stepped back out of Henry's view, back into the doorway. "Come," he said, "and fetch the pink slave."

The fat man hurried after Darius. "Collect Seer Harmon," he said as he left. "Have him bathed and examined."

The robed servant nodded and walked toward the now-snoring body.

Henry swallowed. Adrenaline pulsed through his abused joints. He stepped out from behind the door and slipped into the hall. The spindly shape of Darius, without his cape and hat, strode around the distant corner. The fat man scurried behind him.

Henry put his hand on the latch of the neighboring door and quickly let himself in.

CHAPTER EIGHT

There had been many horrible days in Frank's life, but this was the worst. When he lost his own way in the cupboards and came to Kansas, he had been the one who had suffered most. Though he'd felt awful for his mother. When as a kid he'd nearly gotten Dotty killed in Endor, they'd been rescued by her father. When Henry and Henrietta had disappeared the first time, he'd felt sick. He could have stopped them. He could have nipped Henry's plaster chipping. But he hadn't.

This was worse.

He hadn't again. And he knew why. In his bones, he still wanted to find his way back to his own town, to his own world. Frank would be roaming the cupboards, too, if he hadn't put down roots. He'd be all hypocrite, holding Richard and Henry here. Though he couldn't say he'd expected them to try it with Henry blind.

He'd known someone was lying about Grandfather's key, but he hated inquisitions.

So now they'd gone, all three of them, the key was nowhere to be seen, and Grandfather's room was clamped shut.

Dotty wasn't crying. It was worse than that. She was moving through the house without talking, and when she looked at him, there was nothing in her eyes but confusion. She just couldn't understand him, she couldn't understand what made him make mistakes. The same mistakes.

He wasn't sure he could handle another one of those looks.

Frank shifted his feet in the grass and dropped the shotgun barrels open. He dug in his pocket, fished out two shells, fitted them in, and snapped the barrels shut. Then he pulled the hammers back and puffed out his cheeks.

"Dots!" he yelled.

"We're down!" Dotty yelled back.

Frank raised the gun to his shoulder and sighted in on Grandfather's window. The wind chimes rustled on the front porch, and Frank fingered the double trigger. Exhaling, he squeezed one.

Pheasants burst up out of the fields. They always do. Blake the cat burst out from beneath the front porch. The wind chimes chimed on, but no one listened. Two butterflies that had chosen that moment to flirt between Frank and the house suddenly ceased to exist.

At least they had been together.

Releasing the second hammer slowly, Frank lowered the barrels to the ground and massaged his shoulder. It had been a while since he'd felt that kick. Still carrying the gun, he walked toward the house and the antique gray splintered ladder he had leaned against the porch roof.

He had already attacked the walls into Grandfather's room through the bathroom, above the stairs, and beside the door on the landing. He'd ruined a lot of paint and spread dust through the house, but he hadn't even approached the wooden slats beneath the plaster. It was all futile, and he knew it. But it was better than doing nothing.

He climbed, carefully with the gun, until he'd reached the old shingles above the porch. In front of him were Grandfather's windows. One was uneven in its age but smooth and clear. The other, the one he'd shot, was clouded with scratches. Tiny chips flecked its surface, and paint and splinters stood out around small holes in the trim. Not even the slightest crack was visible, nothing but scuffs and chipping.

Frank dropped the barrels open, pulled out the empty, and flicked it into the yard. He replaced it, snapped the gun straight, and recocked both hammers.

He was about to be rash. All the way rash. Even in his frustration, the corner of his mouth twitched in a smile. This was, maybe, how Henrietta always felt.

He took another step up the ladder, held the gun at his hip, and angled it toward the scratched-up window.

"Dots!" he yelled.

"We're down!" she yelled back.

Then, in a concession to safety, he pinched his eyes shut, turned his head to the side, and pulled both triggers.

It had been a long day.

Frank felt wasps sting him on the cheekbone and on the ear. Not wasps, ricochets.

The kick pushed him back. And then the ancient ladder snapped beneath him.

Have to dig out the pellets, he thought as he fell, and then he landed on his back in the grass. His legs were tangled with the ladder. His feet were in the flowers by the porch. The gun was on his belly.

"Ow," he said quietly.

He tossed the gun away into the grass and lay still. After a moment, he reached up and felt his cheek. A small trickle of blood had already grown sticky. The pellet was just beneath the skin against the bone. Frank felt around until he had it pinched. Then, wincing, he squeezed it out and flicked it into the flowers.

There wasn't a pellet in his ear, just a perfectly round hole up near the top. Bits of wood and paint were stuck in his hair, but he didn't worry about them. He just lay there, feeling his bones ache, his face sting, and listening to the ringing in his ears.

"Frank?" Dotty yelled.

"Nothing!" Frank yelled back. "Be inside in a minute."

For a moment, he watched stiff clouds slide across the sky, and then he pulled his legs free and rolled slowly onto his side, managed to reach his feet, and looked out over the quiet little town of Henry, Kansas. He looked at the town the way a tired fly, stuck in the kitchen, looks at the window screen. A long time ago, he'd tattered his wings against it and chosen a life inside. It hadn't been too bad. Dots had been inside, too. Like warm bread on the counter.

Frank was hungry. He'd spent the morning searching the house for Grandfather's key. He'd flipped mattresses, dumped shoe boxes, smashed a piggy bank, tipped lamps and books and shelves and dolls. While Dotty had made Anastasia and Penelope eat lunch, he'd attacked the bedroom walls, and plaster ash had filled the house. He could still feel concrete grit between his teeth.

He turned toward the house and looked up at Grandfather's window. It was cloudy enough to work in a bathroom now, but the trim was splintered to a ruin, and a piece of siding had split and lost its corner. It made him feel a little better. Even if he had failed, he had done damage. And he'd hurt himself. He should pay a price for his mistake, for letting a bucket of concrete plaster sit and harden in Henry's room.

Frank limped toward the front door. He didn't know what time it was. The sun wasn't low, but it was getting lower. It had to be after supper. Blake was back, and he sat in the grass watching Frank climb the front porch.

"You give it a shot," Frank said. "I gotta sit for a bit."

He opened the screen door and stepped into the house.

"Dad!" Anastasia yelled. He'd left them in the kitchen. They were in the dining room now. "Dad! The raggant's back, and he bit Penny! He's bleeding and he's mad!"

Frank hobbled into the dining room. The raggant was standing in the center of the table with its wings flared and its tail up. His right rear leg was bent, and a dark patch shone on his haunch. Dotty looked at the blood on Frank's face and raised her eyebrows. She was holding a rag on Penny's hand.

"What happened?" Frank asked.

"He squeezed in the cat door in the back," Dotty said. "Got blood on the kitchen floor. I think he was bitten by a dog or something. Maybe a coyote."

"Penny tried to hold him," Anastasia said. "And he chomped on her."

"It's not bad," Penny said. "I think he just wants Henry."

"And he got bit," Anastasia added.

Dotty left Henrietta and walked around the table to Frank. The raggant stretched out his neck and bellowed at her like an angry goose. His wings were almost as wide. Dotty skipped farther away from the table's edge.

"Hello?" It was Zeke's voice at the front door. "Mr. Willis? Are you okay?"

The raggant bellowed.

Zeke stepped around the corner and took his hat off. He was carrying a bat and a glove.

"I was just coming over to talk to Henry," he said to

Frank. "And I saw you on the ground. Are you okay? You fall off that ladder?"

Before Frank could answer, the raggant jumped off the table and hurried to the base of the stairs on its three good legs. They all watched the small animal fold its wings back and strain its neck, its nostrils flaring.

The air moved. Everyone felt it. The raggant's ears rustled, and the room was suddenly warmer. Doors banged upstairs.

Dotty grabbed Frank by the arm. "Are they back?" she whispered.

Frank sniffed. The air smelled wrong, false somehow, he didn't know why. "Don't think so," he said. He moved to the bottom of the stairs and stood behind the raggant. He could hear creaking in the attic.

His shotgun was still out in the front yard, and he didn't have time to get it. He stepped over the raggant and stood on the stairs. Zeke stood behind him.

Someone was coming down from the attic. Someone heavy.

A huge man, dressed all in black, stepped into view on the second-story landing. He was wearing a cape held by a chain around his neck, and a tall velvet hat. In his left hand, he held a long, straight blade. A small barefoot body was draped through the crook of his other arm, partially hidden by the cape. On one dangling limb, there was a blue cast. Frank recognized it. And he recognized the dirty pink sweats.

"Plebe," Darius said quietly. "Where have you en-clapsed my son?"

Frank didn't think to be afraid. He couldn't. His jaw popped, and something burning climbed up into his throat. It was anger. Anger like he hadn't felt in a life-time. This man had Richard.

"Don't know your son," he said. "Put the boy down. You and your costume should get back to the circus."

Darius laughed. Perfectly. Booming behind his ribs.

"So you speak to a seventh? Not a seventh only, but to one stronger than a wizard in his dreamings? To a witch-dog? To your likes, I am none of these. I am a god."

"Excuse me while I get a wreath," Frank said. He was ready to die right here if he had to. So long as he hurt this man first. His hand slid into his pocket and closed around two shells. "Zeke," he said. "Run, grab that stick from the lawn."

Darius took one step down, and the raggant bleated anger between Frank's legs. Zeke backed toward the door.

"I'm glad no one else is here," Frank said. "Wouldn't want my family to have to meet you."

"There are three lives in a room beneath my feet," Darius said. "Girls. A woman. But where is my son?"

Zeke winced and jumped away from the door, suck-ing his fingertips. The wood crackled and hardened around the glowing latch. Zeke tucked his hand beneath his shirt and tried to quickly flip the metal. His shirt burst into flame when he touched it. Yelping, he staggered into the living room and slapped it out on his belly.

Darius took another step.

"Dotty," Frank said. "Leave now. Zeke, go with them."

Zeke didn't budge. Darius lifted the point of his blade to his face and scraped it through his sideburn. Then suddenly, the blade whistled down and sunk deep into the stair between the big man's feet.

Darius spoke, low guttural churnings that sharpened in his throat. They hung from his mouth like creatures, and then exploded through the house.

Someone crashed to the floor in the kitchen, and Anastasia screamed long and hard. Zeke ran toward the noise. Frank didn't move.

Darius licked blood from a fresh split on his lower lip. "Death words will gnaw each," he said, "till you speak me truth."

Sergeant Kenneth Simmons pulled onto the grass in front of the Willis house. Henry, Kansas, was too small to have its own police force, and his had been the closest of the sheriff's patrol cars.

Plus, he knew Frank Willis.

Dispatch had told him that Frank had been seen firing a rifle at a second-story window in his own house while yelling his wife's name.

Sergeant Simmons was fairly certain that there

would not be a reasonable explanation. This was Frank Willis, after all. But there would be an explanation of some kind. Something that would only make sense to Frank. And he had no idea what that explanation might be. Though he did hope it would be good enough to get Frank off with a warning.

He reported his arrival to dispatch, picked his hat up off the passenger seat, stepped out of his car, and screwed the hat onto his head. Unsnapping his holster, he began to walk toward the front door. He was stiff, and his legs moved slowly.

He was glad to see the shotgun lying in the grass. At least that wouldn't be a factor. There could be other guns, but he didn't really think there would be. And Frank was thin. Even if Frank tried to get tough, it wouldn't go anywhere.

Sergeant Simmons was not fat. But he was thick. Thick from his ankles to his earlobes. Always had been. But even with all his bulk, he'd never been able to swing a bat like Frank had. He'd crushed the ball occasionally, but Frank could give it wings.

Wrestling had been his thing. Wrestling and football.

He stepped onto the porch, smiled at the gray and white cat, which ran off, and looked in the screen door. He couldn't see anyone. Not a lot of noise, either.

He rapped on the door frame. "Frank?" he yelled. "It's Ken Simmons. I've got my badge on. We heard you were taking some target practice in the yard. Just needed to check in."

Putting one hand on the butt of his gun, he reached for the door latch.

He pulled it off.

Surprised, he looked down in time to watch ash tumble onto the toes of his boots. Most of the wooden frame was fine, besides needing paint, but a hole the size of his fist had replaced the latch.

There wasn't time to think about it. He dropped the cold metal, slid his hand into the hole, and pulled the door open.

Inside, on the doormat, a gray, horned animal was mostly hidden beneath feathers, shivering in the breeze.

There was a bigger body in the living room.

Sergeant Simmons pulled his gun.

Stepping inside, he swallowed hard, pinched the radio on his shoulder, and requested backup.

Frank was lying on his back in the center of the living room. One arm was draped over his face. Wisps of smoke twisted up off his clothes. His hair was white, curled, and singed in the front.

Beyond Frank, a boy was seated against the living room wall beside the couch. His eyes were open, but his mouth was shut. His body was motionless.

"Zeke Johnson?" Simmons asked quietly. "What's going on here?"

Zeke blinked, but said nothing, and moved nothing.

"Are you the constabulary?" Darius asked.

Sergeant Simmons wheeled and found his gun pointing at a man, halfway down the stairs, wearing a white puffy-sleeved shirt, enormous boots, and the biggest sideburns he'd ever seen. He was also carrying a sword.

"I apologize for not coming sooner," Darius said. "I was in the loft rooms."

"I'm going to have to ask you to put down that sword," Sergeant Simmons said. His gun was pointed directly at the big man's chest.

"Ask? You may ask."

"Put it down," Simmons said. "And stay back. I'll shoot."

Darius smiled. "If you hold nothing more than pistolry, my sword will be enough. My tongue and teeth should be enough."

Darius stepped forward. Sergeant Simmons lowered his gun toward the big man's legs and fired.

A single pulse fired back, muffling and then swallowing the sound of the gun. Sergeant Simmons stumbled like he did when an elevator dropped too fast, but quickly spread his feet and braced himself.

Darius put one hand on the stair rail, lifted his leg, and shook it gently. "Your powder is strong," he said. "But it will not penestrate."

Lifting his sword slowly, Darius took another step.

Sergeant Simmons pointed the gun directly at the man's broad forehead and squeezed off another round.

Darius rocked slowly. A lump grew quickly beneath his pale skin.

Zeke's mouth was suddenly free. "Shoot!" he yelled. "Keep shooting!"

"I am afraid," Darius said, lifting his right arm, "that I cannot allow you to do that again."

Another shot burst through the house, and Darius tottered, shut his eyes, then sat on the stairs. A final round in the chest knocked him flat.

"Kill him," Zeke said. "Quick. He'll wake back up."

Simmons lowered his gun. "Can't do that, Zeke. You know that."

Zeke staggered up and hurried over beside the thick officer.

While they watched, the man's body changed. A mist around it faded, and the man thinned. His teeth were yellow, his legs were long bones loose inside his pants, his hair was thin and stringy, and his ears stuck out like handles. Strangest of all, he was wearing some sort of large white chin strap. Huge goose eggs stood out on his forehead.

His eyes quivered and then opened.

Sergeant Simmons filled them with pepper spray.

"Dad?" Anastasia's voice came from the kitchen.

Zeke hurried toward it.

Simmons holstered his gun and grabbed the quivering Darius by the boot heel. He dragged him down the stairs and into the living room. The skinny, chin-strapped man moved, groaning, trying to sit up. Simmons flipped him onto his face, pulled his wrists

119

together, and cuffed him, reciting Miranda rights as he did.

He updated dispatch, and was told that lights and sirens were already on their way.

Feeling much better, he moved toward Frank. Dotty and Zeke came out of the kitchen with Penny propped up between them. The skin on her face looked almost clear next to her dark hair. Anastasia, frightened, followed behind.

Sergeant Simmons lifted Frank's arm away from his face.

"Is he okay?" Dotty asked.

"He's breathing," Simmons said. "But I don't know about okay. It'll take doctors and blinking lights to figure that. He got himself scorched pretty good, but his arm was up. Good thing for his eyes and face." He looked at Darius. "Who is that guy?"

Dotty's eyes went wide, and she shook her head. "I have no idea. Some crazy wizard." She lowered Penelope onto the couch, brushed the hair off of her face, and then slid down onto the floor beside Frank.

Sergeant Simmons snorted. A wizard. He looked at Darius's back. A wizard. On the other hand, run-of-the-mill psychotics didn't deflect gunshots to the head and shape-change when unconscious.

"I think I hear sirens," Zeke said.

Frank opened his eyes.

So did Darius.

*　*　*

At birth, Darius had been given the name Fred. Not Frederick. Not Frederic. Not even Phred. Fred. His father had been a priest in a very small village and was the sort of man who wore corruption like a badge of honor. Darius had loathed his father, and through a long and complex process of hatred, he'd become surprisingly like him.

But Darius was something different. He was the second son born to his mother by the priest. The first had died. But he was the seventh son born to the priest among the women of the village, though few knew it.

He was a pauper son. He was prone to visions and dreams, and he was able to walk the dreams of others when close to them. He gained much information this way and made use of it as his father had made use of the villagers' confessions.

The story he told his followers, the society he had invaded and taken over in Byzanthamum, was that when he turned twelve, he saw the mage of nature itself swirling around an enormous black oak in the heart of a wood. He had touched it and absorbed the mage into himself. The tree had crumbled in death, and he had wandered the woods blind and mad for three passages of the moon. A black oak was his symbol.

But that was not the truth.

When he was twelve, he had wandered into the woods and disappeared, driven mad by the swirling life he'd seen in a toadstool. Two years later, the whole village was flattened in the night by horrific downbursts of wind. Every soul was cut free from its flesh, and in the morning, the village green was crowded with mushrooms. So was the body of his father.

Now, Darius was spitting and blinking into the carpet. He couldn't see anything, and he was having trouble remembering what had just happened. The thick policeman with the pistol crept into his head between the throbbing drumbeats of an aching skull. His arms were stuck. He twiddled his fingers around and found the chain of the handcuffs. Something began to boil inside of him. Something much louder and stronger than his headache. He was lying on his face, chained.

Darius was strong. He had always been strong. But his strength was wild, untrained and unrefined. He compensated with silk capes, velvet hats, big words, and horrible but expensive wine. He was like a storm in his anger. Uncontrollable. He could light a fire like a small volcano, but he could never put one out. He could tear down walls and rip up trees; he could throw a wind that would shatter stone, but he couldn't calm a breeze. Not without starting a tornado.

He spat again, cursed into the carpet, and jerked his wrists. His mind reached out, grasping for any strength he could find. He reached into the earth and around the house. The grass in the yard began to curl slowly, and hundreds of the closest insects died and dried. The water heater in the basement shorted, and its water went cold. Had anyone been listening, instead of trying to talk to Frank, they would have heard a slow sucking sound like a motorless vacuum, a great collecting of lives, of stories, of words emptying and being swallowed.

The walls began to creak and pop, the floor trembled, and the lights went out. Dotty put her hands on her head and blinked. Sergeant Simmons stumbled and fell to his knees. Anastasia, dizzy, sat down hard. Upstairs, Richard started crying, and a low groan sputtered from the raggant by the door. Zeke put his hand on the wall and looked at Darius's twitching body.

"I don't feel well," Penelope said.

With the strength Darius had gathered, he could have done any number of things most wizards could only imagine. He could have turned blood to water and water to blood. Outside, dead sticks twisted on the ground, approaching life, begging to be serpents. Blake felt the ground grow hot beneath his feet, and he ran, leaping through the curling grass.

Darius just wanted the handcuffs off. On the dark floor of the living room, he arched his spine, threw back his head, and widened his blind and burning eyes. A word formed in his belly and burned in his mind. It coiled in his lungs, and his tongue tensed. He couldn't have held it in if he'd wanted. And he wanted it out.

It roared through him, an ancient word, one of the first words of power he had ever learned, and it sounded like nothing in any modern tongue.

It meant "open." Or "shut."

Every window in the house exploded. Doors slammed. A dog half a mile away snapped his jaws shut on his own leg and couldn't let go. In the irrigation ditch behind the barn, a fish that had swallowed a small safety pin out of curiosity suddenly blinked in surprise. All the frogs belched at once. But Darius had more strength left. He had collected it, and now it came rushing back out. Though his arms had sprung apart immediately, he screamed the word again, and again, three times. Four times. The house rocked with the sound of slamming, bursting, sliding, and shattering. Penelope bit her tongue, and Zeke's teeth cracked loudly. On the Willises' side of Henry, Kansas, every door went haywire. Ovens, safes, refrigerators, and microwaves jerked themselves around rooms, opening and slamming. In the front yard, the patrol car lost its doors. Sergeant Simmons managed to stand, but his gun fired and shot him in the foot while his teeth clattered.

"Out," he said, grabbing at Dotty and the girls while he hopped. "Get out of the house!"

Dotty and Anastasia half carried, half dragged Penelope to the door while Zeke and Simmons managed to careen onto the porch with Frank. All of them tumbled into the yard.

In his darkness, Darius picked up his exhausted body. His eyes were still streaming and still burning. He put his hand to his head and felt the lumps. His anger, though sated, had not completely vented itself.

With a groan of irritation, he put one hand to his head and stamped his foot.

Darius stood still in the living room, fuming, blinking away the pepper pain in his eyes. He wanted to smash the house, kill anything and everything within twenty miles, and tear the sky down. He was as mad as a wasp, but he was much larger and nastier than a wasp. He wanted to sting the world.

The lives around him were no longer in the room, no longer in the house, except for the pink slave on the floor upstairs where he'd dropped him. They were outside the house now, and Darius could tell that the fat policeman was hurt. He would kill them. He could do it now, where they stood, thinking themselves safe.

But he didn't. Something had changed. The earth beyond the house was different, and it held a different sort of life. Beyond the people in the yard, this new place was empty of everything but grass. He had closed the house off from its old place.

Outside the house, he could feel only one song, and the words were *emptiness* and *green*. But inside, there was something more interesting, one clear taste, a flavor, a pull so attractive that he began to forget his anger. Frank had insulted him. The fat policeman had shot him in the head and chained him on the floor, but they were nothing to him now. Nothing to this.

The pull was coming from upstairs.

For the first time in many years, Darius felt afraid. He knew what was pulling him, he'd been dreaming of it since he'd first heard the legends of Endor from a mad medicine man behind his painted wagon, and later when he'd read the same stories scrawled on monk's vellum.

He was feeling the presence of the undying, the life of the last daughter of the second sire, Nimiane, witch-queen of all that had been Endor. Even Merlinis had tumbled before her.

This is what Darius wanted. This, when he first saw the small gateways in Henry's dreams, is what he knew could happen.

But she was stronger than he was. Her life, a slow swirling, swallowing motion, was upstairs and through a doorway. And he was in its current.

He climbed the stairs with all his senses straining, stepped over the snoring, whimpering body of Richard where he had dropped it on the landing, and climbed into the attic.

He stood in front of the cupboards and released his breath. After a decade of searching, he had found three doorways such as these, and he'd paid for them with the lives of others. The wealth in the wall in front of him was unimaginable. But there were greater prizes beyond it.

The cupboards were all open, thanks to his fit of commands, and the room was astir with chaos. There was a horse somewhere, and hateful faeren, bloodshed and murder and war, salt seas, stone, aging, rotting books, desert heat, and a strange southern zephyr. There was home, the sound of laughter, and through one, the unmistakable taste of love.

Above it all, drowning it, drinking it, there was a dark emptiness, a hole into which it was all falling. Into which he was falling.

He shook his head. When he went, when he submitted to the urge, it would be his choice. Ignoring what felt like a rope, tied taut around his insides and reeling him in, he sent his mind through another cupboard. There was a sack of flour, mouse droppings, and a woman sweeping a floor. He probed another and felt himself in a tower, standing in a low, arched doorway, and birds, hundreds of them. Through another, a snake was dying, an ancient serpent unlike any in his world. It was winged, but its wings were shattered, stripped of feathers, and its body had been pierced.

When he sent his mind through the next, he stepped back in surprise. A wizard stood on the other side, probing with his mind, as he was. The wizard had sensed him as well, for he seemed nervous. Darius reached deeper inside the man, surprised that he could. The man was afraid, but beneath that, ashamed. He had some strength, but it seemed twisted inside of him, deformed even.

On his palm, and coursing through him, he had a burning word, a word Darius knew and felt coursing through his own veins.

Horror surged through him, and his head swam. One of the doors had turned him back on himself. Even alone, the humiliation, the terror that came with what he'd seen brought sweat to his face. His real face, the face with the weak chin and the thin hair and big ears.

Quickly, to forget what he had seen, his mind groped for another door and wandered through into darkness. He knew that he felt Endor, the oldest of cities. Or he felt a tomb below Endor, where Nimiane had been imprisoned. But she was not there, and he could not feel beyond the walls and into the place he had only seen in his dreams, a place where the eldest of the undying had gone mad and been imprisoned by their offspring. But no one had been able to bind the young when their minds had shattered. He'd been told they still wandered the streets, drooling, molding light's reflection around themselves, holding whatever shape they desired in their confusion.

He pulled himself back and then straightened, finally letting his eyes and his mind focus on the draw.

A woman sat on a throne in a cold stone room. Rivers of life poured into her, poured into the stones beneath her feet, into the walls and pillars. A cat sat on her lap, the only pocket of quiet. His head spun with the rushing, with the hugeness of the power she had drawn to herself, with the hugeness of the death required to provide it.

He stepped forward, relaxed, his mind no longer groping. It had been grasped, pulled, and his body had followed.

He was standing on the stone floor crowded with the power and life she had poured into it. Rain fell through high windows and ran down his face. She saw him as he was, without any illusion. His illusions would have been pointless.

She was beautiful.

Her mind lashed out faster than he could feel, and it tore through him.

"You seek the life of Nimroth," she said. Her voice was flat and distracted.

Darius was barely hanging on to his own existence, clutching at strength in his own life. He couldn't speak.

"I am Nimiane. He is in me. He is my sire." She looked directly at him, no longer distracted. The river quieted around him. "You are no wizard."

Darius stepped back, horrified that she was searching him, remembering what she would see.

"You are like a man suckled by wolves, strong, hungry, but hunched on all fours, with a tongue twisted in confusion."

Suddenly, she laughed, and her laughter echoed through the room, rattling on stone, dying slowly. "Do not be afraid. You cannot be a man to me, but you will be my wolf. Is that what you have always dreamed? Have you not already named yourself witch-dog? You shall lead my pack."

"Against what land?" Darius managed to say. "In what warring?"

"Against the world. Against all worlds. Together, we shall out-devour death. But first, you shall go out against the home of an old enemy, against his wife and sons, against the land that embraced his feet. There is a grudge-hunger that must be slaked."

He felt her reach into him, and his already-twisted strength twisted further. He fell to the wet stones in pain, and his eyes rolled. He was being split, ripped open, and hollowed. The pain stopped, and something else began. He was being filled. The stones and the sky and even the rain were venting into him, and he could feel her hand guiding the flood. He filled beyond bursting, more than he could ever have grasped for himself. The strength was unbearable, but he was not angry. Anger would have released it all.

She'd finished, and Darius felt too heavy to stand. The world around him was heavier. But he found his knees and then his feet. His hair clung to his shoulders.

His queen was standing, more beautiful than the moon, than a graveyard, than spider's silk.

"Sit," she said, and gestured toward the throne. "Let us call your pack. They are but pups and curs. You shall make me wolves."

Frank was sitting with his back against the side of the patrol car. Penelope was asleep in the backseat with her head on Dotty's lap. Dazed, Anastasia was in the front with the raggant on hers. Frank's skin tingled all over like it was prepping for the worst sunburn of his life. Ashen hairs drifted down onto his nose whenever he turned his head.

Old Ken Simmons had pulled him out of the

house as soon as the earthquake, or whatever it had been, settled down. Zeke and Dotty had carried Penelope.

He wasn't quite sure what had happened, or how. He only knew what was. And what was, was not Kansas. The town was gone. The crops and silos and trees were all gone. The barn and the irrigation ditch were gone. The front lawn, the cop car, and the shotgun he'd dropped by the broken ladder were still there. The rest was all tall, waving grass, without variation, to the horizon. And as far as the horizon was concerned, the sun was on the wrong side. Either it was morning where they were now, or the sun did its business in mirror image to the way it worked in Kansas.

Ken Simmons was leaning on the front of the car, holding his own shotgun and watching the house. Zeke was beside him.

"Zeke," Frank said. "Help me up."

Zeke came over, gripped Frank's hands, and leaned back. When he was on his feet, Frank creaked from side to side and walked slowly over to the sergeant.

"We've got to go back inside," Frank said. "He's got Richard. Doesn't much matter if he's waiting for us."

Simmons nodded.

"No backup coming," Frank said. "Not even crickets, judging from the silence."

Simmons nodded again. "I don't pretend to understand any of this," he said. "But I don't need to. I'm just waiting to wake up."

"Tell me when you do," Frank said. "How's your foot?"

Sergeant Simmons snorted. "Still there."

"Um," Zeke said, and he pointed. "Is that water on the porch?"

They watched as the screen door gently swayed, and water rushed out from beneath it.

Frank hobbled over to his shotgun and picked it up out of the grass. He fitted two more shells into the barrels and levered back the hammers.

"Give the boy a gun," he said, and nodded at Zeke. The water was spilling off the porch.

Sergeant Simmons pulled out his handgun, chambered a round, and showed Zeke the safety. "Point at what you want to hit," he said. "And nothing else."

"Not your feet," Frank said.

The two men limped, carrying the shotguns at their hips. Zeke followed with the gun pointed at the ground.

The grass around the porch had become a fast-growing swamp, and more water poured out the front door every second.

Frank pulled the screen wide and stepped into two inches of water. The living room was a pond, the stairs a waterfall.

"Zeke," he said. "Stand right here and keep your eyes on the back of the house."

Zeke took up his station inside the door as Frank began climbing the flowing stairs. Sergeant Simmons limped behind him.

Halfway up, Frank could see what he'd already suspected. The water was coming out of the attic, romping down the stairs. He took another step and craned his head around the landing. A black cape and tall hat had been dropped by the girls' room. Richard was sitting with his back to the bathroom door. His arms clutched his knees tight to his chest. He was soaking wet, and he was shivering. His wide eyes, watching the flood, wheeled toward Frank in fear.

Frank smiled, but Richard showed no recognition.

"Don't let the hair and face fool you," Frank said. "C'mon."

Richard blinked and jumped to his feet, grinning. His bare feet slapped into the moving water as he lunged down the stairs and threw his arms around Frank.

Frank squeezed his shoulder, but kept his eyes on the attic. "Head right outside," he said. "Go to the car."

Richard didn't say a word. He let go of Frank, slid past Sergeant Simmons, and splashed down the stairs.

Frank didn't think Darius was in the attic. He didn't think he was anywhere around, not with the water running. He'd gone off to someplace. Still, he kept his gun up as he climbed and swept the attic with it before he turned to what had been Henry's room.

The two doors were open, and water was gushing out of them.

He stepped into the doorway, with the water frothing over his feet, and looked at the wall of cupboards—every last one gaping wide. Simmons stepped up beside him.

Neither of them said anything.

The water was surging out of a small, diamond-shaped cupboard by the upper corner of the compass door, splattering off the end of Henry's bed, and washing over the floor.

Frank stepped over to the wall, braced himself, and shut the door against the water, leaning his full weight against it. After a moment, the pressure disappeared, and he let go and stepped back.

The door to Endor was open as well. He squatted down, picked it up out of the puddle, and looked at the screws. They had all snapped. He fitted the door back in place, pushed the bed leg against it, and stood up.

He left the rest of the doors open.

"C'mon," he said. "Let's go talk to Richard."

On the way back down, he looked over at Grandfather's door, thrown wide open.

Not that it mattered. The front windows had shattered, too.

Two police cars and one ambulance were parked beside the hole. The barn was still there, and Frank's old truck was parked beside it, but the house and a chunk of the front yard had been replaced by a smooth-sided hole. For a while, water had poured in from a spot at the back, and the bottom had filled. It was slowing now.

"Smells funny," one of the officers said.

The other tipped his hat to the back of his head. "Septic, you think?"

"No," the first one said. "Salty. Smells like the ocean."

"I wouldn't know. I'm a Kansas boy."

Neither of them noticed the small, very confused crab appear at the edge of the hole and then tumble in.

He had been in tide pools before, but nothing like this. Still, the tide would come. It always did. He could wait.

CHAPTER NINE

Henrietta's wrists were bruised, and she had a scrape on one knee. She twisted her hands slowly, flexing her fingers, grateful that they were no longer tied. The room was small, but it didn't feel dirty. She was sitting on the floor, and the only thing to look at was the thin band of daylight beneath the door.

Before they'd grabbed her, she had screamed and tried to run. But the small men had been faster on the broken floor. When she'd fallen, they'd grabbed her arms and carried her between them. She'd kicked and tried to bite. She'd yelled for Henry and Richard. Finally, she'd tried to talk to the men. She'd begged and explained, but they hadn't responded. They'd never even looked in her eyes.

Through the big doorway, they'd taken her to a small flight of collapsed stairs, where they had left a ladder. One of them had climbed down the ladder first while the other held her arms pinned behind her back. Then she had been made to climb before being repinned at the bottom.

They'd led her through collapsed hallways, over

tumble-down doors, and through gaping windows. Finally, they'd come out into a courtyard, and Henrietta had stopped in her tracks. The two men, each holding a wrist, had stopped beside her. They'd let her look. They'd looked as well, and to Henrietta, it seemed like they were more affected than she was.

With crumbling walls and missing roofs, even in ruin, the city that loomed above her dwarfed anything she had ever seen. Arched walkways soared from tower to broken tower. Armies of pale statues lined rooftops in gapped rows. Windows big enough to swallow barns gaped from still-smooth walls, near seamless to any eye. A belfry, missing its crown, still held its bells aloft where no Kansas silo could have reached, and a slow swirl of crows moved around them. A web of wide paths and rubble was strewn through what had been the courtyard lawns. Fallen gutters and cornices, stone horse heads and angel wings were swallowed by waist-high swaying grass and tangles of flowers. In the center, rising up out of the green, there sprawled a fountain.

The men had led Henrietta toward it.

Marble, shaded with dirt, lichen, and grime, in places painted green with ancient water stains, was frozen in a moment of glory taller than Henrietta's house. Men and women, horses and creatures that she couldn't have imagined were all pulling themselves out of a mountain of rock. Some were laughing, others wept with what had once been joy, but now, hooded with stains and moss, could have been something else.

Perched at the very top, a bearded man sat on the back of a straining ram. Stone vines and leaves wrapped around him and curled through the ram's thick horns.

"A human shaped the font long ago, in the rich times," one of the men had said. His voice was thick, but she'd understood. It was the first thing either man had said. "A man with senses in each fingertip. It has never been defaced."

"A human?" she'd asked. "You're not human?"

He hadn't answered, and the other hadn't even glanced at her. They'd pulled her on, past the fountain, across the courtyard, and out through a narrow breach in a wall to a waiting wagon, loaded with timber. A large but lazy ox had been grazing in his harness. Her wrists and ankles had been twined together, and she'd been seated on and leg-tied to a beam on top of the pile.

And now she was here, after long miles on a near-invisible road, through rolling hills, sometimes wooded and sometimes grassed but always hot and dry.

She'd asked where they were going. If they knew Eli FitzFaeren. If they could take her to him. If they could tell him she'd come. But they'd ignored her and had spoken to each other in low voices she hadn't been able to understand.

Through the entire slow-jolting ride, she'd tried to take note of landmarks—bent trees, stones beside a stream, small, rotten houses, or barns mounded over with brambles. But as the sun had climbed and begun to drop, bent trees had been followed by more bent trees.

The streams were always full of stones, and the hills were spotted with brambles chewing on leaning walls and gapped, gray, and fraying timber.

With the sun pounding down on her face and burning her already watering eyes, she had been forced to squint. But squinting had brought no relief, so she'd lain back, put her arms over her face, and shut her eyes tight.

If she escaped, she would just follow the road.

Henrietta could hear voices. She didn't know how long she'd been sitting in the dark, but she was getting hungry. And thirsty. What she really wanted was an ice cube to pinch between her lips, or rattle on her teeth and stretch inside her cheek. But she knew she'd drink pretty much anything.

She was thinking about screaming, and maybe kicking the walls, when the door finally opened. Turning her head away from the light, she scrunched up her eyes. No one grabbed her. No one even came in to get her. The door was just open. After a moment of blinking, she stepped through it and into the little hall that led back to the front of the house.

One of the men was standing at the other end. He nodded his head at a doorway in front of him and crossed his arms. She walked toward him, a little warily but hoping she didn't look too nervous. She could try to run through him. He wasn't really taller than she was, but she'd already felt his grip. He could probably break her in half.

Instead, she smiled at him. Or leered. But he wasn't provoked. He waited, and when she slipped through the doorway, he followed her.

The room was bright, but a breeze was moving through the open windows, so it wasn't entirely sweaty. Two chairs sat across from a small couch, and a table squatted between them. Behind the chairs, paned windows opened out onto a garden. A goat's horns and eyes were just visible through one of them. The animal was standing in rosebushes.

A woman, with hard lines on weathered cheeks and shot-white hair, was sitting on one of the chairs. A pair of gardening gloves sat on her lap. She looked up at Henrietta and gestured toward the little couch. Her face expressed nothing, but Henrietta thought she caught a smile in her eyes.

"Joseph," she said suddenly. "The ivy has come in the window again. Be kind enough to remove it."

The man moved toward the window, lifted two straggling tendrils of ivy off the sill, and bent them outside.

The old woman looked directly into Henrietta's eyes. "Ivy is a curse," she said. "Doubly so because I find it appealing when it destroys my walls."

Henrietta smiled, but the woman did not smile back.

"There's a goat in your roses, too," Henrietta said.

"Yes," the woman said. "But he won't eat them. He has done so once before and once is always enough."

Turning, she addressed the man again. "Joseph, where is your brother?"

"Gone to drop the timber, ma'am."

"Join him."

"Yes, ma'am."

Without a glance at Henrietta, Joseph left the room and shut the door behind him.

When the door was latched, the old woman relaxed in her seat and looked Henrietta up and down. Her face moved into a smile as bright and contagious as it was unexpected. Henrietta couldn't help but smile back.

"My grandsons are so serious," she said. "They feel safer when I am as well. Please"—she leaned forward and lifted a cloth off a tray on the table—"eat if you are hungry."

"Thank you," Henrietta said. Somehow, though she'd been tied up and carted off by this woman's grandsons and then locked into one of her rooms, she couldn't really manage to be rude. Not to this lady. There was something about her, a complete ownership of her surroundings, a soft strength with a hard edge. Something. Maybe it was just the twinkly eyes, or the white hair on such sun-dark skin. Just looking at her made Henrietta feel oafish. Without meaning to, she found that she was sitting up straight with her hands on her lap and her legs tucked together and crossed at the ankles.

On the tray in front of her, there was a brown piece of wide-grained fish, a bowl of what looked like large curds of cottage cheese, and another bowl of football-shaped olives with the pits still in.

"I apologize for the fish," the woman said. "Joseph believes that every meat should be smoked, and smoked extensively. I suspect him of smoking apples when unattended. He may have even smoked the olives. I haven't yet sampled them. The cheese, however, I can assure you, is all my goat's doing and has had no tainting contact with Joseph and his hickory smoke."

Henrietta leaned forward, bent off a corner of the fish, and popped it in her mouth. It tasted like burnt salt, but she was hungry. She tore off a larger piece, held it on her palm, and picked at it. There weren't any napkins or plates.

"Your name is Henrietta Willis?" the old woman asked.

"Yes," Henrietta said. "How did you know?"

The woman squinted. "It's written on your forehead."

"What?" Henrietta pushed her hair back and felt around with her fingertips. "Where? How?"

The woman smiled. "There's nothing there. You told my grandsons, Benjamin and Joseph."

Henrietta put her hand back down. She could feel her cheeks getting hot. Being embarrassed always made her irritated, and being irritated made her cheeks hotter.

"What am I doing here?" she asked. "I need to get home."

"You are a human who was trespassing in the ruins

of the Lesser Hall of the FitzFaeren. Home is a long way off."

"I wasn't trespassing," Henrietta said. "I was looking for my cousin, and he was looking for Eli FitzFaeren."

"Do you know Eli?" the woman asked quietly.

Henrietta shrugged. "He lived in my house for two years."

"Did he?" The woman picked up her gardening gloves and slapped them against the arm of her chair. Henrietta watched dust rise up and be carried off on the breeze from the window. "Do you know that on the night of ruination, the first and only night that enemies of our people were able to breach our walls, Eli was there, and he had brought a guest? A human guest?"

Henrietta didn't say anything.

"The guest had been there before. He was known to all of us. But he stole—or was given by a traitor—some things of ours that weakened our defenses. Because of him, we were destroyed. Do you know who he was?"

Henrietta swallowed. She thought she did, though she hoped she was wrong.

The woman looked deep into Henrietta's eyes. "He was your grandfather. And to one with the gift of sight, that *is* written on your forehead."

Henry pressed his shoulder blades against the wall. He'd taken off his backpack and reslung it on his front. He was standing on a window ledge, three tall stories above a narrow, cobbled street. Across from him, there was a building that looked like the Boston Public Library, except that it had a dozen or so smokestacks puffing dark clouds out of its roof. Half of the clouds straggled up into an overcast sky while the other half drifted sideways, falling slowly down toward the street or crossing it in midair and filling Henry's lungs.

Careful not to overbalance, Henry grabbed the neck of his white shirt one more time and pulled it up over his mouth and nose.

He could see in the windows of the other building, it really wasn't that far away. The place was full of women, tending to tangled, steaming machinery. Some wore masks while others, men or women, it was impossible to tell, walked around in gray suits like beekeepers.

He'd had plenty of time to watch. When he'd first climbed out the window and pressed his back against the wall, a young woman had noticed him. She'd moved closer to the glass and stared. After a few minutes, she gestured. Reaching high, her hand dove down and smacked on the windowsill. Then she shrugged, questioning.

"Am I going to jump?" Henry had said out loud. "No." He'd shaken his head hard, and she'd made a face and gone back to a pile of pipes.

She still glanced over at him every few minutes.

Soon he knew he would have to do something. Hiding indefinitely wouldn't accomplish much. Climbing out the window had seemed like such a good idea. Now he wasn't so sure. He could climb back in and risk the room and the halls in a quest for stairs. Or he could postpone that and keep walking the ledge, hoping for something. Those were the only options he could come up with. Other than dying or learning to fly.

The city was big, sprawling off as far as Henry could see. Which wasn't actually that far, given the steam and smoke and foggy breath that seemed to be pouring out of every building and slithering around in the streets. And the streets, from where Henry stood watching traffic, seemed like total chaos. Crowds moved on foot. Four-wheeled bicycles rattled loudly on the cobblestones, occasionally by themselves and occasionally carrying some kind of litter between them. Strangest of all were the carriages. At least that's what he thought they were. They were brightly colored boxes on tall wheels, but instead of being harnessed to horses, they were harnessed to barrel-shaped machines that puffed black smoke or white steam out the sides. All of them had a driver, straddling the wheeled engines, and the drivers wore tall hats and coats that matched the carriage color. They were either unable or unwilling to slow down for people on foot, and there was a great shouting and cursing and scrambling wherever they went.

Reaching street level might actually be the easiest part of what lay ahead of Henry, and he knew it. He had to get south, two milongs, through the bizarre ant farm below him, to one of who knew how many post offices in this city. And Darius would probably be there waiting for him when, or if, he did.

The white shirt slipped back off his chin, and Henry left it. It hadn't been helping, anyway. He pulled in a deep breath of the foul air. It was time to do something.

Henry looked down at the street below him, and he looked at the two intersections at the building's corners. It was a full city block. If his legs held out, he would try to walk the ledge all the way around to the other side. There could be fire escapes or ladders or something. If his legs couldn't hack it, or if the ledge stopped, then he would look for an open window. Or break one.

Henry continued sliding in the same direction. Immediately, he knew that sliding wouldn't be enough. He'd reach the other side of the building by tomorrow morning. Breathing slowly, he turned, squaring his feet on the ledge. In order to fit and not overbalance, he had to keep his shoulders angled, one palm against the wall in front of him and the other dragging behind. But at least he could walk, and walking made the building feel less monstrous.

Every twenty feet or so, he had to duck beneath another bank of windows, and each time, the backpack on his belly rubbed against his knees while he shuffled forward. Those were the slow times. But in between the windows, his speed was almost the same as it would have been on the sidewalk. Faster, if the sidewalk was in this city.

Stooping beneath the final windows, he reached the first corner, straightened, slid to the edge, and peered around it. The road below him was hardly a back alley.

But he couldn't see how long the building was on this side because the ledge ended. At least for a while. A huge metal pipe, tarnished green and crusted black, was mounted against the wall, and the ledge had been smashed out to fit it. Henry slid toward it and put out his hand.

The pipe was warm, almost hot. Henry looked up and saw where it cut through two more ledges above him, and where it wheezed steam into the sky. There were two other pipes beside it, each as thick as a large tree.

Henry put his hand behind the first one, between the warm metal and the wall, and he leaned out. The base of the far pipe bent into the wall six feet from where Henry was standing. The middle pipe ended and burrowed into the second-story wall below him. The one closest to him, the one he held, reached all the way down to the first floor, still tucking into the wall well above the heads of the people on the street.

Henry ran his hand up and down its surface. It wasn't slick. The soot scraped off at first, but beneath it, older layers had hardened on. And the metal itself, where bare, wasn't smooth against his palms. The pipe was segmented. Every four feet or so, there was a lip, maybe an inch thick, where the segments were riveted together.

It wasn't a ladder. But it might be possible. Henry looked down at the street. He was a lot higher than the pigeon roost in the barn back in Kansas. This pipe probably ended that high above cobblestones. And he was wondering if he could dangle from it and drop.

Well, even if he didn't do that, at least he might be able to reach a lower ledge and climb in a first-story window.

Sixty or seventy feet off the ground, three hundred in his mind, Henry moved his backpack to its rightful place, wedged his hand deeper behind the warm pipe, bit his lip, and swung his bare foot around to the other side. There was no ledge there between the pipes, but he worked his hand into place, hugging soot and warmth to his chest.

Bending his one supporting leg, he felt for a toehold with the other. Lower and lower, he squatted, until his leg was shaking in panic and sweat dripped off his forehead. His toes splayed out on a hot rivet lip, and he relaxed for a moment. Then, shaking, he fished his other leg off the ledge and braced it on the lip as well.

He'd just committed. There was no way he'd be able to get back up on the ledge. Down was all there was.

Hugging the pipe tight, he tried to look for the next lip. Bending carefully, he reached for it, realized how impossible it was, and straightened back up. What had he done? It was four feet below him. He could reach two, maybe, and that would be an adrenaline-fed stretch. Just to make sure, he tried to squirm back up. It wasn't going to happen.

He didn't have any choice. He was going to have to slide the pipe four feet at a time.

He was going to die. In a city as beautiful as an oil refinery. In a world he didn't like. Barefoot. With his head knocked open on cobblestones. He'd probably land on someone really nice and kill them, too. The only nice person in this place. At least the factory girl wouldn't get to watch.

Henry gripped the pipe with strength he didn't know he had and slid his feet down off the lip, pinching his bare arches against the metal. Plowing soot, he slid in one-inch jerks, relaxing and clenching tight. The lip he had been standing on dug into his thighs, and then his stomach. He didn't care, but it reached his ribs, and he had to. He relaxed his arms, trying to edge his way around it. Instead, it scraped up his chest as he dropped suddenly. He squeezed the pipe hard, grinding to a stop.

He hadn't died. Blowing out relief, he nearly smiled. He'd climbed down one segment. One out of twelve. Or fifteen. Or some other too-large number.

The pipe was getting hot against his chest. And his legs, noodly and sore when he'd first climbed out the window, really weren't up to this. He needed to go faster. And he wasn't sure he could go at all.

Henry clenched his teeth. He couldn't be weak now. He couldn't think about failure. Instead, he focused on the pipe in front of him. He gripped it and slid again.

The next segment did go faster. The third was the fastest, accidentally, and he bruised his heel on a rivet when he slammed into the lip. The pipe rattled and shook, and soot rained down in his hair.

Without giving himself time to worry or to assess his shaking limbs, Henry slid again. And again. Until his raw, black feet dropped onto the second-story ledge, and he eased himself off the pipe and leaned panting against the wall. His arms were scratched and bleeding, and the soles of his feet were worse. His shirt was thick with black mud—soot mixed with his sweat—and the shallow cuts on his belly were stinging like fire ants.

A few people in the crowd looked up at him while they passed, and a boy on the back of a quadcycle waved. Henry didn't wave back.

He really wanted to give up. He wanted to stretch out on the ledge with his head on his backpack and go to sleep. And maybe roll off and never wake up. Whatever he'd gone through strapped to the table, it hadn't left him in pipe-sliding shape. He had never been in pipe-sliding shape.

But he was also feeling stubborn. As much as he wanted to stop, he hated the idea of stopping. He shouldn't have even let himself rest on the ledge.

Swinging his stiff leg back around the pipe, Henry braced himself and began to inch down. Only he didn't inch down. His knees gave out, his legs swung free, and he dropped, hugging the pipe. The next lip ground against him and clipped his chin as he passed. The pipe shook, booming its echo over the top of the clattering, chugging street. Yelling, he managed to get his feet and thighs back against it and felt the friction burn as he tried to stop. The pipe ended, bending into the wall.

Henry dropped free, his hands grazing the wall and then grabbing nothing but air.

Pain shot through his body as his feet impacted on the last stone ledge. His legs crumpled, his body collapsed, his face clipped something solid, and he fell back, limp.

All falls happen slowly, and in a flash. Half the crowd had looked up when the pipe began to rattle and boom. They watched a boy with a bag on his back clutch at the wall and at the pipe, and then tumble into the air, grabbing at the sky.

He didn't fall far.

A red litter, carried front and back by two quad-cycles, was slowing to a stop beside the building. The flying boy crashed into it.

The bright box rocked and leaned side to side, and then forward. But there was no disaster, no collapse, no dramatic spill. If the boy had died, he had done so where the crowd could not see and share in the experience.

Traffic moved on.

Henry opened his eyes. The world was a cloud. In the middle of the cloud, there was a pair of eyes behind glasses. A hand pulled on a beard.

A distant Henry, some other Henry, spoke.

"Can you take me to the post office?" he asked.

The cloud darkened and disappeared. The beard was the last to go.

CHAPTER TEN

"So," Henrietta said. "You don't want me to go?" She looked down at the tray. The fish was gone, and so were half the olives. She hadn't touched the goat cheese.

The woman pursed her lips and shook her head slowly.

"Why?" Henrietta asked. She knew the answer already, but she was stalling. Her grandfather had stolen something, and now this lady was going to take it out on her. She looked at the open window and tried not to glance at the door. She hadn't heard Benjamin or Joseph return. The old woman couldn't be that hard to beat.

The woman straightened in her chair and webbed her fingers in her lap. "I have explained it already. It is the prerogative of a nation to defend itself. We were robbed first, and then cast into ruin. Certain things must be retrieved to enable a restoration. Things taken by your ancestor."

Henrietta furrowed her brow and cocked her head. She was irritated and worried. It was hard not to be sarcastic. Even to this woman.

"A nation?" she asked. "You're a nation?"

The woman licked her lips. She was staring past Henrietta. "The FitzFaeren rose many centuries ago. We are a people first formed half human, half faerie, but we came to see that we had strengths of our own, the powers of both races. We separated ourselves, no longer mules among the faeren or pets among men. And we became great.

"From the time we first laid foundations for our own city until our fall at the hands of traitors and Endorian dogs, we have been governed by queens. The throne and rod were passed from mother to daughter, never through sons."

"Like bees," Henrietta said. "Or ants."

The woman looked at her. "Or certain breeds of tunneling rats, if you prefer. Or southern hive bats."

Henrietta shut her mouth.

The woman sighed. "The ball," she said, "the dance you've seen and listened to in the haunting, it was to be in celebration of my coronation."

She sat motionless, frozen in her pose, distant.

"You were going to be queen?" Henrietta said. It made sense. All of it did.

"I am," the woman said quietly, "the Third Magdalene of FitzFaeren, Queen." She looked deep into Henrietta's eyes. "Regina to a haunted ruin and a broken people. We have taken possession of you, granddaughter to an enemy, a traitor guest. An old debt must be paid."

Henrietta stood up. The queen watched her. She didn't move.

"Okay," Henrietta said. "I'm really sorry. I have no idea what my grandfather did or what he took, and nobody else in my family would, either. But it sounds like Eli would know, why don't you talk to him?"

"Eli," the queen said. "Yes, Eli has been spoken to. Many times."

"Well, talk to him again. I'm sure he'd want to help his queen."

"Oh yes," the queen said. "I'm sure he would. But he has no desire to help his sister. In many ways, that was the beginning of the problem."

Henrietta stared. She wasn't at all sure what to say. She never was when people talked to her about family problems. Even when they were her friends.

"He is here again, lurking in ruined houses beside the river," the queen said. "He is rarely here, but it is still easy for me to feel him. As he feels me."

"So," Henrietta said, "he has to know more than I do. I just need to get home, if I still can. You talk to him, and when I get back, I'll look around for anything. I promise I'll give it back if I find it."

"Sit," the queen said.

Henrietta sat.

"You are our prisoner. You will be released on the following conditions. You will lead myself, my grandsons, and two others back to the house of your grandfather. There, his house will be stripped and searched, and your family's possessions will be turned over to us. If we do not find what we seek, his body will be exhumed and his coffin will be searched as well. That is your ransom. When all this has been done, you will be free."

Henrietta's mouth hung open. "You want to dig up my grandfather? You want all of my family's stuff or you won't give me back? Then what? You'll just kill me? You're not a queen, you're a kidnapper."

Magdalene, Queen of the FitzFaeren, rose. Her trim body tensed, and her eyes hardened. Henrietta waited for her anger, but it didn't come.

"Yes," she said quietly. "But you cannot understand the stakes. I feel more than my traitor brother's presence, squatting in ruins. The earth itself stirs. Its life is leeched in the distance. The forests are complaining. The fields shiver in fear, waiting for death. We were Endor's final conquest before she slept. But she sleeps no more. If Endor rises again, even to a fraction of its former strength, and we are unprotected, our lives will be drunk and poured into her strength like the lives of so many weeds. The FitzFaeren, having survived so much, will finally expire and pass into dust."

The queen paused, breathing heavily. "Our talismans will be recovered, or a heritage, a people, one of the world's goodnesses, will fade forever and never rise again. Believe me when I say I have no thirst for revenge. If I did, my brother would long ago have ceased to draw his sour breath. But I will lay my own life down, even if by doing so, I enabled the survival of just one of my people. And I will just as readily lay down yours. Such are the decisions of a queen."

Henrietta stood up. "I'm leaving," she said. "I'm sorry." She turned to the door. Out of the corner of her eye, she saw the queen's arm rise. Words she didn't know filled the room. The door was being commanded, sealed.

But Henrietta had expected that. While the words were still being spoken, she twisted, stepped toward the window, and jumped.

Her knees caught on the sill, and she fell forward while words slammed the window down on her ribs. She fell through, landed on the goat, and rolled into rose vines. Her mind felt skin puncture and recognized the sound of thorns tearing cloth as she lunged through the garden, and then she was on her feet, grateful she'd worn shoes, and running hard.

"We should turn around," Zeke said. "The sun's going down, and it could get dark fast. Don't want to lose our tracks."

Sergeant Simmons nodded. He turned the bouncing police car to the right and pulled a slow U-turn in the tall grass, back toward the dusty pink horizon.

They had driven five miles in each direction and then followed their tracks back. They had seen nothing. No structures, no animals, no trees. Just grass. A world full of it.

Of course, now that the house had been relocated, there was one structure. And they didn't want to lose track of it. There would also eventually be trees. A very small cottonwood sapling had survived, unmowed beside the house. Two maple seeds were sending down roots in the front. An infant willow was touch and go.

Given the surviving caterpillar population of the transported yard, there would also be two kinds of butterfly and seven kinds of moth. And ants and ground beetles, aphids and ladybugs and spiders and many other things with skeletons on the outside. But no cicadas. Only one had survived the cosmic move, and he was male, destined for loneliness.

Descended from two long-lost and now-expired pets, it was the gerbils that had been making a living beneath the kitchen floor that would really bring change. They would discover a world without predation, without people. A world where gerbils would be the apex. They would grow fat. And they would grow many. Very many.

Sergeant Simmons and Zeke Johnson didn't know any of this as they rattled back down their tracks, racing the light. Just as the man who had first entered the empty world with grass seeds on his boot could never have guessed what he was creating.

Frank watched the car return. Penelope was sitting up, and Anastasia sat beside her. Richard sat by himself. He still hadn't spoken.

Dotty had brought out a blanket and all the cold food she could find. She stood beside Frank, sucking on a cracker. She did not want to go back inside, back into darkness and moisture and the smell of stale seawater.

Frank ran a hand through his hair and watched the scorched strands drift down. He turned toward Richard and awkwardly lowered himself to the ground beside him.

Richard looked up, and Frank smiled.

"What can you tell me, Richard?" Frank asked. "Do you have any idea what cupboard it was?"

Richard shook his head.

"What did they do to you?" Anastasia asked.

Dotty glared at her.

"Was Henry there with you?" Frank asked.

Richard shrugged. "I don't know. I really don't. We were going to go to a Fitz place, but then something sucked me at the wall, and I fainted. Or I think I did."

Dotty reached down and squeezed his shoulder. "Well, I'm glad you're here, honey. I'm glad we got you back."

"He's not back. We're all gone, too," Penelope said quietly. "I need to go to the bathroom."

"Was Henrietta going to go with you?" Frank asked. "She in the room when you fainted?"

"No," Richard said. "Henry didn't want her to come. We didn't tell her anything."

Frank sucked on his lip.

Penelope stood up, rocking. "I have to go to the bathroom."

"Good luck finding a bush," Anastasia said.

"I'm going inside."

Dotty looked at Frank. Frank was watching the police car hop closer.

"Frank?" she asked.

"Hmm?" he said.

"Do you think it's safe for Penny inside? I don't like her in there with all those doors open. With what could come through."

Penelope was waiting.

"Henry and Henrietta gone," Frank said. "And us gone, too."

"Frank?"

"Pick a world, any world."

"Frank, Penny wants to use the bathroom inside."

Frank stood up. The police car stopped in the shorter grass.

Zeke hopped out and shrugged. "Nothing," he said. "Absolutely nothing."

Sergeant Simmons opened his door and levered himself out. His face was pale.

"Keep an eye," Frank said. "I'm steppin' inside."

Simmons nodded, and Frank and Penelope walked to the front steps.

The house was rank. Wet carpets are bad enough, but carpets swamped with seawater are worse. Penelope held her nose and squelched toward the bathroom.

"Don't flush, Pen," Frank said.

Penelope stopped and looked at him. "Why?"

"No water. No sewer. No electric. It won't work."

Penelope sighed. "Right. I forgot."

She went into the bathroom, and Frank crossed his arms and looked around. The last light of the day still hung in the sky outside, but in the house, it was little better than a cave. If the windows hadn't all been smashed wide open, it would have been worse.

Frank walked through the dining room to the kitchen and dug in the junk drawer. It was crammed with pencils and batteries, broken rubber bands, and manuals for appliances they had never owned. At the bottom, he found a little rectangular flashlight. He flipped it on and stared at the small orange spot he'd created on the wall.

The toilet flushed.

"Pen!" he yelled.

"Sorry! I forgot. But it all went down."

"Yeah," he said. "But down where? Tank's not gonna refill, either."

He met Penelope in the dining room.

"Okay," he said. "Tell your mother I'll be right back out. I'm gonna have another look upstairs."

They walked to the front door, and he left her on the porch. Then he turned and climbed the wet flight of stairs up to the second-story landing.

"Frank!" he heard Dotty yell.

"Back in a minute!" he yelled, and walked into Grandfather's room.

The windows were empty. Curtains and glass and wood trim lay on the floor and on Grandfather's bed.

The cupboard was shut. Frank walked straight to it, pried it open, and crouched down with his dim orange light. He saw nothing.

He eased his head and shoulders in and propped himself up on his elbows, squirming forward slowly, inch by inch, with his flashlight in front of his face.

His head was through, inside a cupboard in some other place. A thick layer of dust had mounded in the corners and around the husk of a mouse carcass.

But in the middle, the dust was scuffed up and scraped away. Someone could have come this way. It could have been recent, or it could have been weeks ago. He slid back out and sat on the end of Grandfather's bed. Henry or Henrietta could be through this doorway. Unless someone had changed the combination in the attic. The crazy wizard had closed them out of Kansas. The compass knobs might have been spinning for all Frank knew.

"Right," Frank said. "Let's go look in the attic."

The attic, with only the round window at the end to smash, was stuffier than the rest of the house. Frank stood in Henry's doorway and spotted the cupboards with his dying light. He lost track of the smell of seawater as his senses strained after other things.

Muffled laughter. Heavy footsteps. A dog barking. Wind, coughing, and breaking glass. And through many of the doors, nothing but a black and ancient silence, long unstirred. On the left side of the wall where the ceiling coved, firelight flicked through a rectangular door. He could just see smoke curling out of its open mouth.

"Friendly locals!" someone yelled. "Burn mine, too."

Frank slid down, leaned over the head of Henry's bed, and shut the door quickly. Fire would be a lot more permanent than water.

Straightening back up, he focused on the compass door, open like the others, in the center of the wall. This door was the problem. Was it still set where it had been? Or had Darius's commands respun it? The door was open. It could be set to itself.

He swung the door most of the way shut and looked at the knobs. One of its hundreds of combinations would lead him to his daughter. One of them would lead him to his nephew. Unless they were together. But he didn't think they were, not with what Richard had said, and not with how they'd been interacting before all this had started.

He knew that he and the others couldn't stay in the grass land. But he knew very little else.

Frank turned the right knob one place and clicked the door shut. He tugged on it to see if it would open again, but it was as solid as the wall. He turned the knob back and pulled again. The door swung open easily.

He put his knee on Henry's wet mattress, reached into the opening, and felt around. In the corner, his fingers closed on something dry and wrinkled. He pulled his hand back out. The dried body of a mouse lay rigid on his palm.

Tossing the mouse into another open door, Frank stepped back. Now he knew. The compass locks were set to their own combination. He'd never thought of the central cupboard as another destination.

Shutting Henry's bedroom doors, he walked quickly back down the attic stairs.

Dotty's voice came through the empty windows. "Frank? You okay?"

"Yeah!" he yelled. "Back in a minute."

He'd have to be. His feeble flashlight was dying fast, and the house was getting darker by the second.

Back in Grandfather's room, he fished his body into the cupboard.

The mouse was gone, and he could see his finger tracks.

He pulled back out and crouched on the floor. It might be right. It might be wrong. It felt both.

A shape loomed in the window.

Frank spun, standing. "Gosh, I'm jumpy," he said, and swallowed.

The raggant stared at him, flaring its nostrils. After a moment, it looked down and dropped to the floor. Without hesitation, it limped to the cupboard, hopped in, and disappeared.

"There you have it," Frank said. "I trust you more than me."

Henry woke, and his body tensed, stretching, arching, filling his limbs with morning life. He felt good. His bed felt wonderful. A wisp of mind fog told him that he'd been dreaming. He didn't know if it had been pleasant, but he didn't care. Pleasant or unpleasant, it was gone now. He filled his lungs with warm spring air, and, kicking off his blankets, he sat up.

Sitting there, with his feet on a cold tile floor, his mind stopped.

He had no idea where he was. And he was wearing a dress.

The room was long, with white walls towering up to a black-beamed ceiling. The wall across from Henry was made entirely of windows that rose up from the floor and ended in tall arches. All of them open. Transparent curtains ghosted slowly on the breeze, and golden light flowed through them. The bed he'd been sleeping on was at least as large as his entire room in Kansas, and on the floor in front of him, an enormous porcelain bowl sat on a thick rug. Blue designs and figures were interwoven over its surface, and it was full of cloudy oil spotted with bits of leaves and sticks. He leaned forward and recognized the smell of cinnamon. And cloves. His backpack lay on the floor beside it.

Henry stood and breathed again. His dress was made of tan linen, had no sleeves, and hung to his knees. He didn't see his clothes anywhere.

He walked to the closest window and pulled away the curtain.

A balcony spread out in front of him. It ended in a

low wall, and beyond the wall, the earth dropped away into a deep valley. In the distance, far below him, was a mat of smoke and buildings and silently belching pipes. But where he stood, the sky was a stranger blue than he had ever seen, and the wind was newborn.

A man and a woman with white hair sat on a low bench beside the wall, eating fruit. The man turned and smiled above his beard.

"Join us, pauper son," he said. "There are other refreshments than sleep."

Henry shifted on his feet. "Where are my clothes?" he asked. "I'd like to get dressed first."

"You are clothed already," the man said. "And we have both seen you in your skin-clothes. My wife bathed you twice already, in the night, and I was her assistant."

Henry's ears went hot. He hoped he wasn't as red as he felt.

"Not a good assistant." The woman laughed, and her voice was low and rich, like soft earth. Her skin was smooth and dark next to her hair. "Come," she said to Henry. "Sit with us and talk. There are things we would ask you."

Henry stood, not wanting to sit beside either of them. The man slid off the bench, walked across the balcony, and returned with a wooden chair and cushion, placing them near the stone balustrade before moving back to his wife. Henry followed slowly after him and sat awkwardly in his dress, unsure of how to hold his legs.

The two faced Henry, with a tray of fruit across their laps. Long, dark grapes, peaches, and things Henry didn't recognize were jumbled together.

Henry took a small tangle of grapes and sat down. "Where am I?" he asked.

"You," the man said, "are in our house. Once we lived in the underworld"—he nodded at the valley below—"but now we live in paradise. We sit up here and watch the great city stew in its own flatulence."

"But who are you?" Henry asked.

The man pulled gently at his near-white beard. "You may call me Ron."

"And I am Nella," the woman said. "What may we call you?"

Henry slid the first grape into his mouth and tucked it into his cheek. "My name is Henry York."

Ron sat up. "Your name?" he asked. "You have been named?"

Henry stared at him, blank. "Why wouldn't I have a name?"

"Well"—Ron pointed at his stomach—"the ritual cuts you have only serve one purpose, and a rather dark one. Before you flew away, a bloody naming rite had begun, or been prepared. It can only be performed on the nameless. The named would die."

"I closed them up," Nella said. "The skin is sealed, but I'm afraid that man's adopted mark will be in your flesh forever."

Henry's right hand drifted to his stomach.

Ron leaned forward, and his eyes sparkled. "Your own mark," he said, "is far more interesting. Rare, and one that I am fond of. I have seen it only once before, when I was young, and it was dancing on the flesh of my cousin. Hold out your palm."

Henry pulled his hand away from his body and stretched it out toward them. He watched their faces as they looked. Their dark, unblinking eyes narrowed, and then suddenly sparked with light, each pupil painting a reflection of the dancing fire in Henry's palm.

"You can see it?" Henry asked. But they didn't answer, and his eyes were drawn as well.

The burn had been blurred and damaged by Henry's pipe slide, but as he stared, what looked at first like a scar took shape. And it moved, like a snake beneath his skin. Only it wasn't beneath his skin, it was above it, below it, and through it. And it was every color blended into gold.

Henry's head began to throb.

He heard Ron pull a deep breath in through his nostrils. Then the man spoke. His voice sounded distant, like a pronouncement to be obeyed.

"Henry York," he said. "Dandelion fire mingles with your blood."

A soft hand touched Henry's chin and lifted his face.

"Look away," Nella said. "It is too much for you still."

He looked at her face and felt his mouth fall open. She was a poem, a history. One hundred songs were moving in her eyes, and more spirited through the air around her mouth, crawling like vines, like threads of life. It was beautiful. Terrible.

Nella put her other hand over his eyes and fingered his eyelids closed.

"Enough," she said. "Live to see all the world's songs, or go mad now."

"But there's more," Henry said. "Just another minute."

"No." Nella's voice hardened to clay. And then she laughed. "If you run off the cliff of madness now, then we shall have to keep you here. And I shall always have to bathe your shallow chest. I do not relish it."

She pulled her hand away, and Henry blinked.

"That was really weird," Henry said.

Ron nodded. "The current might carry you away before you learn to swim."

"The whole world is made out of this . . ." Henry didn't know what to call it. "This stuff? With the dandelion, it just looked like one living word, but with you—" He turned to Nella. "There were so many more, all tangled. Thousands of vines growing and turning and changing and talking at once. What part is real?"

Ron smiled. "Which part is real, your skin or your sinew? Your breath or your lungs? What you see is real. What you saw is real. You are a seventh son. You have the second sight. You can see a thing and see its glory. Call it a soul if you want, or a story, or a poem. If you live to an age, you may even learn to shape a thing's glory, to give to it and draw from it in return."

Henry had forgotten his grapes. They dangled from his left hand.

Ron laughed. "It is hard, I know, comprehending this new depth in the world." He held up his hands. "Do you know, Henry, that sounds ripple the air before they strike your ear and you hear them? Imagine seeing the ripples as well as hearing them, sensing every sound twice, in two ways. That is like the second sight. You see things twice, and both are true."

"You both could see my burn," Henry said. "So you have the second sight, too?"

"I have six older brothers, though none still in the flesh," Ron said. "For a woman, it is different."

"Yes," Nella said. "What we see is not always the same, but I have the twain sight as well. It does not come to a woman by birth, but as it wills. And it comes without the violence and spasms."

Ron put his hands on his knees and straightened up on his bench. "I am glad you flew to me, Henry York, and you must tell us the story of your escape tonight. We will have guests who would hear it as well. But now I will find you some clothes. There will be time for stories in days to come. You still have need of much rest."

"Oh," Henry said. "But I really need to get home. I should go today. I'm feeling fine. I need to get to the post office."

Ron stood. His brows furrowed. "You said that to me when you fell. I checked inside your bag and found nothing that needed posting. Your hand, and the cuts on your stomach, show you are no mere messenger."

"I'm from someplace else," Henry said. "There's a doorway in the post office. I don't know how I'm going to get through it, but I have to try."

"We know," Nella said. Her eyes were worried. "You forget that we can see. But your spasms are fresh, your eyes are still fragile, and your mind is not used to its sight. We have done what we can to strengthen you, but there are some things only time can heal, and others even beyond its strengths."

"What do you mean?" Henry asked.

Nella reached out and touched his face. She ran her fingers along his jaw, over his old burns, and then looked at her fingertips and back up into his eyes. Deep into his eyes. After a moment, Henry thought she was going to cry.

"You are fatherless," she said. "Unnamed. Here you are safe. Leave, and you walk toward an old enemy gathering strength like a whirlpool and a new enemy who wields it. You walk toward destruction. Your blood father is—I can see nothing but a blade spinning toward him. The mother of your birth is strong, like a deep-rooted tree, but she bends beneath a wind that could split stone. Moments of joy await you, but beyond them lie betrayal, fear, rage, and horror. Believe your dreams. Yours tell you no lies. There the threads tangle. I can read nothing more."

Nella sat back up and wiped her eyes.

"I don't understand," Henry said. It sounded hollow. "I do have a name," he added.

"You are unchristened," Nella said.

"But I have a name."

Ron's arms were crossed. "We'll find you clothes," he said. "And fill your belly. Do not let us tempt you any more with rest. If you know your path is true, then we will help you on your way."

Henry stood and walked to the low wall. Ron stood beside him. Henry looked down at the clouded city and back to the old man. His beard was rustling in the breeze.

"My fathers built this city," Ron said. "It was mine to defend. I could not fight off the rot." He glanced at Henry and then back over the valley. "When Darius came, I pitied him. He was lost, without direction and without an anchor. He babbled on about his own inadequacy and wretchedness. He could not speak without hurling insults at himself. He begged to call me father, and I was fool enough to let him. He reached his strength. But he never could control it. He fed off the fear of others and confused it with respect. He is the influence in my city now. His fingers drift through the streets like the smoke." He sighed. "I will not pity you, Henry York. My pity is a destroyer."

"Is your name really Ron?" Henry asked.

The old man laughed. "I was christened Ronaldo Thomas Xavier Valpraise, seventh son of Justinian

Valpraise, Lord Mayor of Byzanthamum. I was a hospitaller and architect, patron of pauper sons and orphans. My hospitals are now morgues and factories. I have outlived all my children, and my patronage has created a den of wizardry and darkness. Why have I been left alive? Perhaps only for this moment, Henry York, to wander into the city after years away and catch a falling star before it lodged in hell." He turned and looked Henry in the eyes. He was smiling. "Can you be the redemption for my life?"

"I don't know what you mean," Henry said. "You already saved mine."

Ron didn't say anything. Henry looked back over his shoulder. Nella was gone, and the balcony was empty.

"Why were you in the city?" Henry asked. "Why did I fall at just the right time and land on just the right spot?"

The wind suddenly picked up, swirling around Henry's limbs, rustling in his hair.

When Ron spoke, his voice was somber.

"Nella was given dreams," he said. "She dreamt of your falling. She dreamt of Darius, wielding more power than even he could have imagined and spreading his rot through worlds. Your blood, in you and others, was all that stood against him. She did not want it spilled in our streets and wasted."

Henry's burnt palm itched. He rubbed it with his thumb. "I don't think I like that dream much," he said. "What happened to Darius? Did he lose?"

Ron was silent for a moment. Then he spoke.

"Sometimes standing against evil is more important than defeating it. The greatest heroes stand because it is right to do so, not because they believe they will walk away with their lives. Such selfless courage is a victory in itself."

Henry felt his stomach tightening. His breath was short. "Do Nella's dreams always come true?" he asked.

"In her dream," Ronaldo said quietly, "no one caught you when you fell."

CHAPTER ELEVEN

Frank turned his burned face away from the fire. It, and a few patches on his arms and chest, were producing their own heat. The rest of him was near shivering.

Sleeping in the lawn in Kansas never would have been this cold.

In an ill-fated moment, he had stored the family's sleeping bags in the barn—which was no longer with them. But it wasn't like he could have anticipated that.

Richard had a sleeping bag. Frank had dragged that down from the attic, damp end and all. The rest of the family, along with Sergeant Simmons, were bundled in layers of clothes and wrapped in blankets, lying in a circle around a fire of window frames, trim, and one dining room chair that had been broken, anyway. Frank had been ready to burn everything, but Dotty had not yet been able to process the permanence of their situation. Frank had been lying behind Dotty, but now he had his back against hers and was looking out at the grass bending beneath the sky's very cold breath and stars he didn't recognize. His face was happy. But he could feel his thighs beginning to twitch. And they weren't checking with him first.

"Dad," Penelope said. "I'm freezing. Can we burn anything else?"

"I'll look around in a bit," Frank said.

"I think we should sleep inside," said Anastasia.

Richard sniffed. "I don't want to."

Anastasia sat up, holding her blankets tight. "Well, you're in my sleeping bag," she said. "I mean it, Dad. If something comes through the cupboards, it can get us out here, too."

Frank rolled back toward the fire, and Dotty looked up at him. Her lips were pinched tight.

"Zeke?" Frank asked. "How're you doing?"

"Fine, Mr. Willis," Zeke said. "The girls could have one of my blankets if they want."

Penelope didn't say anything. Anastasia laughed. "Zeke's showing off," she said. "He's just as cold as we are."

Frank shivered and tried to hide it. "What do you think, Ken?"

Sergeant Simmons's mound of blankets was the highest. Not because he had the most, just because he was beneath it. "I've been worse," he said. "One nice thing is that I can't feel my foot."

"Can I just go inside?" Anastasia asked. "No one else would have to come in."

"No." Dotty's voice was firm and quick. "Zeke and

Ken can do what they like. Lord knows your father will. But you girls are not sleeping near those doors. You're not going to go near them."

Frank pulled in a deep breath. It was sharp in his lungs. It may as well happen now. No one was sleeping. "Tomorrow," he said, "we're crawlin' through Grandfather's cupboard."

He'd expected Dotty to wheel on him. She didn't. No one said anything. Not even Anastasia.

"The way I figure," Frank began, "we can't stay here. There's only what's left in the toilets for drinking water, and Pen already flushed one."

"Sorry," Penelope said.

Anastasia snorted. "I wouldn't drink it, anyway."

Frank ignored both of them. "There's a bit of milk left, but with the fridge not working, who knows how long that will last. We've got a box of crackers, some dry cereal, a jar of pickles, and Dot's jams and sauces. That's just about the far limit of things that won't go bad anytime too soon."

"What about Henry?" Zeke asked.

"Well," Frank said. "Going off Richard's story, it feels like Henry was taken. Then Henrietta tried to follow. Can't say if they're in the same cupboard. But something tells me they're not. The wizard came through looking for Henry, so at least he didn't have him. Yet. I don't want to go anywhere near resetting the cupboard combinations. We leave 'em be, and we go through to wherever they lead and hope we find one of them. If we find someplace safe, with food and water, then I'll come back and start looking through other doors."

"Dad," Penelope said. "The guy who came through the cupboards, the guy who did all this, he didn't say he was looking for Henry. He said he was looking for his son."

"Whoa." Anastasia shivered. "Was that Henry's real dad? He'll want to go back to Boston."

Frank listened to the wind, and he watched his wife breathe beneath her blankets. He looked from shape to shape around the fire.

"I don't think so," he said.

"I'll come back with you," Zeke said.

"Maybe," said Frank.

Richard rustled in his bag. "I will as well."

"No," said Frank. "What you think, Ken? See any other choices?"

Sergeant Simmons spoke slowly. "I don't understand any of this. But I have a wife and kids. My boy is starting third base this year. My daughter has a piano recital in August. My baby sister is due with twins in Tulsa. Whatever you do, Frank, I trust you. And I'll follow you. But I can't give up on Kansas. Not for a long time yet. If then. If ever. I'd be alive, but life'd be dead."

Frank didn't say anything. Dotty's arm slipped back beneath the blankets and found his hand.

"My mom will be worrying already," Zeke said. "She'll be sick. But we can't stay here. Not unless Anastasia starts drinking toilet water."

"In the morning, then," Sergeant Simmons said. "There's not much choice."

Dotty sat up. She looked around the fire and then twisted so she could see Frank.

"Why not now?" she asked. "No one's asleep, and I'd rather get it over with than lie here for hours thinking about it."

Two hours later, Anastasia was talking in excitement. Penelope said she felt queasy. Frank thought he might have to carry Richard. Zeke wasn't talking at all. His jaw was set, and he was lost in his own thoughts.

Sergeant Simmons limped in place.

They all stood in Grandfather's room, and Dotty was handing out pillowcases. Frank was holding a long black police flashlight and his shotgun. Each pillowcase contained one blanket and various food items wrapped up inside that didn't seem necessarily useful—dry spaghetti noodles, shortening, split peas, kosher salt. Everyone was still in multiple layers of clothes, so they didn't pack any more. Sergeant Simmons was bulging out of a red Christmas sweater of Frank's. He held his pillowcase over one shoulder and his shotgun over the other.

"All right," Frank said. "I'm first. When I holler, slide me your gear and then come on after. Ken brings up the rear."

"Wait," Anastasia said. "Where's the raggant? We can't leave him behind."

Frank smiled. "He blazed the trail. We're playing catch-up."

Taking a pillowcase from Dotty, Frank crouched. He slung it into the cupboard and then pushed it through with the shotgun. Holding the flashlight and sliding his gun, Frank squirmed through.

In Grandfather's room, there was only darkness, a cold wind in the empty windows, and the sound of nervous breathing.

After a moment, they heard Frank's voice. It sounded distant.

"Right!" he yelled. "Penny first."

In the blackness, Penelope got onto her knees.

The moon was curtained by clouds, and Henrietta walked, feeling her way carefully across hillsides. She had left the road as soon as the old woman's house had been out of sight. When the sun had gone down, she'd wished that she hadn't. Now, she wasn't sure she had a chance of ever finding it again. She could be walking on it, or walking across it, and she would never know.

A cloud's border silvered, and suddenly the ground crawled with the full moon's glare. Henrietta stopped and looked around. She was on a hillside. A clump of trees huddled at the bottom. Another black bulk was sliding across the sky toward the moon. She would run. She would climb the hill before the light was gone, and when she had reached the top, she was going to pick a direction.

She turned, took two slow, driving steps up the slope, and began to run.

Kansas does have some hills, but Henrietta hadn't been around too many of them. She'd only cut the distance in half when the light disappeared. Breathing hard, and pushing her hands against her knees, she slowed to a walk. The fish and olives had worn off a long time ago, and she was thirsty enough to hope that one of these clouds was packing rain. Running didn't help.

She reached the top in the darkness, sat down, and flopped onto her back.

Something slid up her pants, tickling her shin. She jerked forward and slapped at it. Then she felt around, found the long blade of grass, and pulled it out.

She wondered if they were looking for her. Had Benjamin and Joseph gathered up all their friends who knew how to scowl and handed out torches? Were they sweeping the fields? Maybe they had dogs.

Or they might already be back at FitzFaeren sitting around waiting for her. They didn't need to be in a rush. They knew it was her only way out. They might even know which cupboard she'd crawled through. If they knew that, they wouldn't need to wait for her. They could already be in Kansas ripping through Grandfather's stuff, looking for whatever it was they thought he'd taken.

Henrietta stood up. The cloud above her was glowing.

Where were Henry and Richard? They'd said they were going to FitzFaeren to look for Eli. But they definitely weren't here. Benjamin and Joseph would have rounded them up, too. Or maybe they'd played it safe. Maybe they'd hidden in the hall and watched her get captured.

Well, Richard would have watched. Henry was blind. He would have listened and shushed Richard and told him not to do anything.

Henrietta could feel herself getting mad. She didn't want to. She didn't know that Richard and Henry had ever even been here. Except for the fact that she'd heard them planning, and they'd been gone, and the cupboard had been set to FitzFaeren. But the key had been under Henry's pillow. How would that have worked? Would they have unlocked Grandfather's door and then gone back upstairs to slide it under a pillow? Maybe. It wasn't a bad idea. If something went wrong, people could look for them. If nothing did, they'd get back, and no one would notice. Her hand drifted to her pocket, and her fingers felt the stiff shape of the key through the denim. She hadn't been that thoughtful. No one was looking for her. That much she knew. No one could be.

Half the moon appeared, running through a seam in the clouds. Henrietta stood in place and turned slowly, trying to take in everything. To her left was the hillside she had just climbed. Somewhere behind her, she was sure, was the woman's house. She didn't think she could have gotten that turned around. In front of her, the landscape darkened. Trees. A forest of them. The canopies blended together and ate the light. She had come through some woods on her way here, but even if that was the shortest way back, she knew she couldn't take it. There would be animals in there, and she didn't know what kind. Nocturnal forest creatures were not appealing. Of course, animals could stalk her in the open fields, but at least she would have the chance of seeing them before they tasted her. If the clouds weren't in the way.

She turned and looked down the other side of the hill. The forest sprawled in that direction as well, but it wasn't as thick. The trees were scattered around the edges, and, as the light faded again, she could see something long winding through them. It could have been the road. Or at least *a* road.

With the light gone, she started to move down the hill. Down was much better. And faster. Grass rustled around her legs while she walked, and as she neared the bottom, trees began to loom.

The ground leveled out, and she moved to a jog, ducking tree branches in the moonlight and feeling her way with arms extended in the cloud shadows.

Pushing between two trees, she stepped out onto air. And then water.

Henrietta threw both of her arms back, grabbing armfuls of reeds and grass. Her shoulders twisted as she dropped, but she didn't let go. Moving water was pulling at both of her legs.

Gritting her teeth, Henrietta managed to twist around, face the bank, and grip two bundles of grass at the root. Kicking and splashing, she pulled herself back over the lip of the bank and lay panting on the edge.

The night had just gotten much colder and much worse. And now she knew that she hadn't glimpsed a road. She'd glimpsed a river. She'd seen streams when she was tied to the back of the wagon, but no rivers. Not even anything that would qualify as a small river. Rubbing her sore shoulders, she sat up, with her still-dripping feet dangling over the bank's edge.

There was just enough light to see the black band that was the bank on the other side. This was a river. And it was a pretty quick one.

Henrietta sighed and then sputtered her lips. There wasn't much point in going on. She could follow the river into the wood, but why would she? She didn't have any idea where she was in relation to FitzFaeren and the door back to Kansas. She could follow it the other direction back toward the old queen. Or she could turn around and climb back up the hill.

A knot tied in her stomach, and she felt the first stage of panic. She didn't want to express her thought. Not even to herself. But she did. She might never get home. After all, her father hadn't. She might grow up here. Die here. Living with short, very serious, semi-magical people. Something slipped off the bank beside her and plopped into the water.

Henrietta pulled her wet legs up and hugged her knees.

If Magdalene had suddenly sprung out of the reeds, or Joseph with his irritated beard and a torch, she would give them a hug and ask to be shut back in the closet. She could always escape later. But right now, she knew that she couldn't find her way back to Magdalene's house even if she tried.

She wished that she could at least tell herself that her father was looking for her. That he would do everything he could to get her back. But everything he could do would be banging on Grandfather's door and yelling her name and then hugging her mother while she cried. She would have no sisters to annoy, or be annoyed by. There was nothing in this world for her.

But she was thirsty, and the river solved that problem.

Henrietta swung her legs behind her and lay down on her belly. Inching herself over the lip of the bank, she could just reach the surface of the river with one hand. She cupped water to her face and wondered how much bacteria she was drinking. Probably not as much as there would be in a river back home. Unless there were cows around. Or beavers. But she didn't care right now. The water was sweet and cold, and she drank as much as she could in one-palm installments.

The water didn't exactly clear her mind, but it did make her more cheerful. She would make it back to Kansas. There had to be something she could do, even if she had to wait until morning.

But she didn't want to wait until morning. She

wasn't tired. There was too much adrenaline and worry for that. And she was hungry, and she was trying to find some way home without being caught.

Suddenly, she had a thought. Eli wouldn't give her back to Magdalene. Eli would know where FitzFaeren was. Eli might be able to help her get home without being noticed. He didn't like her any, but from the sound of it, he liked his sister less. He might help Henrietta just to spite her.

Magdalene had said he was lurking in ruined houses by the river. Henrietta had found the river.

That meant that Eli was in one of two directions. She had to pick one and follow the water. And she had to pick right.

She wanted to follow the river into the trees. They weren't that dense here, and she still felt like that direction led away from Magdalene. But she also knew that her directions might be completely turned.

Henrietta bit her lip. Which was more likely? That she had gotten turned around in the dark, or that she had kept her sense of direction perfectly while running through hills at night.

She stood up, and began walking along the riverbank, away from the trees. Odds were that she'd gotten her internal compass twisted. She would go directly against her instincts. They'd gotten her into this mess in the first place. Her instincts were not her friends.

* * *

By the time she had picked through three old cottages and one collapsed mill, Henrietta had no idea how long she had been walking. She'd frightened a cat and screamed, but had nothing else to show for her search. The adrenaline was long gone, and her eyes were heavy.

The sky had cleared, leaving her plenty of light, but that wasn't making her any happier. And then she smelled smoke.

It was a wood fire, but there was something else mixed in with it. Something she would have recognized in any world, any time.

Someone was cooking bacon.

Henrietta sped up, still carefully staying back from the river's edge. After twenty yards or so, the smell had gotten stronger, and other things were mixing in with it. Onions. She climbed over a fallen tree, and there, in front of her, wedged between a rock and a rotten tree trunk, was a tiny cottage. It was more of a shed, actually. Looking around, she could see the ruin of a much bigger house, set a little way back from the river. This was almost a boathouse. For toy boats.

Cloth hung over two window holes, but golden light still poured out through the cracks around the edges.

Henrietta could hear the bacon sizzling. And someone was whistling. Smoke was coming out of a hole in the roof.

She walked straight up to the house and stood outside the window cloth, breathing quietly, swallowing down her hunger. Then she put two fingers on the curtain and pulled it back an inch.

A fire on the dirt floor in the center of the room was being smothered by an enormous frying pan. On one half, bacon hopped and arched its back, trying to avoid the heat. On the other, a mass of mushrooms and onions and eggs and chopped potatoes was being stirred and shuffled around by an old man with a knife. His head was bald, and above his ears, white hair straggled away from his scalp. He had a short beard and was wearing gold wire-rimmed glasses.

Henrietta knew his name.

She could see the blanketed door on the other side, but she didn't bother walking around. Instead, she pulled the curtain all the way open and stuck her head in the window.

The man, whistling through his teeth, pulled the pan off the fire and began to sing in a soft, throaty voice.

"Bacon, bacon's all I'm takin'
Tap the ale, pour out the wine
You bring ten hens what all are layin'
And I, my love, will slice the swine."

Henrietta coughed.

Eli didn't look up from his work. He was scraping the egg mixture onto a wooden plate.

"Well," he said, with his head down. "Are you going to come in and eat, or would you rather go for another swim?"

CHAPTER TWELVE

Eli looked up into Henrietta's startled eyes.

"I won't spoon eggs into your mouth through the window. The door's on the other side. Or can you walk through walls?"

Henrietta stepped back and let the curtain fall. She was confused. But she was also very hungry.

She walked around the leaning shed, pushed aside the blanket door, and ducked inside.

Eli was sitting cross-legged on the dirt floor. He was already eating from a wooden plate on his lap, lifting eggs on the flat of his knife. His forehead shone, and the firelight reflected off his glasses.

Another plate, with a small, steaming mound of food capped by four strips of bacon, sat in the dirt waiting for her.

Without speaking, Henrietta dropped to the floor, picked up the plate, and tore a bacon strip between her teeth. It felt at least a quarter of an inch thick.

"Thank you," she said. She had to. It was hard to remember the last time food had tasted so good.

Eli nodded. "I thought you'd get here sooner, but girls are so wretched with direction."

"What?" Henrietta asked. "It was pitch-black. I was running through hills. I'm just fine with direction."

Eli lifted a piece of bacon off his plate and held it up, examining it in the firelight. He didn't say anything.

"How did you know I was here, anyway? Were you following me? If I was so lost, you could have at least helped me out."

"I knew you were here when I saw the philosophers trundle you by, tied up on the wagon."

"The philosophers?"

Eli raised his eyebrows. "Oh yes. They are very astute. The deepest of thinkers. To them, the mysteries of the world are an open book. If only they could learn to read."

"You're joking, right?"

"You are as insightful as they," Eli said. "As to why I didn't help you sooner, the truth is, I only just decided to help you at all. You should eat in silent gratitude."

Henrietta pinched a lump of egg and potato between her fingers and popped it into her mouth.

"You're going to take me back to the ruined hall?" she asked.

Eli chewed thoughtfully. "No," he said. "I don't see the good in returning there. You've seen the night-haunting once before."

"You know what I mean," Henrietta said. "I need to get back to Kansas."

"You can't," Eli said. "The doors have been reset. I checked soon after you met with the great and magnificent queen of the FitzFaeren. She also keeps goats."

"The doors are really reset?" Henrietta asked. She tried to see past the flicker on Eli's glasses. She wanted to see his eyes when he talked.

"They are indeed."

"Will you take me back and show me? I want to see."

Eli laughed. "No. I will not. But you are free to leave as soon as you finish your meal. Or sooner. Wander off in the darkness and find your way home."

Henrietta wavered between doubt and disbelief. She thought Eli was lying, but then she didn't know why he would. He didn't seem to like her. He wouldn't just want to keep her around. She wasn't sure if he was capable of being purely malicious. Probably. Magdalene had called him a traitor.

"You said you were going to help me," Henrietta said. "What are you going to do?"

"Were you hungry?" Eli asked. "Are you eating? Thus, I am helpful."

Henrietta looked at him. "But I can't stay here. How am I going to get home?"

Eli shrugged, chewing.

"What did you give my grandfather?" Henrietta asked suddenly. "What did he take that destroyed this place?"

Eli dropped his plate to the ground. He looked at

Henrietta, and then he looked up and watched the smoke writhe out of the broken roof.

"She probably talked about how it ruined her coronation, too, eh?" He looked at Henrietta. "It's hard to have a conversation with her without it coming up. 'Maggie, how's the corn doing? How's the goat?' " He pitched his voice higher. " 'Oh, fine. But it would all be so much better if my coronation ball hadn't been ruined by my wretch of a brother.' Is that what she said? Something like that?"

"She said she was going to get the things back. She was going to go into Kansas and dig up my grandfather's coffin and look for whatever it is."

Eli cocked his head. "She said that?"

Henrietta nodded.

"Why would she say that?"

Tucking eggs into her cheek and licking her fingertips, Henrietta spoke. "She said she needed whatever they were in order to protect the rest of the FitzFaeren. She said that Endor was drawing power again and was going to swallow them all up like weeds."

Eli rubbed his chin. "I'm surprised she felt it. Most things blaze right past her and never get noticed."

"You mean, it is happening?" Henrietta asked.

"Oh yes," said Eli. "It is happening. Soon fish will be floating in the streams. Grass will curl and slowly turn to ash, never seeding again. Stick around, and you'll curl up, too."

Henrietta set her plate down. "What are you going to do about it?"

"Me?" Eli laughed, took off his glasses, and polished them on his sleeve. "What am I going to do about it? Nothing. Absolutely nothing. A long time ago, I was told that my people, excuse me, the people I once led and that I am no longer a part of, did not need my assistance or leadership. I will do nothing."

"I don't get all this," Henrietta said. "You told me that I would curl up if I stayed here. Did you really mean that I will die? Will you die if you stay?"

With his glasses back on his nose, Eli reached over and took Henrietta's last piece of bacon. She let him. "I'm sorry," he said. "I was unclear. After the grass dies and the fish begin to bake on the banks and the insects dry out and float on the death-breeze, then you will grow very tired, your fingernails will twist and peel back, and your gums will recede. You will lie down or stumble and be unable to rise again. The same will be the case for the larger animals. Dying on the ground, you will be unable to sleep. The life will gradually drain out of you, joining the currents that have been drawn out of the rest of the dead and are being swallowed up or stored by whatever immortal carcass you and your weak cousin set loose through the worlds. Your body will not rot. You will dry and curl and drift away on the breeze. I will die as well. Sometime after you and before the stronger trees. So I do intend to do something. I intend to leave."

He folded the bacon and stuck it in his mouth.

Henrietta swallowed. "You're serious?"

Eli raised his eyebrows. He didn't answer.

"How do you know?"

"I have felt it before. And I have walked through the dead-lands beyond old Endor."

"What about your sister?"

"The queen? You tell me she knows. Let her make her own decisions, for herself and her people. All twelve of them."

"How many are there really?" Henrietta asked.

"Some scattered hundreds," Eli said. "No more than that."

"And you're just going to let them die?"

Eli snorted. "I'm not the one letting them die. They don't have to ask my permission to do that."

"You're awful," Henrietta said. "Where are you going to go?"

"To a place I know by the sea—horrible-smelling fishing village, really."

Henrietta had stopped eating. Eli picked at her plate.

"Why are you going there?"

"You mean, why are *we* going there. I said I was helping you. Of course, I'd forgotten what a plague you are. You may still be on your own. We are going because it is by the sea, and because I know it—I kept a library there for years. Your grandfather was a regular—and because places by the sea have boats."

Eli stood and picked up a rumpled sack from behind him. Without cleaning it, he dumped the large frying pan inside and picked up the two wooden plates, shaking Henrietta's leftovers onto the floor. He slid the plates inside as well and slung the bag over his narrow shoulder.

"What are you doing?" Henrietta asked.

"Oh, gracious stars above." Eli rolled his eyes. "What have we just been talking about? Your incessant questions would almost be bearable if you actually listened to the answers. I am leaving. I am going to attempt to travel to a safer place than this open tomb of a country. And, as I am as magnanimous as Saul, first king of all FitzFaeren, I am taking you."

Henrietta's mouth hung open.

Eli leaned down and looked into her face. His beard grazed her chin. "Shall I write you an invitation and eagerly await your reply?"

"Now?" Henrietta asked. "We're leaving now?"

"Yes. Now. Not later. We act in the present."

Henrietta reached down and rubbed her legs. "But I walked all night. My legs are killing me."

"False," Eli said crisply. "But in five hours, both will be true. Come now, or stay forever."

Eli pulled the blanket down out of the doorway and the cloths out of the windows. He crammed them into his bag and, without another word, walked out of the little shed and into the night.

After a moment, Henrietta jumped to her feet and followed him. The moon was hidden again. She was blind.

"You said King Saul?" she yelled. "Your sister said you only had queens."

"Ha," said a voice from the darkness. "Ha."

She tried to move toward it, slipping on dewy grass. "I'm really thirsty!" she said.

"There's a drink sliding right past you. You already washed your feet in it. It's cold, too."

"Will you wait while I drink?"

"No."

Henrietta licked her lips and swallowed down her thirst. Her toe collided with a rock, and she staggered through the grass and fell to her knees. The sky lightened, and the moon emerged.

Twenty yards away, she could see the cool light glowing on the back of Eli's bald head.

She jumped up and ran after it.

Henry stood, with his backpack against the wall, and watched people open their post-office boxes and retrieve their mail. Apparently, in this place, mail was for the upper classes. Men strode by him wearing multiple capes, each one a different color, and they were always in tall boots. The women were far more frightening. Most of them entered with servants, walked to their box, gave the servant the key, allowed them to open it and retrieve the mail, and then took it all back from them, looked at it, and handed it back to the servants to carry out.

He would have been even more surprised if he had known that most of the women were servants themselves, with under-servants assigned to them to help with the arduous task of mail collection.

A door in the wall opened, and Ron stepped out. He wore a long tan coat that Henry had thought extravagant when they'd left together. But now, after watching a steady stream of overdressed preeners, Ron's coat looked more like a bathrobe. Henry didn't want to think about what he looked like. He was wearing long brown slimlegged pants made out of something velvety and a white oversize shirt with bunchy sleeves and no collar. It didn't really work with his backpack, but at least it wasn't a dress.

Ron smiled and beckoned for Henry to come.

Six women in enormous skirts walked slowly between them. Probably to collect three postcards. Henry waited for them to pass, and then he hurried, wobbling, over to Ron. He was wearing boots—the only shoes Ron had been able to find in a close size—and he was not at all used to them. He didn't think he ever could be.

Ron held the door open, and Henry stepped inside, then stopped suddenly. The room was small, square, yellow, and very full of men in gray uniforms. As Henry entered, they all bowed at the waist and forgot to straighten. Ron looked at Henry and winked.

One man stepped forward, still bent, and gestured toward another door.

Ron turned to Henry and hugged him. He smelled real, like a tree. Henry grunted. And he was as strong as one.

"Stand," Ron said. "No one can ask more."

Henry smiled, but he felt a surge of something inside him—sudden worry. He wasn't just going back to Kansas. Something else was happening. Something else was going to happen. He pulled in a deep breath, blew it out, and watched it rustle in Ron's beard.

"What did you tell them?" Henry whispered, nodding his head at the bent men.

"The truth. That you were the owner of the magic box." Ron gripped his shoulders. "There is more of your blood in the worlds. You will find it running in veins stronger than yours."

"Are you sure?" Henry asked.

Ron shook his head and smiled. "May it be so. But I am sure of this—the fire in you is the dandelion's, the strength in your new sight is like it, sudden, sure, and strong, though it falls quickly to downy dust. But once fallen, it is quick to rise again, reseeded, doubled and trebled and more. It wins by inches and sprints, by both ash and flame."

Henry nodded. He thought he understood. At least as much as anyone could.

Ron slapped his shoulder and turned him toward the new door. The men in gray were still bent.

"You all can stand up," Henry said.

The leader glanced at him through his eyebrows and ducked back down.

"All right," Henry said. He opened the door, waved to Ronaldo Valpraise, and stepped through.

When the door clicked behind him, he was alone in another yellow room. *The* yellow room. This was the place he had first seen, where he had watched gray pantlegs walk around through his attic wall. Suddenly, he hoped Ron wouldn't leave too soon. He wasn't quite sure what he was supposed to do now.

Well, he told himself, *I guess I should start by finding mine.*

The room was long, and the entire right wall was made up of the open-backed boxes. Occasionally, he could hear someone unlock one, slide out their mail, and slap the door shut.

Each box had a little metal tag tacked onto the bottom edge, some with paper slips bearing handwritten names.

Next to him, the numbers were all in the nine hundreds. Henry began walking the room, watching the numbers drop as he did.

He slowed in the one hundreds and then stopped. There, below his waist, was the little open square labeled 77. Two paper tags were tacked beneath it. The top one was blank. Henry lifted it with a finger. The paper beneath it was covered with names, each one scribbled out.

Henry crouched, cupped his hands, and tried to look through. There was nothing to see. Still crouching, he slid his right hand in and felt for the back of the door. This was his fear. There would be no way to open the box from the inside, and no one would hear him yelling.

He'd be left banging on the inside with a broomstick and hoping someone heard.

But his hand didn't find the door. Henry slid against the wall up to his shoulder. Laughing, he pulled his arm out and put his mouth over the hole and yelled.

"Richard! Henrietta! Wake up!" If it was light in the post office, it had to be night in Kansas. Richard would be closest.

"Richard!" He got louder. "Richard! Richard!" It was a little embarrassing. Everyone in the post office had to be able to hear him.

Finally, Henry stood up and stepped back. He couldn't keep yelling indefinitely. And the cupboard was already open. But why would it be open? How could it be open? Henrietta was the only one who would have done that. And that meant that she had to be there. Ignoring him. She was probably even watching him. He knew that she could see through. They had watched the postman together.

He swallowed hard. His ears were buzzing. If she was just sitting there laughing at him, he was going to be very angry.

He crouched back down.

"Henrietta!" he yelled, and felt his throat burn with the volume. "You have to be there. Who else opened this? Anastasia? Say something if you're there. Right now! Reach through. Show me your hand. Do something!"

He stopped and rested his forehead against the top

edge of the box. He could feel something tingling against his skin. And in his fingertips. Leaning back, he looked at his hands.

A whispering motion drifted around their edges. He straightened up and moved away.

He stared at the wall and felt his eyes shifting, growing wet. He was seeing everything. Twice.

The wood in each of the boxes had its own crawling signature, but it wasn't hard to pick out his. In all the crawling, his was a gap in the magic, a black swirling funnel. The slow motion from the other boxes moved around it and disappeared inside. It was like looking at a hurricane on a weather map. If a hurricane could be black, and if a weather map could look real.

Henry's head hurt, but he didn't look away. He looked deeper. He saw more. Beyond the movement in front of him, he could see the wall in his bedroom. Not his wall. The trailing threads and dry, dusty, tired words that made up his wall. His teeth started hurting. Badly. Like something was sliding his gums back and icing the nerves. Hot tears were running down his cheeks. He could taste their salt as they crept in the corners of his mouth, and his nose was running.

Still, he didn't look away. He could do this. Quickly, Henry slid off his backpack. After a moment, he held his breath and tossed it at the hole. It vanished.

Henry stepped forward, wobbling in his boots. Ignoring the backs of all the boxes, he reached into the tiny hole with both hands.

*   *   *

The pressure in his ears was unbearable. He yelled as loud and as long as he could. But he heard nothing. Something burning and sticky bubbled in the corners of his eyes, and his skull throbbed. The pain moved on, bending his clavicles and bowing his ribs.

His face pressed into something wet, and his body folded up behind him. He was still yelling, but now he could hear. He rolled onto his back in the darkness and felt himself falling.

Henry threw up his arms, grabbing for anything to catch himself. Something hard bit into his shin, and he heard a slam. His right hand gripped a door, and something cracked. His left gripped another, closed on knobs, and slipped off. He heard a door slap shut, and he was falling again. But only a matter of inches.

With a bang, he was sitting on the damp floor of his little attic room, and his back was against the foot of his bed. He didn't know why his mattress was wet. A single beam of light shone out of the post-office box above him.

"Henrietta," he said. "Are you in here? Richard?"

The room was busy with small sounds and smells. Through it all, he could tell that Badon Hill was open. Blinking, his eyelids were sticking. He rolled onto his hands and knees and crawled to where he knew his lamp should be. It was lying on the floor, broken.

In the very low light, Henry could see his backpack lumped against his doors. He picked it up, unzipped it, and felt around inside. Grandfather's journals were intact, still rubber-banded together. And beside them, he felt the flashlight.

Henry pulled the flashlight out, flicked it on, and ran the spot across his cupboard wall. They were all open. Well, most of them. Endor was closed down by the floor, and so was one cupboard on the left side. He'd kicked and banged a few shut right around the post-office box, and the door to Badon Hill dangled on a single hinge. He'd almost pulled it entirely off.

The compass lock door was closed.

Henry stood up and pulled his bedroom doors open. Stepping out into the attic, he flicked light down onto Richard's spot. The sleeping bag was gone.

The attic smelled a little funny, and the window at the end was broken. Outside, the sky was preparing for dawn. Or the sun had just set and it was dusk. He couldn't tell which just by looking out the attic window.

"Hello?" Henry yelled down the stairs. "Uncle Frank? Aunt Dotty?"

Henry stood at the top and shifted his feet nervously. Something was very wrong. Richard's bed was gone, the window was smashed, and most of the cupboards were open. Darius had pulled him through the cupboards, but he had assumed that nothing else had happened. Now he wished he hadn't yelled.

He could feel his blood roaring through his veins, and his pulse twitched in his forehead. Listening, he could hear nothing human. A floorboard popped on the first story. Wind rustled in an open window somewhere. And why was the floor wet?

There was no good excuse for staying in the attic. He had to go down. Henry turned off the flashlight. Then he sat down, pulled off his awkward boots, bit his lip, and began feeling his way down the stairs barefoot.

Henry had heard each stair creak many times, and he'd snuck down them often enough. But now, the sigh of nails moving in their cramped homes jumped out at him, pulsing surprise and adrenaline along with his blood. He didn't know this house. Not anymore.

He reached the second-story landing. There was only one window, and it was open. Its curtain was drifting in place. There was a little light, enough for him to see that the carpet was causing the dank smell. Enough to see that Grandfather's room was open. Henry stepped off the stairs and winced as moisture squirted between his toes. He hurried across the landing and knuckle-tapped on his aunt and uncle's door. It wasn't latched. He pushed it open and looked inside. They weren't there, and the bed had been stripped of blankets.

Henry moved back to his cousins' door and pushed it open. The room was empty, and the blankets were gone.

He didn't want to, but Henry took a deep breath and tiptoed across the wet floor and into Grandfather's room.

The cupboard was open, and the bed was stripped. But Henry was trying to process something else.

Something much stranger. Both of Grandfather's windows were smashed, and the wood around them had been splintered. The curtains had fallen or been pulled down. They lay on the floor. A breeze was crawling in, and it smelled much better than the house. Behind the breeze, there was a naked blue sky, dark, but brightening. Beneath the sky, there was no Henry, Kansas.

Henry walked to the window slowly, forgetting everything else. A sea of grass rippled to the horizon. A police car was parked in the front yard, and someone had built a fire near it. A charred chair leg was still sticking out of the black spot in the short grass.

Henry closed his eyes and opened them again. Nothing had changed. Staring, wondering, entirely confused, he forgot to breathe. When his body made him, he choked and coughed. His knees wobbled, and he sat down on Grandfather's bed.

This was not how things were supposed to work. He should be home now, telling Anastasia to be quiet so he could finish his story, making Penelope laugh and impressing Henrietta with his escape and fall. Aunt Dotty should be hugging him, and Uncle Frank should be squeezing his shoulder and saying something that almost made sense. He should be calling Zeke about playing baseball today, maybe even trying to teach Richard.

But they were all someplace else. He looked at the cupboard. Sliding off the bed, he squatted on the floor and turned on his flashlight. The cupboard back was solid. The compass combination didn't lead anywhere.

He stood up. They might not be gone. They might all be stuck here.

They might all be dead here.

Henry pushed away his fear. He refused to think about it. He would go downstairs first, and then outside. If they were here, alive or dead, he would find them. If they weren't, well, if they weren't, he didn't know what he would do.

He stood up and hurried out of the room. He wasn't going to sneak downstairs. He was going to yell. He was going to barge, quieting his nerves as much as he could with false confidence.

It wasn't easy. He thumped down the stairs and yelled at the bottom.

"Anyone here? Uncle Frank, are you okay?"

The front door was open, but the screen was shut. It had a hole instead of a handle. Henry kicked it wide and leaned onto the front porch.

"Hello?"

He let the screen slam in front of him, turned, and walked through the living room. Something soft and smooth flattened beneath his toes, crushed into the swamped carpet. Henry stopped and looked down, lifting his foot. It was a mushroom. The living room floor had sprouted a ring of small mushrooms. In the center of the ring, a dense knot of them bulged up out of the carpet. Henry stared, and staring did nothing to help explain it. But there were weirder things going on than mushrooms in the living room.

Picking his way around the floor fungi, he walked into the dining room. Four cans of tuna were stacked on the table beside a can opener.

He threw open the door to the television room, glanced inside, then stepped back out and moved on to the kitchen.

"Aunt Dotty?"

He hurried on to the mudroom and jerked open the back door.

Sunlight blazed, and Henry stepped backward, kicked his toe with his heel, and sat down with a crash.

He was looking at early-morning Kansas. The thick grass that needed mowing ran down to where the barn hulked in all of its red, flaking glory. Beyond it were the fields of ripening grain. Henry picked himself up off the floor and stepped out onto the concrete block step and then into the yard.

"Uncle Frank?" he yelled. "Aunt Dotty?"

He heard nothing but the yammering of birds, and he turned around.

He almost fell over again. There was no house. He was standing at the edge of a large hole with a pool at the bottom. Yellow police tape had been circled around it, but right in front of him, hanging in the air, there was an open doorway back into the mudroom.

He did not want that door to shut.

CHAPTER THIRTEEN

"I hope you intend to issue kidnapping warrants," the woman said.

"Couldn't say," the cop said, shifting in the driver's seat. "Don't know why we would, though."

The woman turned and glared at him. He just watched the road. He could see the Willises' barn now, and the yellow tape around the hole.

"They have taken illegal possession of someone's child." The woman shook her head. "Law enforcement." She said it like an insult.

The cop didn't want to get into an argument with her. The woman was a lawyer, and arguing is what she did. But he was not at all sure how someone could be charged with kidnapping when their entire house disappeared, along with a sergeant and his prowl car. As far as he was concerned, aliens were the likeliest explanation. And he didn't even believe in aliens.

"That's it right there," he said, and he slowed the car to a stop on the shoulder. "That's where the house has always been. At least since I was born."

"Who is that boy?" the woman asked.

The cop leaned forward and squinted. She was right. There was a boy walking around, looking in the hole.

The woman pulled out a photo, looked at it, and looked back up. "That's Henry York."

She opened her door and got out.

"Henry!" she yelled. "Are you all right? I'm here to take you back to Boston to live with your mother."

The boy straightened up.

"Your father granted custody, so things went much faster than we expected. Come get in the car."

She began picking her way carefully through the yard. The boy turned and ran around to the back of the hole. He looked at her and then at the cop car, and he jumped. When he jumped, he vanished.

"Wha—" the cop said.

The woman ran on her toes to the edge of the hole.

"I can't see him," she yelled. "Hurry! He'll drown."

Henry looked at the woman lawyer trying to walk through the grass in high heels, and then he jumped into the mudroom and shut the door.

He wondered if the door would be visible from the outside, so he locked it. But then, changing his mind, he opened it a crack and listened.

"He's not in there," he heard a man say. "And if he is, it's not deep enough to drown in."

"A child can drown in two inches of water," the woman said. "How would you explain it? I clearly saw him jump."

"I clearly stopped seeing him," the cop muttered. "And that's more than two inches."

"My point exactly, genius. Are you going down there or not?"

"Not."

Henry shut the door quietly and flipped the dead bolt. He stood on his toes and peered out the window high in the door. He wasn't looking at Kansas anymore. The barn was gone, and the fields had been replaced with the endless prairie of this new world.

If he couldn't see them, he didn't think they would be able to see him. But he left the door locked. And he stood there with his left hand on the knob, thinking.

It was strange, knowing that he had a way back to what had been his home. He could open the door, step outside, and be carted back to Boston by a lawyer, attend parentally mandated therapy, and enter the next grade in the fall. He could be safe. Very protected. Too protected. He could leave and never come back. Coming back probably wouldn't even be an option once he stepped outside and the door shut behind him.

Henry swallowed and looked at the burn on his palm. Before he could see it move, he rubbed his hand on his forehead. He wanted to go back to Boston. He wanted to be done with this place, and he didn't care who he was or where his real parents were. He wanted the world to calm down and behave itself. To stop being so dangerous. He even wanted a nanny.

He told himself all of this. He told himself that he

could walk away with the scars he already had and the questions never to be answered, and he could be just fine. Everyone else? Well, wherever they were, they were together. He was on his own. He could go through life never knowing what happened to them. Never needing to know.

But none of that was true. He was lying to himself, and he knew it. He'd never been good at lying. He could feel a warm tingling on his head, sprouting off his palm. Henry lowered his arm and looked at it. This time he watched it grow and swirl.

The world was dangerous. He could be strong, or he could be weak. In Kansas or Byzanthamum. A dandelion had burned him behind a barn, had made him something else. Or he had already been something else, and the dandelion made him notice. There was no place he could go to escape the questions he had. He wouldn't be able to live with himself if he walked away now, without at least trying to find out what had happened to his cousins, to his aunt and uncle and Richard. To this already strange house.

Henry wanted to know who he was. In a way, standing at that door, he was deciding who he was. He wasn't someone who could run away afraid. Not anymore.

He ran his tongue around the inside of his mouth. It was dry and mealy. He let his hand drop off the doorknob, and he turned away, leaving a lawyer and cop staring at a muddy puddle. Leaving the barn and Kansas and Boston. Leaving more than that.

He was hungry. In the kitchen, he tugged open the fridge and then shut it again quickly. There wasn't much in it, and what was inside was starting to smell worse than the rest of the house. He opened a few cupboards and ate a couple handfuls of dry cereal from the bottom of a box. Then he pulled out a glass and walked to the sink to get a drink. The faucet was dead.

He'd made a decision about what he didn't want to do, but that didn't get him any closer to an idea of what he should do. Unsure, he moved back into the dining room and stared out at the empty world beyond the shattered windows. He couldn't get too close in his bare feet. He picked up a can of tuna off the table and looked at it. Tuna didn't sound too bad, and the can opener had already been set out. The covers from a toaster manual and the instructions for an apple peeler had been ripped off and were pinned to the table beneath it. Handwriting covered them, wrapping around the print and illustrations.

Henry sat down, pulled the papers free, and began to grind open the tuna while he read.

Henry/Henrietta—
   We (Frank, Dotty, Penny, Anastasia, Richard, Zeke, & Ken Simmons) are about to head off through the cupboards. Both of you were missing, and a man-witch smashed up the house searching for Henry. And he branched it off into another world. No food

here (we left some tuna) and no water (except in the upstairs toilet tank). We don't know where the man-witch went, but he's not here now.

Henry pried back the tuna lid and pinched out the largest lump. He knew who the man-witch had to be. He didn't know who Ken Simmons was, or how Zeke would have gotten involved.

I haven't changed the compass knobs, and I hope that one of you is through where we're headed. If you come back here and read this, then we missed you somehow. If the two of you aren't together, then it's not over-likely that either of you will read this. One of you is through where we are going, and I'm praying we find you. The other is trapped someplace with a door that doesn't lead back. But if somehow you do find your way back here, you follow us. The knobs are set to the center cupboard (with the compass locks) and we haven't changed them. When everyone else is safe, and if you haven't found us, I'll come back to hunt for you. If somehow you've found another way back here, now you know what's happened and where we've gone. If you go through the cupboard and can't find us, know that we'll always be looking for you and hoping to come to rest in one of two places—Henry, Kansas, or the town Hylfing on the Deiran Coast, where I did my early growing.

If you're alive reading this, but we never live to a reunion, know this—

Henrietta,

You're my sweetness. You're strong. Think twice, and the only things holding you back will be the things that should. Wherever you are and wherever we are, you've got all the love I have. If you grow old someplace without me and find some man who's my better, tuck some tumbleweed in your bouquet for me. I'm nothing pretty, and I've always been out of place, but something of me belongs there. Course, could be a day will come when we'll sit together with the sun on our faces and nothing but peace on our minds. Our mistakes aren't so different, yours and mine, but they'll have settled in the dust back behind us. We'll be all sorts of wise then. We won't talk about them.

See you then,
Dad

(If your mother knew I was writing this, it would bust her up. So she doesn't. But her love's even bigger than mine.)

Henry,

Can't talk to you like a son. Never tried. But I do have something to say. If you're reading this, I'm

glad you got your eyes back. And I hope you figure
out the rest. You're tougher than you might think.
Keep fighting till you lose. There's no shame in that.
Ain't nothing in the world's rule book that says
stuff's got to come easy. And complaining makes
things worse. No matter what you go through, don't
ever just lay down and take it. I've tried that. And
getting back up is as hard as undying. Could be the
same thing. Go to the end, and I'll see you there. Or
after. I'm proud to be your uncle.

Frank

P.S. Whoever shows up first, sign off on this sheet so
the other one knows. And leave two cans of tuna.

Henry hadn't taken a bite since his first one. He
pulled in a deep breath and blew it out slowly. Then he
blinked twice and wiped his eyes. He read the note
through again, then he set two cans of tuna beside it and
put the can opener back on top.

Holding the open can, he leaned back in his chair
and stared out the windows. He could get up and find a
fork, but he didn't want to. He wanted to sit and think
about his uncle Frank. His fingers weren't exactly clean,
but he didn't care about that, either. He finished the can
and set it back on the table. He decided against drinking
the fish juice.

The note would have helped him, except for one
thing. Grandfather's cupboard didn't lead anywhere.

But what would have changed since everyone had gone through?

He had changed. Henry closed his eyes and tried to envision what he must have done in his attic room. He had fallen face-first out of the wall and onto the end of his wet mattress. Then he had rolled and dropped and grabbed and kicked at everything he could reach. He'd nearly torn the Badon Hill door off. He must have messed up the compass locks.

Henry pushed back from the table and hurried up both flights of stairs. He kicked the fancy boots out of the way and picked his backpack up off the attic floor. Carrying it and the flashlight, he burst into his little room. The light was gone from the post-office box. He set the pack on his bed and fished out Grandfather's journals, slipped the rubber band off, and opened the first one to the diagram of the wall and the list of cupboard names. He flicked on his flashlight and spotted it on the page. He ran his eyes over the wall diagram. The center cupboard had no number. The highest number was 98. The list of names stopped at 98. He dropped the journal onto the bed and picked up the other one, flipping to the combination page. The list of combinations was only numbered to 98 as well.

Henry looked up at the wall. How could Uncle Frank have known they were going through the center cupboard? He must have. He didn't say he was guessing. Henry leaned over the bed and tugged at the door. It didn't budge.

For a long time, he stood, chewing on his lip, staring at the wall, staring at the diagram of doors and at the list of combinations. He even counted them, just to be sure. Twice. Finally, he picked up everything, turned, and made his way back downstairs and into the dining room.

He sat down and read Frank's note again, looking for any clues that he had been mistaken, or anywhere that Frank may have jotted down the combination the doors had been set to. He found nothing.

Henry really wanted to break something. He raised his hand to bang the table, but he put it back down, puffing out his cheeks instead. He didn't know what to do. Frank obviously hadn't known that Kansas was just out the back door, and now they had gone off someplace where they would find Henrietta—he hadn't been in the center cupboard—and all live happily ever after. Panicking in the dark, he had messed up everything. At least for him. Well, not just for him. Zeke would probably like to be back in Kansas, and he knew Aunt Dotty would. And whoever Ken Simmons was, he probably hadn't been hoping to spend the rest of his life wherever the center cupboard happened to lead.

That made Henry feel worse. If he hadn't goofed, he should have been able to catch up to everyone and tell them he'd found a way back to Kansas. Now, he was alone, and they were stuck.

Frank had said he should make for Kansas, or for a place called Hylfing. Henry opened the journals again and looked over the cupboard names. Hylfing wasn't anywhere on there. He looked for the Deiran Coast, and for anything that could have been an abbreviation for the Deiran Coast. Nothing.

Henry knew that he had two choices and only two choices. Total. He could go to Boston—and he had already made that decision—or he could go through the cupboards, searching for his family, but more likely just for a place called Hylfing on the Deiran Coast. First, he'd be searching for a world that had a Deiran Coast.

He looked at the tuna juice. He really was getting thirsty.

Henry stood up and walked into the kitchen to get the glass he had left by the sink. When he had it, he walked back to the stairs and climbed slowly, thinking.

He had ninety-eight options. Remove Endor, the old throne room where the wizard Carnassus ate his grubs, and Byzanthamum, and he had ninety-five. But he only wanted to remove those places. He didn't know if they belonged to the same world as Hylfing. Grandfather's journal had said that there weren't that many completely different worlds. All three could be in the same one. But he didn't think that Byzanthamum and Endor belonged together. Darius had heard legends of Endor, but he'd been searching for a way through worlds.

Henry stopped near the top of the stairs. Pieces were falling together. They were the wrong pieces, but still. Darius must have come through into Kansas after Henry had escaped, but he'd been faster than Henry. He was the one who had opened all the cupboards. He had found his way to Endor. Or maybe not to Endor. He'd been looking for Nimiane. He had wanted her freed in the worlds. Maybe he had gone to wherever she was, to wherever Zeke and the girls had shoved her after Zeke had knocked her out. It felt like an age ago, like it had all happened somewhere in Henry's distant childhood, back when he was a baby. But it had only been a matter of weeks.

Henry reached the top of the stairs and stood on the damp landing. How would Darius be able to tell which cupboard the witch had gone into? Maybe he couldn't. But they were both probably through there somewhere. Worse, Nella and Ron had seemed pretty sure that Henry and Darius would be meeting again.

Henry walked into the dark bathroom, set his glass on the counter, and flipped the light switch without thinking. Nothing happened. There was a window in the shower, so he ripped the shower curtain down and threw it in the tub. Bright daylight flooded in through the gapped and shattered panes, and Henry turned and saw himself in the mirror.

Black spots of dried blood were stuck to his lip beneath his nostrils and to the sides of his nose and his cheekbones around his tear ducts. He leaned toward the mirror and saw black tracks leading out of both of his ears. He twisted the faucet handle to wash his face and then remembered why he had walked upstairs in the first place. The only water in the house was in the toilet tank.

Henry picked up the porcelain lid and balanced it on the seat. For a moment, he stared at the black float and the decades' worth of toilet silt that clung to the tank's walls. Then he numbed his mind, dipped his glass, and drank quickly.

It was good.

He didn't finish the glass. He pulled a hand towel off a rack and dumped the rest of the water onto it. Leaning back toward the mirror, he scrubbed at his face.

The blood from his cupboard passage came off quickly. There wasn't a lot of it.

He dropped the towel in the sink and looked at himself in the mirror. His shirt was ridiculous. Wherever he decided to go first, he needed to change his clothes.

A cobweb was stuck to his jaw, straggling off from the new skin around his old burns. He brushed it, but it didn't move. Then he looked closer. It wasn't one cobweb, it was a whole tangle of extremely fine threads. Together, they formed an irregular tube, spiraling in place where his scar had begun to pock. They were gray, and they were deathly. Smaller versions, tiny and ghostlike, crawled out of the other places where the witch's blood had spattered on his skin.

Henry ran his fingers through them, and they were undisturbed. He raised his right hand and saw his palm-flame in the mirror. The gray webs scattered, flattened on his face, spun, and writhed to avoid his dandelion fire. He put his hand down and watched them swirl back into place.

An actual spider, unaware of the consequences of its decision, lowered itself from the ceiling and came to rest on top of the mirror. Henry pinched its thread between his fingers and dangled it in the air. Then he moved it through the ghost-funnels next to his face.

When it touched the first small one, the spider jumped, grabbed at its line, and started to climb. Henry moved it through the bigger one, and the spider twitched and dangled. Its legs folded against its underbelly, and its abdomen shriveled up as all eight legs dropped off. Henry let go of its string, but it clung to his fingertip. He shook it off, scraped his fingers on the sink's edge, and then looked back in the mirror.

He didn't like that at all.

Remembering how Nella had looked when he had begun to really see her, he stared at himself. He wanted to see more than the weird things clinging to his face. But nothing appeared. Nothing but his face-webs and a flash of gold when he raised his right hand.

Henry shivered and left the bathroom quickly. He didn't want to think about what he had just seen. He needed to change. And then he would pick his poison.

Wearing normal shoes felt good. He'd been through a lot barefoot. Henry wiggled his toes. He was even wearing socks. They were a little damp, but better than nothing. Water had found its way through most of the drawers in his nightstand dresser, but his jeans weren't too terrible, and he'd found a black T-shirt that was completely dry.

Henry's backpack was unzipped on his bed. He stood in the doorway, holding Grandfather's journals, looking from the diagram to the wall to the list of names and back to the wall.

He hadn't the least idea where to begin. A brassy-looking door on the left looked interesting. It had some sort of relief of a vine with colored stones as flowers. But he wasn't sure. He found himself more attracted to plain doors, to doors that didn't look as frilly or glamorous as some of the others. To doors that didn't look like they might have Darius or Nimiane behind them.

It was distracting having most of them open. Smells, good and bad, crept through along with warm air or cold. He wanted to shut them all, but he wasn't sure that would be smart. He'd already regretted shutting the most important one.

Badon Hill was the only place he really wanted to go. But it had been boarded up.

Henry stared at the twisted rectangular door. He could pick the smell of Badon Hill out of every other drifting scent. It was its own place. Its wind had its own flavor. The dangling door drifted and rocked, and Henry pulled in a deep breath. Realization bubbled up in Henry's mind. When the faeren had posted their warning, they had closed off the backside of the cupboard. He hadn't been able to smell anything. There had been no breeze.

"Wait," Henry said out loud. He set the journals on his backpack and knelt on the end of his bed. Water soaked up out of the mattress and into his jeans. Henry pushed the door out of the way and felt around inside. Splinters of wood covered the bottom, and when his hand reached the back, his fingers crawled through earth and moss.

It was open again.

Henry didn't know why that would be, but he didn't care. That's where he was going. If he couldn't find a way off the island, then he would come back and try something else. If he found out that there was no Deiran Coast in that world—how, he didn't know—then he would come back and try something else.

Henry flipped through the other journal until he found the combination to Badon Hill. Then he set the compass locks, picked up his backpack, and hurried down the attic stairs. He didn't stop on the second-story landing. He quick-stepped down the next flight, moved through the mushroom patch, dropped his pack on the dining room table, and went into the kitchen to find a pen. He was planning on digging in the junk drawer, but there was already a pen on the counter.

He picked it up and went back to Frank's note. He wrote his own note up the side.

Henrietta—

I left two tunas. The compass door was shut when I came through, and the knobs had been changed. I'm trying Badon Hill first.

Henry

P.S. Good luck.

He looked at his note and tried to think if there was anything he should add. Should he say "Love, Henry"? No. But he did have a thought. He double-checked the journal and then copied the Badon Hill combination next to his note and circled it.

That would be enough.

It was time to load his backpack. The flashlight went in first. A couple pairs of socks, a pair of underwear, a gray hooded sweatshirt, and a long-sleeve T-shirt were wadded into the middle. The other can of tuna went in there somewhere. He didn't know where his pocketknife was, and he didn't feel like looking, so he'd pulled an old-fashioned, plastic-handled, round-nosed steak knife out of a drawer, wound a kitchen towel tight around the blade, and shoved it into the middle of his clothes. He rubber-banded the journals back together, put them in a sealable plastic bag, and dropped it on top of everything else. Then he zipped up.

He felt weird climbing the stairs, knowing that he

might never see the house again. A lot of things had happened to him here. He had changed. But not as much as the house had.

Henry stopped in the bathroom for another drink. He didn't look in the mirror, but he couldn't help looking down at the spider and its scattered legs. He didn't like spiders, but he still felt a little bad. He set his glass on the sink and bent down to pick the dead thing up. The legs stuck to his fingers, and he brushed them off into the toilet bowl. The body was dry and crumbled in his hand. When it was floating with its limbs, he put his hand on the toilet handle but stopped. He shouldn't flush. The tank would empty. Henrietta might need that water later. He might need it later.

"That didn't help," Henry muttered. He banged the lid shut and stood up.

He didn't allow himself to dawdle on the landing. A knot in his stomach was trying to grow and tighten, but he kept his breath even and concentrated on what he was doing, not on what might happen because of it.

Grandfather's room smelled wonderful. The wind from the smashed windows tangled with the breeze that slid out of the cupboard, and Henry stopped and simply felt it. He looked out at the police car and then around his grandfather's room, the room that had been so mysterious for so long. Crouching in front of the cupboard, the floor breeze rustled against his face and filled him with an ache. A longing. Not for anything he knew, but for something. Something that could be had. It was like being hungry without knowing food existed. Or thirsty without ever having heard of water.

Henry wished that someone could assure him that everything would be all right, that he wouldn't die until he was one hundred, and that he wouldn't notice then. Maybe that he wouldn't die at all. But that was Darius's wish. That's what Nimiane had achieved. Death was better than that.

Henry felt like he should pray. He didn't know why, and he didn't remember the last time he had. He took his backpack off and set it in the cupboard in front of him. The breeze was warm on his hands.

"God," he said, and stopped. What else should he say? Fix everything? Kill Darius in his sleep? Make the world soft and friendly?

"God," he said again.

And he crawled in.

Soft earth compressed beneath his palms. Moss pulled away beneath his fingers. He pushed his pack up ahead of him and grabbed handfuls of warm grass. He saw the sky and treetops swaying, grabbing at its belly. He saw the long gray stone, its surface shimmering with warmth, and he rolled out into the sun.

CHAPTER FOURTEEN

The raggant flared its nostrils and sampled the world. He knew it well, and he hadn't been gone long. Much was the same. But the currents had changed. For a person, it would have been like finding a childhood river flowing the wrong direction. Or worse, leaving someone strong for a few days and returning to find them dying. But the raggant was not like a person, and it didn't panic like one. It sat on the thick tree limb and breathed—longer, deeper, louder—and his soul remapped the world. It didn't use any abstractions, like coordinates or dimensions. A spawning salmon didn't need to, even a migrating goose with the intelligence of a walnut wouldn't need to. And their internal compasses were as sophisticated as a bit of fluff when compared to the raggant's. The raggant's was more like a spider's web. If spiders worked in color, knew the stars by how their light tasted, and could see sound.

The raggant didn't have any extra senses. He only had one, and it interfaced everything into an amazingly complicated but entirely accurate caricature of whatever worlds were within his range.

The only thing more intricate and accurate than the raggant was a common bumblebee. And bumblebees only used their abilities to name every individual flower within their flight radius and inflate nectar value by re-classifying every vintage based on temperature, light angle and refraction, time of collection, barometric pressure, period elapsed since previous electrical storm, and mood of flower.

They had the raggant's respect. Though it couldn't comprehend why they would allow themselves to be seen flying any more than a turtle could imagine going around shell-less.

A bumblebee was distracting him now. He dropped off the tree limb where he'd been sitting, pinched off his breath, and flapped madly while his drooping hind end approached the ground. He landed hard on a bed of pine needles and picked his next perch.

Right now, everything he sensed was located in rela-tion to four things—himself, his birthplace, the woman who had raised him, and Henry York. He knew where his self was. The ship he had been born on was just around the next continent and a couple hundred meters below the ocean surface, wedged between a loud rock and some melancholic red coral. The woman was just over the mountains. But Henry York—he had found Henry York. That had been the goal. The first goal. Then he had to find a way large enough and safe enough to lead Henry back through world seams. Now one had opened up, but Henry had gone away just before. And when he'd felt Henry shift, he'd rushed back without planning and stepped on some sort of back-fanged legless thing in the transition. His haunch still stung where he'd been bitten.

The raggant looked at the old ruined temple wall, nestled back in the brush and vines. The crumbling niche in the wall he had come through was completely hidden by leaves, but he didn't need to see it to know it was there. He could sense the flat grassland and the salt water and the flavors beyond each of the cupboards from where he stood. And he knew which one Henry was in. It had been too small for him to fit through—a world of smoke full of people that sounded like peacocks. He had to find another way. There would be one. There always was.

He slowly jog-hopped to build speed, and then jumped, flapping as wildly as he could, just dragging himself in a spiral toward the top of the ruined wall. People were coming. So he hurried and flared his dark wings against the breeze for balance when he landed.

Below him, vine leaves rustled. A white sack dropped to the ground.

Frank pushed through the leaves and fell out onto his pillowcase. He sat up, blinked in the sunlight, sneezed, and turned off the flashlight. Then he stood up, leaned the shotgun against the wall, parted the vines with his hands, and yelled.

"Right! Penny first."

A few seconds later, he pulled out another pillow-case, set it beside his own, and dragged Penny out by the wrists. She stood up beside him and looked around.

"Wow," she said.

Another pillowcase was born. Anastasia slid out through vines and staggered on the soft, needled ground.

"This doesn't look that different," she said.

Frank ignored them both. His daughters chattered while he pulled out Richard, and then Zeke, and then Dotty, and lastly, a limping Ken Simmons, bulging in his Christmas sweater and uniform.

Anastasia and Penelope had already stripped off their extra layers and thrown them onto the pillow stack. Richard was sitting on the ground, and Zeke was pacing a small perimeter, looking around at their new location.

"We should have brought tents," Anastasia said. "This would be just like camping."

Penelope looked at the tall fir trees and the sloped ground rising up around them. "It would be camping," she said.

Dotty pushed her hair back and picked out a leaf. "Try to keep your voices down," she said. "We really don't know where we are or what might be around."

Frank pulled in a deep breath and licked his lips. He reached back into the leafy wall and lifted the loose vines, looking at the stone and the shape of the hole. It had been an alcove once, a niche, and he had seen it before. But only once. A lifetime ago.

Facing the ruined wall, Frank backed up. He bumped

into Anastasia, but he didn't stop. The wall had changed a little. Or a lot, he couldn't tell. The place had been so vividly stamped in his memory for so long that it was hard to submit his memory of the place to the reality. He had filled things in over the years, imagining what he thought he was remembering. The place had seemed so big then. A hidden hollow, with a crumbling temple wall once belonging to the wizards but long thrown down. The vines were thicker and had swallowed the whole ruin, but it was the place.

Shutting his eyes, Frank could still see Dotty's father striding down toward the wall. He could picture him stepping up into the gap. He remembered waiting. And following. And crawling through into a strange bed-room. And a lifetime in Kansas.

His father-in-law had lied to him. Not that he was surprised. But why would he say that the connection had been broken, that the wall had crumbled? Why had he believed him? He hadn't ever. Not really.

Frank sat down hard and looked up at the sky that had been his as a child. He looked at the sharp firs, and then he filled his hands with earth. He lifted the dirt to his face, and he smelled it. It smelled like him, like his arms, like his bed, like what he really was. He was made from this stuff.

His lips were pinched tight between his teeth. His eyes were warm. He wiped them on the backs of his hands, blinked, and looked toward the hills. Beyond them was the sea. Beyond them, he would find the graves of his fathers. And maybe of his mother and brothers. It had been long enough that beyond them, he knew he might find nothing. He sneezed again, and then sniffed.

Dotty looked at him. "Frank?" she asked. "What's wrong?"

Frank just smiled and stood up.

"Frank?"

"I know where we are," he said.

Henrietta nodded slowly and jerked awake. The branches beneath her were moving. She couldn't sleep in a tree, but Eli wouldn't even let her lie down on the ground. He said it would make her feel worse, that the longer she slept on it, the weaker her life would be. So he'd tucked her up in the oldest, strongest tree he could find. And now he was gone.

Her feet had been killing her, but her legs had fallen asleep, so she didn't notice them. She did notice her back, resting against the tree's hard surface, and her tail-bone, which felt like it would be snapping off soon.

"Eli!" she yelled.

"What?"

The voice came from above her, from up in the tree's canopy. Old Eli, with his bag slung over his shoulder, came moving down through the leaves and lowered himself onto her branch.

"I can't sleep here," Henrietta said. "I need to get down."

"You've been asleep for an hour."

Henrietta pulled herself upright and let her legs dangle. She wasn't looking forward to the needle pain when they woke up. "When did you get back?" she asked.

"An hour ago. You were snoring."

Henrietta glared at him. "I was not. Where did you go?"

Eli pulled in a deep breath and yawned. "I have been risking capture and destruction. And without doing much good. We need to move through these hills and over the next ridgeline. Then you can rest again."

"What?" Henrietta shut her eyes and leaned her head forward. "You said we were done. You said we were almost safe." She looked back up.

Eli was chewing on his lower lip. It made his beard move. The top of his head was sunburned.

"I was wrong," he said. "We have to keep going. Now."

He slipped off the branch, grabbed a lower one, and dropped eight feet to the ground.

"How long have we been walking?" Henrietta asked. She stretched her numb feet carefully down to the next branch.

Eli grunted. "Does it matter?"

"Yes. I want to know."

"Why?" Eli asked. "So you can wallow in your misfortune? No one has ever had to walk all night before. You are the very first."

Henrietta dangled, then dropped. Pain shot up

through the arches of her feet and throbbed in her shins. She hopped for a moment and then sat down to rub them.

Eli laughed.

Henrietta wrinkled up her nose at him. "And I'm starving. I could lay down right here and just die."

"You're right. You could. Why don't you try it? I'll come back in a couple years and see what's left. As for food, good I fed you before we started."

"That was last night," Henrietta said. "It has to be lunch by now."

Eli looked up at the sky and squinted at the sun. "Not yet. But maybe you'll get lunch tomorrow. If we start moving now."

Henrietta stood up and puffed her hair out of her eyes. Right now, she wanted to cut it all off. "Fine," she said. "I'm ready. Where are we going?"

"We'll find out," Eli said. He turned and started walking up the slope.

The hill in front of them climbed sharply. Trees were scattered around the rising slope, but higher up, they grew dense, broken only by enormous jutting rocks.

Henrietta tried to stretch her legs while she walked, and she swung her arms to loosen her shoulders. "What do you mean, we'll find out? What are we looking for?"

"We are looking for old mage-doors," Eli said. "These foothills become mountains, and they run the length of the continent. Once, the mountains were the demesne of a single wizard. An order grew around him, and they spread themselves through the ranges, in heights and valleys. They had a choke hold between the northern and southern seas, and the lands on either side saw little of each other without paying tributes for passage. They carved enclaves into the rock and built towers on the peaks, and they connected them all with doorways in stone. Many were disguised, but some were open. And not all were destroyed."

"So we're looking for one?" Henrietta asked.

"Yes," Eli said. "For one in particular. It may still lead us to the coast. One of the old way stations is in a cave not far from here. I meant to explore it while you slept. One doorway led far to the north, where the wizards retreated long ago. But I couldn't approach it. So we seek another."

Henrietta was breathing heavily. "Why couldn't you approach it?"

Eli veered left, marching diagonally up the slope, weaving through trees and rocks. He turned and pointed back across the hill's long face.

"You can see the slope below the cave from here," he said, and he kept walking.

Henrietta hopped up on a rock and looked back. She wasn't sure what she was looking for. But when she saw it, she knew. The green tree canopy was marked by a ring of orange. Inside, the leaves were a paler shade of dead, and in the very center, the trees were gray. Below the tree line, a swath had been burned through the tall grass. But Henrietta had seen farmers burn fields before, and she knew that fire hadn't been used. The grass would have been black. Instead it was gray and shorter than the rest, curled and gray. Dust, ash, stirred above it in the breeze.

She jumped back off the rock and hurried after Eli. "What's happening?" she yelled. "Is that what you were talking about? The life-sucking? Why don't you just shut the door?"

Eli stopped and turned to look at her. His head was bright and sweaty. He took off his glasses and polished them on his sleeve. "If I were to walk past that doorway, or even into the cave, then I would either find myself turned to ash or pulled through and then turned to ash."

"I can't believe you let me sleep so close to it."

"You were in a tree," Eli said. "Trees are strong. On the ground, and I would be carrying you right now. Only I wouldn't. I would have left you."

Henrietta's feet were slipping sideways down the slope. She grabbed at rocks and trees as she passed, trying to brace herself and catch up with Eli.

"I still," she said between breaths, "think that you should, well, just try and shut the door." She looked up at Eli's back. "If that's where everything is coming from."

"I appreciate your sage counsel," Eli said. He turned around and watched her catch up. "When my sister, queen of all living things, blames me for everything now happening to her back garden and goat—if she survives—then I'm sure you could testify to my guilt. 'O Queen, I told him he should just shut the door. That would have done it.' "

"You don't have to be nasty," Henrietta said. "I could help you try."

Eli cocked his head in surprise. "And how would you do that?"

"I don't know. We could roll a rock in front of the cave or something."

Eli leaned back and laughed. It wasn't a mean laugh, but it was patronizing, and Henrietta didn't like it.

"Thank you for your offer," he said. "But it really wouldn't help, even if we both survived. The draw isn't coming from the door. It's pulling from the far north, but it is in concentration through the door. Closing it could only buy pointless time. And only if we could close it. Which we can't."

Henrietta stopped beside him and put her hands on her head to breathe. He smiled, turned directly up the slope, and pushed on.

Henrietta took a deep breath and followed. "So what happened to the wizards, then?"

"You know," Eli said over his shoulder, "you would have a much easier time if you focused on breathing."

"I'm not tired," Henrietta said.

"Liar. You were ready to lay down and die a while ago. Your life was so hard, what with staying up late and missing breakfast."

"What happened to the wizards?"

"I will tell you," Eli said, "if you beat me to the ridge. We really should be going faster."

Henrietta held her breath and started running,

pushing forward with deep, painful strides. The bones in her feet felt like they might spring loose. She ran past Eli and smiled.

"Don't be idiotic," he said. "Just walk faster. Find a pace you can hold."

Henrietta didn't slow down. Eli had been shaking her off for long enough. And she'd let him. And she'd complained too much. A stitch knotted tight in her right side and then on her left. The two of them joined in the center of her stomach and contracted. She spotted a large rock jutting out of the trees at the ridgeline, and she resolved to climb it. That's where she would be waiting when Eli reached the top.

Her legs burned. They were slow, full of acid and sludge, and her lungs wanted to rip wide open. Every part of her wanted to stop, except her will. Her will wanted a different body. One with wings. She slowed, but she wouldn't let her legs stop moving. Only fifty more steps. She nearly tripped on a rock, but caught herself. A branch tangled in her hair and kept some. She closed her eyes and pushed through, ignoring the scratches on her arms and face, and the tugs on her hair. She moved faster, ripping through tangled branches and tripping on low, sprawling trunks and brush. And then she laughed.

She had reached the stone. A sharp face overlooked the hillside, but its back sloped gently into the ridge. The stone was pale where it wasn't covered with dry lichen and cracked and knobby on the side. Even with boiled legs, climbing wouldn't be difficult. She scrambled up onto the edge of the great stone's back. A carpet of scrub oak spread out in front of her, running down toward the valley. In the far distance, beyond much lower hills, she thought she could see the river.

Laughing, happy and relieved that she had actually made it and not just given Eli another reason to be smug, she cupped her hands to her mouth.

"Hey, Eli!" she yelled. "What happened to the wizards?"

"They faded like mist," a quiet voice said, "and went the way of all flesh."

Henrietta overbalanced and nearly fell into the oaks tangled beneath her. Waving her arms, she looked up to the end of the rock outcropping. On the very peak, there stood a man, as tall as any she had ever seen, even taller with nothing but the sky behind him. The man wore leather gloves on his hands. One of them gripped a thick bow beside his waist. A quivered flock of arrow stood up above his shoulder.

Henrietta turned and ran down the back of the rock. She was falling. The ground rose up suddenly, and her tired legs gave out against it. Dust rose, a rock dug into her ribs, pushing the breath out of her.

Strong hands gripped her shoulders from behind, and she was on her feet. She spun and tried to kick, but her body was quickly twisted back. An arm slid down over her head and shoulders. She couldn't move her upper body, so she stomped and found a booted toe.

"Peace, little sister," the voice said in her ear, "unless you wish to be tied." Then it grew louder. "Where is the little Fitzwizard?"

"The birds are tracking him," another voice said. "He's moving along the ridge beneath the trees."

"Follow him. Bring him to the well."

A storm of horses pounded away behind her, but one passed where she could see, gray and speckled black. Standing straight, she wouldn't have reached its shoulder, and she could feel the vibrations in the ground as its huge, hairless hooves drummed by.

Eli wouldn't have much of a chance.

When the horses were gone, she was turned around suddenly and found herself looking into the eyes of the tall man. They were smiling and strangely colored— dark green in the center but with rims of pale blue. His face was rough but clean-shaven, and his hair was black. A scar on his left temple ran back into his scalp, and his hair was streaked gray around it. He looked a little like her father. But not. She'd never been this afraid of her father.

"You are young to keep such company," he said. "What is your name?"

Henrietta didn't want to say anything. She wanted to meet this stranger's eyes with a cold stare and defy them. But she wasn't good at saying nothing. So she lied.

"My name is Beatrice," she said.

The man didn't blink. He leaned closer, staring, until she could smell pepper on his breath.

"That name has not shaped you," he said. "Are you a liar?"

"No," Henrietta said angrily.

"Then what are you called?"

"I am called Beatrice."

The man didn't look away. He spoke again, quietly.

"What is it you are called?"

Henrietta's neck began to droop. She wanted to look down, or up, anywhere else, but he wasn't letting her.

"Henrietta Dorothy Willis," she said.

"And you are called Henrietta?"

She nodded.

"Then come, Henrietta, you will ride with me." He straightened up, put a hand on her shoulder, and led her around to the side of the stone. "Tell me no more lies," he said, "and we shall get along."

He whistled, low and sharp, and an enormous chestnut horse surged slowly up from beside the stone, prancing to a stop in front of them.

"I am called Caleb," the man said, "and this is Chester."

Chapter Fifteen

Henry stood with his thumbs tucked beneath his backpack straps on top of the warm stone slab and blinked in the sun. His breaths were long and slow, and he was savoring them. The only noise was made by the breeze slicing itself through the trees. There had to be insects, though Henry couldn't hear any. If birds had made homes in the trees, they were keeping them all secret.

Henry had only been to Badon Hill once, but he couldn't count how often his dreams had brought him to the tall trees and the breeze coming off the sea. The island hill fell away into mossy shadow on every side of Henry's perch, swallowed by giant trees with their heights rooted in the sky. He was standing on the very crown of Badon Hill, on the ancient rectangular rock, set in the clearing surrounded by the ruins of the old stone wall. Behind Henry stood an ancient tree, weather-worn, with splaying branches and a wide crack in its trunk, a crack that led through a cupboard and into an attic. Far below him, out of sight but not out of smell, there sprawled the sea.

Henry walked down the length of the slab and

jumped off, making his way to the corner, where he knew he would find the bones of the big black dog from his oldest Badon Hill dreams. They were there, the yellowed skull, caged ribs, and others swallowed by grass. He didn't know why he had dreamt it, the dog, running back and forth between the tree and the stone, and digging at both, but he knew that it was important to him. Somehow.

Leaning his back against the warm rock, Henry shut his eyes and let the sun warm his face. Then, with a deep breath, he straightened and opened his eyes. For a second, they wouldn't focus. Threads like jet streams morphed between the trees, knotting them together in a single word, a single story and song. Henry could hear Nella telling him to stop, but he blocked out the pain in his head and the pounding of his heart. He was seeing the raging, laughing life that he had only felt whispered before. And he knew that this storm of names and living words was Badon Hill at rest. Badon Hill, dreaming. His tongue dried and tightened. He wanted to try and speak this language. He wanted words in his mouth to be alive, to take on flesh, wood, bark, sap, leaves, rings of annual laughter and sorrow. He wanted to speak life.

Henry's mouth hung open wide, his joints throbbed, ignored. He turned in place and saw the wind.

It was a single epic creature, a sliding, rushing, legless back. Henry put out his hand and watched it divide around his fingers, around his dancing dandelion fire, and rejoin itself on the other side. It was single, but many. Every tail spun off and found its own personality, shaped another narrative, and then rejoined the rest. Henry put out his other hand. He could grab on. He knew he could. He could be carried away.

Suddenly, the world roared. Henry felt his arms begin to spasm, his eyes rolled back in his head. But even that was no protection. His first sight was gone, but his second sight continued on, carried by something as loud and strong as Niagara. It could rip him apart.

Henry fell to the ground, tucked his legs to his chest, and grabbed his ears. He curled tighter and tighter, breathing hard, trying to push it out of his head, fighting the spasms he felt building in his joints. The trees and wind were shouting their names, their histories, proclaiming their glories with violence.

All went quiet. The world sang on, but Henry's mind stepped out of the roar, reblanketed with simpler perception, perception more easily survived.

Henry opened his eyes slowly. His jaw hurt. It was locked wide open. Grindingly, carefully, he closed it and sat up.

Badon Hill rustled in the breeze, insectless, birdless, content with its quiet life. Henry knuckled his eyes and looked around carefully. His head was drumming. He wished he had brought Tylenol.

In front of him, the gray stone was still blurry. Henry shut his eyes quickly. After a moment, he opened one and squinted at what should have been the flat face of the long, rectangular side of the rock. It was flat at the edges and across the top, but at the center, there gaped a black arch, just peeking above ground level. Henry could see grass running in front of it, but it looked false, an illusion deceiving only his first sight, like Darius's chin. In front of his feet, the ground actually fell away into an uneven stairwell. Henry scooted forward and looked down. The stairs were narrow, descending to the black arch. Henry slid his leg through the grass and held it out over the stairs. Strangely, he felt resistance where ground level was pretending to be. It wasn't merely illusion, but his foot still passed through and settled on a narrow stair. Henry slid forward again and stood. Both feet were on the stairway. He looked around himself. Grass ran up to his knees and between his legs, but he could look through it, at the dark, wet stone beneath his feet. He took another step, and another, wading deeper into the ground. The grass was around his thighs. He didn't like feeling cut in half, so he walked all the way to the stone, with ground level around his ribs, and then he ducked below it.

Henry was squatting at the gaping mouth. He wasn't sure he wanted to go in. Actually, he was sure he didn't want to. But he was just as sure that he didn't want to move on without looking. He pulled off his backpack and went digging for the flashlight. When he found it, he pointed the beam through the arch and saw that the stairs hadn't stopped. They continued down into darkness.

After quieting his stomach's reaction to the idea, he

eased himself through the low doorway. After counting twenty steps, Henry found a floor with his light and then his feet. The ceiling was just high enough for him to stand with his head tilted.

He was in a little oval room. The smooth stone walls were pocked with niches and miniature alcoves, some of which looked as if they held things. On the far wall, a door, as wide as it was tall, was set into the black stone. Its surface crawled with carvings.

A man's head was in the center, the same head that appeared on the faeren's seal. It was big, as large as Henry's torso. The man was bearded, and vines poured out of his mouth and nostrils, tangling with the stone hair on his jaw. Vines and leaves also sprouted from his ears and wrapped around his head like a crown. His eyes, round balls of black stone, were open, but the pupils were funnel-shaped holes, bored back into the man's head. In a circle all around the face, stone hair and leaves and vines intertangled, forming a leafy and serpentine surface. Henry moved closer and focused his light. Throughout the man's beard and the tangled halo, smaller heads had been carved. They sprouted off vines next to leaves, and all of them had their eyes closed in sleep. Henry had counted a dozen, tracing the cool stone with his fingertips, when something rattled at his feet. A snarl of small bones was piled against the base of the door. The skulls were long and wide-nostriled like miniature horses, but at the snout, each had one small horn. Raggant skulls. There were five. Henry shivered.

He was in a grave. Beyond the door, there would be bodies. One, or dozens, but bodies.

Henry slid backward toward the stairs, then turned quickly. He could see sunlight at the top of the shaft. Ducking, he bounded up, gasping for air that hadn't been sleeping with the dead.

Henry erupted from the ground and staggered through the tall grass, looking at the blue sky and then down at the green life beneath his feet.

A bearded man moved in front of him.

Stunned, Henry looked into his eyes. He had black hair and was wearing all white beneath a heavy brown cloak. He was poised, expecting Henry to do something. Henry stepped backward and turned toward the cracked tree. Another man, hairless, taller, thicker, but in the same dress, stood waiting for him. The man raised his hand, and strange words rumbled in his chest. Henry gasped and staggered, struggling to breathe. The air was trying to bind his arms and legs, trying to grip his throat.

Coughing, Henry tripped but kept his feet. The first man was coming toward him. Henry swung his backpack and bumped into the stone. Turning, he scrambled up. His legs were wobbling. His hands wanted to drop what they held, to let his flashlight and backpack find the ground. He gripped them both tighter.

There were four men that he could see, circling around the stone. Henry picked the smallest, took a step on the rock, and jumped toward him. His knees struck the man's chest, and he slammed the flashlight down on top of his head with a crunch of breaking plastic and glass. Together, they tumbled to the ground, and Henry rolled free, scrambling to his feet. The flashlight was gone. Clutching his backpack, Henry ran toward the old stone wall, ragged and tumbled down. He caught his toe as he jumped it and fell again, bouncing and sliding down the slope through the thick grass. Henry pushed himself up and ran faster than he ever had, plowing and tearing the soft earth with each step, down the steep slope of Badon Hill, jumping brush and boulders, rolling in moss when he slipped, filling his lungs with wind and feeding its strength into his legs.

Suddenly, the ground fell away, and he was in the air, legs pumping and backpack swinging. His legs buckled beneath him, his back slammed into the soft earth, and his right arm cracked against something hard. For a moment, blackness hovered in front of his eyes. His burnt hand was throbbing. He grabbed on to the pain, embracing the sharp, singeing itch.

The blackness cleared. His right leg was bent beneath him. He rolled to his side and straightened it out. Behind him was a brown gouge where he had landed and slid. The bank he had fallen off of was at least fifteen feet tall. He had just cleared the path at the bottom. Its thick, mossy surface looked soft, but black, moist paving stones were visible where he had clipped and peeled its edge with his arm.

Henry tried to lift his right hand up from the

ground, but it was tugged back down. He had scraped it palm-down in the dirt, and now green leaves were intertwined above it, pinning it down. Dandelion stems climbed up from between his fingers and exploded into suns, until his hand was buried in gold.

There was no time to marvel. Henry jerked his hand free and scrambled onto his knees.

"Pauper son," a big voice said. The bald man stood at the top of the bank. "Are you the one who is self-called York?" The man's vowels were strange, deep and almost wet. The other three were sliding down the bank. The smallest of them had a trickle of blood on his forehead.

Henry stood up. "Who are you?" he asked, testing his weight on his right leg.

The three men spread out on the far side of the path. Henry was surprised to see them look cautious, almost worried.

"You run like a deer," the bald man said. "If deer struggled to keep their legs."

Henry stepped backward, down the slope. "I can run again," he said. "Who are you? What do you want?"

The man with the black beard spoke slowly. "We were sent to find you. If you be the son of Mordecai. Are you?"

"I don't know," Henry said. "Who is he?"

The beard smiled. The bald man laughed and slid down beside the others.

"Why do you want me?" Henry asked.

The smallest one spoke. "We don't," he said, and wiped his forehead. "But Nimiane, old daughter of Endor, newly wakened, does. And we, who were once servants of Carnassus on his mountain throne, have been given over to serve her." The man's face was young. He looked into Henry's eyes. "She grows strong."

Henry turned down the hill. But they had expected him to. Strange language surrounded him, and he fell facedown. His mouth was sealed tight. A strong hand clamped on to the back of his neck, and a pulse surged into him, wiping his mind. His limbs jerked and relaxed.

"Don't kill him," said a new voice, sharp as frost. "Did you kill him? She'll want his life fresh."

Henry felt himself lifted. His body sagged and swung like a tired hammock as the men walked down the hill. He wasn't in his body. He was somewhere else. Somewhere dark, where the men couldn't find him.

For a moment, he thought about leaving his body behind. He could go up the hill and through the tree. They could put his body in the ground somewhere. Behind a big stone door with a man's envined face to seal it.

His body was leaving, sagging away between the men. He felt a tug of discomfort. He felt suddenly naked, ashamed. He needed his body. He needed to wear it. He had to wear something.

Henry followed.

They dropped him onto wood, wet and hard. It was moving beneath him. He could hear waves, and he knew he was in a boat. Someone lifted his right hand and traced his burn with a finger. Then he was flipped onto his face, and his arms were bound behind his back.

"Club the faeries and throw them over," someone said.

"Why?" It was the small man's voice. "Shouldn't we take them back, too?"

The icy voice made the decision. "Keep one," it said. "Kill the rest."

Henry's face was pressed against a coil of rope. He heard the clubbing, then the splashes. But his mind, already in darkness, was retreating even further away into something else—a memory, or a dream, of another time and another boat.

He was on his back, looking up. One sail creaked and swung slightly across the blue above. Henry tried to move, but couldn't. A big black dog stepped above him, looking down. It looked him in the eyes. There was something strange in the dog's eyes. They seemed to be meaning something, and Henry seemed to be understanding, but he was forgetting it all at the same time. He was happy. The dog sat next to him. Henry could see a man in the back of the boat, steering. He laughed and said something, but Henry couldn't hear. He couldn't see his face. But he knew he liked it. The man stood up, pulled the sail down, and tied it to the mast. The boat bumped, and the man jumped out. Henry still couldn't move, though he wanted to look around. The man came back. He pulled on the mast, and it came out. The dog was already gone somewhere. The man laid the mast down in the boat, and then Henry was up. He wasn't moving himself, but he could see. The man was carrying him. He was looking over a shoulder, watching the water drift away and a rocky pier protecting a dock and the boat. Every once in a while, he saw the black dog bounding beside them. Soon they began moving up, winding back and forth, climbing higher and higher. The man was singing, and Henry was looking down at sun-covered water and the boat. He remembered the boat, right where it sat.

They were in the trees now, and the man stopped to touch some of them. He seemed to be speaking, or changing his song. Henry could see the dog panting and then running back down the hill and then running up behind them. Henry laughed at the dog while he bounced and rocked with the man's steps. They went higher, and the ground behind them grew steeper and steeper. They walked for a long time, but Henry didn't mind. He didn't notice it.

Eventually, the man stopped, and Henry was no longer looking backward. He was looking at an old stone wall. They walked along the outside until they came to a gap. It had been a gate, but the wall was ruined now. The dog leapt through and ran to where the hill ended. Henry and the man followed. The sun was strong here. There were fewer trees. He felt it hot on his face. They came to a great gray stone, and Henry found himself on his back in the grass. He blinked and squinted at the sun. Then he grieved. He did not know why, but grief racked him. He felt it in his chest and stomach. He felt it in his head. Then he was lifted up again and set back down. This time, there was no sun. He was in the trunk of a tree, looking out. He could see the sky and treetops. He could see the great stone and the man walking around it. The dog came and looked at him and left. The man was walking down into the ground at the edge of the stone. Henry shut his eyes. He didn't want to. He wanted to watch what the man was doing. He whimpered. Then he forgot what he wanted.

When Henry opened his eyes, he was looking at the black dog, and the sun was gone. The dog was pushing on him with his nose. Then the dog ran over to the stone, digging and shoving his head into a hole. The sky was gray now, and Henry was cold. He could feel wind on his face, and then water. He cried. The dog pulled his head out of the hole, and Henry watched him bark at the ground. His black coat was wet and slick, and his head was covered with mud. He ran back to Henry and pushed him farther into the tree. Then he lay down with his head on him, and Henry was warm. But the dog jumped up again and ran back to the stone. Henry tried to watch him, but his head fell backward, and he slid deeper into the tree, yelling.

And he was in another dream.

Henry was sitting at a long table. Water was running

off his nose. The table was crowded with food and surrounded with people. Uncle Frank sat across from him,
winking.

"Throw the knife, Henry," Uncle Frank said. "When
he comes, throw it. There's only one chance."

CHAPTER SIXTEEN

Henrietta's legs and hips ached with the horse's motion, and she hadn't even been on it for an hour. Caleb moved up and down easily behind her. She always seemed to be coming down when the horse's broad shoulders came up, and she continued rising when they went back down. It was like being on a trampoline with someone much bigger than she was. Someone who wanted to make her sick.

The horse felt as large as a tractor, and if it hadn't been for the man's arm around her waist, she would have fallen off a dozen times. She'd ridden a horse before, but only an old sway-backed mare that had clomped along the side of the road. This horse was proud. Its tree-trunk neck arched and rippled beneath glossy skin, and it seemed to want every excuse to canter and gallop. As far as she could tell, Caleb was letting him do whatever he wanted. She assumed it was a he.

There were no reins, and Caleb wasn't hanging on to anything. One of his hands kept her on the horse. His other carried a black bow.

"You will meet your little friend again soon," Caleb

said. The bow pointed past her. It looked like it had been made from two long horns. "There is a dead village ahead. The others will bring him to the well."

They were moving along the valley floor. Just around the next bend, Henrietta could see the shapes of houses. Even from that distance, she could see that most of them leaned to one side or another. The roofs looked as patchy as the oldest abandoned barns she had ever dared to explore.

The horse slowed as they approached. Some of the buildings had been tall, four or five stories. Now, none stood above three. Paned windows stared at her with jagged teeth. The walls looked rotten, not with moisture or moss or mold, but with dry rot. They were simply softening and turning to dust. With its thick neck arched, the horse walked down the center street, and Henrietta stared at unhinged doors and collapsing windows. A few of the larger structures had burned, but their blackened bones still staggered toward the sky, remembering, if no one else did, what they had been.

The street opened into a town square. Cobblestones were seamed with dry grass and weeds, but in the center, there was a fountain. It was not as extravagant as the one she had seen in the great ruined courtyard, not by half, but it still watered the pool at its base.

The sculpture looked to have been of a woman, standing twice as tall as Caleb, holding a wide-brimmed bowl on her head. One of her arms was gone, but Henrietta could still see her hand attached to the underside of the cracked bowl. Water trickled down the woman's face and through her robe, leaving the stone greasy.

The horse stopped and slowly pranced in place beside the fountain's edge.

"Magdalene, greeting," Caleb said.

Henrietta spun her head around the square and saw nothing but buildings left unburied.

"Stay on the horse," Caleb whispered, and he dropped to the ground. Henrietta gathered up two fistfuls of mane, careful not to tug.

Tucking his bow through a strap behind Henrietta, Caleb turned and walked toward the fountain. He stopped before he reached it and crossed his arms.

"Call down your birds," Magdalene's voice said, and Henrietta jerked. Chester took one step back and tapped the ground with his front hoof.

"Sorry," Henrietta whispered, and rubbed the horse's neck.

Caleb didn't look back. "Why would I call them down?" he asked. "You have nothing hidden left. Nothing worth hiding."

"They are over our land," the voice said. "Call them down."

"Do you still clutch after these dead valleys?" Caleb's voice was even.

"They still clutch me."

Caleb stood silently for a moment. Then he uncrossed his arms. "Unveil yourself, and the birds descend."

Henrietta blinked. Magdalene, looking just like she

had seated in her house with gardening gloves on her lap, sat primly on the edge of the fountain. Benjamin and Joseph stood on either side of her, and at least ten others like them. They wore short swords tucked into fat belts. A few carried bows.

Magdalene smiled. She did not look at Henrietta.

Caleb raised his right arm and held it out from his side. A huge bird swooped down over Henrietta's head, flared its wide wings, and came to rest on his glove. Its back was dark. Its legs and chest and head were white. It swiveled its head and eyed Henrietta, and maybe Magdalene at the same time. A black stripe ran up around its golden eye and into its black beak.

Henrietta was staring at it, when another flared and landed on the paving stones beside Caleb's feet. Another perched on the fountain peak, bobbed its head into the bowl of water, and shook streams down its back. Two more dropped to the square, before Magdalene finally spoke.

"You have someone who belongs to us," she said.

Caleb laughed. "If you mean your brother Eli, I will cheerfully give him back. He should be in a sack and on his way here already."

"We have no brother." Magdalene's voice was crisp. "We speak of the girl."

"The girl?" Caleb looked back over his shoulder at Henrietta. He moved his arm, and the dark bird flapped up and joined its brother in the fountain. "What ownership do you have of the girl?"

"She trespassed in the Lesser Hall of FitzFaeren. Her grandsire stole certain talismans of the FitzFaeren, of which we are now greatly in need. She is to be held against their return."

"Her grandsire did this?" Caleb asked. He moved back to the horse, took Henrietta by the waist, and lifted her down easily. With his hand on her shoulder, he walked her over in front of the queen.

The queen ignored her, her eyes fixed on Caleb. Henrietta watched the lines on the old woman's well-sunned face. Her white hair was pulled back so tight, it left her forehead smooth.

"You have vision I do not," Caleb said. "Look. Tell me what runs in her veins."

Magdalene licked her lips. Her eyes traveled nowhere near Henrietta's face.

Caleb stepped around beside the queen and examined Henrietta. Benjamin, standing below his shoulder, shuffled to the side.

"I do not doubt you, queen." Caleb pulled off his gloves and rubbed his jaw slowly. "Her grandsire may indeed have taken things without warrant. But have you not seen other blood as well? What vintage runs on her father's side?"

"Keep her," Magdalene said quickly. "For the sake of her father's line. Though her trespass was real."

Henrietta wanted to talk. She wanted everything explained. Why would her father matter? Caleb straightened back up and walked her to the horse. He reached into a pouch at his side and pulled out a brown nugget of coarse sugar. Placing it in Henrietta's hand, he nodded at the big horse and turned back around.

"Now tell me, queen," he said. "Tell me why you would send my sister, Hyacinth, a dream, asking me to come. I have traveled ways best left unstirred, and even now the land dies beneath our feet. My city has need of me. But I have come, through cold mountain tombs, so speak plainly."

Henrietta broke the sugar into pieces. She rolled the smallest one into her palm and held her hand out flat beneath Chester's flaring nose. His lips swallowed up her hand, and his tongue swabbed away the sugar. Henrietta wasn't exactly sure what Caleb had been saying, but she knew she was staying with him. And that was good. Or she thought so. She hesitated with the sugar, and Chester nearly knocked her over with his nose.

"Endor rises," Magdalene said. Henrietta didn't take her eyes off the horse, but she listened. She had a feeling that if she were to tell the whole story about her involvement with the cupboards back in Kansas, Magdalene would be demanding her back. And not just to keep her around.

"Endor sleeps in its own dust and madness," Caleb said. "It is Nimiane that rises, and she does so in the halls of Carnassus in the far north. I have spent these last weeks pursuing death and its currents. How she is free, I cannot tell you, for I stood beside my brother when she was entombed. But I felt her curses in my bones then, and they recognize her voice now. This news is easily spoken, and did not require me to come so dangerously. What more? What that I do not know?"

"We shall fall," Magdalene said quietly. "FitzFaeren goes to its final grave."

Henrietta could hear a general rustling and shifting of feet. She glanced over at Benjamin and Joseph and the men around them. Their faces were red and their jaws were set. In some she saw anger, in others, emptiness.

Caleb said nothing.

"And after us," Magdalene continued, "every mountain people and village. The forests will fade until she has drunk her demon-fill. Your city will crumble into the surf, and your people with it. And after us, the greater kingdoms, the empires of the three seas, they are easily seduced by strength. She will turn her eyes toward them. She will find a throne again, a higher dais, new lands to reduce."

Caleb sighed. "There is a mourning dove nested above my window who sings such songs of death to me every dawn because the sun has risen, and every night because it has set. Will you dig your graves and make your beds inside?"

Henrietta watched the short men squirm. What their queen was saying was making them angry. Caleb was pushing them further. And they were allowed to be angry with him. They glowered, but remained silent.

"Do you deny that she is drawing more power than she alone can hold?" Magdalene asked.

"I cannot say."

"There is another with her," Magdalene said. "We must stand together or each receive our own slaughtering day in turns. And if we fall, we will fall at once, at least embalmed in glory."

Caleb rubbed his stubbled chin. Magdalene said no more, and so he spoke. "Of course you will have all the support we can provide. But that is sparse indeed. What had you in mind?"

Magdalene rose from her seat, and as she did, every man around her dipped their heads. "Make your stand here," she said, "within the halls of old FitzFaeren. We are the farthest north. You are well beyond the mountains and deeper south. If you make your stand there, with your backs to the sea, you will be abandoning us to an early and lonely fate, and only postponing your own defeat. Here, together, we may turn the witch back, or find a quick end."

"Queen," Caleb said, and his voice was strained. "Do you know what you ask? Even now, unripened crops are being gathered within our walls, and villagers struggle in from the mountains with their lives on their backs. We have been preparing for a siege since Nimiane's star rose in a new quarter of the sky. I could not give you twenty of my eldest men, to say nothing of erasing all of our preparations. There is not time. I have traveled through the mage roads to get here, but I would not bring all my people through those ways, nor are they mine to command."

Magdalene looked around at the houses and at the hills behind them, lost in her own thoughts, sampling old memories.

"The blow falls here first," she said quietly. "It has fallen here before."

"I do not think it will," Caleb said. "You are nearer, but many of the ways are still open in the mountains, as you can feel and I have come. Five hundred miles to our foothills is as within her reach as your fallen outposts along your forgotten northern border. Hylfing stood against her once. She was turned back at its walls. There are no old grudges waiting for her here, but no doubt she has filled her dreams with pictures of our blood darkening the sand."

Hooves pounded into the square, and all heads turned. Eleven heavy horses trotted and slowed to a walk. Men dressed like Caleb sat on each one. A bouncing sack dangled over a horse rump behind the leader. Beside them all loped a tall black dog, the size of a small pony. To Henrietta, he looked like a Dane, but his chest and head were broader.

Caleb whistled, and the dog broke into a run. The remaining birds lifted off the ground and found perches on the fountain. When it reached him, the dog lay down at Caleb's feet.

"Queen," Caleb said, and he bowed slightly. "Come to us instead. The council would welcome your people.

You have strengths that we do not, and our walls have never been breached. Now we must go. I would be inside my city's gates before the blow falls, and dark ways lie ahead."

"We will stand or fall in FitzFaeren," Magdalene said.

Caleb lifted Henrietta up onto the horse, pulled out his bow, and swung up behind her.

"May heaven stand with you," he said. "And may it never fall."

Caleb turned Chester away, but quickly turned back.

"Would you have us leave your brother?" Caleb asked. "Or shall we take him?"

"We have no brother," she said again.

The sack squirmed.

Henry was cold. Very cold. His pants were wet and clinging to his legs. His blood had been replaced with frigid water, and greasy coils of brown rope were digging into his cheek. His eyes seemed to be working again, but not well. He tried to push himself up, but his hands were tied behind his back. The floor was rising and falling beneath him, and he could feel water puddling and spilling around his stomach and legs.

Groaning, Henry tried to roll onto his side, at least to get his face off of the rope. He lifted his head up and set it on a gray bag.

The bag kicked him in the cheek.

Behind him, men laughed. Hands reached around

him, and Henry blinked when he saw metal flick toward the bag, and a thick string fall away.

"Faerie," a voice whispered. "Bide a while."

Henry was rolled onto his back, and he propped himself up on the rope. The wind was blowing around him now.

The small wizard was crouching in front of him. His brown hood was up and inflating in the wind. Pale gray eyes stared out of the shadow. He was looking over Henry's face and put two fingers up to the burn scars on his jaw.

"I have a burn like the one on your hand," he said quietly, "but none like these. Are you strong?"

It wasn't a hard question. Henry never felt strong, but especially not when he'd been knocked out, tied up, and frozen in the bottom of a boat.

He shook his head.

"Keep your arms behind you," the young man whispered, and Henry felt a blade slide between his wrists, nicking his skin. The rope fell loose.

The small wizard backed away from him, ducked beneath the sail that flapped above them both, and huddled down in the boat. Henry could see three of them, all hooded. The fourth must be behind him, steering.

The boat itself had only one sail and no deck. It wasn't much longer than twenty feet. Now that Henry could actually see the water around him and watch the prow rise and fall with the waves, he immediately felt ill. An island in the distance climbed and sank with the horizon. Shutting his eyes, he swallowed. He didn't want to start throwing up. Not ever. But especially not now. He didn't know what the young wizard was planning, but vomiting wouldn't help, no matter what it was.

A gust of wind parted the hair on the back of his head and bit into his neck. He shivered as the sail snapped and the boat surged up a wave and dropped.

The gray bag erupted beside him.

A very small man with a pronounced belly bounded up, yelling. He booted Henry in the ear and leapt to the rail, balancing perfectly with the ship's motion.

Henry fell over and covered his head.

The three wizards jumped to their feet, grabbing at the rail and at the mast for balance.

Henry watched flame sprout from beneath the faerie's feet and flare around the ship rail. The wizards yelped, staggering and pulling away their hands even as spray from the bow doused most of the flame.

The fourth wizard jumped forward from the back of the boat and stood facing the fat little man where he balanced.

"Faeries sink like stones," he said. His face was as sharp as his voice. "Drown, or slink back into your sack."

The faerie rolled his eyes in his head, stuck out his tongue, and folded it. Both of his rather thick ears stood out from his wet and tousled brown hair.

As the wizard raised his hand, Henry could already feel the violence of the words in the man's throat. His own body tensed like it was waiting for a blow.

The curse came out of the man's mouth and became

thunder in the air. Guided by the wizard's upraised hand, it tore out a bite of the ship's rail and wall where the faerie had been standing. The faerie was gone.

Henry blinked. The faerie, with puffed-out cheeks, had dropped to the ship bottom and curled into a tight little ball. The air shimmered around him.

The men all spun, looking for the faerie, while he began crawling to the mast with bulging cheeks and a red face. When he reached it, he shinnied quickly up to the top. Henry looked from him to the confused wizards. The small one could obviously see the faerie, and he was stealing quick glances up. The rest hung on to the ship rail for balance and scanned the boat around them.

The young wizard looked at Henry and nodded toward the man that stood closest to where Henry was lying. Then he looked back up the mast. He pointed. "Up there!" he shouted.

The men all looked up. The big bald one leaned back against the rail, and his hood fell away. Suddenly, the smaller wizard hit him in the ribs and flipped him into the sea. Black-beard turned, surprised, and a knife flicked into his chest, burying itself up to the hilt. His legs collapsed, and he slumped into the bottom of the boat.

Only one remained—the one with the icy voice. He turned toward the smaller wizard and smiled.

"Monmouth," he said calmly. "You are only fit for kitchens if you need a blade to do your killing."

Henry braced himself and found his feet. The wizard glanced at him and smirked, tight-lipped. Henry could feel something building, static, tension, something.

The pulse came suddenly, without words. It came from inside the wizard.

Monmouth jumped behind the mast, but was thrown back into the prow as the boat shivered and wood cracked. Henry lunged for the man, but a raised hand stopped him. He felt his throat close and his feet lock in place. His body began to arch backward, grinding his spine.

As the wizard laughed, the faerie landed on his head.

The two of them fell to the ground, with the faerie's legs clamped around the man's throat.

Henry picked himself up and stepped toward the bodies to help, but he froze in confusion. What he saw was more than two bodies. Fire and frost and even lightning all took shape in the air and faded before striking either. Water was turning to ice in the bottom of the boat. Henry's eyes widened and saw even more. The faerie's strength was green. Writhing webs swirled around him and around the wizard's body. All of them met and withered against a cloud of sharp whiteness. But the faerie's threads were fewer, fading.

"Help him!" Monmouth yelled, lunging to the bodies with a lifted knife, its blade already painted dark. The faerie was thrown off and lay limp and panting. Monmouth's knife shattered in the air.

Henry blinked and collected himself. What was he doing? He jumped forward and felt the air around the wizard bite into his skin. Monmouth had both hands suspended above the man's throat, struggling to close.

Henry picked up the gray bag and slid it over the wizard's head. The man screamed, but it was cut off by Monmouth's hands slamming into place.

"Don't kill him," Henry said. "Not like that."

Monmouth looked up, confused, but he didn't stop.

"Kill him now," a throaty voice said. "Now, now, now. Now!"

The world cracked, and Monmouth flew into the air, grabbed on to the sail, and fell into the boat. The bag ripped open, and the wizard stood up.

The faerie bounded past Henry, and flame burst from his hands into the taller man's chest, wrapping around behind him. The wizard stepped back and over-balanced as the boat dropped down a wave. The faerie wrapped himself around the man's shins and pushed him backward through the splintered gap and over into the sea.

The thick faerie immediately ran to the tiller at the back of the boat and swung them slowly away from where the man had fallen. Then he ran to the sail, untied a rope, swung a beam, retied it, and ran to the rail to look for the wizard.

"Ha," he said. "There's one more of the necronancies gone to feed the merpeople. In that water, he'll be ice already, and that's the truth." The faerie turned around and faced Henry. "And you," he said. "I sit inside that spider sack and listen to them jabbering about you. Mordecai's son? Just a bit of paddy's cake, and that's all, standin' there oglin' a fight like it were a bit of puppet entertainment. We should toss you over, too."

Monmouth sat up and put his hand to his head. His features were sharp, and his face pale beneath his jet hair. He was slight and very young. Henry hadn't noticed just how young in all the chaos. He couldn't be eighteen.

The faerie looked over at Monmouth and then up into Henry's eyes. His face was even with Henry's ribs. Bright eyes sparkled above flushed, puffy cheeks, and his brown hair was as thick as fur. His nose looked almost round, like a knob.

"I'm sorry," Henry said. "I'm just slow right now."

"Slow?" The faerie laughed. "Do you even have the sight? Are you a true seventh? What am I doing now?"

The faerie held his breath and stood on one leg.

"You're standing on one leg," Henry said.

"Beginner's luck," said the faerie. "What now?" He stuck out his tongue.

Henry reached out and poked it. The faerie sputtered, grimacing.

"Right," the faerie said, and he took a deep breath and held it, still standing on one leg. His cheeks grew, and his eyes widened. His skin went red and then purple, and the air began to shimmer around him.

"Are you serious?" Henry asked. "You're doing a headstand."

The faerie gasped and dropped his foot. "I knew it."

"I was joking," Henry said. "You were just on one leg again. What are you trying to do? Do you think you're invisible?"

The faerie squinted at Henry and rubbed his belly slowly.

"I don't think," he said. "I am. How're you doing that?"

Henry was confused. "I can see you. I do it by looking."

"He's real," Monmouth said, standing up carefully. "I wouldn't have just done what I did if he wasn't. Probably shouldn't have, anyway. That was Carnassus's son you just tipped over, and he won't be pleased to lose him."

"Carnassus?" the faerie asked. "That old mountain goat will have his own life to mourn soon enough, sending his little wizmancers onto a faerie mound. There are protocols, you know. The committee won't stand for it."

"And what could a gaggle of yelping faeren do about it?" Monmouth asked.

"A gaggle?" The thick faerie marched over to where Monmouth stood. "Shall I gaggle you?"

Henry could hear the two arguing, but he was feeling sick again. Too sick to pay attention. The small boat continued to bob and sink, but with no one steering, the bow slid back and forth as well. His legs were turning to jelly.

"Where are we going?" he asked, swaying. "I need to get back to Badon Hill."

He slumped down into the bottom of the boat and curled his legs against his chest.

"Or the Deiran Coast," he said, and he shut his eyes.

CHAPTER SEVENTEEN

Darius stood in the quiet throne room. Moist, cold air drifted through the high windows and settled around him. His senses were throbbing. He could feel the strength in the stones beneath him. Each one was ready to burst, filled with life that belonged elsewhere. Any more, and they would begin to move.

He pulled in a long, slow breath, noting each droplet that he drew into himself from the air. He was full to bursting as well, teeming with the treasured, savored glories of grasslands and streams, of insects and gnarled trees. Some of the strength had been woven around the rest, to keep him from flying apart. But inside, somewhere, Darius knew that he could never turn back. Despite the cool air, sweat stood out on his broad forehead. His own spark was gone. He had become a mere jar for the stolen lives of others, and he would be forever drawing more.

He looked slowly around at the black, curtained doorways that lined the room, sensing each. There was the one that he himself had come through, leading back into the strange house where his adopted son had been imprisoned.

Not one led to the world he knew. He had come through into a place of legend, a place he had first heard about in the gibbering marginalia in the oldest, most unintelligible books that had belonged to his own adoptive father, Ronaldo Valpraise—a man he had believed to be wise, but had only been a fool, afraid of real power.

This was real power. Nimiane, daughter of undying Endor, sat on the throne a dozen steps from where he stood. Her face, lovely and terrible, was smooth in rest. Her eyes were closed, but the white-faced cat was alert on her lap, and her pale hand moved slightly through its black fur. Darius stared into the cat's eyes and knew that Nimiane was staring back. She possessed the animal, and its vision had replaced her own.

Darius felt life approaching, and then he heard feet slowly climbing the stairs from the hall into the great stone room.

Carnassus, the old wizard, wizened, with flesh like the skin of a withered mushroom, rose into view, leaning on his staff, and stepped onto the thriving stone floor. His neck was thick on his small body, and a long white beard grew from the tip of his chin. He looked up at the gray sky through the windows and around at the doors.

"The boy." Nimiane's voice was flat. Her eyes remained shut. "They have not returned with the boy."

"No," Carnassus said. "They have not. The voyage to the doorway is short, but the seas may be rough."

"They are not returning," Nimiane said quietly. "I had hoped to possess the boy at the first."

Carnassus shifted on his short legs, and his staff tapped the stone. Darius could hear its anger beneath him. "They may yet return," Carnassus said.

Nimiane opened her blind eyes, pulled in a deep breath, and lifted her face toward the roof. "Old man," she said. "Your son is dead. He was strong. I felt his life pass, and I gathered its strength into the stones beneath your feet."

Carnassus didn't move. When he spoke, it was only a whisper.

"What of the son of Mordecai?"

"He lives. But fear the wolf before the pup. You told me Mordecai was dead."

Carnassus pulled his beard and swallowed. "So the faeren claimed. He did not return, so I did not doubt them."

Gathering up her cat, Nimiane stood. "His spark is hidden but not yet gone. Wherever he may be, his dying day will find him. Though we may extinguish the seed before the sire. Prepare the mountain ways. The first blow must fall."

Henrietta lay flat on her back, her limbs splayed. Tall, dry grass swayed around her. There was not a single corner of her body that wasn't clamoring for relief, hoping for healing attention. She had spent nearly an entire day on the back of a horse, and what part of the day she hadn't spent riding had been spent hiking, and she hadn't really slept the night before, and she hadn't eaten anything that counted as actual food since the eggs by the river.

A single rock or clod or bulge of turf was digging into her back, where she thought her kidney used to be. And she didn't care. Wherever it was, her kidney had worse things to worry about, she was sure, and moving the clod would require moving herself first.

She could hear the horses stomping and men laughing as they unstrapped bags and saddles. Someone was singing. How anyone could sing after being shaken and bounced and jostled all day was beyond her. She'd been to a rodeo once, and now she was pretty sure she knew what the bronco riders felt like afterward. And they only had to last eight seconds. She must have lasted eight hours, and it didn't matter that the horse had walked most of the time. It had always been moving.

Something shrieked in her ear, and she jerked despite herself.

Perched on an old log beside her was one of Caleb's birds. It was big, and its head was cocked, eyeing her. As tired and ready for death as she was, she didn't like sprawling beneath the bird. Its black, hooked beak looked needle-sharp, and its golden eye seemed hungry, especially glowing out of the black band around its snow-feathered head.

Groaning, Henrietta sat up and scooted slowly away. "Wait till I'm dead," she muttered. "Then eat whatever you want."

Thinking about the rodeo made her think about Kansas and her sisters and her parents. She wondered how many lasts she would have savored back in Kansas if only she had known—the last ride in her father's truck, the last time her mother handed her a bath towel hot out of the dryer after a shower, the last time she had smelled the ripening Kansas grain, her last barbeque, fireworks, baseball game, movie, or flushing toilet. A world of horse transportation wasn't likely to have plumbing.

Henrietta took a deep breath and blew it out slowly. How often had her father been hunting his memory for lasts when it had seemed like his eyes could do nothing but focus on the horizon? She bit her lip and tucked her hair behind her ears. She had to stop it. No wallowing. She had to live now. Right now. Right where she was.

First making sure that the big bird hadn't moved toward her, she looked around the patchy meadow for Caleb. He wasn't hard to spot.

The big man walked toward her with his saddle over one arm and his black bow in the other. The black dog, pony-size but exuberant as a puppy, bounded around him. Caleb smiled at her and then turned and chirped through his teeth at the bird. It flared its wings wide, wider than Henrietta was tall, and danced in place, spitting its sharp call.

The dog dropped to its belly in the grass, lolling a tongue the size of Henrietta's foot. Caleb set the saddle and bow on the ground and lowered himself onto the log beside the bird. He stroked its belly with the back of his still-gloved hand. It tucked its wings away and bobbed in place.

"What kind of bird is it?" Henrietta asked. "Some sort of eagle?"

Caleb clicked his tongue and glanced at Henrietta. "We call it a Black Sprey," he said. "It has other names. It's smaller than an eagle. Bigger than a falcon. Smarter, too."

Henrietta stared at the flecking on its wings and its white legs and claws. "How many do you have?"

Caleb laughed. "I have as many as I meet. They know me, and they will obey, but I do not have any in cages. They have their own nests and mates and young to tend. There are five with us now."

"Where are the other ones?" Henrietta asked.

Caleb held out his hand, and the bird stepped onto it. He chirrupped with his tongue and teeth and then tossed it into the air. Henrietta felt the wind pushed down beneath its broad wings, and she couldn't help but duck. The bird climbed slowly and then coasted over treetops and out of sight.

"They are feeding," Caleb said. "They only eat fish, and here they must fly far for those. That bird was the first with a catch, the first fed, and now he will be the first to sleep. The others will find him with his head beneath his wing."

Caleb stretched his legs out in front of him and studied Henrietta. "You have flown far as well. How are your bones?"

"They hurt," Henrietta said. "For a while, I was hoping you'd just let me fall off the horse and leave me behind."

Caleb smiled, but only halfway. His eyes were focused on her, and they had their own thoughts. Henrietta shifted where she sat, nervous.

"It will be harder tomorrow," he said quietly. "When the world turns itself back out of shadow and into morning, the horses will have already been watered and kitted. Then we will ride long, deeper into the hills, and there we will find a dark doorway waiting for us, one that I pray will remain passable for another day. On the other side, more miles and more hills await."

"What if the door is shut?" Henrietta asked.

"Then we will be lost in the rough foothills more than five hundred miles from where we would like to be."

Henrietta's eyes widened. "We have to ride five hundred miles?"

"Not if the door is safe enough for life. No more than five remain beyond it." Caleb stretched his arms above his head. "I would ride on through the night if the horses were not so worn. But we will be riding again soon enough."

Watching him, Henrietta couldn't help but yawn. "Do you have any food?" she asked. "I really am hungry."

Caleb stood up quickly and whistled. A circle of men stopped their laughter, and all turned in unison.

"A bowl, when it's hot?" he asked. One of the men nodded, and they returned to their laughing. Caleb sat down. "They are stewing something, whatever herbs and roots they can find to soften salted meat." He pulled in a slow breath and sighed. "Now, I would hear your story."

Henrietta ground the heels of her hands into her eyes and leaned forward, stretching. Where did her story begin? With her grandfather doing whatever it was he had done to collect the cupboards? With the arrival of Henry? With the arrival of her father when he was young? Should she tell him about the witch, about shoving her through one of the cupboards and most likely starting this whole mess?

She took a deep breath, straightened up, and told the truth.

"I don't know where to start."

Caleb picked up his black bow and smiled. "You need not begin at the world's formation." He tucked a horn tip into the arch of his foot, bent the bow an inch, and slipped the string off the top. The bow straightened when he released, but not as much as Henrietta had expected. The black horns still swooped gently back, bending forward again at the tapered ends.

"Does everyone use horn bows here?" Henrietta asked. "My dad got me a bow at a yard sale once, but it was yellow fiberglass."

"I don't know fiberglass, but here we use mostly ash

or yew. My father brought this to me from the southern side of the ocean. I could not string it until I was nine, and could draw it no more than two fingers for three years after, though I tried every day."

Caleb wound the string around the shaft while Henrietta watched, and then leaned the bow on the log beside him. "But you were going to tell me the story of your arrival in FitzFaeren. Have you found a beginning?"

Henrietta brought a thumbnail to her teeth. She didn't think she could lie to Caleb. He'd known she was lying about her name right away. Not that it mattered. She didn't really want to lie. One part of her wanted him to know everything that had happened. She wanted someone to, especially someone who could help her. But another part was nervous about telling him anything. And she didn't exactly like how the story made her look. Grandfather's key had been on her mind all day, digging into her leg from its station in her pocket.

So she drew a deep breath, sighed, and told him what she remembered about her grandfather, and about the arrival of her cousin and the rediscovery of the cupboards. She moved fast, and even while she did, she was surprised at how much Caleb was unlike her. If someone had told her the same story in the same way, she would have been interrupting, badgering and begging for details, demanding explanations, and pointing out inconsistencies. But Caleb sat and watched her face. At most, he ran a hard hand over his rough jaw, but he never looked away from her eyes.

Henrietta was the one who looked away. She found herself telling the grass and the dusk and the trees about overhearing her cousin and Richard and then waking up and thinking they had gone through the cupboards.

And that is where she stopped.

A man, thicker than Caleb but not as tall, walked up to her with a wooden bowl full of stew.

"Thank you," she said quietly, and she meant it. She was grateful, and not just because she was hungry. With the warm bowl in her hands, she didn't have to look in Caleb's eyes. While the story she had told had all been true, her own rashness had been avoided. And when avoidance had not been possible, she had felt blood rise to her face.

She stared into the brown mixture in front of her and looked at her hands.

"I don't have a spoon," she said.

Caleb pulled a small knife out of his belt and handed it to her, gripping the blade.

"What that won't get, you can drink."

The man returned with another bowl for him, and Caleb slipped down into the grass beside his hound, propping his back against the log.

"So you followed your cousin," he said. "Where is he?"

"Not here, I don't think." Henrietta sipped at the bowl, but the broth singed the tip of her tongue. "Magdalene would have grabbed them, too."

"How did you escape the queen?"

"I jumped out her window."

Caleb was ignoring his own bowl, still watching Henrietta's face. Finally, he looked up and away, focusing on something unseen. Her father did the same thing.

"Why did you not return through your small gateway? The halls of FitzFaeren have strange hauntings, but you could have braved it."

"I tried," Henrietta said. "But I got lost. It was night, and I got all twisted up in the hills."

"And you met Eli?"

"I found him, he fed me, and I followed him till you grabbed me."

Henrietta watched Caleb think. Then he drained his bowl, set it beside him, and whistled.

The men turned.

"Where is the little Fitz?" he said. "Bring him over here."

"Sacked?" one of them asked.

Caleb nodded.

Henrietta couldn't help herself. "You still have him in a bag? Why would you do that? He'll suffocate."

Caleb looked at her, but said nothing. Then he stood slowly and crossed his arms.

Two men were walking toward them, from beyond where the horses had been staked. Between them hammocked a lumpy brown sack, bulging and twisting while they walked. The men dropped the sack at Caleb's feet, and they both stepped back.

"You may sit and listen," Caleb said, and Henrietta

knew he was talking to her. "But do not speak or ask questions."

Henrietta felt her ears get hot with embarrassment, but before it could turn into irritation, Caleb had addressed the sack.

"Eli, onetime duke of FitzFaeren, onetime keeper of the libraries of Hylfing, onetime traitor, and onetime friend, would you speak with me?"

Henrietta bit her lip. She had a lot of questions. The sack held perfectly still.

"Respond," Caleb said.

The sack jerked, and Henrietta recognized Eli's muffled voice. "I'm not a potato. I'll talk in the air."

"Use no forces or spells or incantations, and you may be freed," said Caleb. He continued, and his voice hardened. "But be warned. Encroach, attempt to necromance, and you will be resacked. And that only if your heart drums on."

"Fine," Eli said. "Get me out of this filth."

Caleb nodded, and the men stepped forward and began unlacing a seam that ran the length of the sack.

"Why can't he do spells inside the bag?" Henrietta asked.

Caleb turned, looked her in the eyes, and she remembered what he had said. He wasn't angry, but she wished she hadn't asked.

"It is woven from the fiber of sea kelp. Some use spiders' webs. They are stronger, but much too hard to get

in quantity. Both stifle manipulation and tangle any created threads within."

He looked back to where Eli had rolled into the grass
and was climbing to his knees and his feet. His bald head
glowed with heat. Straggling hair plastered over his ears
and onto his cheeks. His glasses were missing, and dust,
turned to silt by his sweat, coated his clothes and spotted
his skin. He looked like an extremely angry chimney
sweep. At least Henrietta thought he did. She had never
seen one.

He puffed his cheeks, muttering to himself, and
Henrietta waited for him to insult Caleb. Instead, he
fished his glasses out of a pocket and tried to bend the
wire frames to straight. Giving up, he put them on. One
of the gold arms stuck out above his ear.

Caleb waited silently. When Eli finally blinked behind cloudy lenses, he spoke again.

"Eli, what rite were you performing when my men
took you?"

Eli squinted and licked his lips. For a brief moment,
he looked like his sister. "I would think it was obvious,"
he said. "I was light-bending. I was invisible, but your
sea-crows revealed me."

Caleb shifted, taking one step closer to the much
smaller man. Then he looked up at the dusking blue in
the sky. Henrietta looked up as well. One early-bright
planet hung above the trees.

"For one such as you," Caleb said, "light-bending re-
quires no rites." He looked down and smiled. "Taste

truth, Eli. You may remember its flavor. It might carry an edge or a bite, but it will never betray you. What rite were you performing?"

"I was summoning strength," Eli said.

"Sour," said Caleb. "Truth is sweeter."

Eli sniffed loudly and rubbed his slick scalp. "If you know, then speak it yourself."

Caleb's look was cold and unblinking. His voice was colder. "My men described what symbols they found— the rite of skulls."

Eli sneered. "You trained yourself in dark power? Your father would be so pleased." He squared his small shoulders. "It was the rite of skulls, indeed. But it would have had no effect. It was begun out of fear. I have no memory of its ending, and I would not have completed it if I did."

"I have seen it completed," Caleb said quietly. "Once. It cannot be forgotten. Why would you begin such a thing?"

"I told you," Eli said. "I was afraid. Do you think I have forgotten who follows when those hawks are flying? I only thought of my own life and the hatred you have always had for it."

"You would turn to Endorian leeching to preserve your life? If you knew I was following, then you had to know I would strike you down for such evil."

Henrietta looked from Eli's face to Caleb's. Eli really did look afraid. Caleb's face was lost in thought. He continued.

"My family has shown you much mercy, Eli. There are many things I could think to blame you for."

A breeze crawled down from the sky, rattling the grass. The two men behind Eli watched him. The men around the campfire were watching as well. Even the dog at Caleb's feet lay still. One horse stamped.

"There are things for which I am to blame." Eli's voice was flat and lifeless. He looked into Caleb's eyes, and neither man looked away. Henrietta fidgeted in the awkwardness. She opened her mouth and then shut it again. After a long moment, Caleb spoke again.

"Eli, the girl escaped your sister, the queen."

Eli nodded.

"And she wandered lost, searching for the ruined hall and the door to her own world."

Eli swallowed, blinking.

"Why did she not find it?" Caleb asked. "Speak truly."

"Because," Eli said, and he glanced at Henrietta. He paused. Henrietta could just see past the lenses in his glasses. The light was fading fast now, and the shadows on his face had deepened, were deepening more. "Because I felt her mind and spun it in circles."

Henrietta scrambled to her feet. "You made me get lost? Why would you do that? You said the doorway had closed behind me. Was that even true?"

Eli shrugged. "Probably."

Henrietta felt tears well up. Anger squeezed them out. She stepped toward Eli.

"Henrietta," Caleb said. His voice was annoyingly calm. "Sit and find silence."

The emotion in Henrietta's veins was not that easy to tame. "You're evil," she said to the little man. "Why would you do that? Why would you take me away from everything, from my family, my parents, my whole life? What was the point?"

A hand closed around Henrietta's arm. It wasn't tight, but she knew it would be if she tried to shrug it off. Her body was turned, and, blinking, she looked up into Caleb's shadowed face. The whites of his eyes stood out bright beneath his brows. He didn't look her in the eyes, he looked around inside them.

He nodded at the log. "Sit," he said. "Your questions will be answered."

Henrietta could not imagine herself obeying. She needed to run and yell, she needed to kick Eli, or something, hard. But for some reason, she found herself calming. She wiped her eyes with the backs of her hands and moved slowly toward the log.

"I am sorry," Eli said. "At least in a way. And her question is not a hard one to answer. I am a man without a people, a tree with wheels and no roots. You feel the blood draining from the land, you feel the crackling in the grass as the lightning builds. FitzFaeren offers me no protection. And I am unwelcome in Hylfing. Both are thanks to her grandfather. But she brings Hylfing into my debt, perhaps even the gifting of a boat or a berth off of these shores. She could earn me the gratitude of a city that banned me from within its walls."

"How is that?" Caleb asked.

"Caleb," Eli said, and smiled. "Are your eyes as weak as that? You owe me thanks. I was traveling to return your kin, daughter to your brother."

Henrietta reeled, nearly slipping off the log. Caleb stood perfectly still.

"Francis," he said.

Eli nodded.

CHAPTER EIGHTEEN

Henry looked around himself. He was wearing his backpack and kneeling in the low mouth of something half-cave, half-burrow. The young wizard was beside him, and the fat faerie stood in front. Henry could look out, down a hill, above a copse of trees, at a rocky beach and the ocean beyond. They'd run the boat aground. Now, it leaned to one side with its hull supported by round stones. Its sails were still flapping. They hadn't bothered to take them down.

When he looked in, over the shoulder of the fat faerie, he still wasn't sure if he should believe what he saw.

The clay ceiling was domed about six feet above the ground, and it was crawling with mud sculptures of faces, most of them contorted into rude expressions. Crude tongues were sticking out, cheeks were puffed, eyes were crossed. One wall was covered as well. The other was littered with papers pinned to its surface with twigs. In the center of the small room, on the fairly flat floor, there was a barrel supporting a tabletop. Around it sat four small men holding cards and squat wineglasses full of something brown. Beyond them, a door frame of sticks had been pressed into the mud of the end-wall. It led nowhere, but the earth was smooth inside it, the only place unmarred by the bizarre sculptures.

All of the little men had wild, thick hair bushing out from their heads. On three of them, the hair was black, as black as their eyes. One wore a beard, another a thick mustache connected to sideburns, and the last wore sideburns that reached all the way down to a bare, pointed chin. The fourth man, the man closest to the door, had red hair, wilder and brighter than any Henry had ever seen. He had more freckles than he had face.

"Are you daft, Frank?" the red-haired faerie asked. "You know what the bylaws say."

"Frank?" Henry asked. "That's my uncle's name."

Frank the fat faerie looked back over his shoulder at Henry. "He must be very proud." Then he turned back. "This is the faerie hall for this district. Access is part of our union privileges, though the committee make us pay for some of the drink."

The red-haired faerie stood up, dropping his cards on the table. His freckles were darkening. "They oughtn't be here, Franklin Fat-Faerie. The committee will have your ears."

"Transfer!" one of the other faeries yelled. "Frank'll be off to the walrus farms!"

They all burst into laughter, and the laughter turned into a muddled chorus of "walrus farms."

Frank crossed his arms above his belly and spread his legs.

"Oh, you're merry lads, aren't you? I know the by-laws, and I've paid my union dues, which is more than I can say for some of you musical lumps. As sub-assistant-treasurer in this archipelago, there are conversations I've been meaning to have. We could have those now, young Loam." Frank paused and stared at the dark-haired side-burned faerie. "Or we could put it off a bit. Would you like to hear why I brung him?"

"It doesn't matter," the red-headed faerie said. "I've never seen an allowance."

Frank snorted, eyeing the taller faerie. "Young Roland, I'll have you remember to which body you're speaking. Five years I've been on Badon Hill while you been scurrying after goats on this little bit of nothing. If I bring man-blood into a hall, you know there's been an importance. And if your mind can't hold your tongue, try using your teeth."

Henry watched Roland's face contort, change color, and then settle back into its original flame. He stepped back, sat on his bench, picked up a glass, and drained it.

The room was quiet, so Frank continued. "I brung him because I am aware that a faerie's purpose is larger than souring the goat milk of fat, already-soured wizards. This boy's name is Henry, and the other is Monmouth, and when they looks, they sees, if you know what I mean." Frank stepped back and put his small, thick hand on Henry's shoulder. The room was still quiet. "Do I need to explain it? Have you forgotten the seasons as well?" The fat faerie sighed and slowed down. "What we're talking about is a couple of seventh sons with both ways of seeing."

Roland's brows dropped, crowding down over his eyes. He stared from Henry to Monmouth and back again. One of the other faeries knocked over his glass.

"A pauper son," Frank continued. "And more. We were set up on Badon Hill waiting for him. He'd been expected and prohibited from walking on that island, as are all men without the birth. But he has the birth. We were never told he was a seventh. Then the five of us were ambushed by mancers from Carnassus. We were sacked, and the other four are forever sleeping at the bottom of the sea."

Roland's mouth hung open. "The wizards stepped on Badon Hill?"

Frank nodded.

"But that's direct encroachment. And they killed faeren?"

Frank nodded again.

"I don't believe that," one of the other faeries said. "How do we know you speak true, Fat-Faerie?"

"I'm not finished," Frank said. "I've got one more thing to say before you call me liar. Would the wizards risk Badon Hill for a boy with little strength and nearly blind eyes, for I must say, so he seems to me? Would they risk darkness for that? This boy is a certain man's son, though he hasn't nearly the mettle. You don't need to have been in this district long to remember the name. Have you heard stories of a green man called Mordecai?"

Frank stopped. The faeries sat in near perfect silence.

"Is it true?" Roland finally asked, looking at Henry.

Henry swallowed. He didn't know. Not really.

"It is," Monmouth said, looking around the room. "And the wizards were collecting him for another."

The faeries ignored him.

"But Mordecai had only six before he was lost," the sideburned faerie said.

"All the same, Loam, this is his son, and he is not one of the six that I knew." Henry was tired of being spoken about, and he was just as curious as the faeries.

"How do you know?" he blurted out. "I mean, are you using magic?"

Roland walked over to where Henry was kneeling. They were nearly eye to eye. His freckled hands closed on Henry's cheeks, prying his face back. Suddenly, Roland winced and dropped one hand away from his jaw. He poked at the old burn scars on Henry's face.

"He's a budding green man, right enough, but what is this? Why would Mordecai's son have death-pox?"

Henry tried to turn his head, to pull his other cheek from Roland's hand. Roland gripped tighter.

"They're burns," Henry managed to say. "From witch's blood. I was fighting her. She got away."

The faeries all laughed. Even Frank smiled.

"Which witch would that be?" Roland grinned.

"She was called Nimiane," Henry said.

Once more, the room fell silent. Roland let go of Henry's face.

"That's not a pleasant jest," Frank said quietly.

"I'm not joking," Henry said.

"Nimiane," said Monmouth, "is the one who sent us to get him."

"Us?" Roland said. "You are in service to darkness?" He turned to Frank. "He is a wizard and an underling to the undying witch?"

"He freed us," Frank said. "And helped destroy the other wizards. Even Carnassus's own son. And he is a seventh."

"I think I should tell you everything," Monmouth said, turning from faerie to faerie, trying to catch their eyes with his. "There really isn't time for more doubt."

"The bylaws prohibit you from speaking here," Roland said. He turned and walked toward the wall littered with papers. Running his hands over them, he read aloud.

"Hand washing, beer rations, hall-expansion guidelines, sanitation proclamation . . . here's one of the first. The committee sent out a couple variations. 'Henry York, aka Whimpering Child, aka WC (hair sample included), is hereby identified as Enemy, Hazard, and Human Mishap to all faeren in all districts, in all ways, and in all worlds. If identified, all faeren are authorized and requested to hamper, hinder, detain, damage, or destroy.' "

Roland picked one strand of hair off the paper and turned around. "Why would old Radulf send that out if he's Mordecai's son?"

"Because," Frank Fat-Faerie said, "old Radulf hated serving Mordecai and was glad to see him go."

"That's a bit treasonous," Roland said. He walked back to Henry, plucked one hair from his head, and tasted it. Then he tasted his sample and nodded.

"What's treasonous," Frank said, "is any mistreatment of Mordecai's blood, when he was our bonded green man, that's what's treasonous."

Henry's knees were hurting. He wanted to lie down. Or stand up. Anything other than what he was doing.

Monmouth coughed loudly and waddled forward on his knees. His pale face was flushed in irritation. "I'm talking now," he said. "I don't care about your bylaws or old Radulf, whoever he is."

The dark-haired faeries all stood slowly.

"Take it back," Roland said.

"Oh, let the boy talk," said Frank. "What can he hurt?"

Roland curled his lip and ran one hand through his hair. "Who are you, then, little wizard?"

"My name is Monmouth—"

"What's that mean?" Roland interrupted. "Mountain mouth?"

"Something like that," Monmouth said. "My father thought I was magical after I received the second sight. He apprenticed me to the wizards four years ago. He didn't realize how much they hate seventh sons. I had to keep it hidden."

"Why?" Henry asked suddenly. "The hate, I mean."

Frank swiped a glass off the table. "Because," he said, "the sevenths have a right to be touching what they touch. They don't need all the rigmarole of the wizards. The sevenths, especially the green men, are like man-faeries."

"Green men?" Henry asked.

Monmouth looked at him. "Seventh sons that are connected to growing things. Green things. Like your dandelion." He raised his right hand, and Henry stared at the wizard's branded palm. "My aspen tree."

Henry closed his hand tight over his own burn. Monmouth had looked at it, he'd recognized it.

"Not long ago," Monmouth continued, "a woman appeared in Carnassus's throne room. She was weak, and some advised Carnassus to crush her quickly. But he did not, and she grew stronger daily. Now, were all the wizards to turn against her at once, they would have no hope. She leeches life to herself from everything capable of dying, from the world itself. She is a parasite."

Frank looked at the other faeries and raised his eyebrows. One of them nodded. Roland spoke.

"We have heard of this farther south. But we have not felt it."

"I do not know where on the map we are," Monmouth said. "We traveled through a doorway prepared for us and then sailed to Badon Hill."

Frank shifted his belt farther below his belly. "In a straight line, with only your legs or a sail to carry you, two weeks would pass before you found Carnassus in his perch. We are in the far north."

"It doesn't matter," Monmouth said, shifting his weight. He looked at his palm and then ran it through his hair. "Every place will feel it in turn. She will drink what she can and pour out the rest. Only two, maybe three days ago, a new wizard arrived, stronger than any I have ever seen. Stronger than Carnassus himself. He is called Darius, and he has been filled by the witch. Now, even now, or very soon, he is to be sent out with lesser wizards behind him. The witch was once defeated by Mordecai, and out of hatred for his memory, they will begin with Hylfing, in the far south. After, they will turn to the empire. She will find a new seat and create a new Endor. Whether out of spite or fear, I can't say, but we were sent to collect the boy called Henry, the son of Mordecai. She told us all that his blood was meant to be the first spilled, that it would serve as a christening for her second coming."

Henry opened his mouth in surprise. Hylfing was in this world. He had to find his way to Hylfing, but he would be running toward the witch. It might be destroyed before he got there, along with his family. It might be destroyed right after he got there.

"They cannot reach Hylfing quickly," Roland said. "They can be stopped."

Frank puffed out his cheeks and crossed his arms. "They have opened the old ways, you nit. They reached Badon Hill quickly."

Roland scowled at Frank and then turned to Monmouth. "Why are we to trust you? You helped to capture the boy beside you and assisted in the deaths of our brother-faeren."

"If Mordecai once overthrew Nimiane, then I wanted to find his son and help him," Monmouth said. "Help him do it again."

Henry's mouth went dry. His throat tightened. Monmouth's gray eyes were staring right through him. "I can't do that," Henry said. "I just need to get to Hylfing and meet my family. That's where they were going. I need to get them out of there."

The fat faerie raised his eyebrows and looked around at the other four faeries.

"And so we came here," Frank said. "To the closest hall of faeren. He's nothing next to Mordecai, but he's his son, and the witch and wizards are after him. We owe him some abetment."

"That's for the committee to decide," Roland said quietly. "Mordecai abandoned us, and a notice has been issued on him." He nodded at Henry. "We can't just ignore that, even if we are on some forsaken outpost. The notice must be officially waived in committee after appropriate appeal. Or other action will be taken. The committee will decide. We'll send him back to the Central Hall. Radulf can hear you."

"Radulf," Frank said loudly, "is a one-toed sloth. The union code is clear on pauper sons and green men. The pauper sons formed the union in the first place. Ralph Radulf will drag things out, table motions, move to recess, and then just bury him alive in some hill somewhere for further deliberation!" The fat faerie's voice rose even further. He stood on his toes. "Endor wakes, Roland! Nimiane, daughter of Nimroth and every other ancient life-sucking death-demon, is looking for him, Roland! She sends her wizards to Hylfing now, Roland! Let's do more than call the committee!"

The fat faerie dropped back to his heels, sputtered his lips, and waved his hands above his head. Finally, he stuck out his tongue and was quiet.

Roland chewed his lower lip and then rubbed his freckled nose. "You may be right, Franklin, but I'm the one who'll have my hair sheared for a mistake. That one," he pointed at Monmouth, "is free to go, so long as he doesn't return to the wizards. But the WC is off to Central. You and I will escort. Loam here will act in my absence."

"You mean drink and play cards in your absence," Frank muttered. Loam smiled. "Well," he continued, "if we must, we must. Fix the door, then."

"I'm coming as well," Monmouth said. He looked at Henry. Roland shrugged.

*　*　*

Henry hadn't seen the buckets behind the table. He didn't know how many more there were, but Roland pulled out two. They were battered and rusty, and he set both of them on the table. One was full of black dirt, the other of water.

Singing quietly under his breath, Roland cupped his hands in the water, turned to the stick door frame, and dribbled it down over the lintel. Filling his hands again, he rubbed the water first on one post and then the other. When that was done, he filled his hands with black earth from the second bucket and nodded at Frank.

"Turn them around," he said.

Frank couldn't turn them around, not kneeling side by side in the doorway. So he pulled them both into the room and had them stand.

Henry creaked gratefully to his feet. His toes throbbed as blood rushed back into them. Inside, they both turned their backs to Roland and examined the mud sculptures around the entrance. Just above it, Henry recognized the man from the seals on his letters and from the tomb on Badon Hill. This time, his beard and eyes and crawling vines were all crudely formed with mud. It was still unnerving.

"Right," Roland said. "Lead them backward. Loam, scrape the door clean when we've gone."

Someone pulled Henry's backpack. Another hand gripped his arm. He was led around one side of the table, Monmouth around the other.

Monmouth was held back. Henry was being taken first.

Henry watched Loam holding Monmouth tight, making certain that he did not turn his head.

He stepped backward into the smell of roots and compost. Utter blackness surrounded him, carried by a warm underground wind. His mind slipped away, back to Kansas, behind the barn. He was watching the storm roll in, watching dandelions sprout up around him, watching their fire and listening to the stories in their names. He was on Badon Hill, smelling trees and moss and sharp sea air. He was falling off a building in Byzanthamum.

Henry opened his eyes. Light flicked from somewhere behind him. He blinked, but could see nothing. Darius was in this world, going where he was trying to go. He put his hand to his stomach. He could feel the sealed-up lines even through his shirt. He did not want to see Darius again.

"Roland?" a voice asked. "Fat Franklin? What are you doing? Who are they?"

"They are pauper sons, both green," Frank said. "We've brought them because they need our help."

Roland cleared his throat. "The Central Committee needs to assemble. I didn't know what to do with them."

A hard, acidic voice rattled in Henry's ears. "Who are you, Roland, to summon the committee?"

And another. "Since when do provincials summon anything?"

"Misters Braithwait and Radulf, sirs," Roland said quickly. "I apologize. But there was a notice—"

"Since," Frank's voice rang out loudly, "the before-unknown seventh son of Mordecai arrives, pushed before a storm of darkness. Nimiane of Endor, once entombed, sits in Carnassus's seat."

"Yes," the first voice said, "we have been informed. But she seeks no quarrel with us. This boy, the small one, a notice has been issued, has it not? Is he not the Whimpering Child who disturbed and unearthed and dusted off this old evil before releasing it? Hold him in a lower borough. Hold them both. We will deal with them in time. The committee is slated to meet at week's end."

Hands grabbed Henry from all sides. He tried to struggle, but strange speech slid into his ears, and his legs went limp. He fell, but did not reach the ground. Small shoulders were propped beneath his arms. He was being carried. Half of him at least. His knees dragged on the ground behind him.

"Week's end!" he heard Frank yell. "Do you hear that, Roland? Good we have taken action! The elder faeren will sit in committee by week's end. The relief is overpowering. I wonder the witch-queen hasn't surrendered herself already! I hope we have room for her on the agenda!"

The voice died as Henry was dragged gradually down through the tunnels. His eyes were foggy and unfocused. No matter how much he blinked, he could see nothing more than the occasional smudge of light around him.

He heard a door open, and he was thrown inside.

Shortly after, a body landed on top of him, and the door slammed.

"Monmouth?" Henry asked.

The body grunted.

Henrietta, though tired beyond her experience, had not fallen asleep easily. The lumpiness of the ground and coarseness of her cloak-blanket would not have bothered her. The lumpiness in her mind was the problem. Caleb had refused to answer any of her questions. He had merely smiled at her and promised to answer her in the saddle tomorrow.

But she hadn't been able to stop asking herself the questions tonight. Even when she did fall asleep, she didn't think she had. Her dreaming mind asked as many questions as her mind awake. The only difference was that it imagined answers.

Caleb was her uncle. This was her father's world. She was traveling to meet a grandmother that she had never heard anything about. Caleb had only said that she was happy, but not well.

Did she have cousins? How many? What were they like? Would she hate them? Would they hate her? Would she ever see Kansas again? Could she learn to keep hawks? What had her grandfather done to FitzFaeren? Was Eli really evil?

And there was the witch. Would her new world even survive? Had she helped destroy it before she'd ever seen it?

She was sitting on a tall horse, not as heavy as Caleb's, cloaked in gray, holding a horn bow, smiling down at Henry and Anastasia and Penelope and Richard. And Zeke. Then she woke with a jerk.

Caleb was lifting her body. He laid her on the log. She teetered and sat up.

"Stay there," he said, and he turned and ran.

The sky was gray, dully anticipating the dawn, and men were yelling. Horses neighed and stamped.

Not far from her, a dappled mare lay on its side, dead. Its eyes were rolled back in its head and a clot of dried blood hung from one nostril.

"Caleb?" she yelled. "What's happening?"

Then she noticed the tall grass all around her. It had curled. Even in the dim light, she could see that leaves on the trees were mottled and dry.

She stood up, holding the cloak tightly around her shoulders. Hooves pounded, and Caleb came roaring toward her, running beside his great chestnut. As he approached, he kicked off the ground and swung onto the horse's back. He had no saddle, it was on the ground near Henrietta's feet, and no bridle to speak of. On the horse's hooves came the black dog. The horse stamped and puffed beside her, and Caleb reached down, gripped her forearm, and pulled her awkwardly up in front of him.

"Leave the tack!" Caleb yelled. "Weapons only!"

Other horses and riders were already galloping away, down the gentle slope toward a break in the trees. Caleb clicked his tongue, the chestnut crouched its rear legs and sprang forward. Henrietta had thought it was going to rear and shake them off, but instead, they were pounding down the hill, Caleb's hand pressing her head down as they tore through branches and then leapt a stream.

The birds were screaming in the air, and the enormous black dog passed them and rushed ahead, leaping logs before they did.

There was no talking above the drumming of the heavy horse hooves and the snapping of its hocks ripping through grass and brush. Caleb held her tight with one arm as the horse puffed like a train between her legs. Other riders were stopped ahead. The dog rushed into them and then backed out, nosing in circles through the grass. It pawed a dead quail, then nosed another small animal, a rabbit or gopher of some sort.

Caleb somehow brought his horse up. Turning sideways and pawing at the ground, it stopped as two more riders joined the group. Behind one of them was tied a body wrapped in blankets. The other led a horse on a lead. On it were two more bodies.

When the horsemen had all gathered, Caleb spoke.

"We will eat as we go. Forgive me, all of you. We should have pressed on through the night, but I did not fully understand the danger. It would have been better for the horses to collapse beneath us than to lose those three." He nodded at the bodies. "Pray for them as we ride. I hate to think of their strength poured into the enemy." The chestnut turned, stamping. "We push hard, but if the mounts die, they must do so beyond the doorway."

The men nodded and turned their own horses. Some were saddled, some were bare. The horses' eyes were all wide, and their nostrils flared broader than Henrietta's fist. The men's faces were as hard as stone.

Caleb clicked his tongue again, and the horse gathered itself and galloped toward a break in the trees, this time not as quickly. A black shape crept into Henrietta's vision, and she looked down to see the dog running beside them.

"How did they die?" she asked. She had to yell to be heard, and her throat was tight.

They leapt a log and a smaller stream, and Henrietta's face bounced off the horse's neck. She would have fallen had Caleb held less tightly.

His voice was calm. "They and the horse drank from the stream. Two of the birds fell as well."

This did not clear things up for Henrietta. All the horses had drunk from the stream the night before. She'd been given water from it as well. "How is this happening?"

"Sorcery," Caleb said. "The wizards' new mistress has begun in earnest, and we are caught too far north. If the horses are slow, some of us may die before the sun sets."

"Are they behind us?"

"Not yet. But soon. Tomorrow, maybe, or in a few hours. And it is not likely that they will be behind us.

They will be in front of us, in the hills around my city." She heard Caleb blow out a long breath. "She is much stronger than I had hoped. Her draught flows through the ground and through watercourses. The weakest things have already given up the struggle and faded. The stronger leave, or they will die as well. We will not touch any water until the world grows green again."

Henrietta remembered the night before. "Is Eli coming with us?"

"He made his decision. He cloaked himself and fled in the night on a stolen horse, ever afraid that death may overtake him. That is still a terrible thing in his mind."

"Aren't you afraid of dying?" Henrietta asked. She knew she was.

"I have ridden with death, and walked beside it. Some say I have sought it. The search would not have been difficult, but I look for the death of my enemies first. That is much harder to find."

After a moment, Caleb continued. "When I am called, I will go. But that call has not yet come."

CHAPTER NINETEEN

The room was dark with a smudge of light near the top. Henry still couldn't see. The darkness was crawling with movement and wiry shapes, but nothing clear.

He held up his hand, looking for the golden burn on his palm. It was there, bright and crawling, sharper and cleaner and faster the longer he looked at it. It made his head hurt again, throbbing behind his eyes and at the base of his skull. But now when he looked up, he could see.

The walls were solid, earthen in parts, planked with carved wood in others. If he left his eyes anywhere for long, all of it began swimming into strands, woven in place, shaped by strange words he could not speak, though he knew they could be spoken.

"There's so much magic," he said slowly. "Everything. All of it is magic."

Monmouth groaned on the floor. He had a lump on his forehead, just below his dark hairline. Streaks of dirt stood out on his pale face. He put his right hand to his head, and Henry watched the burn on his palm. It was green, with flicking, twisting silver.

"You're in a faerie mound," Monmouth said. "Everything in the world has its hidden glory, its magic. Here it'll be doubled and trebled. They can make things real on many levels."

Henry blinked, wondering how long he could keep seeing without his head exploding. The door was made of tightly bound reeds. The ceiling was green clay, and a single lamp hung from its center without a chain. He could see the twisting strands that held it up, but he knew they would disappear if he relaxed to his normal sight. The whole place would.

He shut his eyes to let his head recover. "What are we going to do?"

Monmouth's voice was tired, pained. "Apparently, we are waiting for a committee meeting."

"Does your head always hurt when you, you know, see?" Henry asked. He was grinding his knuckles against his eyebrows, and the pain was actually a relief.

"No," Monmouth said. "It did. Years ago. But you grow into it. Right now my head hurts because someone clubbed me when they dragged us off."

"Why?"

"Because I resisted. They tried to numb my legs. They had to use an older technique."

"What are we going to do?" Henry asked again.

"Henry," said Monmouth. "I'm going to sleep."

"Why?"

"Because my head won't hurt in a dream. Talk to me there."

"What?" Henry asked. But Monmouth didn't say anything else. "Monmouth?"

After a moment, the young wizard's relaxed breathing filled the darkness. Henry stood, shifted his eyes, and ignored the pain in his skull. He walked to the door and pushed on it. There was no handle or latch, so he couldn't pull.

His aching head quickly became impossible to ignore, and looking around made him dizzy. He could see the room in at least three different ways, dark and muddled, shaped and clean, and crawling with sculpted magic. None of them helped him, so he lay down on the floor and closed his eyes.

They were grateful.

"I waited," Monmouth said. "Your dream is strong. I couldn't keep my own when it came."

"What?" Henry asked. They were both sitting on the floor in the center of the room. The room was bright and clean. Nothing was writhing. The walls were earth and plank and no more. It was far more sensible than the reality.

"Your imagination is stronger than mine," Monmouth said. He smiled, and Henry could see that the lump was gone. As Henry thought of it, it appeared. Monmouth grimaced, and his hand shot up.

"Ow," he said. "Do you mind? I don't have to have it here."

"Sorry," Henry said. "I didn't mean to."

"Take it away, or I might as well be awake."

Henry tried. Nothing happened. He couldn't dream it away when his mind knew it was really there.

"I'm sorry," he said again. "I don't think I can."

Monmouth stood up. "Right. Well, at least it's not as bad here. I already tried to get out. The room is charmed to keep us in."

"But we're dreaming," Henry said. "How can they keep us in?"

Monmouth smiled. "You're more than just a body, Henry York."

"You mean our minds? That's where you dream, right?"

"Your mind is part of your body. This is different. You can shape dreams, but real ones come from outside of you. You learn to travel through them and to ride them, forcing them toward truth if you like, or into fantasy. I've never really been good at it, but there were dozens of old books and scrolls on dream-walking in Carnassus's library. I read most of them."

Henry looked around the room. Dreams had always been strange to him. Now that he'd been pulled out of one by Darius, and accurately dream-walked Badon Hill, he was prepared to believe anything Monmouth said.

He stepped over to the door and reached out his hand to feel the tight reeds. In Byzanthamum, Nella had said something about dreams. She'd told him to believe his. *How do you believe a dream?* he wondered. *It doesn't say anything.*

The reeds felt almost fused together. They probably were. He turned back to Monmouth. The wizard was massaging his head. The lump was smaller, but it grew when Henry looked at it. Then he looked at Monmouth. Really looked at him.

Monmouth looked back, first with anger and then with surprise. Something changed in him, shrouded what Henry was trying to see, but only for a moment. It didn't matter. Henry could still see. Monmouth looked like Nella had, a collection of strong green strands, living words all moving slowly, written on top of each other, tied together, growing together.

But in places there was darkness, stiffness, and stagnation—death, fighting with the rest.

Monmouth's eyes were narrowed. "What do you see?" he asked.

Henry blinked. "What do you?" His head wasn't hurting. He could do this in a dream.

"I see fear and confusion," Monmouth said. "And damage. There is some strength, but it's all unguided and without purpose, outside your control. And you have a sinkhole in your face. In your jaw. It's small, but it's stronger than the rest of you, and it's growing. What do you see?"

Henry swallowed, wishing he could pull clothes over everything. "I"—he paused—"I don't know."

"You're not quite as strong as I thought," Monmouth said. "I don't mean to be rude, it's just that I thought you must be incredible if the witch wanted you so badly."

Henry put his back to the door and slid down with his knees against his chest. "I know," he said.

"Did your father really defeat the witch?"

Henry shrugged. "Never met him." He closed his eyes and leaned his head back. "I'm going to sleep."

"You can't go to sleep. You're already dreaming. Why would you want to?"

"It won't have to hurt in a dream."

Henry dreamed that he fell asleep. And so he did.

This time, Monmouth wasn't there. For a moment, Henry could see a faint ghosting of his outline, but he blocked it out quickly. His own shape, equally faint at first, grew stronger until he was looking down at Henry York, sleeping with his knees hugged against his chest. As for himself, the self that was seeing, he was without any shape at all. He lifted what he knew were his arms, but saw nothing. And then, slowly, the head of a stemless dandelion bloomed in midair.

Henry turned, stepped over himself, and walked through the door.

One faerie stood outside, leaning on the jamb, yawning. His arms were crossed, and a stick with a knobbed root end was tucked under one arm.

Henry moved past him and wandered down the corridor. Lamps hung from the ceiling low enough that he ducked around them. Then he wondered if he had to at all. He felt like he had a head to move, but he wasn't sure if he did.

He was looking for stairs or ramps, anything leading up. The corridor was strange. Though extremely earthy, it didn't seem at all dirty. The floors were slate, unlike the dirt floor in his room, and the upper walls were green clay sculpted into panels, sometimes complicated friezes and occasionally a jumble of contributions without any theme whatsoever.

Everywhere he went, the lower walls were paneled with a pale wood, pickled unnaturally white, almost whitewashed, and many of the doors were the same. Others were made of reed, like the one he'd walked through, but still tinted white.

When he found stairs, he went up, hunched into the tightly spiraling space. Two faeries trundled down and straight through him without hesitation, though both shivered as they moved on.

Henry climbed until he had found another level, this one busier, and then he climbed again. The tint of the clay changed, grew smoky, streaked with brown and even red in places, but everything else seemed cut from a mold, though the halls rose and fell and bent and curled beyond the ability or desire of any human architect outside of a madhouse.

Finally, on his fourth level, passing by a group of laughing faeries, he saw a broad, low door. The knob at first looked like iron, but at second glance appeared to be wood with the bark still on, perfectly grown to a functional shape.

Hanging on the knob was a large wooden sign with

carefully painted black letters. Strangely, the painted letters seemed to be in imitation of those on a typewriter, though the artist hadn't been able to resist adding little flourishes on each *t,* and the whole thing had been fancily underlined.

❦ PRIVET ❦

Do Not Enter Through, Knock On, or Obstruct Entrance.

(Violations Will Be Parsed)

At first Henry wondered if it might be a bathroom, but then he walked in.

The room was posh. Thick red carpet, like an overgrown lawn, covered the floor. A large, round window made up of triangular panes was set into the end. The walls, pale green here, had been smoothed into perfectly rectangular panels. In the center of each, there was a face, the same face, but expressing different variations on a theme—serious. Or maybe pompous. It was fat-cheeked and heavily browed, and it was also sipping a drink in a deep chair by the window.

The faerie that owned it was rather slim, and the heavily featured face was balanced on an oddly slender neck. His hair was cut close on the sides and was bald on the top. He was clean-shaven and wore round, black spectacles. Most remarkably, he was wearing a satin fuchsia bathrobe that had obviously once belonged to a woman.

Henry remembered his first encounter with Eli and wondered if there was something in faeren blood that made stolen bathrobes attractive.

Two other faeries sat across from him in less comfortable chairs. One had a young-looking face, but his hair was both the color and texture of straightened steel wool. The other was older and fat, much fatter than Frank. His head was completely bald, but he made up for it with an enormous rounded beard below a bare upper lip.

All three of them held glasses full of something thick and yellow, like eggnog. They contemplated it silently.

After a moment, the fat one spoke.

"Who does the milking?" he asked. For all of the softness in his body, his voice was sharp. "The mares," he added, and lifted his glass.

"Flax," said the fuchsia faerie. Henry recognized both of their voices from the corridor when he'd arrived. Frank had yelled at them.

"The fermenting?"

"Colly handles that. He is improving."

The fat faerie nodded slowly, and then, flaring his nostrils, he sniffed at his drink.

"Ralph," the young faerie asked, "I think we should be discussing the boy. I didn't come here to drink mare's milk."

The fuchsia faerie turned in his chair, looking out the

window. "Who," he said quietly, "ever invited you to call me Ralph?"

"Apologies and prostration," the young faerie said. He obviously didn't mean it. "Chairman Radulf and Mr. Braithwait, what do you intend to do with the boy? Franklin Fat-Faerie is already creating a froth among the younger set, claiming that he's the seventh son of Mordecai. He needs to be dealt with, and soon."

"He is the son of Mordecai, is he not?" the fat one asked. Henry had him pegged as Braithwait. The other one had to be Radulf, the one who'd sent him his "a lert."

"He is," Radulf said, "though no one could ever explain to me how an infant could escape when his father could not." He sighed. "Incompetence."

Henry moved closer, put his dream hands behind him, and leaned against the wall.

"Has he been christened?" the young faerie asked.

"If he had, young Rip," Braithwait muttered, "you wouldn't need to ask. A lot of things would have regressed around here."

Rip? He looks like a Rip, Henry thought. *Or like someone who did a lot of ripping.*

Rip, if that was his name, ran one hand through his coarse hair, scratching his scalp. "I still don't understand why you didn't simply kill Mordecai."

Radulf sipped at his milk and then wiped his mouth delicately on his pink sleeve.

"We were bonded to him. Killing him would have created . . . problems."

"Breaking that bond would have destroyed us," Braithwait said.

"Yes." Radulf nodded. "Permanent storage was the superior option. The faeren would patiently hope for his return, and we could enjoy a life of freedom without human overlords of any type, self-governing for the first time in an age."

"But surely," Rip said, "entrapping him broke the bond as well? And you tried to kill his son."

"We did not try to kill his son," Radulf said. "His son disappeared before we could. And a careful constitutional case could be made that handling Mordecai as we did was in fact in keeping with our bond. Considering his enemies, we probably saved his life."

"But you will kill his son now?" Rip asked. "You can't risk a christening. You're not strong enough to hold against the power of a naming, and I'm sure Mordecai would take issue with your constitutional nuances."

Radulf swirled his glass, leaving a creamy film in the thick bowl. "He won't get the chance," he said. "By week's end, Hylfing will have been crushed, the last of his blood will have been poured out, and we will—"

Radulf looked directly at Henry. Henry flinched and slid to the side. Radulf's eyes did not move. They were fixed on the spot where Henry had been standing.

Henry followed his eyes and nearly choked in surprise. A large clump of dandelions had grown out of the clay wall. A dozen golden faces glowed in sprawling bloom.

Radulf stood. "He's here. Rip, was his room not sealed?"

"It was. In every way."

The little bureaucratic faerie pulled in a long breath. "Fetch his body now. He has volunteered himself for an early judgment. We have enough already to condemn him."

Henry turned and ran through the door. In the corridor, he couldn't find the stairs. So he shut his imaginary eyes, blocking everything else out, picturing himself with his knees tucked up against his chest.

He dreamed himself waking.

Henry stirred, straightened his legs out, and opened one eye at a time. Monmouth was crouching in front of him, chewing on a straw.

"I've never even heard of that," he said. "Not in any of the books." He laughed and threw the straw at Henry. "We were in the dream, and you just folded up and ghosted off. I tried to follow, but you pushed me back."

Henry blinked at the room as it was, swerving back and forth between perceptions. With concentration, he could keep it normal, just dirt and wood, and none of the magic that made it.

"Find anything out?" Monmouth asked, straightening up.

Henry nodded. "Yeah. The faeries did something to Mordecai, my father, the guy everyone thinks is my father." His mind ran over the rest. "And they're coming for me," he added.

Both of them heard voices, just moments before the door burst open. Five faeries plowed into the room, led by Rip. He pushed Monmouth into a corner and picked Henry's backpack off the floor. The other four surrounded Henry, each latching on to a limb. There would be no thrashing around and kicking. His legs and arms all stiffened in the faeries' grip, and they carried him into the corridor as rigid as a log.

He tried to yell, but his jaw was locked shut. The door to the room slammed, and Henry could do nothing but stare at the ground as it passed beneath him. After more turns than Henry could count, he was shoved through a door, and his limbs suddenly relaxed. Before he could move, rough hands grabbed him, and he was stripped, even his shoes and socks. Shivering in his underwear, Henry tried to stand, but two faeries pushed him down into a chair in front of a very small table and took up positions behind him. The room wasn't much bigger than a closet. A single lantern, suspended above the table, filled the little clay-walled space with light. There were no wood panels.

The door opened again, and a faerie in a battered yellow hat entered unsteadily, looking both tired and surprised. He was chewing on a cork, his gray coat was dirty, and an empty green bottle dangled in his hand.

"What's this?" he asked. "I wasn't notified."

"You have been now," said one of the guards, and the two of them stepped through the door. "You're the committee-appointed representation, Tate," the faerie added, and shut the door behind him.

Henry shivered again. The room really was cold. The faerie looked at him with what could only be disappointment.

"They know it's my day off," he muttered. "It's my week off. I haven't worked a case since the hooked moon." He sat down, took his hat off, and set it on the table in front of him. He scrunched up his lips around the cork. "Not this year, actually. Well." He looked in Henry's eyes. "What have you been doing to get Radulf's knickers in a twist?"

The faerie didn't look much older than Fat Frank, but he seemed far more tired. He had a short beard around his chin, a subdued red, but the hair on his head, pressed into a ring where his hat had been, was nearly brown. He fished a lump of bread and a few slices of cheese out of his pocket and dropped them on the table.

"I haven't been doing anything," Henry said. "Everything's been done to me." Looking at the bread and cheese, he tried to remember the last time he had eaten. He couldn't. Oh. Tuna. He pointed at the food. "Do you think I could have some?"

"Right," the faerie said. "Surely. I've got more." He slid the bread and cheese across the table. "My name is Tate, and it's probably best if you tell me everything, though it won't matter. Reality rarely does in this sort of thing, and if old Braithwait and skin-and-malice Radulf are against you, then I'm your friend. And, if it's pride speaking, oh well, but I was always a bit magnificent in debate. What are you doing?"

Henry had ripped the bread in half and tucked the cheese between the pieces. His first bite was already jammed into his cheek.

"That's rather clever," Tate said. "Never seen it done. What's it taste like?"

"Tastes like bread and cheese," Henry mumbled.

"At the same time?"

Henry nodded. The bite scraped down his throat. "It's called a sandwich." Remembering one particular bit of trivia from his one-on-one games of Trivial Pursuit, he added, "Invented by the Earl of Sandwich. He was addicted to gambling, so he ate this way so he could play at the same time."

Tate's eyes were wide, and his mouth hung open in an impressed smile.

Henry took another bite and chewed. "What are we supposed to do?" he asked. "They couldn't hurt me or kill me, could they? I haven't done anything."

"Kill you?" Tate asked. "Why would they do that? The faeren haven't executed a human since, well, I can't even remember. I mean, they've killed wizards, but that's hardly the same thing."

The door burst open, and the faeries stepped back inside. The food was taken out of Henry's hand, and he was lifted out of his chair. Tate rose to follow.

"Of course it depends on what they say you've done, but I guess we'll find that out soon enough."

Henry wasn't stiffened this time. His legs dragged behind him as he was hurried through the corridor.

"Cheese between bread," he heard Tate muttering. "Beautiful."

Double white doors opened in front of them, and Henry was dragged into a large hall with vaulted, beamed ceilings and hundreds of lanterns. Three enormous stone fireplaces hulked cold along the far wall. There were also hundreds of the faeren—men, women, and patches of children—seated on benches. More were pouring in through large doors in the back. Every eye followed him. Scattered through the room, he heard laughter.

Henry felt his whole body blush.

"Committee of Faeren for the Prevention of Mishap, District R.R.K., now in session!" a voice yelled. "Sitting in emergency session according to the *Book of Faeren*, Section Six, Article Three! Ralph T. R. Radulf, Esquire, the Ninth, presiding from the chair!"

Henry was dropped onto a stool in front of the crowd. Two faeries stood behind him. In front of him was a long table on a raised platform. Seven faeries sat behind it. Henry immediately recognized the three from his dream.

Radulf was seated in the middle in an enormous black chair. Tate was squeezing behind the table toward one empty seat.

Radulf lifted a mallet and banged it loudly on the table five times.

"Let the minutes show all members present in the matter of the boy, self-called Henry, self-styled pauper son, hereafter Whimpering Child, hereafter WC."

Clacking filled his brief pause. A round woman was seated at her own low table on the other side of the platform. She was typing.

"Seventh son of Mordecai!" someone yelled from the back. The crowd rumbled.

Henry took a deep breath. He was as confused as he was worried and afraid. He thought about running. But where? He didn't know the way out, and he was surrounded by faeries who were apparently capable of turning him into a limp rag or a stiff post anytime they liked.

Radulf banged his mallet again until the crowd quieted. "William Tate, committee-appointed defense."

Tate waved at the crowd and pulled out another lump of bread and a knob of cheese. Henry wasn't exactly confident in his defender. As he watched, Tate fished a small knife out of his jacket and sliced the cheese. Then he tore the bread in half and, grinning at the crowd, made himself a sandwich.

Radulf banged his mallet. "The chair addresses William Tate."

Tate looked up, chewing. "Yes, Your Majesty?"

The crowd snickered.

"Pray, what precisely are you doing?" Radulf asked.

"I'm eating." Tate said. He held up his sandwich. "It's called a gambler. Man who invented it gambled."

Radulf sighed, took off his glasses, and polished them, scowling. "Let the charges be read."

Rip stood up, holding a piece of paper out in front of him. "The District R.R.K., acting on behalf of Region Zed, asserts, alleges, and declares that WC, despite notification, admonishment, and warning, did knowingly and with malice, persist in actions that roused, released, and/or assisted in the awakening of an imprisoned evil; that due to said actions, the demon sometime called Nimiane, onetime witch-queen of Endor, has risen, strengthened, and even now assaults this district's human sister in the south, the town of Hylfing."

Henry felt the air go out of the room. Tate put down his sandwich and looked at him.

"What is the committee's recommended judgment?" Radulf asked.

Rip cleared his throat. "The committee humbly requests death, expungement, and the complete and permanent severance of body and soul by traditional means."

The room was still.

One woman typed.

Henry fell off the back of his stool.

CHAPTER TWENTY

Somewhere behind the clouds, the sun was up and blazing. For hours, Caleb had pushed his horse as much as he was able, slowing all the way to a walk as rarely as possible and only when the terrain required it. Henrietta's bones rattled like the arrows in Caleb's quiver. Her back and legs ached, and the smell of horse sweat was always beneath her.

Despite the clouds, the day had gone from warm to hot to stifling. The morning breeze had been cool at first, but now it was a moist wind, and it made Henrietta's skin feel greasy.

The grass around them was brown and, in some places, curled. Smaller trees had lost their leaves; others were mottled and spotted. Only the largest trees had remained green.

Along the ground, she'd occasionally seen dead birds and rodents, even a young deer. Now, the smaller animals were as frequent as the dark stones scattered over the hillsides. And when they crossed streams, her eyes always found the floating fish. Bunches of them packed the little eddies behind rocks or branches, where the currents couldn't reach them.

Henrietta's mind was on Kansas and her family. Despite all the aches and pains, despite the heat and weariness and strangeness of the world around her, despite her fear, what she felt more than anything else was complete worthlessness. Why hadn't she learned? Why didn't her mind ever work well before she did something? Regret, that's what her bones ached with. And cold anger with Eli. She'd been stupid, but he'd tricked her. She might have been able to get back, but now she'd never know. Even if the cupboards were still set to FitzFaeren, no one could follow her. The pain from the key digging into her leg kept reminding her of that.

"What did Eli do?" she asked.

Caleb said nothing. The chestnut was climbing across a slope, picking a way between stones.

"Magdalene said that he gave something to my grandfather that he shouldn't have," she added.

"I do not know the whole story," Caleb said. "Nor do I need to. But as a matter of state, their feud was somewhat public. Eli was the elder brother, Magdalene was his sister, six years junior. In the early days, FitzFaeren was ruled by kings."

The horse broke into a trot.

"But the kings were forever desiring expansion," Caleb continued. "They even rode out against Hylfing and various strongholds of the faeren. They lost much, both in trade and in lives, and after the conquesting folly of three kings, all killed in the field, a woman inherited the rod. Under her, the scattered FitzFaeren found comfort, and they built themselves into greatness. Their artists and architects, poets and musicians were the greatest for many nations around. They still rode to war, but never as the aggressors, and they found peace with their neighbors. Some of their adventurers traveled out through the shadows of the worlds and brought back talismans and relics, twelve of them, and around their strength, they built the Halls of FitzFaeren, protecting themselves against every kind of enemy. In that queen's old age, she named her daughter her successor and made her sons dukes. And so it was for three hundred years."

"And Eli didn't like that?" Henrietta asked.

"When his queen-mother died, his sister was very young, a child really, but the landed families still desired her over him. They did not care that he was peaceful, a great sculptor himself, and a scholar. In the week of her coronation, three of the greatest talismans disappeared. And on her coronation night, FitzFaeren fell to the witch-dogs of Endor. It was Endor's final conquest. People said it was Eli's doing."

"Was it?" Henrietta asked.

"He came to Hylfing, and we took him in, along with some remnants of the library he had saved from the ruined halls. But then he was discovered to be collecting darker volumes as well, studying at the feet of old

Endorian power, the power of demons, not men or the faeren. He said he studied only to know his enemy, but his enemy had already fallen, and some of the books went missing, given away to a man thought to be a wanderer. My brother Francis, your father, followed him and was lost."

Raindrops spattered on Henrietta's forehead. She wiped them off on her sleeve.

"So yes," Caleb continued, "I believe that Eli betrayed the FitzFaeren, if not with open-faced malice, at least with folly and self-lies."

Henrietta was extremely thirsty. She stuck out her tongue, hoping for a raindrop. None came. "Magdalene says he gave the stuff to my grandfather."

"Yes."

"That would make my grandfather bad."

"At the least a fool," Caleb said. "Perhaps nothing more. Many people meddle with things beyond their strength and nature. It can begin as foolishness, but it must end soon and in wisdom, or in evil and a fall. The desire to touch what should not be touched is as old as the world itself, and is at the root of all its hardships."

Henrietta thought for a moment. She wondered how different she was from her grandfather. If at all.

"What were the things Eli gave away?" she asked.

Caleb sighed. The horse turned beneath him. They were entering a grove of small trees. The rain quickened for a moment, and dry leaves rattled beneath it as they passed.

"A stone. A hilt. And a shaft."

"A shaft?"

"An arrow," Caleb said, "fletched with the feathers of a desert seraph, pointed with a tablet shard brushed by God's own breath, and shafted on the core of great Moishe's rod, first found and flown on the ancient field of Ramoth Gilead, killer of kings."

Henrietta tried to turn around on the horse. She couldn't see his face. "You believe that?"

Caleb laughed. "I don't know. But even if I found it lying in the road, I would never touch it for fear of being struck down."

"And Grandfather took it?" Henrietta asked, as much to herself as to Caleb.

Caleb drew the horse up, and relief poured through Henrietta's body, though she was sure it would not last long. They were in a clearing surrounded by smaller, dying trees. In the center, one towered over the rest, still green. Horses slowed down around them. After a moment, the dog appeared and threw itself down on the ground, panting.

"Ride on," Caleb said. "We will catch you."

The horses continued on. Caleb dropped off the side of the chestnut, told Henrietta to stay on, and began walking toward the large tree. He didn't look at all stiff to Henrietta. When he reached its trunk, he placed his hands on its bark and looked up into the branches. Henrietta could hear him, but only slightly, and it sounded as if he was singing. Then he stepped back and pulled a knife out of his belt. It had a straight blade and a silver handle wrapped with black leather. He swung his arm suddenly and with tremendous force. Henrietta flinched onto the horse's shoulders. He had struck the tree, burying the blade deep in the wood. Leaving the knife behind, he turned and walked back to the horse and Henrietta.

"Are you going to leave your knife there?"

"Yes," he said, swinging up behind her. "The tree was a marker established by my fathers. I did not want to see it drained by their hated one."

"Did you do something magic?" Henrietta asked.

The horse began moving again. Henrietta's eyes stayed on the knife.

"Some would call it magic," Caleb said. "But only because they cannot do it."

"What did you do?"

"I told it not to be deceived, not to give its strength away."

Henrietta wiped fat drips off her face and pushed her hair behind her ears. She needed a shower. It felt filthy. "Why'd you stick it with the knife?"

"So it would not sleep. It is awake now. As awake as a tree can be."

The horse moved into a trot again. They were leaving the grove behind.

"Were you singing?" Henrietta asked.

"In a manner. I spoke so that it would listen."

"How do you know how to do that?"

Caleb was distracted. There were more animals on the ground than they had seen, and bigger ones. Some kind of wildcat not far from a skunk. Farther on, she saw her first badger.

"My father taught me," Caleb said suddenly. "He could do much more, but I learned some."

"What could he do?"

Henrietta heard something rattle behind her. Caleb had pulled an arrow from his quiver.

"He would not be riding away from this scourge, for one. He would be leaning against it and calling the world around him to lean as well. He would walk to its center and find its source, and the greenness would follow him."

"We can't do that?" she asked.

"We can't do that," he said.

She looked down. Beside her, she could see Caleb's bow in his left hand, one finger holding an arrow in place, already notched.

"What's wrong?" Henrietta asked.

His voice was tentative, distracted. "Everything. Something. We'll see."

The trees were growing thinner now, and the ground was becoming more broken. Caleb kicked the horse lightly and let it pick its own path. They could see the last of the other horses disappearing over a small rise. The dog had run ahead.

Caleb's arm was no longer around her.

Through the trees and off to one side, a horse's

scream pierced the wood. Snarling followed after, and the baying of a dog.

"Hold on," Caleb said. "Grip with your knees. Grab his mane if you need to." The horse broke into a gallop, as much as was possible through the trees and boulders. She wondered if he needed to steer the horse at all.

Then both of his arms came back around her. In his left was his thick black bow with the heavy-shafted arrow on the string. Fingers from his right were around the arrow's notch. Henrietta could not hear anything other than the pounding of the chestnut's hooves as she hugged the horse's neck. Something came over the rise toward them. It was a riderless horse. On its rump was a large gray wolf. Two more ran beside it, lunging at its legs and shoulders, snapping at its neck. Then from over the rise came another shape. It was Caleb's black dog. The horse spun and kicked, but the wolf's teeth were in its saddle, and the kick missed. The horse screamed again.

Caleb's chestnut lengthened its stride as it wove, pounding through the trees toward the animals. They were closing fast. Caleb's body twisted sideways behind her, and she leaned back against his chest, ducking her head as he drew back his bow. She saw the shaft fly and bend its course through the air. The arrow passed just above the empty saddle and through the wolf's body, scraping off its feathers as it went. The animal dropped limply onto the hooves of the kicking horse and spun into the dirt. The other two wolves did not break concentration, though Caleb was bearing down on them from one side and his dog from the other. Caleb's bow bent again, and a second wolf dropped, kicking dust and writhing with the feathers pluming its shoulder. Then they were past them. Galloping up the slope and around the trees, a snarling broke out behind them.

"What about the other one?" Henrietta yelled.

"The dog can manage one wolf. Look for Eli."

"Eli?"

"That was the horse he stole."

As they reached the top of the rise, Henrietta frantically looked around. She saw nothing. Caleb slowed his horse to a walk, looking from side to side as they picked their way through the trees. Ahead, the other horses were returning. Caleb saw something she did not and changed their course, plowing the horse through underbrush. On the other side, beneath a tree, was Eli. The only blood visible was on his palms. Caleb slid off of the horse and put his hand on Eli's chest. Eli opened his eyes.

"Oh," he said. "I fell out of the tree. I jumped and grabbed a branch, and the wolves chased my horse. Then I fell."

"Are you all right?" Caleb asked.

"I believe so." Eli blinked. "I have never been attacked by wolves. It was not the experience I expected."

"What did you expect?" Henrietta asked.

"I expected to die. Is the horse dead?"

"It should not be."

"The wolves?"

"Three killed if I know my dog."

"The she-wolf?"

"I did not see one."

"She was back a way. They were circling her and broke off when I rode right into them. I do not know how they would miss my coming." Eli stared at his hand. "Or how I could miss them."

"It is hard to sense anything now. We walk through the clamor of death." Caleb put another arrow to his bow and stood up. "Which way?" he asked, and he whistled through his teeth. Henrietta heard a horse coming, and then it appeared, still bucking and kicking at the air. There was blood on its flanks and scratches on its neck and shoulders. Eli was trying to stand up and point for Caleb at the same time. Caleb followed his hand and began picking his way slowly through the underbrush. No more than thirty yards away, he stopped. Henrietta could see the top of a large rock in front of him. Then, as he crouched down, he disappeared. Henrietta followed quickly.

The wolf was large and beautiful, a dark gray, nearly unmottled. She lay on the ground with her head leaning on the rock, exhausted, tongue limp and lolling. Behind her lay three pups, all dead. One had been chewed. The wolf's yellow eyes rolled toward Caleb, but her tongue remained draped out the side of her mouth as she stared. Henrietta watched her uncle set his bow on the ground and crouch in front of the long animal. Her lip curled, and the smallest of snarls crawled out of her throat. While Henrietta held her breath, Caleb whispered to the she-wolf, and she stopped. Then he dropped to his knees beside her.

Henrietta exhaled and bit her lip. Caleb was stroking the wolf's head. Slowly, he worked himself around behind her and placed his back to the rock. The wolf was stretched out on her side, legs extended, head in Caleb's lap. Her tongue was still out of her mouth, but her eyes were shut. She wasn't dead. Henrietta could hear her breathing. Caleb looked up at Henrietta, but his hand did not stop its motion along the wolf's neck, and he did not speak to her. Instead, he bent over as far as he could and whispered in the wolf's ear.

Henrietta was silent. She didn't think Caleb would like it if she said anything at all. Instead, she stepped closer and waited to see if Caleb would tell her not to. He did not, so she crept closer still. The wolf's eyes opened, and her body bent, spasmed, trying to stand up. Henrietta froze, and Caleb whispered again. The long charcoal body relaxed, and Caleb looked at Henrietta and nodded. She got down on her knees and reached her hand out to the wolf's shoulder. The yellow eyes opened and looked at her, but the body was motionless beyond the soft rise and fall of its ribs. She felt the animal's neck and head, gently rubbed behind her ears, and then, growing bolder, she ran her hands down the wolf's legs, stroking the lean bones, and feeling her pads.

When Caleb nodded at her to stand up, she didn't want to.

"We must go," he said. His voice was no louder than normal, but it felt like a shout. Henrietta stood, tucked her hair behind her ears, and looked down at the pups. She moved toward them, but her uncle shook his head. Caleb slid out from beneath the wolf, lay her head down on the ground, ran his hands down the length of her body twice, and then placed one hand on her head and one on her ribs.

"Go," he said quietly to the wolf, and Henrietta watched her ribs rise and rise in one long, deep breath and then sink. She did not breathe again. Henrietta walked in front of Caleb to the horse. She was trying not to cry.

Eli was back on his horse, and the other riders were around him. Caleb slid up onto his horse, grabbed Henrietta, and pulled her up in front of him.

"Eli," he said. "You are a liar and a coward and a thief. You think you have no master, and so you are lawless in your self-worship."

Eli flushed. "I have no love for myself."

"Self-loathing and self-worship can easily be the same thing. You hate the small sack of fluids and resentments that you are, and you would go to any length, and betray anything and anyone, to preserve it."

Henrietta was shocked. She watched Eli's face darken, and then grow white with anger. He opened his mouth, but Caleb raised his hand to stop him.

"Swear fealty to Hylfing now," he said. "Eli Fitz-Faeren, belong to something other than your puffed self."

"I—I don't know," Eli stammered.

"It was not a request." Caleb's voice was bone-hard. Henrietta felt fear surge through her, and she couldn't even see his face. "If you do not, I will spit you to a tree. Your theft could have cost a life from among my men. If you felt the sudden growth in danger and did not tell us . . . three more lives have already been added to your tally. Swear." Caleb paused. "Now."

Eli sat, frozen. Henrietta heard Caleb draw another arrow from his quiver.

"Please don't," she said suddenly. "Don't kill him."

"Peace, Henrietta," Caleb said. "Be still when you have no understanding."

Henrietta bit her lips.

Thunder tumbled slowly across the sky. The rain had made up its mind. It came down hard, needled and stinging, warm but cooler than the air.

"Eli?" Caleb asked.

"I swear," Eli said quietly. Henrietta strained to hear him in the rain. "Before God and these witnesses and all the witnessing world, I swear to serve Hylfing, pursuing its good, its purity, and its peace." Avoiding Henrietta's eyes, he looked up at Caleb. "Will that do?" he asked sharply. "Or did you have something else in mind?"

"That'll do," Caleb said. "What awaits you if you break this oath?"

"An arrow, I presume."

"Something sharp, anyway," Caleb said. "Right—" Caleb turned to the others, but Eli interrupted him.

"You realize, of course," Eli said, his hair limp and wet, "that I remember you when you wept to be suckled. As a babe in a soiled nappy."

Caleb laughed. "I cannot remember you as anything. Anything at all. But let us change that."

The men all smiled, but briefly.

Caleb pulled a cloth out of his cloak. "Blind the horses. We are within a mile of the old gateway. The death will worsen as we approach, so there will not be another moment for stopping. Come what may, we will ride to the door and through. Do not fall to the ground. That is where the drain is strongest. Once we are in, if a mount or rider stumbles, there will be no time for a rescue. Do not breathe until you are in the light. Follow on my heels with weapons ready. We do not know what waits for us before, in, or through the evil door."

The men all pulled out scarves and rags and bandages and bound them around the horses' tossing heads. When the horses had quieted, the men drew blades or notched arrows on bowstrings. Caleb nudged his chestnut to a trot, guiding him through the brush with his knees.

The rest followed in a line.

Henrietta had a knot in her stomach. Her body no longer ached, or maybe it did and she failed to notice. In days of wild adventuring, she had reached a new level of nerves. They were riding toward something that could kill them. Three bodies were already wrapped in blankets.

Even Caleb's body felt tense behind her, and the horses whickered as they went. The black dog trotted with his nose up and ears high.

The grass around them was more than curled. As they rode, it went from brown to gray, and all of it was battered down in the rain.

Henrietta's wet hair was slicked back, and she didn't bother to wipe the running water from her face. Instead, she sucked at it with her lower lip. It was her first drink of the day.

She didn't need to ask Caleb where they were going. Ahead, she could see for herself. They were heading for an outcropping of stone surrounded by leafless trees. A funnel of gray death was traced toward it on the ground. Soon enough, she could see the open door.

Thunder rattled the sky in the distance. She saw no lightning. Her eyes were on a growing black mouth, just a little too symmetrical to be a cave. She swallowed hard as the ground leveled out in front of them. Dead ground. Gray ground. Every blade of grass, twisted into wet, ghostly corkscrews, lying back, pointing toward the door.

Caleb clicked his tongue, and the chestnut surged. For the first time, Henrietta thought of the birds and squinted into the rain.

"I released them," Caleb said in her ear. "Long ago.

You may see them again. For now, prepare to hold your breath. If you grow dizzy, cry out and clutch the horse's neck. Do not fall."

Henrietta nodded.

"Be stubborn," Caleb said. "As stubborn as a stone mule."

She clenched her teeth and expanded her fistfuls of mane. She could do that.

Caleb continued, and his voice was a chant. "Your life is your own, your glory is your glory, but you will lose it if you keep it for yourself. Grasp it for the sake of others. What might you do with it? Do not let the demon woman take it. Do not breathe." The words did not stop, but Henrietta could no longer understand them. They were no longer for her.

The door was in front of them. The horse slowed, but not much, as Caleb guided it in. Henrietta caught her breath and entered dead, rushing darkness with her eyes open wide.

She felt the pull immediately, like a hook set in her guts, tearing its way out. Gasping, her breath was gone. The horse's hooves sparked on stone, and others clattered behind her. She wanted to breathe, but she couldn't open her mouth. She wouldn't. Something would come out if she did. Something important. Her skin felt stretched, peeling. They were in a broad, circular room, a polygon, each wall a doorway. Faint light came through some of them. The chestnut surged toward one in the darkness, and Caleb corrected it, angling toward another. Henrietta felt her eyes pulling her that way, her hearing—

She opened her mouth to breathe, and sickness filled her. She was turning inside out, leaning, falling off the horse. A strong hand closed over her mouth from behind and pulled her up. She was pinned against Caleb's chest. Her eyes burned as she shut them.

Something clattered to the floor behind them, and they were through, into rain and much louder thunder.

Henrietta threw up through Caleb's fingers. He moved his hand, and she threw up again, down the horse's shoulder, and again, finally, on the ground. Then she sat up and realized she was crying.

Caleb had turned the horse and was watching others emerge. One. Coughing. Two. Strong. Three. The horse stumbled out of the doorway with Eli on its back. It staggered sideways and crashed to the ground with twitching legs. Eli rolled free into thick brush.

"Up, Eli!" Caleb yelled. The rain and thunder drowned him out.

The chestnut moved toward the fallen man, and Caleb slid off its side.

Caleb was on the ground and had lifted Eli up behind Henrietta before she could even think to object. Three other horses bounded into the rain, and a fourth carried a limp rider, who tumbled to the ground. No others followed.

Caleb reached up and slapped Henrietta across the face.

"Wake up!" he yelled. "Hold! Eli, take her to the house you knew as my mother's. Take her fast. You will not betray my trust."

"Wait!" Henrietta yelled. "Where are you going? Don't send us alone!"

"Go!" Caleb yelled. "The wizards are through ahead of us. On the ridgeline." He pointed back. The cave mouth was set between boulders near the top of a long slope that climbed into a ridge. In the wind and the rain, Henrietta could see nothing. And then she saw cloaks, dark cloaks moving down toward the doorway. "They are coming! Go now!" Caleb slapped his horse's rump, and she felt its strength tense beneath her. But there was no strength behind her to hold her on. She clutched and wobbled. Caleb was running toward the man on the ground, carrying his bow in his hand. An arrow was still on the string.

Henrietta turned away, terrified, bouncing onto the horse's neck.

Away in front of her was a rolling plain, divided by a river. Straddling the river mouth, she could see a small city with pale walls and spires.

Beyond it stormed the sea.

"The city of your fathers," Eli said behind her. "My city. May it weather the tempest."

Lightning struck beside them.

CHAPTER TWENTY-ONE

Hands lifted Henry back onto his stool. Quiet voices rustled through the room.

"The accused will stand for committee examination," Radulf said.

The hands grabbed him again, this time pushing him to his feet.

Henry wobbled. They wanted to kill him. And he was standing in front of hundreds of people in his underwear.

Braithwait eased his bulk around the table, stepped off the platform, and made his way toward Henry. He was carrying a wooden pointer.

The round faerie stopped and stroked his thick beard.

"Who is your father?" Braithwait asked.

"I don't know," Henry said. "You tell me, you're the ones who—" Henry's throat tightened. It didn't merely tighten. It closed off entirely. Radulf sniffed from behind the table.

"Answers only," Braithwait said, and poked Henry in

the chest with his stick. He turned around, pacing. "So, you do not know who your father is?"

Henry tried to speak. His mouth wouldn't open.

"Let him talk!" someone yelled from back.

"Look at him! He's Mordecai's boy right enough."

"Same nose!"

Radulf banged his mallet and scowled. When the room was quiet, he nodded to Braithwait.

"We presume from the chaotic, unfocused nature of your ah, how shall I put it, aura, that you are nameless. Is that correct? Has a christening or other naming rite ever been performed over you?"

Henry still couldn't speak. He shrugged. He knew he had a name, but he was pretty sure no ritual had come with it.

Braithwait stood in front of him and bobbed on his toes. "Could you explain, for the benefit of the committee and those assembled here, the meaning of the primitive symbol on your belly? It appears to be a type of brand, a mark of possession. And I should warn you, such things are not in truck with anything other than dark corruption and evil. How did you acquire it?"

Henry chewed on his tongue. His jaw was beginning to ache. Fear and worry were moving into panic. He looked up at Tate. The faerie wasn't even watching. He was slicing more cheese.

"I warn you," Braithwait said. "Your silence shall be interpreted by this body as an admission of guilt." The faerie's voice rose, rumbling up to a roar. "Have you bonded yourself to darkness? The scarring on your body and face make it seem so! Did your continued actions, after notification from this body, result in the unentombment of a witch, excuse me, *the* witch-queen of Endor, bloodthirsty in rage and madness? Speak up, boy!"

Braithwait brought his pointer across Henry's stomach.

He winced and tried to double over, but could not move. He tried to grab at his stomach, but his arms were locked in place. He could only look down and watch the stinging stripe welt up, joining and crossing the scars made in Byzanthamum.

The crowd had begun to rumble. They were more than rumbling, they were roaring.

Henry shut his eyes, trying to absorb the sudden pain, to drive it away. He could hear the yelling and the banging mallet. Over it all, he could make out the voice of Fat Frank.

"I'll cut off your hand, Braithwait! Touch him again, and off it comes!"

Men and women shouted, babies cried, and the mallet banged.

Somewhere under and through all the noise came the sound of typing.

As the din of the crowd ebbed into muttering and complaints, Henry opened his eyes and looked around.

A chair scraped back, and Tate rose to his feet. Then

he climbed onto his chair and, from there, stepped onto the table.

Radulf banged his mallet. "Chair addresses William Tate!" he yelled.

"William Tate addresses Chair!" Tate yelled back. And he stuck out his tongue.

"Contempt!" Radulf yelled. "Let the minutes show contempt!"

"Aye," Tate said. "Let them." He turned to the stenographer. "Bertha Big-Foot," he said, and the woman looked up. "Have you a pencil? Might be best to include a picture."

The crowd roared with laughter, and Tate moved into a series of gyrations, faces, and contortions that Henry had never seen, movements that could not have been possible for human joints.

Tate's ears inverted. He shut his eyes and reopened them, bulging and white. Swollen lips protruded, and a thick tongue slid out between them, sputtering a long and profoundly moist raspberry in Radulf's direction. Then he fell on his face, grabbed his heels behind his head, and rolled to the center of the long table, where he uncoiled, springing into the air and landing on Radulf's mallet.

Radulf was blotched purple. "Any faeren child," he said when the cheering had quieted, "could put on such a display. There were times when faeries would be moved by such things, but that time has passed, William Tate. It passed with your father. This"—he jerked his mallet from beneath Tate's feet—"is not a circus. It is in fact an emergency session of some moment."

Tate grew very serious. "Aye," he said. "As momentous as a kitten's piddle. I can see that." He raised his arms for the crowd to be quiet, unmoving from his spot on the table. When the room was as quiet as it ever had been, he spoke. "Faeren big and little, round and knobby, I have one thing to say." The crowd waited patiently while Tate examined them. "Mordecai never died. And when he returns, as he must, don't ask me to explain what the faeren in one of his districts did to his seventh son."

Something crashed toward the back of the room, and a cloud of soot rose from the farthest fireplace. Faeries jumped to their feet and parted, opening a path through the crowd.

Henry was just able to lean, watching the crowd stir and shift.

Into the front stepped the raggant, black with soot and wheezing small clouds from its nostrils. It walked directly to Henry, limping slightly as it came. Then it turned, sat down on Henry's toes, lifted its nose in the air, and sneezed.

Henry laughed, and the laughter unlocked his jaw.

The crowd stared in silence.

Radulf banged his mallet and shouted, "Committee to adjourn and be deliberate. Accused to be enclosed in quarantine and trebly sealed. Sentence to be posted in the main hall by moonset."

The committee members rose and exited quickly through the side door. Benches skidded as the crowd of faeren pressed forward to stare at Henry and his raggant.

Henry was shoved into a different room. It was smaller, and the ceiling was lower, carrying two lanterns. He staggered across a coarse rug on the center of the floor and turned around. A faerie threw his clothes and backpack at Henry's feet, and then the raggant tried to enter.

One guard bent and wrapped his arms around the creature's belly. The raggant bellowed, flaring his wings into the faerie's face and raising a swirl of soot. The faerie held on, and the animal twisted, swinging its head and clipping him with a blunt horn to the jaw.

The faerie clutched his face, and the raggant dropped to the floor. Two other faeries jumped on it. Bellowing, snorting, flapping madly with its eyes rolling and nostrils chuffing, the animal tried to drag the faeries in, tried like a small, black, wildly angry train engine with wings. It slid backward, and the door closed. Henry could still hear the snorting bellows, mixed with the sounds of faeries yelling in what sounded like pain.

A large cushion, like the sort Henry had seen used for a dog's bed, was lumped in the corner.

Henry dropped his backpack beside it and then shivered in the still room. He wasn't sure what exactly there was to do now, but he could start by putting on his clothes.

He slipped on his jeans and shirt, then dropped onto

the cushion to work on his shoes and socks. When they were on, he leaned back in the corner and looked around the room. He had no idea how committee meetings usually went, but he was pretty sure he had just experienced something abnormal. Most of the crowd had seemed to be on his side, or at least amused by Tate and his bizarre routine. But he was sure Radulf and Braithwait and Rip wouldn't care at all for what the crowd thought.

Henry picked up his backpack and unzipped it. Inside, he fished around until he'd found the kitchen knife and his one can of tuna. Opening it was going to be a trick.

Eventually, after blunting the knife, Henry managed to perforate the lid of the can halfway around. Then he bent the lid up and folded it back, sucking for a moment on the small cuts the metal left on his thumbs.

He quickly picked the can clean, even collecting remainders out from beneath his nails, and then he drank the juice without hesitation. That, and a couple bites of cheese and bread, were serving as lunch and dinner and probably breakfast.

For a moment, he wondered if that had been his last meal.

"Don't think about it," he said out loud. He could feel worry and gloom descending on him. "Think about something else."

But what else was there to think about?

Uncle Frank? Aunt Dotty? His cousins? Baseball?

Boston? The first time he'd tasted soda or felt the ball connect with the sweetest spot on the bat?

He stood up. He took the small knife and walked to the clay wall. He would write a message.

The clay was harder than it looked, like it had been fired somehow, but his knife still broke the surface.

It was easier than cutting open a can of tuna.

HENRY PHILLIP YORK came fast enough, as high up on the wall as he could reach, but what else should he say? What else was there to say? Faeries are ridiculous? I'm still hungry? Beneath it, he added (SEVENTH SON OF MORDECAI).

Henry leaned against the wall and thought. No one had ever trained him for this sort of thing. Everybody should have some famous last words ready. They should make you come up with some at school.

What would Uncle Frank say?

Finally, he started carving. It didn't take him long. He only had so much wisdom to pass down.

HENRY PHILLIP YORK
(SEVENTH SON OF MORDECAI)

IF THEY'RE PITCHING FAST
CHOKE UP.

He stepped back and looked at it. It was okay. Very Uncle Frank. And if they weren't actually his last words, at least it was good practice. Almost smiling, he sat back down on the cushion and set the knife beside him in case he thought of anything else.

For a while, he picked his teeth. Then he shut his eyes and tried to imagine himself in the barn, looking out over the fields with the raggant beside him. His mind got there quickly, but it wouldn't stay put, always slipping right back to where he was.

His grandfather had written out his own last words. It had taken him two volumes, but that was the sort of guy he must have been.

"Not very Uncle Frank," Henry said, but he still dug into his backpack and fished out the two plastic-baggied, rubber-banded books.

He'd always been impatient with his grandfather's writing, the style, the wordiness, the indirection. But he had time on his hands now, though he didn't know how much, and he needed to distract himself.

He'd flipped through the pages of both volumes many times, glancing or staring at diagrams that didn't make much sense at all, and scanning pages for his name. This time, he settled into the back third of one of the books and resolved to make sense of what he read.

The first thing he looked at was a diagram done in pencil with a few ink notes in the margins. At the top, Henry recognized the small outlined shape of his wall. There were no cupboards on it, excepting a central rect-angle with two dots that he took for the compass knobs. At the base of his wall, the floor was drawn out to make the space look three-dimensional. The other walls had been left off. The pencil had traced the attic stairs but nothing else until farther down and forward. Then there was another floor and the angled outline of what had to be Grandfather's cupboard. A dotted line ran directly between it and the central door in the attic. Where that line intersected with the attic floor, there was a crude, childish arrow. Two other dotted lines ran up from the arrow, one to either side of the cupboard wall, level with the compass door. One terminated in a small circle, the other in a *T* with a rounded trunk but sharper crossbar.

In the margin was written, *Crude, but more detail unnecessary. Three from FitzF were needed. No more.* Farther down, there was another note: *Two years of adjustments, uncounted ritual before more than 75 percent of cupboards functional.*

Henry understood enough to realize that the illustration was supposed to help explain how Grandfather's cupboard accessed the attic cupboards. But it didn't do much other than reconfirm what he already knew—the cupboards were magic.

He glanced down to the first paragraph below the illustration.

Eli provided the relics, and the arrow was by far the most potent. He paid a great price for it, and I have been in his debt since that day of destruction. Him I have wronged even more than you, Frank, and for all of my labor and years, I have done so little good with my achievements.

There is not one soul that I can name that has been helped by these doors, with the exception only of the boy.

The boy? Henry turned the page, scanning quickly.

Voices in the corridor muffled through his door. He looked up.

"Didn't happen," someone said, and the door opened.

"Of course not," said Fat Frank, and he stepped into the room. Tate, with his yellow hat on the back of his head, and Roland, freckled and flamed with hair, squeezed through behind him, and the door shut with a snap.

The fat faerie smiled. "Good to see your drawers back on."

Tate yawned and dug his chewing cork out of his coat pocket.

Roland was looking at Henry's words on the wall.

"What did they decide?" Henry asked. "What's going to happen?"

Frank puffed his cheeks. "What they decide and what happens are not likely to be the same thing."

Henry looked around at all of their faces.

"They haven't decided anything yet," Tate said. "Moon won't drop for at least seven hours. But I wouldn't be too worried. I thought we did pretty well."

Roland pulled at his ear and then ran both hands through his thick hair. Frank nodded at him.

"I," Roland said. He was blushing, but it was hard to tell. "I thought I should, well, I wish I hadn't drug you here. Not the way I did."

"Well, there was a notice on me," Henry said.

Roland nodded. He looked relieved.

Frank crossed his arms and sniffed loudly. "Don't be too soft on him, Henry York. He should have known better."

"Well, you said you wanted to throw me into the sea with the wizards," Henry said. "That would have been worse."

Frank raised his eyebrows. The other two faeries looked at him. "Did I?" he said. "Of course, there's mitigation for that. I'd just heard my fellows drowned from inside a sack, and then my blood was all boiling from the fight. Can't stick words to their meanings in a time like that."

Roland's freckles broadened into a grin.

"What am I supposed to do now?" Henry asked.

"Wait," Tate said. "The mob is with me. The committee won't dare go against them."

"We should bolt the borough now," Frank said. "Before the sentence. Could be all friendliness, but it won't matter if Hylfing has fallen."

"Shouldn't go to Hylfing anyhow," said Roland. "Not the way the wind is blowing. Run beneath the wizards' hammer? It'd be kinder to leave Henry here alone with the committee."

"I have to go to Hylfing," Henry said. "No matter what. That's where my aunt and uncle and cousins will all be."

"Not to mention your mother," Tate said. "And brothers and sisters, though I couldn't say how many are left."

Henry's jaw dropped. "My mother? She's alive?"

The faeries all looked at each other. Tate shrugged and flipped his cork between his fingers.

"As far as we know," he said. "Haven't actually kept up on Mordecai's family over the years. Should have, but haven't."

"What's her name?"

"Hyacinth," Frank said.

Henry rolled the name through his mind. He was feeling an entirely new sensation, a new kind of nervousness. And it planted goose bumps all up and down his spine.

"I need to go to Hylfing," he said again.

"You can't help," Tate said. "Wait and go with the committee's blessing, maybe even support against the wizards. I don't want to break you out of here."

"You have to try," Henry said.

Tate's eyebrows went up into his hat, and his bearded jaw slid forward. "I have to? Why do I have to?"

"Because," Henry said, "I don't know how long there will still be a Hylfing to get to. And," he added, "even if I wait, I don't think the committee is going to be nice to me, even if every faerie here wants it. I listened to them talking in a dream. That's why they rushed my trial, or whatever it was."

"You dream-walked out of the room?" Roland asked. "How?"

"I don't really know," Henry said. "I had a dream that I was in the room dreaming, and I got out in that one. The second dream."

Roland stepped back and cocked his head.

"It doesn't much matter," Frank said. "What did you hear?"

Henry recited virtually the entire conversation verbatim, watching the faeries' expressions as he did. At first their eyes were narrow, almost skeptical, but they widened quickly. Mouths opened, and Roland turned white between his freckles. His Adam's apple bobbed like a yo-yo.

Henry took a deep breath and finished. "When the dandelions grew out of the wall, they knew I was there, and Radulf said they had to have the meeting right away."

"Good Lord," said Tate.

Frank said nothing. His jaw was locked shut, and his eyes were wet with anger.

"Good Lord," Tate said again. "Good Lord have mercy."

Roland sat down on the floor. Henry was surprised to see tears on his cheeks. He didn't even bother to wipe them away. "We betrayed him," he said quietly. "All these years drifting on account of cutting our own anchor."

Frank pulled in a long breath. "The christening!" he said suddenly, and clapped his hands. "There's still hope if they fear the christening! Oh, they want you dead, all right, Henry York, because it's you or them now."

Roland looked up and sniffed. Tate stood motionless in thought.

"We have to get to Hylfing now!" Frank said. "Now! Tate, where's the closest union hall on that bit of coast?"

"There's one just outside the south gate, but it'll be jammed with faeren," Tate said. "And they won't have exactly posted the Hylfing loyal just there. All hostiles."

"So where, then?" Frank asked.

Tate's eyes came back into focus. He looked at Henry and then at Frank. "Used to fish just up the coast from the bay. Kept a boat there and everything. From there, we can hoof it down or sail."

"Right," Frank said. "Off we go, then. Who's on shift in the main hall?" he asked Roland.

"Pius and Colly," Roland said, standing up. "Pius is solid through, but Colly'll be mush for Radulf. He'll need distracting."

"Hold a moment," Frank said, and he slipped out the door.

Henry listened to his hushed voice as he spoke to the door guards. There were three loud thumps, and he slipped back in.

"Asked me to knock them so they'd get off a bit lighter," he explained. "Up now."

Henry collected the journals and his backpack. He tucked the knife back inside, but left the empty tuna can.

Frank led him to the door.

"Monmouth," Henry said. "We can't leave him."

The fat faerie scrunched up his face in irritation.

"And the raggant," Henry added.

Faerie eyes rolled, but Henry didn't care. His heart was pounding, and questions he didn't have time to ask were racing through his head.

He stepped over the legs of his faerie guards and into the hall. As the door swung shut behind him, he looked back into the room.

"Choke up," he said quietly, and hurried down the corridor.

CHAPTER TWENTY-TWO

Darius stood on the ridgeline and let the wind swirl around him. The rain parted above his hooded cloak. He felt . . . still. Every crackle of tension in the clouds, he savored. An offshore wind was colliding with cold salt breath from the sea. The clouds frothed into dark mountains in their struggle. Litter by litter, miles up in the biting sky, they birthed lightning and groaned thunder.

All of it was building. Inside him.

The little pale city was a village compared to Byzanthamum. But it was a beginning.

The storm he had drawn sprawled over hundreds of miles. He could bring it all together. It could fall in one crushing blow, sending shattered walls into the ocean. Pounding life into sand.

The old Darius would have rushed to a finish. Now, he held his strength back. He knew he couldn't hold it forever. It must be released. He must destroy. But he could taste each life passing, he could relish each blow, each death.

The refugees outside the walls had already been

killed. But at least five thousand more lives waited inside the walls.

Every life has a flavor.

It was a thought. Not his. At least it hadn't started with him.

She was inside his head. Behind his eyes. Through his whole body.

I am greater than a cat, he thought.

You are a dog.

He nodded, shut his eyes, and filled his lungs with the storm.

I am your witch.

"My queen," he said aloud. He looked down at the fragile city, the city that had caused his mistress to stumble. It was nothing, and yet a man from within those walls had taken her eyes. Another had bound her in darkness.

Grapes can be trampled. Or they can be plucked singly and crushed between the teeth, moistening the tongue.

One blade of lightning fell within the walls. One unseen body crumpled, broken. Thunder climbed the ridge and quivered in his bones.

Darius relaxed, caught his breath, forced it level.

His nostrils flared. It was good, sowing the wind. He closed his eyes. Holding . . . death . . . back. Within.

The riders had been interesting. Bold fools, traveling through the dark ways. It was like riding through a dragon's mouth. Only one horse had survived, crossing the plain in a frenzy, balancing two riders. Some small strength had even deflected the lightning.

In the end, it wouldn't matter. Every life would be accounted for. The townspeople, the animals, even the men beneath him, all but a few of the strongest wizards. As for the rest, he would let the weaker wizards expend themselves against the old, charmed walls, and if they managed to enter, then so be it. Come what may, his wrath would fall, and even the lightning would be silent in fear.

He smiled. Feeling the death of the lesser wizards the riders had managed to kill had been pleasurable to him, but not so much as the end he'd given the riders.

Darius raised his arms, fingering the wind. As he did, a single shaft pierced through it, an unwavering black arrow.

The thick-shafted arrow struck Darius in the chest, and for a moment, he felt pain. He felt the storehouse of power inside him surging to break free, to tumble down the slope flattening trees and stone.

He closed his hand around the arrow. The wood and fletching faded to dust and were carried away on the wind. Darius pinched his fingers over the wound and felt the metal head come to them. He pulled it out, dropping it to the stone at his feet.

There was a life to be sensed and ended. One of the riders no doubt. Within bowshot. Darius closed his eyes, but he felt nothing more than the awkward power of the other wizards.

A whisper. Maybe an animal, maybe a man with some small shielding around himself.

Darius opened his eyes and pushed back his hood. Down the ridge beneath him, boulders had long ago tumbled together, trees growing at angles to find the sun between them.

The sky split, and lightning fell on the boulders like hail, clustering, linking, sprawling, splaying into charges and tongues. The trees toppled. The boulders shattered. Higher up, more stone fell away and tumbled down.

Thunder shook the ridge. It shook Darius. Wizards were pushed to the ground by its drums. Darius took one step back and closed dizzy eyes.

The storm returned to its building swirl. What whisper of life there had been had now passed out of the world.

Or beyond sensing.

Henry's ears were ringing with nervous excitement. His mouth and lips were dry. He took a deep breath and hurried on, close behind Frank and Roland. Tate was following him.

They'd gone up stairs, and down more. They'd gone through long, curling corridors with floors that rose and fell beneath his feet.

If he really tried, Henry thought he could get motion sick.

They'd passed only one group of faeries. Frank and Roland had made them face the wall and asked how their evenings had been progressing. Everyone had said, *Quite well, thank you, but a little boring,* not having seen anything at all of interest. Except two of them. They had turned and run, but they hadn't gotten far.

Henry thought they'd been stored in a closet, but he wasn't exactly sure.

Henry watched Fat Frank glide through the halls, sensing every corner, stair, and doorway as they went. Frequently, the faerie stretched out his arms, allowing his fingertips to drag along the wall or across the planks of a door. He was as nimble as he had been in the brawl on the boat, and his head was perpetually swiveling, cocking even, like he was hearing and smelling his way more than seeing. Beside him, Roland loped, his lean body looking slow and awkward next to Frank's constant motion. Tate remained in the very back with Henry, trotting and breathing loudly, apparently unconcerned with any degree of stealth.

Monmouth's door hadn't even been guarded, and he was asleep on the floor when the faeries opened it. He sat up, blinked twice, and then was immediately on his feet, grinning.

They'd gone back the way they had come, and then off into new chambers, beyond what Henry had seen. The place was like a city, and some of the corridors they crossed were as wide as roads, though Frank seemed to avoid them whenever possible. They were always filled with chatter, shouting, and even singing.

Some of the faeren people were more nocturnal than others, but Frank knew where they congregated.

Henry had actually begun to sweat when Frank suddenly froze in place. Henry and Tate ran into his back while Roland took several more steps before managing to stop.

Frank shook his head in disgust. "Shall we bang a drum while we go?" he asked quietly. "We don't have long. Someone will rat to the committee soon, if they haven't already."

Tate wiped his forehead. He hadn't been a terribly active faerie for quite some time. Monmouth seemed unaffected by the exercise. Henry knew he couldn't possibly look as calm as the young wizard, and he couldn't erase the stitch in his side, or stop puffing.

"When do we get the raggant?" he asked.

Frank snorted. "We don't. Don't know where it is."

Tate slapped Henry on the back. "Never go looking for a raggant, boy. It threatens them. That being their job and all."

"It found you once," Frank said. "It'll track you again." The fat faerie didn't wait for any argument. "Now, if we're gonna get to the way rooms, it's time to cross the main hall. Follow close, and stop when I stops." He looked at Henry and Roland. "No barging into me or staggering on, right?"

Henry smiled, but Roland blushed.

"Now," Frank said, and raised a thick finger to his

lips. He widened his eyes and shook his head wildly. Then he turned, moving silently down the corridor and around a bend. Fifteen feet on the other side, there was a large door. Frank touched the hinges, seemed satisfied, and pulled the door open just wide enough for a pencil.

Tate stepped forward and tapped his arm. When Frank looked at him, he pushed him back out of sight, motioned for Roland to keep Henry and Monmouth back, and then threw the door open.

Yawning loudly, he walked in.

Henry pressed himself back against the wall. Frank's hand pressed him even further. He twisted to make room for his backpack and could see nothing. But the voices were perfectly clear.

"Who is that?" Tate asked. He sounded tired but prepared to enjoy himself. "Colly? Pius?"

"What are you doing here, William Tate?" The voice was sour and quick. "Central Mound is closed. You know that. It's been regulated. Do you have a blue stamp for night access?"

"Ha!" Tate said. "No, young Colly. No blue stamps. But then I don't want access. I was just coming to give Pius here a message"

"What?" asked another voice. "What message?"

"The committee is ready to declare. They should be sealing up the sentence now." Henry had absolutely no idea what Tate was trying to accomplish. But he wished he could see his face, because his voice became wildly exaggerated. If voices could wink, Tate's was winking heavily. "They'll need someone to run post it on all of the levels." Wink. "Someone who understands the importance of the case." Wink. He didn't add *Someone who knows how to type and can fake a seal,* but he may as well have. "So," Tate finished, "why don't you just run along, then, Pius. It wouldn't hurt to be available."

"Um—"

"Wait a limp," came Colly's voice. "What are you trying to pull, Tate? You're not going anywhere, Pius, lad. Nobody's gonna pull a switch while I'm around."

Tate laughed. "Ridiculous," he said. "The idea. Well, if you won't do it, Pius, it shouldn't be hard to find someone to ruin—ha—I mean run, the posting."

Fat Frank rolled his eyes. Henry still didn't understand.

"William Tate," Colly said. "I've a mind to arrest you right now."

"On what grounding?" Tate sounded shocked.

"Conspiring to commit anarchy and disrupting the notification of justice."

"Colly," Tate said seriously. "You're over-acting. Maybe reading into things a bit too much? What have I said? But I'll stop bothering you both. One way or another, the committee will need someone—hard to find anyone at this hour—and I should be there to help."

"Oh no you don't!" Colly yelled. Tate cried out in pain. "Pius, you keep an eye on him. Don't let him off the ground till I'm back with Chairman Radulf!"

Roland and Frank wedged Henry and Monmouth

deep behind the door. Feet pounded, and a large faerie lumbered past, even more awkwardly than Roland.

Before he was out of sight, Frank had Henry and Monmouth out from behind the door and through the doorway. Roland pulled it shut behind him.

The hall was a large oval, and its ceiling was domed earth, held up by enormous beams. With a lot of light, and time, Henry would have noticed that the beams had no joints, and that the wooden webbing that ran between them was actually a root system. The faerie mound was crowned by a single enormous tree, and its roots had been trained for centuries.

Henry didn't notice. He was looking at the very center of the large room, where Tate lay facedown on the stone floor, groaning at the feet of a confused faerie. Beside both of them, there was a black hole unguarded by any rail. Stairs descended into it.

Tate propped himself up and grimaced, rubbing the back of his head.

"Down you go," he said. "Not much time. Even Colly might realize what's happening before too long."

"What is happening?" the confused faerie asked. "Is that the boy?"

"It is," Frank said.

The confused faerie coughed, and his eyes moved from faerie to faerie to faerie to Monmouth and finally to Henry. Panic was painted all over his face.

"Are you for Mordecai?" Frank asked.

The faerie nodded.

"Are you for the faeren?"

He nodded again.

"Then you're for him," Frank concluded, smiling. "Oh, and the wizard's a friend."

The faerie looked at Henry, at Monmouth, and then back at Frank. "Really?" he asked.

Tate and Roland nodded with Frank.

"Well, that's all right, then," the faerie said.

Roland gripped Henry's arm, leading him toward the dark hole of a stairway.

"Wait," the confused faerie said. "Do you have a blue stamp?"

"Oh yes," Frank said. "But it's in my shoe, and the laces have knotted."

The faerie thought about this. "All right, then," he said. "Go ahead."

Frank stepped around behind him. His arm was so fast, Henry hardly saw it move, but the confused faerie crumpled to the floor. His legs folded up underneath him, and his cheek found its rest on the stones. He looked happier that way. Like he was really understanding life for the first time.

"Sorry, Pius, lad," Frank said. "But it will be better for you in the end."

"Maybe," Tate said. He put his hands on his knees and steadied himself. "That Colly can hit."

"We need to move," Frank said. "Lickety-lickety. Down the hole. Roland, stick between the boy and the wizard. Tate, follow if you can." He looked back at the wobbling faerie with a smile. "If you can't, kiss old Radulf for me."

Fat Frank stepped onto the stairs and quickly disappeared into the gaping black throat in the floor.

"C'mon, then," Roland said. "If it gets too much for you, just shut your eyes."

"What?" Henry asked. "If what gets too much?" His feet were already on the top step. Roland gripped his arm with one hand and Monmouth's with the other. The hole was large, but the stairs, spiraling down around the edge, were not at all wide, especially for three bodies.

"We're going to the center of the mound," Monmouth said. "It's not meant for people."

"It's not that bad," Tate said. "Sort of the magical trunk to the magical tree. The corridors and halls are all branches and twigs to this shaft. Everything funnels through here."

Monmouth wobbled on his feet and quickly shut his eyes. "Don't let yourself look at it, Henry." He rubbed his forehead. "It's too much."

"Oh, it's wine to us," Tate said. "But you have to have a head for it."

"Hullo?" Frank's voice echoed up from the blackness.

Roland tugged Henry and Monmouth forward. Henry felt Tate's hand on his shoulder behind him.

The darkness was tangible, cool as a mist but not wet. And then they were inside it, and the world was empty.

"Can't we have a light?" Henry asked.

"Wouldn't help," Tate said quietly. "You couldn't see it."

Henry swallowed and felt the fog slide down his throat. He kept his shoulder against the wall. "Light won't travel through it?" he asked, simply to keep his mind off what was happening. "But sound does."

Tate sent out a chuckle that grew until it filled the darkness. "For a seventh son, you don't know much. For the son of a faeren legend, you know nothing. You are standing in enough brightness to feed a forest for a century. This is all light, all around you. Light at rest. It is our strength, the soul of our people."

"Monmouth?" Henry asked. "Did you know that was possible?"

Monmouth was silent for a moment. "No," he said. "I still do not. It is beyond me."

"That's the spirit," Tate said. "An example to wizards everywhere. We are beyond you."

Henry's foot hit bottom, and he stumbled forward.

"Alive?" Frank's voice asked.

"Both," Roland answered.

"Good. Welcome to the roots. The way rooms are this way."

Henry was dragged forward, a door opened and shut behind them, another opened and slammed, and still they moved on in darkness. Finally, he began to see.

Light was active around head level in the corridor. The darkness settled and dissipated until the walls were bright and only the floor was hidden, and Henry's feet with it. He felt like he was walking without them, on his shins only.

Frank found a door in the wall, pushed it open, and stepped aside, waiting for everyone to enter.

Henry stepped in and squinted at the brightness inside.

The room was large, circular, and lined with shelves. There were no lamps that Henry could see, no source of light at all. But the room was as blinding as the sun on snow.

"This is active light," Frank said. "That means it's shiny."

The other faeries laughed, but Monmouth and Henry both tucked their heads down, tears streaming down their cheeks. Henry's eyes hadn't adjusted, but he wasn't sure they ever would, so he looked up.

The floor of the room sloped gradually down toward the center. Looking at that low point, he almost expected to see a floor drain like in some basement back home. Instead, there sat a broad, smooth stone, six feet across, with two shallow indents carved into its surface a couple feet apart.

The shelves all around the room were lined with jars, from floor to the high ceiling. Near the door, there was a large cabinet, like an old card catalog in a library. Tate and Frank were pulling out drawers and flipping through stacks of small papers inside.

Roland, his hair a vivid pumpkin in the extreme

light, had collected rough sticks from somewhere and was walking down toward the smooth central stone.

Monmouth had finally looked up as well and stood blinking beside Henry.

"Weird, huh?" Henry said.

Monmouth nodded. "How did we come to be here in the first place?" he asked. "We didn't arrive down here."

Roland looked up from what he was doing. "You come in the branches," he said. "Go out the roots." He balanced two sticks taller than he was in the indents on the stone and then set a knobby crossbar over the top.

Tate had found the paper he wanted, and he and Frank had moved on to scanning the shelves. When they found the right jar, Henry watched the faeries move down to the precariously balanced doorway. Tate and Frank dipped their hands in the jar and rubbed water over the surface of the sticks. Then they poured out a small puddle on the stone between them.

Tate slapped wet hands on his cheeks and then replaced the jar on the shelf and the paper in the cabinet.

"Right," Frank said. "Now's the time. It's not likely that we're heading for any pleasantness, but head we must. Tate?"

Tate nodded, stepped up to the doorway, pulled his yellow hat down tight on his head, turned sideways, and slid through.

For a moment, Henry could see him on the other side. He turned, looked back, and vanished.

"Roland," Frank said.

"I'll wait," said Roland. He looked worried.

Frank shook his head.

Roland approached the door, sniffed loudly, and walked through with his shoulders square. Just before he disappeared, Henry thought he saw him trip.

"Monmouth," Frank said. "Special wizard guest. If my father knew a wizard was seeing the roots of the mound, he'd be likely to die. He's already done that anyhow, so it'd be no great loss." Frank nodded toward the door.

Monmouth took his place in front of the door and inched forward. He was taller than the doorway, so he ducked his head, bent his knees, and shuffled into nothingness.

Fat Frank looked at Henry, pursed his lips, and rubbed his knob nose with the back of his hand. "Well," he said. "You've been no end of trouble, I can't lie. I hope you have the zing to make all this worth it. I don't want to ruin my life just to hustle toward the end of yours."

The two of them looked at each other.

Henry walked to the door and turned sideways like Tate had. They were going toward Hylfing, toward danger. He was hurrying to get in the witch's way, to see Darius again. Ronaldo and Nella had known he would. His hand drifted toward his stomach, feeling the raised-up scars on his belly.

"You know," Henry said. He was talking more to himself than the faerie, trying to believe something. "A man once told me that sometimes winning a fight isn't as important as standing in the right place, facing what needs to be faced. And sometimes standing in the right place means you end up dead. And that's better than not standing at all." Henry twisted around and looked into the fat faerie's dark eyes.

"Oh," Frank said. "That's a dark bit of philosophy for a lad. Think that way, and all you'll ever get is your name written on a bit of stone. What I say is, don't go playing unless you can win. Only sit down to chess with idiots, only kick a dog what's dead already, and don't love a lady unless she loves you first. That's Franklin Fat-Faerie's—"

Henry was gone.

Frank puffed out his cheeks and pulled a thread from his pocket. "Well, Franklin, that boy's not all cotton fluff, is he?" He began tying the thread around one of the supporting sticks. "He's got it pretty well figured, and you know it. We're all going to get ourselves dead, and only the gulls will want our after-bits. But," he added, tugging gently on the thread, "I'll do my dying standing on the right spot, beside the son of Mordecai, even if he is a bit of a nunce."

Frank stepped back, scanning the room once more, looking for anything that could give away their direction. "Nonsense, Frank," he said. "That's like saying losing's all right so long as you find the person that was supposed to kill you. All I need to do"—he stepped into the doorway—"is get that boy to a christening, even if he's got but five minutes of life left. That's the goal, Franklin. Then it can be hooves up, if you like, though I'm sure you won't."

Frank the fat faerie stepped through and disappeared. Then one of the legs of the doorway jerked and fell. The rest followed, clattering in the empty room.

With no ways to brighten and no eyes to blind, the young light slowed and settled, puddling over the sticks and the center stone.

There it slept.

CHAPTER TWENTY-THREE

Henry slid through, grazing his legs against rocks on both sides. He was glad he'd copied Tate.

And then he felt the wind. And the rain. The smell of salt water surrounded him. He was standing in the dark, but a single slice, a crack full of gray dawn drew him forward. He had to take off his backpack in order to squeeze out of it, and he found himself standing on a beach covered with round stones the size of melons. A small boulder pier hooked out into the sea, or the surf would have been pounding over him. As it was, the pier was overwhelmed by the towering swell, just managing to trip the waves from the open sea. Spray climbed into the sky, taller than the cliff at Henry's back.

"Henry!" someone yelled. He could barely hear anything. He moved farther out into the gusting rain and peered up the cliff. Monmouth and the faeries stood at the top, hooding their eyes and staring at something in the distance. Monmouth was the one calling for him.

Henry slipped his way up the wet rocks until he stood beside them. Monmouth pointed, and Henry tried to shield his eyes from the downpour.

In the distance, set on what looked like a peninsula, he could see what could only be a walled city. It was small and light, the color of sand, standing out against the black clouds behind it.

Lightning flicked above the city, never absent for more than a few seconds, but the only thunder came from the surf.

"Now what?" Roland yelled. "We should have gone closer!"

"Too late now!" Tate yelled back. His hat was drooping over his ears in the rain, but the wind stood the brim straight up in the front. "Walk or sail?"

Frank scrambled up next to them.

They all turned, looking out at the great froth-topped salt hills in the sea and then back to the pale city, crowned with lightning.

"Die now or die later?" Monmouth asked.

"Later!" Tate shouted. "The boat wouldn't make it out of the harbor."

Henry huddled closer so he could hear. The others turned their backs to the wind beside him and leaned together.

"Faeries sink!" Roland yelled. His red hair bristled like wire, struggling against the storm.

Henry wiped his eyes and shivered. "Is all the lightning from the wizards? It's just striking over the city."

Monmouth nodded. "The city can't last long." Henry could barely make out what he'd said.

"We'll see!" Frank yelled back. He was easier to hear. "Hylfing's got some old strength left in those stones."

"How are we going to get inside?" Tate asked, flipping the collar up on his coat and pocketing his hands.

No one answered him.

Henry unzipped his backpack and pulled out his already-wet hooded sweatshirt. At least it would keep the rain from stinging his skin and cut some of the bite from the wind.

Frank began walking along the cliff's edge. The rain bounced off his head and shoulders, shattering into little droplets. All the faeries looked different wet. Their wild hair flattened and clung to their cheeks and tangled with their beards. Their clothes clung to skinny legs.

Frank set a quick pace, occasionally jogging or even running. Roland and Monmouth didn't seem to struggle to keep up. Monmouth wasn't even breathing hard. Or Henry couldn't hear him above the wind. Tate straggled behind Henry, wheezing. That stood out well enough.

The landscape wasn't too difficult. The cliff height climbed occasionally but stayed fairly level. Just inland, hills turned into near mountains, all of them treed. Despite the cold and the spray, Henry was grateful they weren't trekking over the steeper terrain, always staying within a few dozen feet of sea level.

Following the coastline, the city occasionally disappeared as they looped in around a bay or cape. Each time the city reappeared, Henry hoped that it would look bigger. Instead, it seemed perpetually distant, until finally, feeling their way around a large rock promontory, the city had clearly grown. Henry could make out the shapes of the taller buildings, a cathedral spire, a round-topped tower. And as the lightning danced around them, still untired, he could hear the thunder.

"See," Frank said cheerfully. "The towers still stand. Hylfing has faced darkness before. There are words stronger than stone woven through those walls."

"How much stronger?" Henry asked.

No one answered. The group stood, dripping, watching the storm assault.

"I think we're going to find out," Frank said.

After that, Henry didn't need to be told to hurry. His tired muscles ignored themselves, and his burning lungs made a truce with their pain. He pushed himself, and even Frank hurried to keep his pace.

If his real mother was alive, she was in there. If he had brothers and sisters, they were within those walls. If his aunt and uncle and cousins had survived, this is where they had said they would meet him.

Henry didn't know what he could do. He only knew where he needed to be, where he was supposed to stand.

As they grew closer, the thunder began to sound more like the war it was. It cracked like a whip and boomed like artillery. It jagged and staggered in its own echoes. Finally, as they rounded a point, the harbor opened up below the cliff in front of them. Hylfing sat on the other side.

Frank had them all take cover in a grove of gnarled, wind-salted trees as they surveyed the situation.

They could try to swim the harbor to the city docks and hope they made it and were allowed in. They could attempt the gate, which seemed just as unlikely, or they could try to climb the wall, which seemed even worse.

Masts from two ships stood out from below the harbor water. Not one ship still rode the surface.

"I think we have to swim," Monmouth said.

"Faeries sink," Roland reminded him.

"Henry," Monmouth asked. "Can you swim?"

Henry shrugged, shivering, blinking away rain. "I had lessons a long time ago, but I haven't tried recently. And that's a lot of water."

"You don't want to be in the harbor," said Frank. "A strike to the water could kill you."

Tate pulled off his hat and twisted it hard, wringing out the water even as more fell. Then he sank to the ground and propped his back against a tree. "I don't suppose," he asked, "that this is a good time to wonder why we came?"

The thunder stopped.

No one noticed at first, but the longer the lull lasted, the stranger it felt to all of them. Henry pushed aside branches, letting his eyes roam over the plain outside the city walls. He saw nothing. On his second pass, he caught the motion of something dark, a man in a cloak walking out from the distant trees at the foot of the ridge and toward the city. When he'd seen the first, he saw another. And another. And a dozen others, spread across the plain, all walking toward Hylfing.

When the men in robes were close enough, arrows rose up from unseen archers within the walls and plummeted through the wind toward the advancing wizards. Thunder reawakened, and the city's bells chimed against it, mingling with the shouts of defenders.

In all the noise, Henry heard something behind them, rustling the underbrush. Voices.

Henry turned, and through the trees came four men in black robes, carrying swords.

Tate swore.

Roland and Frank both jumped to their feet as a wizard's curse rang out. The blow fell, a downburst of air, bowling them back to the ground.

Henry's mouth hung open in shock. He couldn't move. But a hand, Monmouth's, grabbed him, pulling him behind a tree. The trees and brush crackled and snapped with magic, muffling the shouts of Frank and Tate, and strange voices using stranger words.

Henry picked up a short, thick stick, stood up, and stepped out from behind the tree.

The small wood was burning, and Henry saw everything in one frozen moment, swirling strength, the birth of smoke, a splitting tree. Two small bodies, dead. One with a yellow hat, still burning. The other facedown, broken, limbs splayed unnaturally, crowned with hair like an angry sunset.

Three large bodies, wizards, with robes smoking where they lay.

Henry choked in shock, in anger, unable to move.

There were more than four wizards. A whole crowd of them were moving forward cautiously. Henry could see Monmouth and Frank where they had ducked behind trees. They looked at him with shocked eyes. The wizards looked at him. All of them.

"No," Henry said. Something hidden inside him snapped, and warm strength surged through his veins. A word crawled out of his angry blood and onto his tongue, a living word. Yelling it with all the lung he had, Henry threw his stick at the wizards, harder than he had ever thrown a ball.

The stick spun through the air, and as it did, it burst into green and golden flame, a spinning galaxy of bursts and blades. The swirl surrounded Henry, too. Green and gold spun and twisted out of his fingers, following the thrown sun—living fire, laughing like dandelions standing tall in a fresh-mown lawn, like dandelions that have cracked concrete with nothing but roots, like dandelions unafraid to be turned into ash, or cut or poisoned, ready to be born again.

The stick split around the sword in the raised arm of the first wizard and struck him in the chest.

He crumpled, his black robe, his black life, and the

lives of those beside him, all swallowed by hungry color. The flame shattered and rushed through the wood, chattering on trunks, and sparking through needles and bark. And then the color was gone from Henry's hands. Gone from his blood. Five wizards slumped lifeless over the bodies of Tate and Roland. The rest had ducked away.

Henry stood, weak and clammy.

Monmouth and Frank hit him at a run, dragging him through the underbrush and ducking around trees, toward the harbor. Flame crackled and burst in a ball around them, knocking them to the ground. But they were up again and running with smoking hair, and Henry in between them.

"Idiot," Frank said. "Idiot."

Flame crackled again, farther behind them.

"They won't wait long," Monmouth said between breaths.

"Nope," Frank managed. "But they might be nervous after that bit of foolery."

Henry stumbled along, blinking and dizzy. He felt like all the blood in his body had drained out of his feet.

They were out of the cluster of trees, running along the cliff beside the water.

"Daft," Frank muttered, and managed to twist and slap Henry across the face. Frank stopped, and Monmouth stopped as well, watching the trees behind them.

Frank sputtered, flushed with anger and burned skin, dripping with rain. He shoved two fingers into

Henry's mouth and grabbed his lower jaw. The grip hurt, but the pain focused Henry's eyes.

"Two faeren dead for you, Henry York," he said. "Likely another soon." He slapped Henry again. "You get into the city," he said. "Get to your mother. Be christened. Rouse your father. Do you hear me?"

"They're coming," Monmouth said. "They know we've stopped."

"Do that," Frank said. "And there just might be a city here in another week. Die, and everyone does."

"Frank!" Monmouth yelled.

The fat faerie gripped Henry's jaw even harder, pulling Henry's face all the way down to his.

"Write my name on a bit of stone," Frank said, and he kissed Henry on the forehead.

Monmouth was moving, backpedaling.

Frank put both hands on Henry's chest and pushed him off the cliff.

Henry choked on his own yell, limbs flailing as he fell backward.

"Live, Henry York!" a voice yelled, and Henry hit the water.

Below the surface, the world was calm. No wizards. No wind.

No air.

Henry wasn't sure that was a problem. He could stay down, simply drifting, and the world would never be crazy again.

His mind was numb and confused, but his lungs were not. In a flash, panic replaced his confusion. He could see the surface. Orange light flicked in sheets above it. He kicked toward it and discovered that he couldn't move his right arm.

It was stuck in a backpack strap.

Henry struggled, tore the backpack off, kicked it away, and climbed toward the surface in a frenzy.

His face burst into the wind and rain. Gasping, he looked up at the cliff's edge. He couldn't see anyone, but even through the wind, he could hear shouting.

Bobbing, treading water with near-useless limbs, sinking and surging and swallowing and spitting, Henry turned and looked across the harbor toward the city walls and the dock. It was a long way off, and the water, though less angry than the open ocean, was still far from calm.

His head was ringing with the ache of what he'd done in the wood and the breathlessness of nearly drowning, but he managed to kick off his shoes and start a slow crawl across the water, making for the rigging of the closer ruined ship.

The waves grew as Henry left the shelter of the cliff behind. He struggled more and more to stay on course and keep his head above water. In his previous life, he'd never been allowed to swim without a life vest. He'd hated it, but now he would have given just about anything for something large and orange and puffy with an embarrassing strap through the crotch. But he only had his sweatshirt, and it was bogging him down. He would have tried to get it off, but as exhausted as he was, he knew he would only get tangled up and sink.

A dozen times he told himself that his arms could no longer move, that his legs were going to cramp, that he should just stop and rest. But there was no place to stop, and the only kind of rest was permanent. If he tried to float, the waves pushed him where they wanted, and they wanted him down.

From the water, he couldn't see what was happening on the plain in front of the city, but he could still see arrows tailing through the wind. As he watched, his hand rubbed against something in the water. It wasn't alive, so he gripped it, spat out a mouthful of harbor, and looked at what he'd found.

It was a rope. He looked up at the ship's mast, still many yards away, and then at the rope in his hand. He pulled on it. It wasn't taut, and at first he was only straightening out a lot of slack, but it still moved him forward. And then the slack was gone, and he slid through the water toward the mast. When he reached it, he grabbed on to the leaning timber and let his limbs go limp in the water. He looked back at the cliff and at the city dock. He was more than halfway there. The other ruined ship was farther out toward the harbor mouth. From where he was now, he couldn't stop until the long dock.

Above the city, lightning flashed. Henry felt a tingle in the water as the jagged bolts fell and the thunder rumbled beneath the water's surface.

If lightning struck anywhere in the harbor, he could easily be dead. If it was at all close, he would be.

Wrapping his legs around the mast, he managed to struggle off his sweatshirt. Then he braced himself against it and pushed off with all the strength he had left in his legs.

Without the sweatshirt, his arms felt free, strong again, but only briefly. His muscles stopped working with oxygen and began to work with acid. His stomach was tightening into a knot, as much with fear as exhaustion.

Henry closed his eyes, breathed as evenly as he could, and kept his arms moving. If lightning struck the water, he might never notice.

He winced with the thunder.

Henry opened his eyes and saw that he had drifted off course, but he was closer to the dock than he had expected. He shifted, releveled his breathing, and set out again.

When Henry reached the dock, he scanned the cliff on the other side of the harbor for any sign of life.

Three men in black stood on the cliff's edge, their robes gusting with the wind.

Henry tried to pull himself onto the dock, but the platform was too high, and his arms had lost all function.

Instead, he moved from pylon to pylon, toward the sharp bank that grew up into the city wall. When he reached it, he managed to find a handhold and foothold and struggled up out of the water, scrabbling at the heavy, planked surface. He rolled onto the dock and lay on his back, panting, his eyes shut against the rain and his ears ringing with thunder.

If he'd been watching, he would have seen lightning strike the water.

After a moment, he rolled onto his stomach and clambered onto his knees and then up onto his bare feet. He teetered in the wind as he moved along the dock toward a short set of stairs that led to a black door recessed into the wall.

He fully intended to knock.

The wall was made of smooth stone, and Henry could see no mortar. It was tall. He reached the stairs and put his hands down in front of him to climb.

"Stand!" a voice yelled. Henry pushed back up and stood. He looked around for the speaker. There were slits in the ceiling above the door. Henry saw the tip of an arrow.

"Watchword?" the voice asked.

"Um," Henry said. He was feeling wobbly again. "I— I just need to see Hyacinth." The name tasted strange on his tongue.

"The city is under siege. We'll not open the door without the watchword."

Thunder boomed, and the door rattled on its hinges.

"I just swam the harbor. I need to see her." He swallowed. "I'm her son."

"Which one?" the voice asked. "I don't know you."

"Henry. I've been missing."

"Missing? Since when?"

Henry thought about this. "Since forever," he said, and he lay down on the steps.

Behind him, the door opened.

CHAPTER TWENTY-FOUR

Henry opened his eyes and looked into a face spattered with blood. A low, stone ceiling arched above him. An open door and slit windows let in the daylight, such as it was. He was out of the rain, but he could still feel the wind. The face smiled at him, a wide smile set into a strong jaw. It reminded him of Henrietta's.

"I'm your uncle Caleb," the face said. "You have been long awaited."

Henry struggled to sit up, but the man pushed him back down. Two other men stood behind him. He looked at them.

"He swam the harbor?" he asked. They both nodded.

He looked back into Henry's eyes. He looked inside them. "You've struggled to death's brink today. Well done."

Then he stood up and moved toward the door.

"Take him to his mother's house. He needs nothing but sleep, and his cousins can attend him. Other reunions must wait out the day, but send a message to his mother where she hospitals."

The men threw a cloak over Henry, propped him up

on either side, and led him out through the doorway and into the swirling rain. They descended one flight of stone stairs, crossed under an arched walkway, and entered the streets. Henry's bare feet slapped on the cobblestones and splashed in rivers of rainwater.

The roofs of the buildings were rounded, and most of the walls were of stone. The streets were narrow and winding. Most of the buildings' windows were smashed and shattered, even where assembled from small panes. And many of the buildings themselves were crumbled and charred. Some still smoked in their ruins, steaming rain.

"Henry," one of the men said. "I'm afraid we cannot be spared for long. And we are exposed in the street. We must go more quickly."

"I can't," Henry said.

"Right."

Arms wrapped around him, and he was folding over someone's shoulder. He watched their heels as the running water parted around cobblestones. He watched until his eyes closed, and then he was looking into Frank Fat-Faerie's dark eyes. Small, thick fingers were hooked into his lower jaw, and the faerie was alternating between slapping his face and kissing his head.

Rouse your father.

When Henry woke, he was facedown in a soft bed. And he wasn't wet.

The room was dark, and the sound of thunder was

muffled. He could hear glass rattling. There was some light in the room. Behind him.

He rolled over.

At the foot of the bed, there was a small table holding a lamp. Beside it sat Henrietta.

She smiled. "That wasn't that bad," she said. "They thought you would sleep all day. It's only two in the afternoon."

Henry squinted. "Henrietta?"

She nodded.

"Did you get the tuna?"

"What?"

"I left you two cans like your dad said."

"You're not making sense," she said. "Do you know where you are?"

Henry slid back in the bed and looked around.

"Hylfing?" he asked. "How did you get here?"

"It's a long story. I went through FitzFaeren." She thought for a moment. "Do you know why it's ruined?" She didn't wait for an answer. "Because Grandfather took some things from them that they'd always used against Endor."

Henry rubbed his eyes. "Right," he said. "He used them to make the cupboards work."

She cocked her head. "You know about the arrow?"

"The arrow?" he asked. "What arrow?"

"Some special arrow. I can't make it sound as cool as Uncle Caleb, so I won't even try. There was a sword hilt and a stone, too. He stole all three. How did you know what he did with them?"

"I read something about it in his journal."

"Where are the journals?" she asked.

He looked around the room. "In my backpack."

"Where's your backpack?"

Henry blinked and rubbed the corners of his eyes, thinking. "It's in the harbor."

Henrietta sat perfectly still. "And the journals are inside?"

Henry nodded.

For a moment, the two of them looked at each other, thinking about what that meant.

Henrietta slipped a hand to her face, tucking hair behind her ear. She smiled with tight lips. "It's good to see you again, Henry. For a while, I didn't think I would see anyone again. Ever."

Henry pulled in a deep breath. "It's good to see you, too."

"It's not really a good time to be here," Henrietta said. "We're not even allowed out of the house. Henry—" She sat up, slapped her hands on her knees, and leaned forward. "You can see! When did your eyes come back?"

Henry's mind moved back through the blur of the last few days. "In Byzanthamum," he said. He opened his mouth to say more, but shut it again. He didn't know where to begin, and he didn't want to tell his story. Not until he had finished it.

The door opened, and Henrietta jumped to her feet. "He's awake," she said, and slipped quickly out of the room. The door shut behind her.

"Good morning," a woman said. Her voice was soft. She walked behind Henrietta's little lamp and moved toward a dark wall, gathered up curtains, and threw them back.

Three big windows, each made of thick, circle-swirling, blown-glass panes, let in the gray storm-light. Water ran down the outer surface, following the swirls.

The woman turned and looked at him. She was tall. Her hair was nearly black through, with soft streaks of gray. She was wearing a heavy apron, spattered with what could have been blood. Henry didn't care what she was wearing. He didn't want to look away from her face and her eyes. They were very gray eyes.

"I had thought to watch you sleep," she said, and her voice sounded almost sad. "Others can tend the fallen for a while."

She drew a chair to the side of his bed and sat down. She was beautiful and tired. Her eyes were deep, her voice, her motion, deep with a slow, terrible joy. A joy despite sadness. A joy built on sadness.

She stretched out a slender arm and pushed Henry's hair up off his forehead to stare in his eyes. Her touch was cool.

"Do you know who I am?" she asked.

Henry nodded, opened his mouth, and then swallowed.

The light in her eyes answered him, and her hand slid down to his jaw. A finger felt his burns. Henry saw pain flash across her face, but she didn't flinch away. Her cool fingers were still, and he felt nervousness and fear fade from inside him, replaced with something else, something he didn't recognize.

He watched tears pool slowly in his mother's eyes. They built and fell, and she didn't bother to wipe them away. His own eyes grew hot in imitation.

"When you left," she said, "you had no name. Your father took you to prepare for one that we had chosen. It was to shape you."

Henry wiped his cheeks. "What was it?"

He listened to her slow breath and watched her watching him. Her brows lowered a fraction on her face, and she shook her head.

"I will never speak it," she said. "To tell it to you now would be a lie. I will not gift you with something stillborn and buried long ago. We could not know what you were meant to be. We held only a kicking child, full of laughter, who jumped, even in the womb, at the voice of his father and cried at the kissings of his sisters."

She took his right hand in hers and looked at his palm. After a moment, she looked up and smiled.

"Your blood is all green and gold," she said, "with the strength of dandelions." She stood up. "And their strength is in their laughter, for they fear nothing."

"That's not me," Henry said.

Hyacinth bent down, wrapped her arms tight around her son, and he knew they had never let go.

"That is you," she said, "to those with eyes to see."

She kissed him on one cheek and then the other before she straightened.

"I must go, but I will come back to you soon. Your sisters are nervous to meet you."

"Now?" he asked.

Hyacinth smiled again, but Henry could feel her sadness. "There may be no other time."

She reached the door and looked back at him.

"How do you know for sure?" Henry asked quickly. "I mean, how do you know I'm your son?"

"Because I am your mother," she said. "And you have your father's soul."

She opened the door. "And his nose," she added.

"Am I going to be christened?" Henry asked.

She stood still, surprised. "Now?"

He didn't answer.

Her eyes brightened. "Yes," she said. "Tonight, even if the sea climbs the walls and wizards are the guests, I will set a christening feast for my son. We shall have some dandelion laughter."

When she had gone, Henry swung his legs out of bed, blinked at the linen pants that he hadn't been expecting, and stretched his body cautiously.

He hadn't come to Hylfing to lie in bed. That's not

why Tate and Roland had died. At least he hoped not. He had to do something. Fat Frank had told him to get christened. Why that was important, he didn't know. The other faeries, Radulf and Braithwait and Rip, had talked about it in his dream. They hadn't wanted him to be christened. What had Rip said? They couldn't risk it.

This is what Ron and Nella had seen and talked about. Why Ron had caught him when he fell. Darius was here. This was where Henry needed to stand. Maybe, this was where he needed to die.

Henry looked around the floor for shoes. There weren't any. As he crouched to look under the bed, he heard laughter outside his room, and the door opened.

Girls poured in. Girls and Richard.

Penelope hugged him before he could say anything. Anastasia joined in while Richard stood on one leg, and then the other, smiling and picking at his dirty blue cast.

Henrietta stood back with her arms crossed, clearly pleased with herself. Beside her stood two other girls, one who was taller than Penelope and had long, straight auburn hair, and the other Henrietta's size with hair like Hyacinth. They were both smiling, but looked worried.

"You've got sisters!" Anastasia yelled.

"And brothers," Penelope said. "But you'll meet them later."

Richard stepped in and stuck out his casted hand. Henry laughed and shook it. Then he stepped in front of the two new girls and tried to look less nervous than he felt.

"Hi," he said.

"I'm Una," said the tall one, and she hugged him. "I remember when you and father left."

"I'm Isa," the smaller one said, and hugged him around the ribs. "You look like James."

"He looks like all of them," Una said.

"But like James the most."

"Who is James?" Henry asked.

"He's the youngest," Una said, and she tucked her hair behind her ears exactly how Henrietta did. "The youngest besides you at least. He's a sailor."

"He's small," said Isa.

"James is?"

"You are."

"You're smaller," Henry said.

"I'm a girl, and I'm still older than you. I was almost two when you left."

"Oh." Henry didn't know what else to say. Five girls were all standing around looking at him. Plus Richard.

"Zeke's here as well," Richard said suddenly.

"What?" Henry asked. "How?"

"And a policeman," Anastasia said. "I don't remember his name."

"Do you really want the whole story?" Henrietta asked.

Henry shook his head. "Sometime. But right now, I just want to go look at what's happening."

"We're not allowed outside," Anastasia said.

"Is Zeke outside?" Henry asked. He knew the answer,

but he still waited for his cousins to nod. "Then I'm allowed outside."

All around them came the sound of great bells ringing.

"I wouldn't go out," Una said. "Uncle Caleb said the bells would only ring if the wall was broken. We should stay here."

Henry looked around at all of them. "I need to go," he said. "I'm supposed to." His voice wavered.

"Are you afraid?" Una asked.

Henry swallowed hard. "I haven't thrown up yet," he said, and he left the room.

Darius's head was dipped to his chest. The seventy-seventh wizard had fallen, killed by someone outside the walls. It was a strong number. Sharp around its edges. Darius would stir the anthill.

Looking up, he stared blindly across the plain. He had no need of his eyes anymore. Hylfing had seen lightning since its birth. It had been built and strengthened and preserved by men with a loathing for wizards and wizardry. With every strike, the walls almost grew stronger, though many houses and buildings had been burned inside.

With a groan, he released strength. It trickled from his fingers, but quickly grew to a rush, and then a torrent, peeling the skin on his hand back to the bone. With a struggle, he resealed the dam inside him. His skin reclosed. The pulse ran through the ground, racing through rock and earth, and as it reached the city wall, he called it up with strange tones, speaking an ancient earth-rape he had never before heard.

The ground split and twisted beneath the wall. It was severed, and a portion fell back into the city.

He could hear the cries and feel the shattering of bones. Bells began ringing, but his mind ignored them. Darius released another river of stolen strength across the plain, and the crack and shattering of stone marked the birth of a second breach.

Henry stood, shivering in the street. His cousins and sisters—real sisters—had followed him through the house, refusing to give directions. At the door, little Isa had given him a cloak and a pair of boots. They were too big for him.

The house was on a hill, and while the cobbled street wound its way through other houses on its way down, Henry could see over them, all the way to the river that separated the city, and to the wall. He could see the gaps and the crowd of men in dark robes pushing through them. In the other direction, from the cathedral spire, the bells were beating out an alarm, competing with the never-ending thunder.

For the second time in a single day, Henry ran toward a fight. This time, he wasn't even holding a stick.

By the time he'd crossed the bridge, he began to slow down. Archers had pushed the wizards back out of one of the gaps with swarm after swarm of arrows, but the dark-robed surge in the other was growing. Flame and balled lightning crawled over the rubble and through the streets.

Everywhere Henry looked, he saw men taking cover behind stones and in doorways, only to fall back again, retreating to new shelter. Still, Henry ran forward in the middle of the street, trying not to slip on the wet cobbles. One hundred yards from the wall, Henry stepped into a doorway and looked out over the shifting conflict.

Bodies, with and without dark robes, were scattered through the rubble, and four figures were running from the other breach. In the center, a tall man drew back a bow even while he ran. Beside him came two others. Both were carrying what looked like rifles. One was thick, dressed like a policeman and limping, the other was lean and hunched while he ran. The fourth was smaller and ran in front, burdened with a long, rectangular shield.

As they approached, wizards shifted to face them. Henry watched in shock as Zeke Johnson banged the long shield down across stones, and the men all ducked behind it.

The tall man stood the longest, and three wizards fell in the rubble with his arrows in them before he huddled with the others, flame curling above them.

Then they were up again, pushing forward, still with only the tall man letting fly his black arrows. Henry could see three quivers on his back.

Other men were pushing forward now, and wild

arrows rattled in the stones. Arrows that met their purpose made no sound at all.

Henry's eyes were shifting. A dozen wizards made a stand in the rubble, combining their strength. The men on the outside were lashing out with wind, sending arrows bending away useless with raised hands and knocking the city's defenders to the ground as they showed themselves. Henry could see others inside the group, calling down bundles of lightning, cracking whips of light madly at walls that hid the city's archers, or balling the power up and bowling it through the streets, searching for life. If any defenders crept too close, then balls of flame sought them out as well.

Zeke's wide shield approached the wizards slowly, shaking in the wind and thunder, shading the men behind it from rolling flames. Lightning never reached it, though the wizards tried. Henry could see the tall man with the bow forcing it away, though his strength did not match any one of the wizards. When Zeke lowered the shield, the tall man's arrows flew, and two shotguns blazed.

Two wizards fell to wounds Henry could not see. A long arrow from behind the shield found its way through the twisting wind and through a wizard's chest. The clustered group of dark blowing robes edged slowly back, leaving behind the bodies. As they did, Henry moved forward.

Three more fell, and Henry watched the wind's

strength shrink and the shield move forward. Another turned and ran for the breach, but tumbled into the rubble with a shaft between his shoulder blades.

All around Henry, dozens of archers moved into the open streets and began to let fly. Henry could hear the twang and hum of string and feather, and he watched as the last of the black robes were brought down inside the walls. The rest were through the breach and onto the plain.

Men swarmed down the streets, filling the breach with arrows while others shifted rubble and pulled away bodies.

"Uncle Frank!" Henry yelled. Frank didn't hear him. He was rolling a stone back toward the wall. Henry hit it beside him and looked up at his uncle. His forehead was red. Singed and curled white hair was plastered onto it with rain.

"Fill the breach!" the tall man shouted. "Killing barrels!"

"Henry York," Frank said. "Brother Caleb said you were here." He grinned. "I'm glad to see you while we're both still pullin' breath."

"He's your brother?" Henry asked.

Frank smiled. "And brother to your father. Can't shake me. I'm still your uncle, Henry. By blood."

Caleb strode over to them, and Henry looked from his face to Frank's. They were alike. But very different. Henry braced himself to be sent running home, back up the hill to bed.

"Can you shift stone?" Caleb asked. "Both breaches need filling."

Henry nodded. Zeke and the policeman were too far away to be heard, but Zeke dropped a rock and waved.

"Push coming!" someone yelled.

Shouting echoed along the wall while men dropped to their knees and bellies.

Again, fire filled the breach, and lightning laid men low. But this time, the archers stood their ground at the wall, and the wind bristled with arrows.

Henry rolled and lifted and stacked stone until the sun was gone and darkness, almost as heavy as faeren light, settled on the city.

Still, with hundreds of nameless men, Henry worked by lightning light, his bones vibrating with the dwindling thunder. The storm was regathering.

The wizards had drawn back. And though no one understood it, it was welcome.

Henry stood beside Zeke, and they stared at their hands, with flapping skin where blisters had been born and died in a matter of hours. Every drop of rain stung what it touched.

Zeke looked at Henry, and Henry looked at Zeke. Henry had thrown his cloak away to work, and now he was as wet as he had been in the harbor. Zeke had lost his baseball hat, and his face was filthy with smoke and grease. Rain beaded up on his cheeks. His eyes were as calm as they had ever been, despite the madness they'd seen, and burn spots had welted up on his forearms where he'd leaned against the flame-heated shield.

"We're still here," Zeke said.

Henry nodded and looked out at the darkness beyond the walls. For how long? Someone with strength beyond all the wizards stood out in the hills. He thought he could feel him pulling at the wind, though he couldn't quite see it. He wasn't even sure if the wizards he'd watched die would have been able to call down lightning on their own. Someone had handed it to them.

Two stone walls, *U*-shaped, had been erected from the rubble, quarantining the breaches. Wizards who entered the breach would be standing in a space surrounded by stone, below the bows of men on the intact walls. Killing barrels.

Uncle Frank and the policeman walked over to Henry and Zeke, carrying their shotguns. The policeman limped.

"Coupla shells left," Frank said.

The policeman nodded. "They'll be gone by breakfast."

"Henry." Frank put his hand on the cop's shoulder. "This is Sergeant Ken Simmons, who thought he would come along when the house was ripped from Kansas land. He does good work with a shotgun."

Sergeant Simmons stuck out his hand to shake, but when he saw Henry's torn fingers, he slapped him on the back.

Caleb was moving toward them. All three of his

quivers were empty, and he stooped to pick up arrows as he walked. He ran his hand over the shaft of each, muttering something to the head and breathing on the feathers before he kept them. Some he dropped back on the ground.

"The quiet will not last," he said when he reached them. "Return to the house and rest and eat while you can."

"And you?" Frank asked.

"I will search beyond the walls," Caleb said. "There is one strength behind this, and I do not know why he bides. But while he bides, I may find a way to strike."

"His name is Darius," Henry said. "He's a seventh son."

Caleb raised his eyebrows. "You know him?"

"He pulled me through the cupboards." Henry shook his head, thinking Caleb wouldn't understand. "He kidnapped me and tried to make me his son." He pulled his shirt up, and his pale, wet scars stood out in the dark. "I escaped."

Caleb crouched and ran his fingers over the tangle of scars on Henry's belly.

"A tree?" he asked. Caleb stood up and stepped backward, toward a shadowed doorway. In a flash, he spun, grabbed something near his waist, and pulled it out of the shadow.

Surrounded by shimmering air came Frank the fat faerie, pulled by his nose, grimacing, sputtering pain, and kicking.

"Who is this?" Caleb asked, crouching.

"That's Frank Fat-Faerie," Henry laughed. "He's alive! Can you see him?"

"I can smell him," Caleb said. "More or less. I do not have the full gifts, but I have enough to know when a faerie is blinding vision."

Caleb let go of the faerie's nose and gripped him by both ears. "Listen well, Frank Fat-Faerie. Faeries will not walk unseen in my city, not in these times and not with the district committees as they are. I do not trust the faeren. Make yourself seen."

The shimmer disappeared. Uncle Frank and the others all blinked. Caleb dropped the faerie's ears.

"What business do you have in Hylfing when the wizards attack?"

"Well, sir," the faerie said, "my busyness involved saving your nephew from wizards, sir. Saving him from faeren corruption, sir. And saving him from wizards again, sir. Bringing him to the city of his fathers, sir, and in other ways manifesting extreme faeren nobleness and loyalty." The faerie's face was flushed with anger. He looked at Henry and nodded toward Uncle Frank.

"Is that your uncle Frank?" he asked. "I like him. Much better than some I could mention, who're eager to grab faces and accuse. But then it's hard to go wrong with a Frank."

Caleb laughed, and the others laughed with him. "What else have you got hidden in that doorway, Fat-Faerie?"

"A young wizard, sir. But a good one. He's badly hurt in his gut."

"Monmouth?" Henry jumped toward the doorway.

"Mushrooms," Monmouth said quietly. "Not a tree. Darius's strength began with mushrooms. His brand is poison."

"Mushrooms," Caleb said. "That makes more sense of his strength, though it may not help me."

"Caleb?" a voice cried. Henry watched old Eli hurry toward them through the shadows.

"Eli," Caleb said. "You look pure and unspoiled. How have you passed the battle?"

"With Lady Hyacinth," he said. "In the hospital. Ask her if you doubt me. But now she sent me to tell you that the table is set, and the priest waits."

"Priest?" Caleb asked.

Eli nodded. "For the christening."

"And about time," said Fat Frank.

CHAPTER TWENTY-FIVE

Hyacinth was very happy. But she was a wise woman, and an old enemy had returned. She did not think her happiness would last.

There was a window in her room, a large window that saw the sun's path most of the day. She had borne nine children, and for each of them, she had tended a sapling tree on its sill. She had woven all of the magic of motherhood into those trees, and as they grew large enough, she planted them in the courtyard behind the house. There were five trees in the courtyard now. Three had died when her oldest sons had fallen. Her daughters' trees blossomed every spring and were still small. The trees of three living sons led strange lives. Their leaves changed and fell, not in Hylfing's autumn but whenever autumn found her sons. And when spring sun was on their faces in some far part of the world, leaves budded and grew through any winter that might fall on their mother's house. But there was one tree, more twig than sapling, that still sat in soil in Hyacinth's window. It was Henry's tree, though it had never known his name. Not once had it ever produced a leaf or bud, and yet it had never died.

She looked at it and ran her hand over its surface, humming. It was supple, wick with hidden life.

Downstairs, she heard loud voices and knew the others had arrived. She turned and walked to the stairs.

Uncle Frank and Caleb carried Monmouth into the house.

Zeke and Henry stopped in the doorway and stared into the front room. Richard, in baggy clothes, came and stood beside them. Tables had been brought in from somewhere, strung together, and set. There was a dusty bottle of wine, larger than Henry had thought possible, and huge plates of cold meat. Aunt Dotty was bustling around the table with a steaming bowl of apples in each hand. Her face was flushed red, like the first time Henry had seen her, and her hair, once pulled back, fell down onto her cheek.

When she saw Henry, she set the bowls down and rushed to him. She was softer than his mother, and she wrapped him in the smell of apples. She smiled and kissed him and couldn't speak, and then led him to an old white-haired woman, already seated at the table. The woman was blind and spreading smiles through the room.

Henry's cousins and sisters were seated around her.

"Your grandmother Anastasia," Dotty said, and the

woman found his face with her hands, squeezed his cheeks, and kissed his head. Little Anastasia sat beside her.

Monmouth was tended and laid on cushions in the corner, where he slept. Fat Frank refused a seat and instead crouched nervously by the door, fidgeting and gnawing on his fingernails.

The wine was being poured. Henry's mother took him by his elbow and directed him to a seat as she had already done for Richard. Zeke was on Henry's left, and his uncles were seated at either end of the long table. A bowl of warm water and a cloth were passed for washing. Another bowl of water, wooden, sat in front of Henry, and he rinsed his fingers in it. The seat beside him was empty, and his mother stood behind it, pushing hair away from a glowing face. She was saying something, but Henry was a little dazed. He watched the smiling, serious faces. He watched the fat faerie squatting nervously by the door.

Then a man in black, a priest, stood up beside his uncle Caleb and spoke while everyone was silent.

"A table laden in the face of enemies," he said. Henry heard little else. The man continued, and when he had finished, everyone laughed. Henry laughed as well and didn't know why. He didn't need to know, because it was real, and it came from within and without. Henry watched the food on the table travel around and the people at the table smile and take of it. He smiled, but he could hear little of their words. His mind and his eyes were sensing other things. He heard rain on the windows and wind through the cracks of the house. He watched the thunder shake his glass and felt the sea pounding the coast. And none of these things were as loud as his uncles' laughter. Zeke was talking to Caleb, and Caleb was telling him that he would give him a bow. Hyacinth was smiling at Henry, and Grandmother Anastasia stared toward the ceiling. Her smile was gone, and her food was untouched. Uncle Frank was trying to explain baseball and ketchup to whomever might listen.

And Henry found that he was eating as well, and drinking something extraordinarily red out of his glass.

The eating passed quickly. The mounds of food grew smaller. Henry was full, and he felt warm.

Caleb stood, and the conversation quieted.

"My nephew, brother-son, eats with us today. He returns to us in a storm. Some of his brothers sleep in the earth, as do some of mine, and others, now away, he shall someday meet if this storm breaks. He is the seventh son of a seventh son and more. His inheritance is rich. May he make it richer for those behind him. His father, long lost, is gone, but his mother tonight shall name him."

All eyes, especially Henry's, went to his mother. She stood slowly, smiling, but her eyes were sad.

"I have long lacked this son and knew not what had become of him, as I know not what became of his father. But now I know in part and am grateful even for the providence that took my son away an infant, because he has retrieved a lost brother and uncle."

Dotty began crying, but Hyacinth continued.

"A name is meant to shape and mold. To destine. And yet my son has already found shape. This is not the naming of an infant. This is the naming of a young man with feet already on a path. His name shall still be Henry, and it is a good name. He has dwelt away from us in the home of another father, descended from another line. This house would honor that, and we would not try to remove the mark of his young exile. It has shaped him and is woven in his story. So he shall have the name that those other fathers bore. He shall be Henry York. But another name he still lacks. It is the name on which he will stand, the river on which his other names will travel."

Grandmother Anastasia pushed back her chair and stood up, weakly, still staring at the ceiling. She opened her mouth to speak, swaying as she did.

"This is Henry York, seventh son of Mordecai Westmore, seventh son of Amram Iothric, in the line long faithful to the Old King, farmers of the earth, husbands of the sea. Through him shall kingdoms find new birth. Through him shall the earth find balm for hidden wounds. He shall not be a man of blood, though he shall shed it. He shall not be an angry man, though he be angered. An old enemy has risen through him, but he shall be its curse. It marks his flesh, but he shall break its back. He shall be called Maccabee, for his strength has been hidden away, but it shall become a hammer that burns in the night, both green and gold."

The room was silent as Grandmother settled into her chair, smiling. She began to eat.

The priest rose to his feet and walked slowly around behind Henry. He set his wineglass on the table and picked up a plain wooden bowl filled with water. Henry twisted in his seat, looking up at the priest and his mother.

"I think I might have washed my hands in that," he whispered.

"Even better," the priest said.

"Is it holy water?" Henry asked.

The priest smiled and bent his mouth to Henry's ear. "It will be when we've done." He straightened back up.

"Who fathered this child?" he asked.

"Mordecai Westmore," Hyacinth said.

"Who bore him?"

"I did."

"What path is meant for his feet?"

"The one true path."

"What God shall walk before him?"

"The true Gods shall be the God before him."

"What shall be his life?"

"Death."

"What shall be his end?"

"Life."

"What is his name?"

Hyacinth paused, looking down at Henry and then at his grandmother. "Henry York Maccabee," she said. "May he be a true son to a true father."

Henry felt a tingle in the air, like metal in his mouth. Beside the door, the faerie squirmed and covered his ears.

The priest cupped his hand in the wooden bowl, and it rose dripping.

Fat drops splattered on his plate, and then Henry felt the wet beneath the man's palm settle on his already wet head. The priest's voice rang out in a slow but short chant, rolling an unknown, ancient tongue into a song that Henry felt he knew. A song his bones could recognize. Then the priest handed Henry his glass.

"So he is, and so he shall be," the priest said. "All of you, drink."

With water dripping off his nose, Henry drank, and he watched as the rest of the table did as well, even Zeke and little Anastasia, who coughed, and the policeman.

The wine made his eyes water.

Henry had been christened.

Upstairs, on the sill in Hyacinth's window, there was a sapling that knew Henry's name. A single bud stood out at its tip. By morning light, it would spread its first leaf.

Henry looked around at the table, and the table looked around at him. He wasn't sure what had happened, but he was glad he was still Henry, though Maccabee was a little strange. The rain rattled on the windows, and laughter once again spread its way down the table. Isa and Una jumped up to fetch pies, but wind stopped them.

The door to the street blew open, and rain and wind spilled into the room. Frank the faerie cowered beside it.

While Henry watched, a tall shape, cloaked and hooded, stepped into the doorway. Panic froze him.

Darius had come.

The man stepped into the room, dripping, and looked about himself. No one moved. Henry waited for Frank, for Caleb, for anyone to do something. His heart was in his throat. The hood turned, and Henry could see black hair beneath it. The man was looking for him.

Pressure surrounded Henry, holding him still, holding them all still, a magic that didn't want them to move.

"Knife!" Fat Frank sputtered. "Throw a knife!"

An enormous weight sat on Henry's chest and pinned his arms to his sides. But he fought it. He broke it. He leaned forward and grabbed the blade of a long knife from a platter of meat. He didn't know how to throw a knife, but it didn't matter. His hand was hot. The blade was hot. He twisted in his seat and threw it.

The man looked at him.

"No!" Caleb yelled, and Henry watched the blade spin toward the man's head. He didn't move as the knife, threaded with Henry's gold, passed above him and stuck in the wall above the door.

The pressure was gone. People around the table gasped for air.

Grandmother Anastasia laughed.

The man reached up and pushed back his hood. His face was hard, and wet hair hung around it. He looked like Caleb, but younger and older at the same time. Like Frank.

"There is no magic stronger than naming," he said. "But only my son had strength enough to move."

"Mordecai!" Hyacinth cried, and she was in his arms.

Beside them, Fat Frank burst into tears.

Darius walked across the plain, and the world died into silence around him.

He has come.

"Yes," he said.

Begin the end.

"How is this possible?" Caleb asked, laughing. "Now, of all times, Mordecai, you walk through the door of a house so long empty of you."

"Faerie magic," Fat Frank said, wiping his eyes. "When I heard the committee feared a christening, I knew what they'd done. They'd laid you up in a barrow, no mistake there, and left an unchristened child, the fools."

Mordecai looked down at the short, rounded faerie. "You told him to throw the knife," he said. "You've betrayed your own and revealed their magic."

Fat Frank snorted. "My own? The way I see it, the committee betrayed the rest of us, not to mention you."

Mordecai smiled and looked around the room. "Francis?"

Uncle Frank nodded. "It's been a long while since we threw stones at the bishop's dog."

Mordecai laughed. "And who is this tainted wizard in the corner?" He pointed at Monmouth, still sleeping.

"He's a friend," Henry said. "He helped me get here. I'm glad I didn't hit you with the knife," he added. "I was trying to. I thought you were Darius."

"Who is Darius?" Mordecai asked.

Beneath them, the ground shook. Wineglasses tipped and spilled on the table.

Bells began ringing.

Mordecai looked to Caleb, confusion on his face. "What strength is this?"

"Nimiane of Endor has risen," Caleb said. "She possesses a wizard called Darius. He is more than my match. I stalked him once, and even struck him with an arrow handed down to us from the Old King. It turned to ash in his flesh."

Mordecai pushed his face into the top of Hyacinth's head. "Reunion must wait. I will not be lost again."

She released him, and he walked quickly to where his mother sat smiling in her blindness. He kissed her, and she grabbed his arm.

"You were hidden for a while," she said. "But I walked with you."

"You did," he said. "Thank you."

Both of his daughters stood in the doorway to the kitchen. He moved to them. "You were too young to remember me," he said. "But soon, we shall know each other." He kissed them both on the head and then the cheeks.

"Mordecai," Hyacinth said. "Are you not weary? Should you go into battle weakened?"

"I have had nothing but rest for years on end. The weariness in my bones cannot be shaken off with more. Men who can fight, come. Father priest, stay behind. There will be wounded in need of you. My son, you and I have had one adventure together that is now ended. We will have another, and briefer, tonight. The last blood of Endor waits on us."

CHAPTER TWENTY-SIX

By the flash of lightning and the glow of burning houses, Henry could see that the wall was down from breach to breach. The wind blew against them as they struggled down the hill to the bridge. Unlike the last time, Henry could see no hurrying shapes, no black robes standing out in the flames.

"He is strong," Mordecai said. "As taut as a bowstring."

The three brothers hurried at the front of the group. Sergeant Simmons limped beside them. Zeke and Richard were on either side of Henry. Fat Frank danced around and between them while Eli followed behind. Caleb had not allowed him to stay.

Mordecai sniffed the wet air, now laced with smoke. "The life is all but out of this place. His fingers touch it all. Have we nothing?"

"Nothing but ourselves," Caleb said. "I have already wasted an heirloom against him."

They crossed the bridge in silence, bows drawn and shotguns leveled. The streets were empty of everything but rain. As they moved forward, archers stepped out of doorways and alleys and followed them.

"Mordecai returns!" Caleb yelled, and more men poured from the shadows. "You must be our talisman, brother," he added quietly. The earth rumbled again, and another stretch of the wall toppled in the distance. With a rush of hot wind, houses sprang into flame ahead of them. The rain steamed on the street.

"I may be no charm against this," Mordecai said. His voice was quiet.

Henry stopped suddenly and turned. Eli tried to step around him, but Henry grabbed his arm.

The little man shrugged his hand away. "If I must die, I must die," he said. "But must I be gripped?"

"Eli," Henry said. "You gave away talismans from FitzFaeren."

Eli cleared his throat. "It may have been foolishness, but I have no desire for your judgment now. At that time, they were mine to give."

"I don't care," Henry said. "But you did give them to my grandfather, didn't you?"

Eli nodded. "FitzFaeren was to have the doors at our disposal. Travel within a world is open to many with magic—wizards, faeren—but from world to world? Time to time? Our people would have been greatly strengthened."

"Whatever," Henry said. He looked around. The group was continuing slowly down the street, scanning every intersection. "Was one of them an arrow?" he asked.

"Yes." Eli wiped his forehead. "The Arrow of Ramoth Gilead. Some called it the Arrow of Chance. It had not been flown for an age and had no value as a weapon. But oh, the threads all twined within it, the stories in that shaft. They took on a life of their own, a life that could not be killed. Our charms drew on that life. I have never seen or touched it. None of the FitzFaeren have. It's in a sealed case."

"Where is it?" Henry asked.

Eli looked at him. "I don't know. And you could never open its case."

Henry thought for a moment. "What were the other two things you stole?"

"I didn't—"

"No. Of course not. Sorry. What were they?"

"A sword hilt and a stone. They were both—"

"Are they in the Kansas house?"

Eli pulled in a deep breath and pursed his lips.

"Right," Henry said. "Tell my father and uncles not to die. I'll be back as soon as I can."

Henry turned toward the lower city and cupped his hands. "Fat Frank!" he shouted. "I need you!"

The thick faerie came bounding back up out of the darkness. Eli sniffed, and the faerie made a face at him.

"Come on," Henry said, and ran back up the street. The faerie looked confused, but stayed beside him.

"Tate said there was a faeren hall by Hylfing," Henry said quickly.

"By the south gate," Frank said.

Henry stopped. They were well out of Eli's earshot. "I need you to help me find it. I need to get to Badon Hill now, and then back again fast."

Frank blinked. "Why?"

"I can't explain right now, but will you help me? We have to hurry."

Frank nodded.

"Good," Henry said. "Where's the south gate?"

The two of them ran. The faerie easily, but just fast enough to burn Henry's legs and lungs. While the bells rang and fire grew behind them, they climbed the hill back to the house.

How was he going to do this? Just getting there was going to be near impossible.

"It's down the hill and turn to the other side," Frank said.

As they passed by the house, Henry looked at the door still thrown wide open. A shape stood in the road with arms crossed.

"Henrietta?" Henry asked, and she jumped.

"Henry? What are you doing? I thought you'd gone with—"

"Just come on. I think I'm going to need you."

"I should—" she began.

But Henry hadn't even slowed down. He and the

faerie had turned into a side street and were disappearing quickly.

"We have to go now!" Henry yelled back from the darkness.

Henrietta stuck her head back into the house. "Pen, tell Mom I'm going with Henry. He says he needs me. I won't get in the fight. I think."

She didn't wait for an answer. It was more notice than she usually gave.

Henrietta caught her cousin and the faerie on the next turn, after slipping twice on the dark cobbles.

"What are we doing?" she managed.

"The arrow Grandfather stole from the FitzFaeren," Henry said.

"Yeah?"

"We're getting it."

"We are? How? We can't get back to the house, and even if we did, how would we find it?"

Henry thought about the diagram he'd seen in the journal. There had been a line drawn between the compass door and the door in Grandfather's room. And there had been a circle, which could have been a stone, and a *T*, which could have been a hilt. And an arrow, which hopefully had nothing to do with directions.

"There was a diagram in the journal. I think I might know where it is."

"You might know?"

"Well, I can't double-check, because it's at the bottom of the harbor."

"You two should hush," said the faerie. "Unless you'd like to be shot in the dark. The south gate's ahead, and the guards will be tetchy."

Both of them shut their mouths, at least from speech, but they couldn't quiet their breathing or the slap of their feet on the road. They could only hope the wind did that.

The wall at the gatehouse loomed suddenly in front of them, and a voice cried out.

"Hoy there! How goes it?"

"Ill!" Frank yelled. "There's a breach fifty yards wide in the eastern wall. And yet it goes well, for Mordecai has returned."

"Mordecai?" the man asked. "Then why do you flee?"

"We're not running away," Henry said. "But we have to get outside the walls."

"I can't open the gate. Caleb's laid a strict law about that."

Henry didn't want to wait any longer. There wasn't time to convince anyone. "We'll jump," he said.

"Off the wall?"

"Yes. How do we get up?"

The man became a shape in the darkness. "You're children."

Frank's voice raised hackles. "I am not a child."

"Children and a whatsit," the guard said. "I can't let you out."

"There's a stair behind the gatehouse," another voice said from the wall. "I hope you know your business."

Henry pushed into the shadow and felt his way carefully around the small building. When he found the stone stair, he scrambled up quickly. On top of the wall, a few men had gathered from their posts. All carried bows.

Henry peered over the battlement and immediately wished he hadn't. The darkness of the ground made it seem several ages away.

"It's higher than the hayloft," Henrietta said beside him.

Henry gritted his teeth, swung one leg over before he could think about it, and then the other. He twisted onto his belly and scooted backward. For a moment, he dangled with his fingers on the lip of the stone. And then he dropped.

His feet dug troughs through the mud of a steep slope, and his body slammed against it before sliding into brush.

He coughed, trying to get his wind back, and twiddled his toes and fingers to see if everything was working.

Henrietta crashed into him.

Fat Frank somehow managed to keep his feet, slid past, and grabbed on to the brush to steady himself.

"Up if you're alive," he whispered. "If we're going to do this, then there's no time to hurt. No time to feel. Up."

Henry and Henrietta managed to find their hands and knees and then their feet. Frank moved carefully off into the darkness, and they followed close behind.

As he moved farther into the brush, he began whistling a tune.

After a moment, his tune whistled back.

Frank stopped and turned in place.

"Who goes?" a voice whispered.

"Franklin Fat-Faerie, District R.R.K., Region Zed, Badon Hill detachment."

"Poem?"

"I don't have one," Frank said. "We haven't time. We've got news for the mound. For right now. I'm in the union. I've a right to come in."

"This is a conflict zone. The hall is operating under martial protocol. *Book of Faeren*, section 7, article 2. Poem?"

Frank took a deep breath. "There once was a man named Tiggle, whose wife always walked with a wiggle. And whenever she wiggled, Mr. Tiggle, he giggled, and those giggles all turned into Tiggles."

"It's a bit off," the voice said. "At the end. Not warlike. Too many syllables, I thought."

Henry stepped forward. "Mordecai has returned," he said. "And I am his son. If you don't open the hall now, you'll be the one with the wiggle."

"And we'll giggle," Frank added.

After a moment, a different voice spoke. "There's nothing in the notifications about a return, and there's not much I can do without committee authorization. Not in a conflict zone."

"Now," Henry said. "Do it now."

"I can't—"

Muffled voices cut him off. A group of bushes shifted and lifted to the side. Henry looked down into a lit hall, just like the one he had already visited. Only this one was much larger and was crowded with above twenty faeren.

He slid down inside and looked around. He knew he was covered in mud, but he didn't care. Henrietta and Frank followed.

"I need a doorway to the Central Mound now," Henry said. "Right now."

A smaller faerie grabbed two buckets and hurried to the back wall, where multiple stick doors were imbedded. The remaining faeries all watching him silently.

"I am Henry York Maccabee," he said. "I am the seventh son of Mordecai Westmore, who has returned. He was betrayed and entrapped for twelve years by faeren on the committee of this district. He will repay you all."

Eyebrows rose. Lips were licked. Beards were scratched.

"Is the door ready?" Henry asked.

The small faerie finished rubbing his water and dirt and nodded quickly. Henry grabbed Henrietta's hand and pulled her through the crowd, beneath the ceiling of grimacing faces. When they'd reached the back wall, Henry turned around. Fat Frank was pushing his way through after them.

"If you would convince Mordecai of your loyalty," Henry said, "or maybe just water down your guilt, he is struggling against wizards at the eastern wall."

He stepped backward, bringing Henrietta with him into the darkness.

*   *   *

As the world began to reform, swirling through focuses, revealing the mound-magic and then sliding into paneled walls and green clay ceilings, Henry turned and began shouting.

"Mordecai has returned!" he yelled. "He stands in the breach at Hylfing!"

"Where are we?" Henrietta asked. "I can't see anything."

Frank stepped around beside them. He grabbed some earth, spat in his hand, muttered a few words, and dragged it over Henrietta's eyes. She blinked, wiped away the goop, and rocked back in surprise. Five faeries stood facing them, armed. The corridor split into five ahead of them.

Henry looked at Frank. "Get to a way room. Prepare a door for Badon Hill right away. And one for Hylfing," he added. Frank ran down a corridor on the right, and Henry turned back to the guards. He was actually surprised that he had made it this far. If he made it out of the mound at all, he would be shocked.

"Do you have an alarm?" he asked them.

They all nodded, shifting on their feet and regripping their small clubs.

"Sound it," Henry said.

Not one of them moved.

Henry stooped down and gathered up a fistful of dirt. He looked at it, looked at them, and raised his eyebrows.

"Sound it," he said again.

One of them hurried to a root on the corridor wall and pulled it three times.

Nothing happened.

"Will I hear anything?" Henry asked.

Suddenly, the ground shook, and light surged out of all the corridor mouths, carrying the sound of an army of bells.

"Take me to your hall!" Henry yelled over it. "Run! We'll keep up!"

They wove through the quickly crowding corridors. Babies were crying, women were yelling, men were being angry.

"To the hall! Mordecai's returned!" Henry yelled every time they pushed through another group, before sprinting to catch up with their guides on the other side.

"What were you going to do with the dirt?" Henrietta asked while they ran.

"What?" Henry asked. "The dirt?"

Henrietta nodded.

"I don't know. I think I could have grown a dandelion. Maybe."

When they reached the hall, it was already in an uproar. The place was filled, shoulder to shoulder, with worry and anger.

Henry plowed his way through the doors into the same room where he'd been dragged in his underwear.

Radulf was already behind the table, banging away with his mallet. And he was wearing his fuchsia robe.

Henry walked to the platform, left Henrietta standing beside it, climbed up, stood on a chair, and then stepped onto the table.

He walked to its center and kicked the mallet out of Radulf's hand. Then he turned and faced the crowd, preparing to shout over the alarm.

He didn't have to. The alarm stopped.

"Of all the brazen——" Radulf began.

"Quiet!" Henry yelled. "By order of the green man!"

The room was still.

"You returned for your execution?" Radulf asked.

Henry ignored him. "What is the seal the committee uses?" he asked. "What face is carved into every one of your halls? Now look at mine. Really look. The committee stamps their letters with a face they hate. They hate Mordecai and every other true pauper son and green man."

Faeren guards were moving toward Henry. Radulf leaned back in his chair and crossed his arms.

"Mordecai has returned!" Henry yelled. "I am his son, and he returned from his sleep this night. He returned at my christening. Do you know what that means?"

A murmur ran through the crowd. Many of them obviously didn't.

"Mordecai," Henry hurried on, "was betrayed and entrapped by faeren on this committee, and he has returned. This committee even condemned me, his son. He has returned, and the faeren will be judged!"

They understood that.

A guard grabbed at Henry's ankle. He moved back. Another one was climbing onto the platform. Rip and Braithwait had entered through a side door, and the crowd was parting around them.

"Right now," Henry yelled, "Mordecai struggles to save Hylfing from the wizards. When he has finished, this is where he will come. Show your loyalty, or wait for his judgment. It is your decision, but make it now. The faeren in the Hylfing hall have joined the fight, and a way room has been prepared. Join them now, or stay and wait. See how he repays those who sit on their hands. Go now!"

Henry jumped off the table and grabbed Henrietta by the arm. She looked stunned, running her eyes over the crowd and the hall and even Henry.

"We have to beat them down," Henry said. "Or we'll take too long." He grabbed a young faerie, a girl, by the shoulder.

"Can you run to the way rooms?" he asked.

"I'm fast," the child answered, and she turned and ran, darting through the mob.

The crowd was all confusion. *Let them sort it out,* Henry thought.

The girl was indeed fast, and by the time they'd reached the stair down into the Central Mound, few faeries were ahead of them.

"No farther," Henry told her. The tiny girl stood and

watched as Henry gripped his cousin by the hand, and the two of them descended into the darkness.

"Wow," Henrietta said when they had been swallowed.

"Yeah," said Henry. "Ask me about it later."

At the bottom, Henry felt around for a door. When he'd found one and opened it, he called for Frank. When there was no reply, he felt for another.

"Frank!" he yelled again, and began to move on. A crowd of faeries was descending the stairs behind them.

"This way!" Frank's voice echoed back, and Henry and Henrietta pushed forward in the dark.

"What is this stuff?" Henrietta asked as the blackness sank to the floor around them.

Henry smiled. "Light," he said.

Two doors were open, two way rooms prepared.

Fat Frank stood in the hall, waiting to direct traffic.

"This one's Badon Hill," he said, pointing to his right. "And this one is Hylfing."

Henry stopped long enough to send the first of the faeren into the Hylfing room, and then the three of them slipped into the other and shut the door.

Henrietta threw her arms up over her eyes and staggered back against the wall. Henry, squinting, led her down the sloping floor to the balanced sticks.

"We might need some light," Henry said. "On the other side. Torches or something."

"Torches," Frank said. "Ha." He hurried to a shelf and rejoined them, carrying a limp sack.

"You won't find any faeren on the other side of this one," Frank said. "I'm the only one from that hall still alive."

Henry stood in front of the stick doorway, took a breath, and stepped through, still holding Henrietta's hand.

Darius had not been expecting faeren. He had never encountered them in Byzanthamum. They were pests, harder to sense, but weak. He didn't care to fight them anymore than he cared to fight flies. It was not yet time to enter the city alone. He looked forward to that. He'd even saved himself a horse.

He sent the wizards forward again and strengthened the wind at their backs to weaken the arrows and spread the flame. He needed some of them alive. At least until the faeren were gone.

Henry stood in the dark and smelled the earth around him. It was Badon Hill, but Badon Hill below the surface. The smell of his cupboard without the wind. He walked forward to the mouth of the small faerie hall and heard Frank sniff behind him. He was thinking of his dreams, of what he had seen below the stone at the top of the hill. The raggant bones and the carving of a green man. This hill had been his father's cage.

He looked out at the towering trees. There was a moon here. They were far enough north to be out of Darius's storm, and the breeze was sharp but soft.

Henry didn't know which side of the island he was on, but he knew which way he had to go.

Up. To the top.

"This is beautiful," Henrietta said.

Henry filled his lungs to bursting and nodded, digging his feet into the mossy slope. It was soft, green breath silvered over with the moon's silence. He had to remind himself to hurry, and his mind drifted back to when he'd first seen the magic of Badon Hill, the roaring, surging potence of its story, of the living words that were its glory.

"Is there a path or something?" Henrietta asked.

"Yes," the fat faerie said.

"But we're in a hurry," said Henry, "and we need to get to the top." He thought he could see where the island peaked in front of the stars. The faerie hall had been well up on the island. He was grateful they didn't have to climb all the way from the bottom.

As he pushed himself, Henry savored the sharp pricks of the clean air in his lungs. Soon, the trees thinned around them, and Henry could make out the broken-down stone wall standing out in the moonlight above them. When they reached it, they walked through the ruined gate and stood beside the long barrow stone.

Henry didn't let himself stop to stare at the cold,

breeze-dusted sky, crowded with an audience of stars. He walked to the old, cracked tree and knelt beside its trunk.

He felt nervousness, like he had when he'd first crawled through the cupboards. It felt like he was returning to something unknown, something that was no longer him.

He closed his eyes and wedged himself into the crack, reached forward, felt his hand touch Grandfather's carpet, and scrambled into the room.

Kneeling on the floor, he shivered. The bed was there, the open door, books, a lamp, another life, a chapter buried. The sky outside the shattered windows was gray but un-sunned. Predawn.

Henry sat on the bed and waited for the others.

Henrietta crawled through and stood quickly, rubbing her arms. Frank somersaulted out after her.

"Okay," Henry said. "The diagram in the book had a straight line between this cupboard and the compass locks. Where that straight line crossed the attic floor, Grandfather had drawn an arrow. We need the arrow."

"So we go upstairs and pull up floorboards?" Henrietta asked.

"Right," Henry said. "I have a knife, but nothing else."

"There's a hammer in the junk drawer." Henrietta laughed, surprised. "And I think I might know which board it's under."

Fat Frank was looking around the room and out at sprawling grass fields. "This is where you lived?" he asked. "Dismal place."

"Oh no," Henrietta said. "This isn't Kansas. Kansas isn't, well, Kansas has wheat. And people."

On the landing, Henry climbed his attic stairs, and Henrietta descended to look for a hammer.

The faerie followed Henry.

In the attic, the only light trickled in from the broken round window set into the end, and it wasn't enough. Henry opened his bedroom doors and tried to envision a straight line from the compass locks down to where he imagined Grandfather's cupboard would be.

He couldn't even see the seams between the floorboards.

"Need light," he muttered.

The faerie fished the limp sack out of his shirt, swung it around his head, kicked it twice, shook it, and then pulled a string and dumped it out.

Blackness dribbled to the floor and then sprang into white light. The attic blazed, experiencing real natural light for its first time.

"Too much," Henry said, blinking. "I can't see."

"Oh, don't worry," said Frank. "It found the window. It will fade."

Henry got down on his hands and knees and examined the floorboards. None of them had nail holes.

Henrietta rose up out of the attic stairwell and handed Henry a hammer. The light was already softening.

"You can carry light around?" she asked.

"We can, too," Henry said. "In flashlights. Which one were you thinking?"

Five feet out from the doorway to Henry's room, Henrietta crouched down and pointed. The floorboard didn't just have nail holes, it had nail heads and hammer dings in the wood around them. "I always wondered why this one had been nailed down," Henrietta said. "I thought maybe it squeaked. But then every floorboard up here squeaks."

Henry ran his hand over the battered wood and looked at his clawed hammer. He wasn't exactly sure how to start. He flipped it to the claw and slammed it against the floorboard.

The faerie laughed, jumped around him, and took the hammer from his hand.

"We don't have that much light, nor that much time."

He crouched over the floorboard, his belly on his thighs, and swung the hammer with sharp accuracy. The claws bit into the wood around a nail, and with a jerk and twitch, the nail screamed and rattled to the floor. Again and again the faerie swung, and each time he jerked a nail free.

Finally, as the light faded to orange, he wedged the claw into the seam between the floorboards and threw his body against it. With a crack and squeal, the board rose. Henry and Henrietta grabbed on to it, snapping it up.

Beneath it, there was a long silver case. It was open. And it was full of water.

Inside it, there was something that, at some point, could have been an arrow.

Henry reached in, hooked a finger beneath it in the water, and lifted it out carefully.

He let it rest across his palms, and the three of them stared at it.

The shaft was badly bent, and the wood was soft and fraying around cracks. There were only two feathers. One actually. One and a half. Water dripped from both of them, and Henry thought he could see hints of orange in their color. But they were ashen.

The tip was sharp stone, but one of the barbs was missing, and Henry wasn't sure if it was on straight.

"Well," Henrietta said. "It was a good idea, Henry."

CHAPTER TWENTY-SEVEN

Henry stared at the arrow, and his heart sank. Fat Frank crouched in front of him, and his eyes were excited.

"Look at it!" he said. "See what you're holding."

Henry looked back down. This time, he really looked.

He almost dropped the arrow.

Strength swirled around its fringes, but beyond that, Henry could see something else. The stone tip was white-hot and alive, crawling with an unquenchable story. Henry slid his hand away from it, down onto the shaft. It was straight and thick in his hands, growing without increasing, burning without being consumed. And it was fletched with three long, fiery feathers, cold feathers, mothers to the wind.

Henry swallowed and blinked, and once again, he held a twisted, rotting ruin of an arrow.

"Which is real?" he asked.

"Both," the faerie said. "The two are married. You see its story, its shaped name, and living glory, and you see the wood and stone decayed. They are twined to one and will not be separated. We must go. You were right to come. This arrow must fly."

"But how can it?" Henrietta asked. "Even if it's magic, you still couldn't hit anything with it."

"We'll see," Henry said, and he stood up, holding the arrow in the middle, hoping nothing would fall off. Henrietta grabbed the case and dumped out the salt water pooled in the bottom.

The three of them hurried down the stairs and back into Grandfather's room.

Henry held the arrow to his chest, and for a moment, he panicked. Grandfather had used the arrow to make some of the cupboards functional. The door might be closed. Dropping to his knees, he stretched his hand into the cupboard, holding his breath, feeling for the back, afraid that he would find it. He felt moist earth, a worm, and night air. Relief flooded through him, and he crawled quickly back up into the moonlight of Badon Hill. When the others were beside him, he began to run, now holding the arrow away from his body.

"Careful!" Henrietta said.

He knew. Don't run with scissors. But he also knew she was more worried about the arrow than him. He wasn't sure he could break it if he tried. They plowed and slid down the side of Badon Hill, and Henry brushed his free hand over tree trunks as he passed them. In this light, in this moment, he felt like he could talk to them if he tried. If he knew the words.

Sitting impatiently in the little faeren hall, the cousins watched Frank prepare a doorway back to the mound.

And then they were through, back into the upper branches of the Central Mound.

The corridors were as bright as they were silent. There were no guards to be seen, and most doors hung open, revealing beds unmade, food uneaten. Occasionally, they heard the voices of children.

Henry laughed as he ran. How many faeries had he sent? Worry crept in. Had they helped? Could they help? Or would they fight on the wizards' side? If he'd frightened them too much, they might have.

He wondered where the committee members were. They wouldn't have gone to help, though they probably had gone somewhere else. Somewhere very far away.

Henry followed Frank as the faerie rushed down the stairs into the Central Mound, panting but unweary. He had an arrow, an ancient talisman in his hand, and that brought its own strength.

"I can't believe this is light," Henrietta said as they entered the darkness, and Henry laughed again. He didn't say anything.

The way room back was empty.

They hurried, squinting, down the sloping floor and through the doorway without a beat of hesitation.

Two faeries sat in the hall with their arms crossed.

They both jumped when Henry appeared.

"Why are you not at the wall?" Henry asked. "What are your names?"

They ran out of the hall in front of them.

Henry climbed up slowly and stepped into underbrush and storm-darkness.

He could see very little, and he'd forgotten the rain, and the wind had grown. The clouds flashed with lightning, but he couldn't see the forks. They were on the other side of the city.

Together, Henry and Henrietta slogged through the mud and the brush while Frank rushed ahead to the wall and the gates.

The gates were open.

The guards were gone.

Henry pulled in a deep breath and looked at the streets ahead. They still had a city to cross.

Frank Willis looked around for his brothers. The city below the river was burning.

Caleb and Mordecai had stood in the street as hundreds of families had retreated across the bridge. Even the faeren had fallen back. The alleys on the other side of the river were probably as full of them as they were of cowering archers.

The last Frank had seen of his brothers, Mordecai had fallen to his knees, drawing lightning to himself. Absorbing strikes. Because of him, the bridge was still intact.

Frank was crouched behind one of the pillars in the center of the bridge. He could see where Sergeant Simmons lay across from him, unconscious he hoped, but he had lost all track of Zeke and Richard and Henry.

When the faeren had come, it had looked like the tide had turned. They had even held the wall for a while, held the entire breach.

And then Darius had come again. The tall wizard, who moved for nothing, and stood in the swirling carnage like he was made of the rock beneath him. No arrow, no faerie, not one of Mordecai's blows had reached him, and his wind had pushed the fire through the city. Mordecai had only just prevented it from crossing the river.

Frank had a bow and a quiver full of salvaged arrows. But they were still slung beside him.

His shotgun had one more shell, and it was time to find his brothers.

He stood, looked across the bridge and through the street and flames. And he began humming. It was a simple tune, a protective charm of a war song, one lost from his boyhood. His mother had called it a breastplate.

Frank was not unhappy. He was home, where he belonged. And if his home was going to be destroyed, he was grateful that he had seen it again, that his life, rather than fading into dust on a couch in Kansas, could be laid down here.

He moved across the bridge and onto the street lined

with fire. Cobblestones were dry from the heat, even as more rain fell.

His arrows rattled behind him as he walked.

All the way at the end of the street, through the shimmering distortion of the heat, he could see the remaining wizards gathering. In front of them sat a tall man on a horse.

Frank kept moving forward, scanning the walls and the side streets, wherever people could be hidden.

After more than one hundred yards, he stopped and stared into an alleyway. The buildings around it had already burned themselves out.

"Mr. Willis," a voice said.

"Zeke?" Frank hurried to the alley, glancing down the street.

"Have they come?" another voice asked. "Shall we stand?"

Frank stepped into the shadow and laid down his shotgun. Caleb was leaning back against a wall with his legs splayed in front of him, his horn bow across his knees.

Beside him, Mordecai slumped.

Zeke was crouched in front of them both, holding a bow. Behind him, wide-eyed, sat Richard, his arms full of quivers.

Caleb opened his eyes, and Mordecai raised his head. "Have they come?" he asked again. "Shall we stand?"

"No," Zeke said.

"But they are coming," Frank said. "Are you wounded?"

Mordecai smiled. "Our wounds are the wounds of

exhaustion. Of being overpowered. But we are not yet dead, and I do not want to be made a liar."

"A liar?" Frank asked.

"I told my wife I would not be lost again."

"Is Darius himself coming?" Caleb asked. "Or is he still unsure of his victory?"

"He is coming," Frank said.

"Then we stand on the bridge," said Caleb.

He stood, and the two of them pulled Mordecai to his feet.

They hobbled into the street, and Zeke and Richard followed.

Below them, the wizards were approaching.

When they reached the bridge, Frank called into the shadows for water. A man hurried forward with a skin, and Frank handed it to his brothers.

He turned to Zeke and Richard. "Now it is time for you to fall back to the house," he said. "If it comes to it, you'll have your own last stand there. Go."

Richard turned, but Zeke only backed up into the shadows.

Mordecai pulled in long, slow breaths, straightened up, and squared his legs. Caleb stood beside him, leaning on his bow. Frank leaned on the shotgun.

After a moment, Frank hurried forward and lay on his back among the pillars on the bridge. He was careful to spread a leg visibly into the road. Darius would know he was there if he was hidden or not.

There are men who would have scruples about shooting an enemy in the back. Frank Willis was not one of them.

When Henry and Henrietta reached the top of the hill in front of the house, they stopped in shock, looking down over the burning lower city.

"Look to the bridge," the faerie said behind them.

Two figures, both tall, stood on the near side of the bridge, with their feet spread and their shoulders square. Up the road from the other side came a single horseman.

"Where's my dad?" Henrietta asked.

Henry was already racing down the hill.

Darius sat still on his horse. Half the city had fallen. He had only to cross the bridge, to trample the two weary lives in front of him. He nudged his horse forward and stopped even with the first thick posts in the railings. His cloak rolled and flapped in the gusts that burst through the streets. His mouth opened and spoke. He did not choose his own words.

"You are of a blood I do not love," he said. "You cannot stop me."

"Likewise," Caleb said. He closed and opened his fingers around the grip on his bow. There was a shaft on the string.

Darius listened to the words that poured out of him.

"I am Nimroth. Blackstar. Mountains have bowed to me. Your knees, your souls, will bend."

"You are not Nimroth," Mordecai said. "Mountains may have bowed to him, but our grandsires made sure that they bowed to the ground. He is under them still."

After a moment of silence, Darius opened his mouth to speak again. This time, he spoke with a woman's voice.

"I am Nimiane, dread queen of Endor. Nimroth lives in me for I am his daughter." Darius said this without flinching, without even noticing. His soul was being crowded out.

The horse sparked a hoof on the cobbles, snorting.

"That much we know," said Caleb. "Why have you come?"

"To settle old grievances. To collect a debt from your diminishing clan. It is a debt they will pay."

"We owe no one," Caleb said. His right hand found the bow string.

"Do you think an arrow can find my flesh? Do you think there is a bow that can pierce me?"

"Yes," Caleb said.

The woman in Darius laughed. "You are not your father. Nor are you your brother. You are not even equal to your brother's son. He at least drew my blood when I was weak and entombed in the prison his father gave me. He is also the one who opened the way to my freedom. The father's seals were broken by the son, but that will not prevent him paying his portion of the debt." Darius nudged his horse a step forward. "Speak to me, Mordecai. Have you learned of that betrayal?"

Mordecai's voice was heavy. "Darius," he said. "I do not know you, but she has filled you past return. You cannot but die, even if you defeat us. And you shall not defeat us. Do not set foot on the bridge."

Caleb shifted his feet and drew the bow back to his cheek. Raindrops ran down the string and dripped off the arrow's feathers onto his lips. Caleb held the bow drawn, and his arms did not shake.

The horse tossed its head, but did not move.

Caleb's voice rang out. "This shaft was taken from the tomb of the Old King, and the bow was made for his brother kings in the South, who set the ancient stones. Try its strength if you dare."

"I dare," the woman's voice said, and Darius rode onto the bridge.

Henry ran past alleys and shadows crowded with watching men. He ran straight for the bridge.

He saw Darius ride forward.

He saw the shotgun blast from the side, and the horse rear. He saw Caleb's arrow fly and turn to ash in the air. He saw Uncle Frank thrown from the bridge and his father grasp Darius's own wind and hurl it toward the ramping horse.

The animal staggered on its hind legs, and for a moment, Henry thought it would topple.

"Henry!" Eli jumped out of a shadow.

The small old man ran after him.

The horse stamped, regaining itself. Darius's hood had fallen back, and the woman in him laughed a rich, long laugh.

"I have braved the arrow of the Old King, the Old Dead King, and I live. I will always live. I have stood your blow. Can you stand mine?"

Henry ran onto the bridge with Eli behind him.

Darius looked at him and smiled.

"That blood I have tasted," she said. "Shall we begin with the young and move on to the vintage?"

The blow fell.

Air as hard as rock crushed Henry from above, and he crumpled on the cobblestones. His body slid forward, toward the wizard. His life was being drawn out through the burn on his face. His blood, his newfound fire, was being taken from him. Henry struggled. He could see the gray lines of his life, dying green and gold, straggling toward the wizard, and they dragged him behind. Suddenly, another strength stretched above him, purple and rich, twisting and green, his father's vines drawing him back, intertwining with his own.

Eli jumped over him, yelling, racing toward the wizard.

Henry was released.

His father and uncle were above him, pulling him back off the bridge.

"Here," he said, and he handed Caleb the arrow.

Eli screamed, and Henry rolled over in time to see his small body fold and tumble in the street.

Caleb placed the bent and rotten arrow on the string. Mordecai stepped forward, drawing strength from the wind, from the river and the stones, pulling down the cold breath from the cloud-mountains. Henry saw it all. He saw the serpentine wind rush down in bands thicker than trees. He saw twisting river words rise from beneath the bridge like a waterfall undone, and a wall of seamless, roaring strength climbing in from the sea. His eyes burned with the sight, and pressure built in his skull. It was too much. His eyes were teetering toward blindness, overpowered. His ears were going to burst and bleed with the crackling magic. But Henry leaned his mind against it, fighting to stay conscious. He knew that it had to be more than his father could bear to hold.

Darius rode forward to the center of the bridge, smiling at Caleb. "And where is this one from?" Nimiane asked.

"Ramoth Gilead," Henry said. He saw shock on Caleb's face, and a single flash of fear in the tall wizard.

Suddenly, Darius hurled his strength toward them and pounded down lightning at Caleb. But Mordecai had thrown his own. Wind struggled with wind, lightning tangled with lightning and fell to the bridge, thunderless, crackling stone.

In one motion, Caleb drew the arrow to his lips and let it fly.

The arrow veered and twisted. But Henry saw another, white-hot, fly true through the crackling wind.

The two arrows met, and together, they drove into Darius's throat.

The wind died, but the rain continued on.

Darius slid from the horse's back and landed in the road. Henry blinked. He could barely see the wizard's body for all the ghostly, tangled web of stolen life that swirled around him beginning to unravel. All of it gray, like the strands on Henry's face, it expanded, jerking loose, snapping fear, struggling free, accelerating, growing. In a flash, Henry realized what would happen. He saw all that was about to explode, and he knew that he, his new life, his family, would all be washed away. Henry raised his hands and pushed what little strength he had against it.

Mordecai stumbled toward the fallen wizard.

Darius sputtered. Something in his mind drew back. A waterfall, a deluge of strength, roared inside him. He could hold it no more.

All the power gathered, all the life stolen and poured into Darius, burst out in a rushing spirit-wind of death.

With the last of his strength, Mordecai threw himself against it, dropping to his knees with both hands raised. Cobbles cracked and aged to dust in front of him. Henry watched his father's twisting vines grab his own and spin into a wall against the fury, but they were bending back, unable to hold, dying and joining the gray. And then the storm of death turned, pouring away down the street, through the wizards, through the flames.

What was left of the eastern wall collapsed. Trees fell, and in the darkness, the ridge rumbled, and its face slid down to the plain.

The sea crashed on the cliffs, but struggled against no thunder. Rain fell faster, stronger than fire.

Uncle Frank climbed up from the river, and Henry crawled toward the body of Eli FitzFaeren. Onetime traitor, onetime friend.

The bridge around the body of Darius of Byzan-thamum, seventh son to a priest, was covered with mushrooms. They'd spread through and down the street and over the bodies of the wizards.

The dead horse was covered with them, and they were growing on Eli.

Henry brushed them off.

His father crouched beside him. His face was white, bloodless, but the struggle was over, a weight was lifted.

He smiled at his son, slid his arms beneath the small body of Eli, and stood up.

He turned back. Hundreds of men and faeren drifted out of the shadows.

"Who will carry him to the house of Hyacinth?" Mordecai asked.

Through the rain, a crowd moved forward. Henrietta walked in front of them.

Uncle Frank stepped over the railing, nodded at Henry, and turned to look for Sergeant Simmons.

Caleb stood tall over the body of Darius and looked at the ivory chin and the warped and rotten arrow beneath it.

The mushrooms had not gone near the shaft. The chipped-stone point stood out of the wizard's neck. Caleb bent, gripped it, and pulled the rest of the arrow through. Then he shrugged off his cloak and wrapped it carefully around the shaft.

Mordecai watched Eli being carried up the hill, and then he turned to his son.

"Well done," he said. "I had wondered where you'd gone."

Uncle Frank called for them as he helped a thick Sergeant Simmons to his feet.

Zeke, Richard, Henrietta, and the fat faerie came and stood by Henry, and no one said anything until Uncle Frank and his two tall brothers returned with the policeman limping between them.

In the crowd, voices were beginning to spread quietly through the memory of what had been lost.

The lower city burned. The eastern wall was gone. Hundreds of fallen waited burial. And yet, Hylfing lived on. Caleb no longer stood alone, but walked with brothers. Mordecai had returned.

Someone began ringing the bells, and they sounded new.

Silent, the brothers climbed the cobbled hill, and the others walked with them.

When dawn came, Henry was standing on the roof of his mother's house. She had stood with him for a while, under a cloak, in the rain and the now-slow sea breeze. Together, they had watched the clouds begin to break and part in front of the laughing stars. Dotty had come and held him for a moment, kissed him, and left him to his thoughts.

Zeke had stood with him, and Richard, but they had both gone inside. The house had been awake through the night, the women treating wounded, and Hyacinth had gone out through the dark to grieve with those who had lost.

After eating, Mordecai and Caleb had ridden up the ridge to the wizard door, and Caleb had carried the Arrow of Chance with them.

They had returned before the sun, beneath the graying sky. Carnassus and the remaining wizards had all been found dead, lying in the ancient, arched throne room. The witch was gone.

Now, as the sun rose through the scattered rain, only Henrietta stood hooded beside Henry, and the two of them looked out over the blackened lower city, out over the white-lined sea. They watched the sun rise over the ridge, above the shattered eastern wall.

After hours of silence, Henrietta shivered and spoke. "You're different, Henry York."

Henry swallowed and blinked away everything he was feeling. This was where he was from. This place that had almost been destroyed. This wounded family, now partly healed. This city by the sea.

But there were already things he missed, things he had only just found. The barn. The combine-combed fields and the smell of Kansas grain as it ripened. Baseball.

"I'm still scared," he said.

Henrietta smiled and looked at him, wiping rain from her wet forehead, tucking back her hair beneath her hood.

"Yeah," she said. "But now you're scary."

Henry smiled and leaned over the wall. "If you have some dirt, I'll show you a trick."

Henrietta laughed, and shivered.

Something was moving through the air in front of the ridge.

It was struggling.

"What's that?" Henry asked.

The animal grew in the air, wavering above the charred streets in the lower city, dragging its dangling hind end as it avoided houses and climbed above the hill.

It was Henry's turn to laugh, but not so loud that the raggant might hear him.

The creature circled the house and landed on the roof behind them.

Henry and Henrietta bit their lips, and neither turned around.

A moment later, the raggant sat on the wall beside Henry, spread its wings against the wet breeze, shut its eyes, and raised its nose.

Its job was done.

CHAPTER TWENTY-EIGHT

Henry spent days in the streets, working like he had never worked. But those days were also filled with meals like he had never eaten, laughter and singing like he had never heard, nights full of stories, and the sleep of a body and mind used like tools and not like treasures.

He dreamed, but only one that he remembered after waking. In that dream, he sat with Ron and Nella on their balcony overlooking the city of Byzanthamum. Neither said a word, but they smiled, and together, in his dream, they sat for a lifetime and did nothing but watch the smoke slowly fade away until a new city breathed below.

Though his days were full of tasks, not one passed without a visit to the roof. There, the raggant always joined him. Together, they would choose a wall, or let the wind choose for them, and they would stare—at the sky, the sea, the trees, the city, the world—and Henry would listen to the raggant breathe, and to the wind breathe through its wings.

Sometimes, Henry was worried. Sometimes, he was afraid. Always, he knew he loved too much of the world, of two worlds, and he knew that roots only belonged in one.

Soon after Darius's fall, Uncle Frank, Henrietta, Zeke, and Sergeant Simmons all followed Henry as he led them back to Grandfather's room in the old house.

When he led them downstairs, through the dining room, the kitchen, and out the back door into the bright Kansas sun, Uncle Frank had laughed, Zeke had whooped, and Sergeant Simmons had hurried out, wiping his eyes. Zeke and Simmons had walked off together, waving and laughing.

They would all see each other again. Soon. They'd even picked a day.

Eli, duke of FitzFaeren, was buried in Hylfing beneath the cathedral floor. Magdalene, her grandsons, and many others traveled through the wizard doors to attend.

Magdalene formally requested the right to remove the body if the Halls of FitzFaeren were ever restored.

She did not ask for the arrow. After her mother's death and before her coronation, the Arrow of Chance had been under the duke's authority.

Frank and Dorothy Willis gave it to her.

Tate and Roland were buried privately, according to a faeren custom nowhere established in the *Book of Faeren*. Not even Mordecai and Henry were permitted to attend, and Fat Frank would say nothing of it beyond simply asserting that it had been the sort of affair that would have kept both reveling late, and that gamblers had been served.

When the settled day came, Henry rose in the predawn without being wakened and helped his mother plant a tree in the courtyard.

Then he and his father had walked out the south gate, found the local faeren hall, traveled to the distant regional mound—full of extremely respectful faeries—and from there to Badon Hill in the far north.

His father carried a long, narrow wooden box.

Beneath the young blue sky of a morning still hung with a waning moon, the two of them knelt on the wet earth of Badon Hill and felt for old, moss-covered bones with their hands, slowly filling the box. When they finished, the sky was lighter, and Mordecai pulled from his cloak a smooth red cloth Hyacinth had woven and laid it over the top. The box was closed, and Mordecai lifted it up and set it on the great gray stone. He leapt up beside it and sat down. Henry followed him, and there they sat, the sun warming as it climbed.

When it hung well above the trees, Henry spoke.

"Could the faeren trap you again?"

Mordecai looked at his son. "Yes. With cleverness, deception, and betrayal, any man could be entrapped. The magic of the faeren is very powerful, though they take it for granted and are easily distracted. Their hill magic is the greatest they have. They can enclose whole cities of theirs in a hill, and if you went to it with a shovel, you would never find it. The hill has not been hollowed out, but used to create a new place that is only connected to this world through certain doors, which they hide."

"So they trapped you in a hill."

"They trapped me in this hill. Its magic added to the binding, but they failed to kill you. A christening has its own pull, its own terrible potency. They would have been better off with chains than with magic in the face of a naming."

Henry tasted the sunned air. "I'm not sure I understand."

Mordecai laughed. "Do you understand how the ground pulls you down, or why the earth has never been drawn into the sun, or how a crawling worm morphs into a butterfly? We can give names to these things, but that is not understanding."

"What was it like?" Henry asked.

"Like a lifetime of fitful, troubled sleep."

When Mordecai believed the time was right, the two rose and entered the barrow beneath the great stone. Mordecai carried the bones of his faithful dog, savior to his infant son, and through his infant son, himself. Beyond the stone-carved green man, they entered a corridor that circled back on itself in a ring. Lining the walls were the stone beds of Mordecai's ancestors.

Henry stood where he would have been held as an infant and watched his father lay the bones of the dog to rest. And then he listened to him sing. His father's voice carried through the halls and vaults and returned from distant chambers. Henry never knew the dog, except in his dreams and by its son that his uncle Caleb kept, but the song, and the memory of the song, made him feel as if he did. His father's words had been in a language he could not understand, but they had been words that he could see. Through those words, Henry loved that dog, the dog that had pushed him into the tree.

When the song had faded, the two reentered the living world and found the others already waiting for them.

One at a time, Henry's laughing family crawled through the crack in the great tree of Badon Hill and found themselves in the shattered old house and the empty world around it.

Henry, Kansas, is a town where lost people find themselves, or find that they are lost. In the summer, there are frogs to catch in the ditches, baseball to play in fields that no one mows, and three kinds of ice cream at the gas station.

On the edge of town, there is a barn, an old brown truck, and a steep-sided pond with a fence of plastic webbing around it.

Behind the barn, while the sun dropped, stood Henry York Maccabee and his uncle, Frank Willis.

In front of them, wheat rolled, impatient for the harvest. The air was fat with its smell. The heads shifted in the breeze, rolling gold, rasping bristles in a lie of softness. The long grass around Henry was dry as well, all gone to seed.

There were no dandelions, but there was one wrinkled and stiff piece of paper.

Henry picked it up and read it. It was from lawyers, and it said that he would be reclaimed by the third of July.

Yesterday.

Uncle Frank filled himself with the rich air and looked at Henry. "A lot can happen in two weeks." He smiled.

Henry blinked. Two weeks. That was all it had been? For a moment, he thought about dropping the letter back in the grass. Instead, he folded it up and slid it next to an envelope in his pocket.

Frank turned and walked slowly around the corner of the barn. Henry followed him.

It was only twilight, but in the minds of those who lived in Henry, Kansas, it was dark enough for fireworks. A small house, painted the same shade of dying green as the grass in its backyard, watched the fire in the sky and listened to the laughter of those around it. It was the house where Zeke Johnson lived, but he was thinking about moving. Though the backyard was small, it was crowded with people. There were three tall men laughing, and girls, and boys, and mothers. There was a man wearing a fresh police uniform, and a pleasant woman hanging nervously on to him, looking around at the people she had heard so much about and which she hadn't really believed existed.

Monmouth was eating a hot dog and watching the blue screaming fire trail back down from the sky above the city's field. Caleb was standing next to Zeke, who had his arms around a slender blond woman, his mother. Caleb was laughing, somehow unable to watch the fireworks. The woman was smiling, and she did not want to stop.

But before the fireworks ended, while the streets of Hylfing would be free of prying eyes, all of the guests left, and Zeke and the blond woman followed them. A train of people carrying bulging pillowcases made their way down the street, seen only by a gray and white cat that hurried to catch them.

When they reached the barn at the edge of town, they walked around the pond, where the house should have been, and at the back, hanging in midair, there was a door, propped open with a baseball bat.

At the door, there were hugs, and the policeman and his wife said good-bye. Then sacks of clothes and old photos and peanut butter, but mostly mitts and bats and balls, as well as helmets, were passed through the door, and the policeman watched as it swung shut and disappeared. Then he looked at his wife, and they looked up at the fireworks. There were three exploding in the sky at once. They kissed and made it four. It was the Henry, Kansas, finale.

Sergeant Simmons was humming as they walked,

barely limping, back to where he'd left the car. In his hand, he held a letter that Henry had asked him to mail.

On the other side of the door, up two flights of stairs, through a cupboard and the byways of the faeren, things were different. The sun was low but shining after a slight rain, and a breeze was blowing in from the sea. A train of people crossed the bridge, but did not climb the cobbled hill. They turned down a side street and made their way to the city wall and then to the green fields beside the river.

Soon, the city heard the sounds that it would come to love. The crack of a bat and laughter, and the sound of the first ball hit far enough to reach the water.

Uncle Frank rounded the bases.

GRATITUDE

My parents for the treble-read
My wife for the treble-listen
Jim T. for the confidence
Random House for the making
You for the reading

ABOUT THE AUTHOR

At the age of twelve (and thanks to a house fire), **N. D. WILSON** spent nearly a year living in his grandparents' attic. The ceilings were low and baggy, and a swamp cooler squatted in a window at one end. Inviting crawl spaces ran the length of the attic on both sides. If there were cupboards in those walls, he never found them. But not for lack of trying. He loves barns, still checks walls for hidden doors, and is certain that dandelions are magic.

N. D. Wilson and his wife live in Idaho, along with their four young explorers. For more information, please visit www.ndwilson.com.